Wild Margaret

by

Charles Garvice

Double 9
BOOKS

Wild Margaret
by Charles Garvice

ISBN: 978-93-69077-97-7

Published by

DOUBLE 9 BOOKS

2/13-B, Ansari Road
Daryaganj, New Delhi – 110002
info@double9books.com
www.double9books.com
Tel. 011-40042856

ABOUT THE AUTHOR

Charles Garvice (1850–1920) was a highly prolific British novelist known for writing over 150 romance novels during the late 19th and early 20th centuries. His works, often characterized by themes of romance, adventure, and melodrama, were immensely popular not only in the UK but also in the United States and around the world. Garvice was considered one of the most successful novelists in England during his time, with his novels frequently serialized in magazines and widely read in both English-speaking countries and abroad. In addition to writing under his own name, Garvice also used the female pseudonym Caroline Hart. His storytelling often featured strong heroines and captivating romantic plots, appealing especially to a predominantly female audience. Arnold Bennett referred to Garvice as "the most successful novelist in England" in 1910, acknowledging his significant influence on popular fiction. Garvice was born to Andrew John Garvice and Mira Winter, and after his death in 1920, his legacy continued to shape the landscape of romantic fiction well into the 20th century.

CONTENTS

CHAPTER I

When the train drew up at the small station of Leyton Ferrers, which it did in the slowest and most lazy of fashions, two persons got out. One was a young girl, who alighted from a third-class carriage, and who dragged out from under the seat a leather bag and a square parcel instead of waiting for the porter, who was too much engaged in light and pleasant conversation with the guard, to pay any attention to such small cattle as passengers.

The other person was a young man, who sauntered out of a first-class carriage, with a cigar in his lips, and his soft traveling cap a little on one side, and with that air which individuals who have been lucky enough to be born with silver spoons in their mouths naturally acquire, or are endowed with. Standing on the platform, as if it and the whole Great South-Northern Railway system belonged to him, this young gentleman at last caught sight of the porter.

"Hi, porter!" he called, and when the man came up, quickening his pace as he took in the tall, well-dressed figure of his summoner, the young man continued with a smile, "Sorry to tear you away from your bosom friend, my man, but there's a portmanteau of mine in the van, or should be."

The porter touched his hat, and was going toward the van, when the young man called after him:

"See to that young lady first," he said, indicating with a slight nod the young girl, who was struggling with the bag and the parcel.

Somewhat surprised at this display of unselfishness, the porter turned like a machine, and addressed the girl; the young man sauntered down the platform and, leaning over the fence, surveyed the June roses in the station-master's garden with an indolent and good-tempered patience.

"Any luggage, miss?" asked the porter.

"No; nothing but these," said the girl. "Here is the ticket;" then she looked round. "Can you tell me how far Leyton Court is from the station?"

"Little better than two miles and a half," replied the porter.

"Two miles and a half—that means three miles," said the girl, and she looked inquiringly at the road and across the fields, over which the dying sun was sending a warm, rich crimson.

"Yes, miss. Will you have a fly? There is one outside," he added, with a touch of impatience, for it seemed highly improbable that more than twopence—at the most—could proceed from his present job, while sixpence or a shilling, no doubt, awaited him from the aristocratic young gentleman still lounging over the garden fence. The girl thought a moment; then, with the faintest flush, said:

"No, thank you. I will leave my luggage; there will be something, some cart——"

"Carrier's cart goes to the Court every evening!" broke in the porter, and, seizing the bag and the parcel, and dropping them in a corner with that sublime indifference to the safety of other people's goods which only a railway porter can adequately display, hurried off to the other passenger.

The young girl went with a light step down the station stairs, and having reached the road, stopped.

"How stupid of me!" she said. "I ought to have asked the way."

She was turning back to worry the porter once more when she saw a finger-post, upon which was written, "To Leyton Court," and, with a little sigh of relief, she went down the road indicated.

Meanwhile the porter had got the portmanteau, and stood awaiting the passenger's pleasure.

After a minute or two, and in the most leisurely fashion possible, the young man turned to him.

"Got the bag? All right. I'm going to Leyton Court." The porter touched his cap. "Is there anything here that can take me?"

"There's a fly, sir," said the porter, nodding toward the road, where a shambling kind of vehicle on its last wheels, attached to a horse on its last legs, stood expectantly.

The young man surveyed the turn-out, and laughed.

"All right; take the bag down to it. Wait! here's a drink for you. By the way, where can I get one for myself? No inn or anything here?"

"No, sir, nothing," said the porter, with almost pathetic sadness. "Nearest is at Parrock's Cross, a mile and a half on the road."

"Then I shall have to remain thirsty till I get to Parrock's Cross," said the young man, with an easy smile. "Do you think your horse can get as far as that, my friend?" he added to the driver.

The man grunted, mounted the box, and the Noah's ark rattled slowly away.

The young man lit another cigar, put up his feet on the opposite cushions, and surveyed the scenery, through eyes half closed, in perfect contentment, good humor, and indolent laziness. Presently they came abreast of the young girl, who was stepping along with the graceful gait which belongs to youth, and health, and good breeding.

"Now, I wonder where she is going?" he said to himself as he looked at her. "If she were a man now, I would give her a lift; as it is——By George! she's pretty though. Pretty? She's lovely! I wonder whether she'd take the fly from me, and let me tramp it instead of her? Don't dare ask her! I know what she'd do—give me a look that would make me wish I were fifty miles under the sea, and not say a word. What a devil of a stupid world it is!" And with this reflection as a kind of consolation, he made himself a little more comfortable, and closed his eyes completely.

It was a lovely evening. Some days in June, as we miserable Englishmen know only too well, are delusions and snares, cold as December or wet as October, but it was late in the month and really summer weather; and as the girl walked along the smooth path, which a shower had made pleasant, the trees shone in all their midsummer beauty; the birds sang their evening hymns; the flowers loaded the air with perfume.

It is good to be a girl, it is good to be young, it is good to be beautiful, but it is best of all to be innocent and happy, and she was all these. To save her life she could not help singing softly as she walked through all the splendor of this summer evening, and so she joined the birds in their evening hymn to the tune of "Oh, Mistress Mine!" stopping now and again to gather a spray of honeysuckle or a particularly fine dog-rose, of which the hedges were full.

The fly rattled on its way and came in due course to Parrock's Cross; and the horse, no doubt with a sigh of relief, pulled up of its own accord at the door of the village inn.

The young man woke up—if he had really been asleep—jumped out without opening the door and sauntered into the inn.

"Give the man what he likes, and me a bottle of Bass," he said to the landlord, and he threw himself down on the rustic seat outside the door.

The landlord brought the ale, touching his forehead obsequiously, for like most country people he knew a gentleman when he saw him, and the young man took a huge draught.

"That's very good beer," he said, nodding. "Get another bottle for yourself. How many miles is it to Leyton Court?"

"Not more than a mile, sir," said the landlord, touching his forehead again, for a man who was not only a gentleman but who was going to Leyton Court was worthy of all the respect that could be paid him.

"Is that all? Look here, then; I shall walk it. That contrivance reminds me too forcibly of a hearse; besides, I want to stretch my legs." He stretched them as he spoke; they were long legs and admirably shaped. "Tell the man to take the bag on. Here's five shillings for him."

"The fare's half-a-crown from the station, sir," said the landlord.

The gentleman laughed lazily.

"All right. Tell him to put the other two-and-six in the poor-box."

The landlord laughed respectfully, and the young man, left alone, leaned back on the seat and drank his beer in indolent content. Presently the girl passed on the other side of the road.

"Hullo!—there she is again!" he said. "I wonder where she is going? I dare say she's thirsty. It's a pity she isn't a man, for I could ask her to have a drink. Do you know that young lady, landlord?" he asked.

The man shaded his eyes and looked after the girl.

"No, sir," he said. "No. The lady's a stranger to me, sir; a perfect stranger."

The young man smoked his cigar and watched the graceful figure going down the road in the twilight with a touch of interest on his handsome face. He seemed in no hurry to pursue his journey by any means; and when he rose, at length, he yawned and stretched himself.

"Could you give me a bed here to-night, landlord?" he asked.

The man eyed the ground doubtfully.

"We're plain people, sir——" he commenced.

"I like plain people," broke in the young man with a laugh, the music of which never failed to call up an answering smile on the faces of those who heard it. "I don't mind roughing it; I'm used to it. I'm not sure that I shall want one; but if I should——"

"We'll do our best to make you comfortable, sir," said the landlord, touching his forehead again.

"Right!" exclaimed the young man, carelessly. "Well, don't be surprised if you see me back in—say a couple of hours. Straight on to the Court, I suppose?"

"Straight on, sir," said the landlord, and swinging his stick with a careless, happy-go-lucky air, the young man started off.

Slowly as he walked, his long legs soon overtook the young girl, and he passed her again, as she was standing on tiptoe to get a flower from the hedge. He half stopped with the evident intention of reaching the blossom, which reared itself tantalizingly just beyond her reach, but he thought— "she won't like it perhaps; think I want to intrude myself upon her," and walked on. She had not turned her head.

Probably the loveliness of the evening had the same effect upon him as it had upon her, for when he had got out of her hearing he began to sing, for, you see, he was young and handsome, in good health, and—I was going to say innocent, but pulled up in time.

In a quarter of an hour the road grew wider, and opened out on to a village green. Two or three houses were dotted about it, and an inn with the sign of the Ferrers Arms swinging on a post. A little further stood a pair of huge iron gates, with a lodge at the side of them.

"That's the Court, I suppose?" he said to himself. "Now for the tug of war! Lord, how I wish myself back in London!" and he flicked his cap onto the back of his head, and laughed ruefully.

Some children were playing on the green, and two or three men lounged on the settle outside the inn. Suddenly one of them rose, just as the young man came abreast of the door, and as he made way for the man to pass, a dog ran out from the inn and caused the man to stumble. The fellow uttered an oath and raised his heavily-booted foot. The kick struck the dog in the side, and with a howl of pain he fled behind the young man.

Now a moment before his handsome face had been a picture of indolent good temper, but at the kick and the howl his face changed. The lips grew set, the eyes stern and fierce. He was not a good young man—alas, alas! it will be seen that he was a thousand miles removed from that—but his heart was as tender as a woman's, and he loved dumb animals—dogs and horses in especial—with that love of which only a strong, healthy, young Englishman is capable.

"You brute!" he said, not loudly, but with an intense emphasis, which caused the man to pull up and stare at him with an astonished scowl.

"Did you speak to me, guv'nor?" he growled.

He was a tall, wiry-looking ruffian, and his voice seemed to proceed from the bottom of his chest, and the glance he shot at the speaker came from a pair of evil-looking eyes, deeply sunk beneath thick and black brows.

"I did!" said the young man curtly; "I called you a brute!" and he stooped and comforted the dog.

The man eyed him up and down with a vindictive glare.

"Can't I kick my own dawg?" he demanded, with a most atrocious attempt at a sneer.

"Not when I am near," said the young man, quite calmly, but meeting the glare of the evil eyes with a steady firmness.

"Oh, I can't, can't I?" retorted the man. "You get out of the way and I'll show you, curse you!"

The young man stepped aside, apparently to leave the dog exposed to the threatened assault, but as the man lifted his foot the young fellow thrust his own forward, and launching out with his left hand, dealt the man a blow which sent him a mass of arms and legs against the doorway.

The dog fled, the group of idlers who had remained seated, listening to the colloquy, sprung up and drew near, exchanging glances and staring at the pair.

The young fellow stood in the easiest of attitudes, with something like a smile on his lips, for the man's attitude of complete astonishment as he leant against the doorway was rather comical.

"That was a good 'un," cautiously whispered one of the men, looking at the young fellow admiringly. "'Tain't often Jem Pyke gets it like that, are it?"

The man called Pyke pulled himself together, and stretching himself glared round him; then his eyes rested on the young fellow, and he seemed to remember.

With an oath he made ready for a spring, but the young fellow raised his hand.

"Wait a minute, my friend," he said, almost pleasantly. "If you are anxious for a fight, say so, and let us have it comfortably. I haven't the slightest objection myself."

"Curse you, I'll—I'll kill you!" gasped the man.

The young fellow laughed.

"I don't think you will, my friend. I'm afraid you'll be disappointed, I really am; but if you'd like to try——"

He threw his cigar away, and, taking off his light shooting jacket, tossed it on to the settle.

As he did so his back was turned to the road along which he had come, and he didn't see the young girl, who had been near enough to witness the scene from its commencement, and was now kneeling down by the dog and murmuring womanly words of pity and sympathy.

"Let the gentleman alone, Jem," said one of the men. "'Twas all your fault. What did you want to go and kick the dawg for? Beg the gentleman's pardon, and go and get your beer."

For all response Jem commenced to turn up his sleeves. Two or three of the men got between them, but the young fellow waved them aside.

"Don't interfere, my men," he said pleasantly. "Your friend is dying for a fight, I can see, and a little exercise will give me an appetite. Just stand back, will you?"

The next instant Pyke rushed at him, and the first blows were delivered.

The girl heard the sound of them, and, with a cry of fear and horror, started as if to run across to them, but her heart failed her, and she shrank back against the hedge, looking on with hands clasped, and her face white and terrified.

The man Pyke was a giant in length and strength, but he was in a rage, and no man who is in a rage can fight well. The young fellow on the other hand was, now, in the best of humor, and thoroughly enjoying himself, and he parried the furious onslaught of his opponent as easily as if he were having a set-to at a gymnasium. The blows grew quicker and smarter, one from the young man had reached Mr. Pyke's face, and had cooled him a little. He saw that if he meant to win he must play more cautiously, and drawing back a little, he began again, with something like calculation. Like the blows of a sledge hammer his fists fell upon the chest of the young fellow, one struck him upon the lip and the blood started.

With a smile the young man seemed to think that it was time to end the little drama, and planting his left foot firmly forward, he delivered one blow straight from the shoulder. It fell upon the bully's forehead with a fearful crash, and the same instant, as it seemed, he staggered and fell full length to the ground. A murmur of consternation and admiration—for the blow had really been a skillful one—arose from the group of onlookers, and they crowded round the prostrate man.

"Dang me if I don't think he's killed 'im!" exclaimed the ostler, lifting Jem Pyke's head on his knee.

"What do you say?" said the young fellow, and, pushing them aside, he bent down and examined his late foe. "No, he's not dead. See, he's coming to already. Get some water, some of you—better still, some brandy. That's it. There you are!" he added, cheerfully, as Pyke opened his eyes and struggled to his feet. "How are you? You ought to have countered that last shot of mine, don't you know. You don't box badly, a little wild, perhaps, but then you were wild, weren't you? and that's always a mistake. Well one of us was bound to win, and there's no harm done, though you've got a bump or two, and"—putting his hand to his own face—"my figurehead isn't improved. There," and under the pretense of shaking the man's hand, he slipped half a sovereign into the wiry palm. "Get yourself a drink—and good-morning," and with a laugh and a nod he was striding across the road, when, seeing the pump at the head of the horse trough, he called to a boy to work the handle, and with his pocket-handkerchief washed his face and head, coming out of the impromptu bath with his short chestnut hair all shining like a Greek god's.

Then he strolled across the road, and—for the first time became aware that the young girl from the station had been a spectator of the scene.

He pulled up short within a few paces of her, and the two stood and looked at each other. She had the dog in her arms, and on her face and in her eyes was an expression which baffles my powers of description. It was not fright nor disgust, nor admiration, nor scorn, but a little of each skillfully and most perplexedly mingled. Women hate fighting, when it is inconveniently near to them; on the other hand they love courage, because they have so little of it themselves, and they adore a man who will stand up in defense of one of themselves or a dumb animal.

The girl had longed to turn and fly at the first sight and sound of the awful blows, but she could not: a horrible fascination kept her chained to the spot, and even when the fray was over she still stood, trembling and palpitating, her color coming and going in turn, her arms quite squeezing the dog in her excitement and emotion.

The young man looked at her, took in the oval face, with its dark, eloquent eyes and sweet, tremulous lips, the tall, graceful figure, even the plain blue serge, which seemed so part and parcel of that figure; then his glance dropped awkwardly, and he said, shamefacedly:

"I beg your pardon; I didn't know you were looking on."

The girl drew a long breath.

"You ought to be ashamed of yourself," she said, sternly, with a little catch in her voice.

He raised his eyes a moment—they were handsome, and, if the truth must be told, dare-devil eyes—then dropped them again.

"It—it is shameful," she went on, her lovely face growing carmine, her eyes flashing rebukingly, "for two men to fight like—like dogs; and one a gentleman!"

He looked rather bewildered, as if this view of the proceedings was something entirely novel.

"Oh, come, you know," he said, deprecatingly, "there isn't much harm done."

"Not much! I saw you knock him down as if—as if he were dead!" she said, indignantly. "And you—oh, look at your face!" and she turned her eyes away.

As this was an impossibility, he did the next best thing to it, and put his hand to his cheek and lips.

"I don't think he's hurt much," he said, excusingly, "and I'm not a bit. I think we rather enjoyed it; I know I did," he added, half inaudibly, and with the beginning of a laugh which was smitten dead as she said, with the air of a judge:

"You must be a savage!"

"I—I think I am," he assented, with a rueful air of conviction. "But, all the same, I'm sorry you were here! If I'd known there was a lady looking on I'd have put it off! I'm afraid you've been upset; but don't worry yourself about either of us! Our long-legged friend will be all the better for a little shaking up, and as for me——The dog isn't hurt, is he?"

"I—I don't know," she said.

He came a little nearer, and took the dog from her, noticing that in extending it to him she shrank back, as if his touch would pollute her.

"No; he's all right!" he said, after turning the animal over, and setting him on his legs. "He ought to have some of his ribs broken, but he hasn't! I'm glad of that, poor little beggar," and for the first time his voice softened.

The girl looked at him with grave displeasure.

"I am afraid he is the best Christian of the three," she said, severely.

"By George, I shouldn't wonder!" he muttered, with the ghost of a smile.

She gave him another glance, then, without a word, raised her head loftily and passed on.

He lifted his hat and looked after her, then tugged at his mustache thoughtfully.

"So I'm a savage, am I?" he said. "Well, I expect she's about right! What a beautiful girl! I'm a savage! By George, the old man will say the same if I present myself with this highly-colored physiognomy. I'd better go back to the inn, and turn up later on."

As he stood hesitating, the fly crawled up with the bag; the man had pulled up within view of the fight, and had enjoyed it thoroughly.

"Here, wait! I'll go back with you! I've decided to stay at your place for the night," said the young fellow; and he jumped in.

"Not hurt, I hope, sir?" said the man, as he turned the horse. "It was a right down good fight, sir; it was, indeed!"

"Not a bit! There, hurry up that four-legged skeleton of yours! I'm as hungry as a—a—savage," he concluded, as if by a happy inspiration, and throwing himself along the cushions, he laughed, but rather uneasily.

CHAPTER II

The girl, without looking behind her or vouchsafing even a glance of farewell, walked on until she reached the great iron gates. There she rang the bell which hung like a huge iron tear, within reach of her hand, and on the lodge-keeper coming out, inquired if Mrs. Hale were in.

"Mrs. Hale? Yes, miss; she is up at the house," said the woman. "You are Miss Margaret, I expect?"

"Yes," said the girl; "my name is Margaret. I am Mrs. Hale's granddaughter."

"She has been expecting you, miss. Keep along the avenue and you'll come to the small gates and see the Court. There are sure to be some of the servants about, and they'll tell you whereabouts Mrs. Hale's rooms are."

The great gate swung heavily back, and Margaret passed through. The avenue wound in and about for nearly half a mile, and she was thinking that she should never get to the end of it, when at a sudden turn a sight broke upon her which caused her to stop with astonishment.

As if it had sprung from the ground, raised by a magician's wand, rose Leyton Court. You can buy any number of photographs of it, and are no doubt quite familiar with its long stretching pile of red bricks and white facings; but Margaret had seen neither the place nor any views of it, and the vision of grandeur and beauty took her breath away.

Far down the line of sight the facade stretched, wing upon wing, all glowing a dusky red veiled by ivy and Virginian creeper, and sparkling here and there as the sunset rays shone on the diamond-latticed windows. The most intense silence reigned over the whole; not a human being was in sight, and the girl was quite startled when a peacock, which had been strutting across a lawn that looked like velvet, spread its tail and uttered a shrill shriek.

The size and grandeur of the place awed her, and she stood uncertain which direction to take, when a maid-servant, with a pleasant face and a shy smile, came hurriedly through a wicket set in the closely-cut box hedge, and said:

"Are you Miss Margaret, please?"

"Yes," she replied.

"Mrs. Hale sent me to meet you, miss. This way please." And with a smile of welcome, the girl led her through a narrow alley of greenery into a near courtyard which seemed to belong to a wing of the great house. An old fountain plashed in the center of the court and all around were beds of bright flowers, which filled the air with color and perfume. Up the old red walls also climbed blue starred clematis and honeysuckle, through which the windows glistened like diamonds.

Margaret looked round and drew her breath with that excess of pleasure which is almost pain.

"Oh what a lovely place!" she murmured involuntarily.

The servant looked pleased.

"It is pretty, isn't it, miss?" she assented. "Of course it isn't the grand part of the Court, but *I* think that it's as beautiful as any part of the terrace or the Italian gardens."

"Nothing could be more lovely than this!" said Margaret.

Then she uttered a low cry of loving greeting, and, running forward, threw her arms round an old lady, who, hearing her voice, had come to the open doorway.

"Why Margaret—Madge!" said the old lady tremulously, as she pressed the girl to her bosom, and then held her at arm's length that she might look into her face. "Why my dear—my dear! Why, how you've grown! Is this my little Margaret?—my little pale-faced Madge, who was no taller than the table, and all legs and wings?" and leading the girl into a bright little parlor, she sank into a chair, and holding her by the hands, looked her over with that loving admiration of which only a mother or a grandmother can be capable; and the old lady was justified, for the girl, as she stood, slightly leaning forward with a flush on her face and her eyes glowing with affection and emotion, presented a picture beautiful enough to melt the heart of an anchorite.

"Yes, it's I, grandma," she said, half laughing, half crying. "And you think I've grown?"

"Grown! My dear, when I saw you last you were a child; you are a woman now, and a very"—"beautiful" she was going to say, but stopped short—"a very passable young woman, too! I can scarcely believe my eyes! My little madcap Madge!"

"Oh, not madcap any longer, grandma dear," said the girl, sinking on her knees and taking off her hat, that she might lean her head comfortably on the old lady's bosom, "not wild madcap now, you know. I am Miss Margaret Hale, of the School of Art, and a silver medalist," and she laughed with sparkling eyes, which rather indicated that there was something of the wildness left notwithstanding her dignity.

"Dear, dear me!" murmured the old lady. "Such a grand young lady! You must tell me all about it. But there, what am I thinking of? You must be tired—how did you come from the station, dear?"

"I walked," said the girl.

"Walked! Why didn't you take a fly, child?"

The girl colored slightly.

"Oh, it was a lovely evening and I was tired of sitting so long, and—and—flys are for rich people, you know grandmamma," laughingly, "and although I am a silver medalist, I am not a millionaire yet! But indeed—" she added quickly—"I enjoyed the walk amazingly, it is such a lovely country, and my things are coming on by the carrier. And now I'll go and wash some of the dust and smuts away, and come back and tell you—oh, everything."

The old lady called the maid, and the girl, still shyly, led Margaret to a dainty little room which overlooked the flowered court, which filled it with the odors of the clematis and honeysuckle and sweetbrier.

Margaret went to the window, and leaning over, drew in a long breath of the perfumed air.

"Oh, beautiful! beautiful!" she murmured. "Ah! you should have lived in London for five years to appreciate this lovely place. Mary—is your name Mary?"

The maid blushed.

"Why, yes, miss! Did you guess it?" she replied, almost awed by the cleverness of this tall, lovely young creature from London.

Margaret laughed.

"Most nice girls are called Mary," she said; "and I am sure you are nice."

The girl blushed again, but, rendered speechless with pleasure, could only stare at her shyly, and run from the room.

When Margaret came down it seemed to the old lady that she was more beautiful than before, with her bright soft hair brushed down from her oval face, and her slim, undulating figure revealed by the absence of the traveling jacket. Tea was on the table and a huge bowl of Gloire roses, and the whole room looked the picture of comfort and elegance.

"Now tell me all about it," said Mrs. Hale, when the girl had got seated in a low chair beside the window, with her teacup and bread and butter. "And you are quite a famous personage, Margaret, are you?"

The girl laughed, a soft, low laugh of innocent happiness.

"Not famous, dear," she said, "a very long way from the top of the tree; but I've been lucky in getting one of my pictures into the Academy and gaining the silver medal, and what is better than all, my picture is sold."

This seemed to surprise the unsophisticated old lady more than all the rest.

"Dear, dear me!" she mused. "Who ever would have thought that little wild Madge would become an artist and paint pictures——"

"And sell them, too," laughed the girl.

"How proud your poor father would have been if he had lived," added Mrs. Hale, with a sigh.

A swift shadow crossed the girl's lovely face, and there was silence for a moment.

"And you are quite happy, Madge? The life suits you?"

"Yes, quite, dear; oh, quite. Of course it is hard work. I paint all day while there is light enough, and I read books on art—I was going to say all night," and she smiled. "Then there are the schools and lectures—oh! it is a very pleasant life when one is so fond of art as I am."

"And you don't feel lonely with no kith nor kin near you?"

"No," she said. "Three of us girls lodge together a little way from the schools, and so it is not lonely, and the lady who looks after the house—and us, of course—is pleasant and lady-like. Oh, no, it is not lonely, but—" her eyes softened—"but I am glad to come down and see you, grandma—I can't tell you how glad!" and she stretched out her long, white, shapely hand— the artist's hand—so that the old lady could take it and fondle it.

"Yes, my dear," she said. "And I can't tell you how glad I am to have you. It seems ages instead of five years since we parted in London and I came down here as housekeeper to the earl—ages! And the change will do you good; I think you want a little country air; you're looking a trifle pale, now that you have settled down a bit."

"It's only the London color," said the girl, smiling. "Nobody carries many roses on his cheeks in London. What lovely ones those are on the table, grandma, and what cream! How the girls would stare if they saw and tasted it. You know we drink chalk and water in London, grandma!"

"Bless my soul!" exclaimed the old lady.

"They carry it round in cans and call it milk, but it is chalk and water all the same," she said, laughingly. "And now, dear, you must tell me all about yourself—why, we have done nothing but talk about foolish me since I came! Are *you* quite happy, grandma, and do you like being housekeeper to a grand earl?"

"Very much, my dear," said the old lady, with a touch of dignity. "It is a most important and responsible post," and she stroked the smooth white hand she still held.

"I should think so," said Margaret, with quick sympathy. "Keeping any kind of house must be a tremendous affair, but keeping such an enormous place as this—why, grandma, it is like a town, there seems no end to it!"

The old lady nodded proudly.

"Yes. Leyton Court is a very grand place, my dear," she assented. "I suppose it's one of the grandest, if not *the* grandest, in the country. You shall go over it some day when the earl is away."

"The earl, yes," said Margaret. "It was very kind of him to let me come."

Mrs. Hale tossed her head.

"Oh, my dear, he knows nothing about it!" she said. "Bless me, the earl is too great a person to know anything about the goings on of such humble individuals as you and me. I am my own mistress in my own apartments, my dear, and am quite at liberty to have my own granddaughter stay with me."

"Of course," said the girl quickly. "And is he nice?—the earl, I mean."

"Nice!" repeated the old lady, as if there were something disrespectful in the word. "Well, 'nice' is scarcely the word—I've only seen him half a dozen times since I came, so I can't say what he's like; but he was very pleasant then—in his way, my dear."

Margaret opened her eyes.

"Not half-a-dozen times in five years? Then he doesn't live here always?"

"Not always. He is in Spain or Ireland some parts of the year, but he lives at the Court during most of the summer. You see, my dear, great folks like the Earl of Ferrers keep to themselves more than humble people. The earl has his own apartments—you can see them from the drive; they run along the terrace—and his own particular servants. Excepting Mr. Stibbings, the butler, and Mr. Larkhall, his valet, and the footmen, none of us see anything of his lordship."

"He is quite like a king, then?" said the girl musingly.

"Quite," assented the old lady approvingly; "quite like a king, as you say; and everybody in Leyton Ferrers regards him as one. Why, the queen herself couldn't be more looked up to or feared!"

The girl pondered over this. You don't meet many earls and dukes in the National Art Schools, and this one possessed an atmosphere of novelty for Margaret.

"And does he live here all alone?" she asked.

"All alone; yes."

"In this great place? How lonely he must be!"

"No, my dear," said the old lady. "Great people are never lonely; they are quite—quite different to us humble folks."

Margaret smiled to herself at the naive assertion.

"I thought he would have had some relations to live with him. Hasn't he any sons—children?"

Mrs. Hale shook her head.

"No, no children! There was a son, but he died. There is a nephew, Lord Blair Leyton, but he and the earl don't agree, and he has never been here, though, of course, he will come into the property when the earl dies, which won't be for many a long year, I hope."

"Blair Leyton! and he's a lord too——"

"A viscount," said the old lady. "I don't like to speak ill of a gentleman, especially one I don't know, but I am afraid his young lordship is—is"—she looked round for a word—"is a very wicked young man, my dear."

"How do you know?" asked Margaret, nestling into the comfortable chair to listen at her ease.

"Well, Mr. Stibbings has spoken of him. Mr. Stibbings—a perfect gentleman, my dear—is good enough to drop in and take a cup of tea sometimes, and he has told me about young Lord Blair! You see, he has been in the family a great many years, and knows all its history. He says that the earl and the young nephew never did get on together, and that the young man is, oh, very wild indeed, my dear! The earl and he have only met two or three times, and then they quarreled—quarreled dreadfully. I daresay the earl feels the loss of his son, and that makes it hard for him to get on with Lord Blair. But he is really a very wicked young man, I am sorry to say."

"What does he do?" asked Margaret.

The old lady looked rather puzzled how to describe a young man's wickedness to an innocent girl.

"Well, my dear, it would be easier, perhaps, to say what he *doesn't* do!" she said at last.

Margaret laughed softly.

"Poor young man," she said gently. "It must be bad to be so wicked!"

The old lady shook her head severely.

"I don't know why you pity him, my dear," she said.

"Oh, I don't know," said the girl, slowly. "Perhaps some people can't help being bad, you know, grandma! Oh, here are my things coming! now I can show you one of my pictures!" and she jumped up gleefully, and commenced unfastening the brown-paper parcel. "I did think of carrying it, but I am glad I didn't, for it was warm, and I met with an unpleasant adventure on the road, when the parcel might have been in the way. Oh, I didn't tell you, grandma! I saw such a terrible fight—a *fight*! think of it—as I came here."

"A fight, my dear?" exclaimed the old lady.

"Yes," nodded Margaret; "between two men; and what made it worse, one was a gentleman."

"A gentleman, Margaret! Gentlemen don't fight, my dear."

"So I thought," she said, naively; "but this one does anyway, and fights very well," she added. "At least, he knocked the other one down—a great tall fellow—as if he had been shot."

"Bless my heart! where was this?"

"Oh, just in the village here. The man—he was an ill-tempered fellow, I'm sure, with such a dreadful face—kicked a poor dog, and the gentleman, who was near, fought him for it."

"Good gracious me! And, of course, you ran away?"

The girl laughed rather strangely.

"No, I didn't, grandma. I ought to have done so, I meant to do so, but—well, I didn't. I wish I had, for the creature had the impudence to speak to me!"

"What—the man?" aghast.

"The gentleman. He came across the road and begged my pardon. I'd got the poor dog in my arms, you see, and I suppose—well I don't know why he spoke, but perhaps it was because, being a gentleman, he felt ashamed of himself. If he didn't at first, I think he did when he went away," she added, with a laugh and a blush, as she remembered the words that had flown like darts of fire from her lips. "Oh, it was shameful! His face was cut, and there was blood"—she shuddered—"on his collar! He was a very handsome young man, too. I wonder who he was. Did I tell you he came down by the same train as I did?"

Mrs. Hale shook her head.

"No one I know, my dear," she said. "None of the gentry hereabouts would fight with any one, least of all a common man. A tall man, with an ugly face——"

"Oh, very ugly and evil-looking—I think they called him Pyke."

"Pyke—Jem Pyke!" said Mrs. Hale. "Oh, I know him; a dreadful bad character, my dear. I'm not surprised at his kicking a dog, or fighting either. He's one of our worst men—a poacher and a thief, so they say. I wonder he didn't get the best of it!"

"He got the very possible worst of it," said Margaret, with an unconscious tone of satisfaction. "There's the picture, grandma! And where will you hang it?"

It was a clever little picture; a bit of a London street, faithfully and carefully painted, and instinct with grace and feeling.

The old lady of course did not see all the good points, but she was none the less proud and delighted, and stood regarding it with admiring awe that rendered her speechless.

"You dear, clever girl," she said, kissing her, "and it is for me, really for me? Oh, Margaret, if your poor father——"

Margaret sighed.

"Get me a hammer and a nail, grandma," she said, after a moment, "and I'll put it in a good light; the light is everything, you know."

A hammer and nail were brought, and the picture hung, and the two went out into the garden, and presently the girl was singing like a nightingale from her over-brimming heart. But suddenly she stopped and looked in at the window of the room where the old lady had returned to see the unpacking and uncreasing of the clothes which had traveled in the unpretending Gladstone bag.

"Oh, grandma, I beg your pardon! I forgot! Perhaps the earl won't like my singing?"

Mrs. Hale laughed.

"The earl! My dear, he is right at the other end of the building and could scarcely hear a brass band from here! But come in now, Margaret, and have some supper. You must go to bed early after your long journey, or you won't sow the seed for those roses I want to see in your cheeks!"

When she woke in the morning with the scent of the honeysuckle wafting across her face, Margaret could almost have persuaded herself that Leyton Court was a vision of a dream, and that she should find herself presently on her way to the art school at Kensington amidst all the London noise and smoke. To most Londoners the country in June is a dream of Paradise; what must it have been to this young girl, with the soul of an artist, with every nerve throbbing in sympathy with the sky, the flowers, the songs of the birds?

Like a vision herself, her plainly made morning dress of a soft, dove color and fitting her slim young shape with the grace of a well-made garment that can afford to be plain, she ran down the oak stairs into the parlor. But Mrs. Hale was not there, and Mary, who glanced with shy admiration at the lovely face and pretty dress, said that she had gone to see the butler.

"You will find her in the pantry, miss, if you like. It is at the end of this passage, to the right. You can't miss it, miss."

But Margaret did miss it, for her idea of a pantry was a small place in the nature of a cupboard, whereas the pantry at the Court was a large and spacious room, and Margaret, seeing nothing to answer to her idea, opened a door, entered, found herself before another door, opened that, discovered that she was in a round kind of a lobby surrounded, like Blue Beard's chamber, with other doors, and all at once learned that she had lost herself.

It was a ridiculous position to be placed in, and an annoying one, for she felt that her grandmother would be vexed by Margaret's venturing out of their own apartments.

But she did not know what to do; it was impossible, having turned round in the circular lobby and lost count of the door, to regain it again, and in a semi-comic despair, she opened the door opposite her, intending to walk on until she met a servant of whom she could ask her way back to Mrs. Hale's wing.

She found herself presently and quite suddenly in a short corridor, at the end of which a stream of varicolored light poured from a stained window; there was the reflection also of gilt carving and velvet hangings, and rather awed, Margaret was for turning back, when she saw a footman pass with noiseless footsteps across the thick Oriental carpet at the end of the corridor.

She called to him, and hurried after him, but before she could reach him he had disappeared as if by magic, evidently without hearing her suppressed voice, and she found herself standing at the entrance to a magnificent picture gallery, which seemed to run an interminable length and lose itself in a distant vista of ferns and statuary.

Margaret literally held her breath as she peered in through the velvet curtains.

There, line upon line, hung what was no doubt one of the collections of the kingdom—and she within the threshold of it.

Her mouth, metaphorically, began to water; her large dark eyes grew humid with wistfulness.

What cream is to a cat, water to a duck, *pate de foie gras* to a gourmet, an Elziver to a bookworm, that is a picture gallery to an artist.

She could resist the temptation no longer. The place was crowned, as it were, with silence and solitude: no one would see her or know that she had been there, and she would only stay five—ten minutes.

Eve could not resist temptation—being doubtless fond of apples; Margaret could not resist, being fond of pictures. And yet, if she had known what was to follow upon this visit to Leyton Court, if there had only been some kind guardian angel to whisper:

"Fly, Margaret, my child! Fly this spot, where peril and destruction await thee!"

But, alas! our guardian angels always seem to be taking bank holiday just on the days when we most need them, and Margaret's angel was silent as the tomb.

Pushing the heavily-bullioned curtain aside she entered the gallery, and an exclamation of surprise and delight broke from her lips.

It was a priceless collection: Rubens, Vandyke, Titians, Raphael, Michael Angelo, Cuyp, Jan Steen; all the masters were here, and at their best.

The soul of the girl went into her eyes, her face grew pale, and her breath came in long-drawn sighs, as she moved noiselessly on the thick Turkey carpet, which stretched itself like a glittering snake over the marble floor before the pictures.

What jewels were to some women, and dress to others, pictures were to Margaret.

She was standing rapt in an ecstasy before a head by Guido, her hands clasped and hanging loosely in front of her, her lovely face upturned, a picture as beautiful as the one upon which she gazed, when she suddenly became aware, without either seeing or hearing, but with that sense, which is indescribable and nameless, that she was not alone, but that some one else had entered the gallery.

The consciousness affected her strangely, and for a moment she did not move eye or limb; then, with an effort, she turned her head and saw a tall figure standing a few paces from the doorway.

It was that of an old man, with white hair and dark—piercing dark—eyes. He was clad in a velvet dressing-gown, whose folds fell round the thin form and gave it an antique expression, which harmonized with the magnificence and silence of the gallery.

The eyes were bent on her, not sternly, not curiously, but with a calm, steadfast regard, which affected her more than any expression of anger could have done.

She stood quite still, her heart beating wildly, for she knew, though she had never seen him, that it must be the earl himself.

CHAPTER III

Margaret stood perfectly still, her eyes downcast, yet seeing quite plainly the tall patrician figure enveloped in the folds of violet velvet.

What should she do? Pass by him without a word, or murmur some kind of apology? How upset and annoyed her grandmother would be when she heard of her trespass, and its discovery by the earl, of all people. And the earl himself, what was he thinking of her? He was, no doubt, setting her down, in his mind, as an ill-bred, forward girl, who had intruded out of sheer impudence! The idea was almost unendurable, and smarting under it, the color came slowly into her face and her lips quivered.

Meanwhile, the earl, who had been indifferently wondering who she was, moved slowly, his hands behind him, along the gallery and toward her. His movements nerved her, and bending her head she made for the door, but slowly. The earl may have thought that she was one of the higher servants, but as she came nearer—for she had to pass him to leave the gallery—he must have seen that she was not one of the establishment, which was far too numerous for him to be familiar with.

"Do not let me drive you away," he said, in a low-toned, but exquisitely clear and musical voice, which had so often moved his fellow peers in the Upper House.

"I am going," said Margaret, flushing. "I—I ought not to have come."

She had never spoken to a nobleman in her life before, and did not know whether to say "my lord" or "your lordship," at the end of her sentence.

"Ought you not?" he said, with a faint smile crossing his clear-cut features.

"No—my lord," she faltered, venturing on that form; "I—I came here by accident. I lost my way. I am very sorry."

"Do not apologize," he said, bending his piercing eyes on her face, and smiling again as he noticed her abashed expression; "it is not a deadly sin. Are you——" he hesitated. It was evident that he did not want to add to her distress and confusion, and was choosing his words—"Are you staying here?"

"Yes," said Margaret; "I am staying with Mrs. Hale, my grandmother, my lord."

"Ah, yes!" he murmured. "Yes. Mrs. Hale. Yes, yes. You are her granddaughter. What is your name?"

"Margaret—Margaret Hale," she said.

"And how long have you been here?" he asked.

"I came last night, my lord," said Margaret.

"Last night? Yes. And you were on a voyage of discovery——"

"Oh, no, no!" she broke in, quickly. "I was looking for Mrs. Hale, and— opened the wrong door; when I came into the corridor outside I saw the pictures, and"—her color rose—"I was tempted to come in," and, with an inclination of the head, she was moving away.

His voice stopped her.

"Are you fond of pictures?" he asked, as one of his age and attainments would ask a child.

"Yes," said Margaret, simply, refraining even from adding, "very."

His glance grew absent.

"Most of your sex are," he said, musingly. "All life is but a picture to most of them. The surface, the surface only"—he sighed very faintly and wearily, and was pacing on, to Margaret's immense relief, as if he had forgotten her, when he stopped, as if moved by a kindly impulse, and said: "Pray come here when you please. The pictures will be glad of your company; they spend a solitary life too often. Yes, come when you please."

"Thank you, my lord," said Margaret, quietly, and without any fuss.

Perhaps the reserved and quiet response attracted his attention.

"Which was the picture I saw you admiring when I came in?" he asked. "You were admiring it, I think?"

"It was the head by Guido, my lord," she answered.

He looked at her quickly.

"How did you know it was Guido's?" he asked, and he went and stood before the picture, looking from it to her.

Margaret stared. How could it be possible for any intelligent person not to know!

"It is easy to tell a Guido, my lord," she said, with a slight smile. "One has only to see one of them once, and I have seen them in the National Gallery fifty—a hundred times."

He looked at her, not curiously—the Earl of Ferrers, famed for his exquisite courtesy, could not have done that—but with a newly-born interest.

"Yes? Do you recognize other masters here? This, for instance," and he raised his hand; it stood out like snow in front of the violet velvet, and a large amethyst on the forefinger gleamed redly in the downward light.

"That is a Carlo Dolci, my lord; but not a very good one."

"Right in both assertions," he said, with a smile. "And this?"

"A Rubens, and a very fine one," she said, forgetting his presence and grandeur, and approaching the picture. "I have never seen more beautiful coloring in a Rubens—but I have not seen the Continental galleries. It would look better still if it were not hung so near that De la Roche; the two clash. Now, if the other Rubens on the opposite side were placed——" but she remembered herself, and stopped suddenly, confused and shamefaced.

"Pray go on," he said gently. "You would hang them side by side. Yes. You are right! Tell me who painted this!" and he inclined his head toward a heavy battle piece.

"I do not know, my lord," said Margaret.

He smiled.

"It is a pleasant discovery to find that your knowledge is not illimitable," he said. "It is a Wouvermans."

Margaret looked at it, and her brows came together, after a fashion peculiar to her when she was thinking deeply, displeased, or silent under pressure.

"Well?" he said, as if he had read her thoughts; "what would you say?"

"It is not a Wouvermans, my lord," she said.

The earl smiled, and stood with folded hands regarding her.

"No, my lord. That is, I think not. It is not even a copy, but an imitation—oh, forgive me!" she broke off, blushing.

"No, no!" he said, gently; "there is nothing to forgive. Tell me why you think so? But I warn you—" and he smiled with mock gravity—"this picture cost several thousand pounds!"

"I can't help it," said Margaret, desperate on behalf of truth. "It is not a Wouvermans! He never painted a horse like that—never! I have copied dozens of his pictures. I should know a horse of his if I met it in the streets, my lord," and her eyebrows came together again in almost piteous assertion.

He looked at the picture keenly; then, with a slight air of surprise, he said:

"I think you are right! But it is a clever forgery——"

"Oh, clever!" said Margaret, with light scorn.

"Are you an artist?" he asked, after a second's pause.

"Yes, my lord," she said, modestly.

"Yes! Ah, I understand your inability to keep outside the gallery. An artist"—his piercing eyes rested on her downcast face—"my pictures are honored by your attention, Miss Hale. Permit me to repeat my invitation. I hope you will pay the gallery many visits. If you should care to copy any of the pictures, pray do so!"

"Oh, my lord!" said Margaret, and her face lit up as if a ray of sunlight had passed across it.

There was no ill-bred admiration in his gray eyes, only a deep and steady regard.

"Copy any you choose," he said. "As to the De la Roche——"

He paused, for a hurried footstep was heard behind them, and Mrs. Hale's voice anxiously calling "Margaret."

At sight of the earl she stopped short, turned pale, and dropped a profound curtsey.

"Oh, my lord! I—we—beg your pardon! My granddaughter lost her way——" then she seemed unable to go any further.

The earl turned to her with the calm, impassive manner he had worn when Margaret had seen him first.

"Do not apologize, Mrs. Hale," he said. "Your granddaughter is perfectly welcome. She is an artist, I hear?"

"Yes, my lord," faltered the old lady, as if she were confessing some great sin of Margaret's.

"Yes, and a capable one I am sure. She will probably like to copy some of the pictures. Please see that she is not disturbed."

Then, leaving the old lady overwhelmed and bewildered, he inclined his head to Margaret and moved away. But as he raised the heavy curtain at the end of the gallery, he turned and looked aside at her with a grave smile.

"The De la Roche shall be re-hung, and the false Wouvermans removed." Then murmuring "would that it were as easy to depose every other false pretender!" he let the curtain fall and disappeared.

Margaret stood looking after him, her brows drawn together dreamily, and seemed to awake with a start when, with a gasp, the old lady turned to her, exclaiming:

"Well, Margaret! To think that the earl—that his lordship—that—that——When I came in and saw him with you here I felt fit to sink into the ground! Oh, my dear, how ever did you come here?"

"'My wayward feet were wont to stray,'" quoted Margaret, with a laugh.

"What do you say?"

"Oh, it was only a line from a poem, grandmamma. I lost my way, and the earl came in and found me——"

"And—and spoke? And he wasn't angry? My dear, if I had been in your place, I should have longed for the earth to open and swallow me up!"

Margaret laughed softly.

"Of course you mustn't pay any attention to what he said: you mustn't take advantage of his offer about the copying of the pictures. Copy the pictures! Good gracious! as if you'd take such a liberty!"

Margaret opened her eyes.

"I certainly did think of taking it," she said.

"Oh, dear, no; it would never do!" exclaimed the old lady. "It was only politeness on his part to make you feel at your ease, and to show that he wasn't angry. As to his meaning it, why of course he didn't!"

"I had an impression that great noblemen like the earl always meant what they said; but that's only my ignorance, grandma, and, of course, I'll do as you wish. But," with a wistful glance down the gallery, "I had looked forward to painting some of them."

"Well, never mind, my dear," said the old lady soothingly; "you can come and look at them—sometimes, when the earl's out or away from the Court. It would never do for him to find you here again."

"No. I suppose next time he wouldn't find it incumbent upon him to be polite. Well, let's go now, grandma," and she turned with a sigh.

"Not that way!" exclaimed Mrs. Hale, in a horrified whisper, as Margaret went toward a door; "that leads direct to his lordship's private apartments."

Margaret laughed.

"It is quite evident that I mustn't venture out of your rooms alone again, grandma, or I shall get into serious trouble!"

"That you certainly will. But it's excusable, my dear; there aren't many places so big, and such a maze like. It took even me a long time to find my way about."

She opened the proper door as she spoke, and nearly ran against a portly gentleman, who was dignified looking enough to be the earl's brother.

"Bless my heart, Mr. Stibbings!" exclaimed Mrs. Hale. The butler puffed out a response in a hushed voice—everybody's voice was hushed at Leyton Court—then looked at Margaret and made a respectful bow.

"My granddaughter, Margaret, Mr. Stibbings," said the old lady, proudly.

The butler appeared surprised. He had taken Margaret for a visitor, and had been wondering how on earth she had got into the place without his knowing it?

"In—deed, Mrs. Hale! Glad to see you, miss."

"Yes, Mr. Stibbings; and, would you believe it, she's been in our picture-gallery, and——"

But Mr. Stibbings seemed too hurried and full of suppressed excitement to attend.

"Mrs. Hale, ma'am, you'll scarcely credit it, but——" he drew nearer and lowered his voice to a whisper.

"Bless my heart!" exclaimed the old lady. "Dear, dear me! What is to be done? Will he stay, do you think? You'll let me know at once, there will be a great deal to see to——"

"Yes, yes," said the butler. "I'm going to find out. He has only just been announced. I don't know yet whether the earl will see him. Extraordinary, isn't it?" and he hurried on his way.

"Ex—tra—ordinary!" responded the old lady, staring at Margaret.

"What has happened, grandma?" asked Margaret, with a laugh.

"It's no laughing matter, my dear!" said the old lady, gravely. "Lord Blair Leyton has come."

"Has he?" said Margaret, with less interest than the matter deserved.

"Yes, and who knows what will happen? Perhaps the earl won't see him; perhaps they won't meet after all."

"I suppose they won't kill each other if they do, will they?" said Margaret.

The old lady looked at her aghast; such levity was terrible.

"My dear," she said, "you don't know what you are talking about. Kill each other—the earl and his nephew! Why, how ever could you say such a thing? Great people never fight, let alone kill each other."

CHAPTER IV

Meanwhile, Mr. Larkhall, the valet, had gone to the earl's sitting-room and made the announcement:

"Lord Leyton, my lord!"

The earl raised his steel-gray eyes, and, frowning slightly, said, "Lord Leyton?" without any expression of surprise.

"Yes, my lord," said the valet, with the proper impassiveness of a high-class servant.

The earl kept his eyes on the floor for a moment, then nodded as an indication that Lord Blair was to be shown in, and Mr. Larkhall went out to the drawing-room, where Lord Blair was waiting.

He was looking remarkably well this morning, and there were no traces of his encounter with Mr. Pyke on his handsome face, which with its prevailing suggestion of brightness and good humor, seemed to light up the grand and rather too stately room. He was dressed in that very comfortable and somewhat picturesque fashion, which is the mode nowadays, and his shapely limbs displayed themselves, not without grace, in knickerbockers and a shooting jacket of a wide check, which made his broad shoulders look even more vast than they were. Take him altogether he presented a very fine specimen of the genus man, at its best period, when youth sits at the prow, and pleasure sings joyously at the helm.

"This way, my lord," said Mr. Larkhall, and the young man followed the valet into the earl's room.

As he entered, the earl rose and looked at him, and notwithstanding the sternness of his face, a gleam of reluctant admiration shone in his eyes. He held out the thin, white hand.

"How do you do, Blair?" he said.

Lord Blair shook his hand.

"I hope you're well, sir?" he said, and the light, musical voice seemed to ring through the room, in its contrast to the elder man's subdued tones.

The earl waved his hand to a chair, and sank back into his own.

Then a silence ensued. It was evident that the earl expected the young viscount to account for his presence, and that Lord Blair found it rather hard to begin.

"Not had the gout lately, I hope, sir?" he said.

"Thanks, no; not very lately," replied the earl.

"I'm glad of that," said Lord Blair. "I shouldn't have liked to worry you while you were ill—and—and I ought to apologize for coming uninvited——"

It was palpable that he was not used to apologizing, and he did it awkwardly and bluntly.

The earl waved his hand.

"You are always free to come to the Court, Blair; you know that, I trust?"

He did not say that he was welcome, or that he, the earl was glad to see him.

"Thanks," said Lord Blair. "I shouldn't have come if I hadn't been obliged—I mean," with a smile at his clumsiness, "I mean I wanted to see you particularly on business——"

"Business?" said the earl, raising his eyebrows slightly. "Would not Messrs. Tyler & Driver——"

Tyler & Driver were the family solicitors.

"No," said Lord Blair; "I didn't think so. The fact is, sir, that I'm in a scrape." He said it with an air of surprise that made the earl smile dryly. "Yes; I suppose you'll say I always am. Well, I dare say I am. By George, I don't know how it is, either, for I'm always trying hard to keep out of 'em."

"Is it money—this time?" inquired the earl, with an impassiveness that was worse than any exhibition of ill-humor.

"Yes; it's money this time," assented Lord Blair laughing slightly, but coloring. "The fact is——" he paused. "I don't know whether you saw that my horse, Daylight, lost the Chinhester stakes?"

"I don't read the racing news," said his lordship gravely.

"Ah, I forgot. Well, it did. The fool of a jockey pulled at him too long, and—but I'm afraid you would not understand, sir."

"Most probably not," was the dry response.

"Anyway, he lost, and as I'd backed him very heavily—too heavily as it turned out—I lost a hatful of money. I've had a run of ill-luck all the season, too," he continued, as cheerfully as if he were recounting luck of quite another kind. "So I find myself completely up a tree. I don't like asking you for any more money, I seem to have had such a tremendous lot, don't you know, and it occurred to me that there was that Ketton property, and I could raise the money on that."

The earl's face darkened.

"Of course I know I needn't have troubled you about it," went on Lord Blair, "but I promised you I wouldn't raise any money without letting you know, and so—well, here I am," he wound up cheerfully.

The earl sat perfectly still and looked at the carpet.

"Blair," he said, at last, "you are on the road to ruin!"

"It's not so bad as that, sir, I hope," said the young man, after a rather startled stare and pause.

"You are a spendthrift and a gambler," continued the earl, his face hardening at each word.

Lord Blair's face flushed.

"That's rather strong, isn't it, sir?" he said, quietly.

"It is the truth—the plain truth," retorted the earl, quickly. "You are twenty-five, and you have run through—flung to the winds, destroyed— nearly all your own property. Only Ketton remains, and that is, you tell me, to go. What do you expect me to say? Have you no conscience, no sense of decency? But, indeed, the question is unnecessary, you have none."

The young man rose, and on his handsome face came a look that bore a faint resemblance to that on the old man's.

"What do you mean?" he asked, shortly.

The earl raised his eyes.

"With this ruin impending over you, you come to me to ask my sanction of the last step, and on the way here you amuse yourself by indulging in a vulgar ale-house brawl with one of my people, outside my gates—within sight of the house!"

Lord Blair sank into the chair, and smiled.

"Oh, that," he said, easily—"oh, that was nothing, sir. The fellow deserved all he got and more. 'Pon my word I couldn't help it. It was—but you've heard all about it, I daresay?"

"I have heard that you had a vulgar quarrel with one of the worst characters in the place, and indulged in a fight with him, sir," said the earl, his eyes flashing for a moment, then growing hard and cold. "But I forget.

You say it was nothing. That which I deem a degradation, the future Earl of Ferrers may regard differently. But this I may be permitted to ask: that you will choose some other locality than Leyton for the exhibition of your brutality."

A hot response sprung to the lips of Lord Blair, but with an effort he choked it back.

"We won't say any more about the affair, sir," he said, "except that if it were to be done again, I'd do it!"

"I don't doubt you, sir," said the earl, coldly.

There was a pause, then the young man rose.

"I take it I can raise the money on Ketton, then?" he said.

The earl stared at the floor moodily.

"Hartwell gone, Parkfield mortgaged to the hilt, and now Ketton. What next, sir? Thank Heaven, you cannot play ducks and drakes with this place, or you would do it, I suppose! But I could forgive you all you have done if you had spared Violet."

The color mounted to the young man's face, and he bit his lip.

"In her, and her alone, lay your chance of salvation. You flung it away as ruthlessly as you have flung away your property. You have ruined yourself and broken her heart, and you sit there smiling— —"

As if he could endure it no longer, Lord Blair rose.

"Broken her heart! Broken Violet's heart!" he repeated, with mingled amazement and incredulity. "Good Heavens, who told you that? I don't believe she has a heart to break! We—we broke off the match by mutual agreement. She was quite jolly about it! She—oh, come, sir, you don't know Violet as well as I do. I'll answer for it she thinks herself well out of it; as she is, by George! Any woman would get a bad bargain in me, I'm afraid."

"I wish that I could contradict you," said the earl grimly. "I pity any woman who trusts herself to your tender mercies. As for Violet Graham, I am glad that she has escaped; but your conduct was dishonorable— —"

The young man's face paled, and his hands clinched with a passion of which he had shown no trace during the fight of yesterday.

"That will do, sir," he said, in a low voice. "No man, not even you, has the right to use such a word to me! I tell you it would have been dishonorable to have married Violet for her money; it was more honorable to keep from it. I'm going. As to Ketton, it's my own— —"

"For the present," put in the earl, with fearful sarcasm.

—"And I can do what I like with it. I'd rather sell it twenty times over than marry Violet Graham, and get her money to save it! Good-bye, sir!" He was going out of the room with this brief farewell, but at the door he paused, and striding back held out his hand. "Look here, sir," he said, his voice softening, a gentler light coming into his eyes. "Don't let us part like this! Heaven knows when we shall meet again, if ever we do! I may have to clear out of England! I've some thoughts of going in for sheep farming out West, or I may break my neck at the next steeplechase. Anyhow, let us part friends."

The earl waved him to the chair.

If he had grasped the extended hand the warm heart of the young man would have forgiven all the hard words that had been spoken—forgiven and forgotten them.

"Sit down, please. You are right. Words are of no avail between us. In regard to your proposition, I am averse to it. I will give you the money. What is the amount?"

Lord Blair looked surprised, then grave.

"Thanks, sir," he said. "But I would rather you didn't. I have had too much from you already. I'm ashamed to think how much. I'm a spendthrift and a fool, as you say, but for the future I will spend only my own. I'm not ungrateful for all you have given me! No, but—I can't take any more from you."

The earl's lips came together tightly. He bowed.

"I have no right to combat your resolution," he said, "or to prevent you ruining yourself in your own fashion. After all, it matters very little whether the Jews have Ketton now or later; they will get it one time or the other, doubtless."

"I'm afraid they will," said Lord Blair, with a short sigh; then he rose. "Well, I'm off, sir."

"Stay!" said the earl; "our quarrel—if it can be called one—is over. You will oblige me by remaining for one night at least. I do not wish it to be said all over the country that we could not exist for twenty-four hours under one roof, as it will be said if you go at once. Stay, if you please."

"If you wish it, sir, certainly," said Lord Blair, not very joyously. "But I'm afraid I shall bore you dreadfully, you know."

"The boring will be mutual, I have no doubt," said the earl grimly. "I may remind you that we need meet only at dinner."

"That's true," said Lord Blair frankly. "Well, until then, I'll walk round the place."

Then earl inclined his head, and rang the bell which stood at his elbow.

"Lord Leyton will remain here to-night," he said to Larkhall, and that exemplary servant, holding the door open for Lord Blair to pass out, hurried off to tell Mr. Stibbings and Mrs. Hale the extraordinary news that the future earl was to sleep at the house which would some day be his own.

Lord Blair had spent a remarkably bad quarter of an hour; but before he had got half way down the broad staircase, with its carved balustrades and magnificent cross panelling, he began to shake off the effects with that wonderful good-humored carelessness which had lost him nearly all his lands, and won him so many hearts.

He went down the stairs into the hall and looked round him with a smile, as if his interview had been of the pleasantest description; then he lit a cigar and, with his hat on the back of his head, went out into the warm sunshine.

He walked along the terrace and across the lawns, and then as if by instinct found his way to the stables. And be it remarked, and it is worth noting, that he had not—as many a man in his position would have done—given one glance at the magnificent place with the thought that it would some day all be his.

Strange to say, for an heir, he didn't wish the earl dead. Blair Leyton hankered after no man's property, not even his uncle's; whatever sins may have been laid to his charge, he was innocent of that love of money which is the root of all evil.

So without a spark of envy or covetousness or ill-will, he went to the stables and, nodding pleasantly to the head groom, went into the stalls.

Of course the man knew who he was—the news had spread all over the Court in five minutes!—and was respectful, and in a second or two more than that; for Blair's manner was as pleasant with high, low, Jack, and the game all round.

"Some good horses," he said.

The man shook his head doubtfully.

"Some, my lord," he assented. "But not what they ought to be for so big a place—begging your lordship's pardon. You see his lordship the earl only has the carriage horses—and them only once now and again—and there's nobody to ride. I try to keep 'em up, but a man loses heart like, my lord."

"I understand," said Lord Blair, sympathetically. "It's a pity. Such a fine hunting country."

"Ah, isn't it, my lord!" said the man with a sigh. "If the earl 'ud only take the hounds—but there"—and he sighed again.

Lord Blair went up to a big black horse and smacked him, a little attention which the animal responded to by launching out viciously.

"Nice nag!" said Lord Blair, approvingly.

"All but his temper, my lord," said the man. "He's as crooked-minded a hoss as ever I see."

Lord Blair laughed.

"He's straight enough in other ways," he said. "Put a saddle on him and I'll take a turn."

The man hesitated a second.

"He's an awkward one to ride, my lord," he ventured.

"So I should think," said the young man, cheerfully; "but I like them awkward."

The horse was saddled and brought out, and immediately commenced to verify the character bestowed upon him.

"Ill-tempered dev—beast, I'll take him back, my lord," said the groom; but, with a laugh, Lord Blair got into the saddle, and as the horse reared brought him down in so neat a style that the groom's misgivings fled.

"All right, my lord," he said, with an approving nod.

"Yes, it's all right," said the young man, with another laugh. "He's rather hot just at present, but he'll come back like a lamb, and I shall be hot, I expect," and off he rode.

"There," said the groom to a circle of his helpers, "that's my idea of a young nobleman! There'd be some pleasure and credit in keeping a stable for him."

"What a pity he's such a bad young man," murmured a maid-servant, who had crept out to look on.

"He may be a bad young man," retorted the groom sententiously, "but he's a darned good rider."

"He's dreadfully handsome," said the girl, with a little sigh, as she ran in again, and they unconsciously expressed the general opinion of the two sexes of Blair, Viscount Leyton.

The announcement that the young lord was to remain the night at the Court threw Mrs. Hale into a state of excitement.

"I must see Mr. Stibbings about the lunch and dinner at once, and there's the room to prepare. I shall have to leave you to yourself to-day, my dear," she said to Margaret. "Bless me, if I'd only had an hour or two's notice I could have got something nice for dinner. The earl doesn't care what it is, and often sends the things away untouched; but a young man from London, and used to the dinners they get there at the London clubs, is very different."

"Don't mind me, grandma," said Margaret. "I suppose I can't help you at all?"

"You?—Good gracious me, no!" said the old lady quite pityingly.

"Then I'll get my hat and go into the garden," said Margaret.

"Do, my dear; but keep this side of the house, mind, and do not go in front of the earl's windows."

"Very well; I'll take care," laughed Margaret. "I suppose if the earl should happen to catch sight of me twice in one day it would be fatal!—or would he only have a fit?" But Mrs. Hale, fortunately for her, did not hear this.

Margaret went out into the garden, and carefully kept out of sight of the great windows. She was very happy, and now and again she would break into song. The garden attached to this wing was a large one, and filled with flowers, and when she came in to lunch she had a large bunch of roses and heliotrope and pinks in her hand.

"There was no notice—'Do not pick the flowers!' grandma. I hope I haven't been very wicked?"

"No, no, my dear," said Mrs. Hale, who was in a fine state of flurry. "What a beautiful bouquet you have got!"

"Isn't it?" said Margaret, pinning a red rose in the bosom of her dress. "Where shall I put these?" and she looked round for a vase.

"Anywhere you like, my dear. Oh, Margaret, how nice they would be in Lord Leyton's room! It would make it seem more homely like; do what you will, a room that hasn't been used for months does look cold and formal."

"Doesn't it?" agreed Margaret. "And there is nothing like flowers to take off that effect. His lordship is welcome to them; so there they are, grandma."

"Yes, thank you," said Mrs. Hale, hurriedly. "I'll ring for Mary, unless you wouldn't mind running up with them; you'll arrange them decently, while she'll just throw them into a vase."

"Very well. Show me the way, Mary, to Lord Leyton's room," said Margaret as Mary entered.

Mrs. Hale had given him one of the best rooms in the house, and Margaret, who had never seen such an apartment, was lost in admiration of the silken hangings which stood in place of paper on the walls, and the old and priceless furniture.

She arranged the flowers in a deep, glass dish, and placed it on the spacious dressing table.

"His lordship ought to be pleased, miss," said Mary, shyly, as they were leaving the room.

Margaret laughed.

"I daresay he will think them very much in the way and throw them out of the window. I hope he won't throw dish and all," she said.

As she entered Mrs. Hale's sitting-room, she saw Mr. Stibbings approaching.

"I have been looking for you, miss," he said. "I have had a table put in the gallery, as his lordship directed, and his compliments, would you like any blinds put to the windows to shade the light?"

"Grandma, he did mean it after all," said Margaret, delightedly. "How kind? Oh, thank him, Mr. Stibbings! No, nothing more. I've got a portable easel and everything, and the light will do very well. Grandma, I may go now?"

"Yes, I suppose so," said the old lady, absently; "but mind, dear, if you hear the earl coming, you must get up and go away at once."

"Very well," said Margaret, with a smile, and she ran up and got her folding easel and painting materials. Mr. Stibbings wanted to place a footman at her disposal, but she laughingly declined, and with her impedimenta under her arm, and her paintbox in her hand, she made her way after lunch to the gallery.

"In the future, when I hear any one remark—'as proud as a lord,' I shall correct them and say—'kind as a lord,'" she said to herself. With all the eagerness of an artiste she set up her easel before the picture and commenced at once; and in a few minutes she had become absorbed in her work, and was lost to everything save the burning desire to catch something of the spirit of the great original she was copying.

"It is almost wicked to be so great!" she murmured. "How can I do more than libel you, you beautiful face?"

The afternoon glided on unnoticed by her. She heard a great bell booming overhead in a solemn fashion, but she gave it no attention beyond the thought, "the dinner or dressing bell," and went on with her copy.

She was so absorbed that she did not hear some one who had entered the gallery, and it was not until the some one stood close beside her that she knew of his presence.

With a start she looked up, and for a moment saw nothing but a handsome young man in evening dress.

His beauty—of the manliest type—gave her a pleasant sensation—she was an artist, remember—but the next moment she recognized him.

It was the young man whom she had called a savage; the gentleman who had fought Jem Pyke. Her eyes grew wide and her lips opened, and she sat and stared at him.

As for him, his astonishment equalled and surpassed hers. He had seen her back as he was passing the door of the gallery, and being unable to resist the temptation to ascertain what the face belonging to so graceful a figure was like, he had entered and softly approached her.

Margaret was a beautiful girl, but she was never lovelier than when under the spell which falls upon an artist absorbed in her work.

The clear, oval face grew dreamy, the large eyes softer and mystical, the red lips sweeter with a suggestful tenderness.

It was the loveliness of the face as well as the recognition of it which struck him—Blair Leyton, of all men—dumb and motionless.

They looked into each other's eyes while one could count fifty, then, with an embarrassment quite novel, he spoke.

"I've disturbed you?"

"No," said Margaret, and the word sounded blunt and cold in his ears. Who could he be, and how did he come here? Yesterday, fighting on the village green, this evening at Leyton Court. Then it flashed upon her: it was Lord Leyton! "No, I didn't hear you," she added.

"I came in quietly so as not to disturb you," he said, regaining some of his usual composure, but not all of it, for her loveliness dazzled, and her identity with the girl who had so sternly rebuked him yesterday, bewildered him.

"You—you are an artist?" he said.

"I have that honor," she said.

He looked at the copy.

"And a very good one! Your picture is better than the old one."

"You are *not* an artist, evidently," she said with a smile.

"No," he admitted; then a light shone in his eyes. "Oh, no, I am a savage!"

A burning blush covered her face, and she took up her brush.

Mr. Stibbings appeared between the velvet curtains.

"Dinner served, my lord."

Lord Blair Leyton nodded impatiently without turning.

"Are you staying here?" he said.

"Yes," said Margaret, going on with her painting.

He stood looking at her, at the beautiful, intelligent "artist" face, at the dove-colored dress, at the pink-white hand with its supple, capable fingers.

"Are you not going to dinner, my lord?" she said, unable to bear his silent presence any longer.

"I beg your pardon!" he said with a little start. "I was waiting for you."

"For me?" she said, turning her face to him with wide-eyed surprise.

"Yes," he said; "we will go together. You are coming, are you not?"

"I?" she said, then she laughed; "I am Mrs. Hale's—the housekeeper's granddaughter, Lord Leyton."

He reddened and bit his mustache.

"And you are not coming?" he said. "I am very sorry. I——"

"Dinner is served, my lord," said a footman in a low voice from the doorway.

Lord Blair uttered an impatient exclamation, which, as it was something remarkably like an oath, was fortunately unintelligible.

"Have you forgiven me yet?" he said, humbly.

"Forgiven?" said Margaret, as if she were trying to discover to what he referred. "Forgiven?"

"Yes! That affair of yesterday—the set-to, you know," he explained.

"Oh!"—the monosyllable dropped like a stone from her lips—"I had forgotten."

"That's right," he said, quickly; "if you've forgotten you have forgiven. I assure you——"

"Dinner is served, my lord," said a solemn voice.

He turned sharply.

"Confound it all——"

"Whether I have forgiven you is not of the least consequence, my lord," said Margaret, "but the earl will certainly not forgive you if you keep dinner waiting any longer," and she bent over her canvas with an air of absorption which shut him out of her cognizance completely.

He stood for a minute, then with an audible "Confound the dinner!" strode off.

CHAPTER V

Margaret did not raise her head from her work as Lord Blair Leyton moved reluctantly and impatiently down the gallery, but when the echo of his footsteps had died away she looked up with a slightly startled and altogether strange expression.

To her astonishment and disgust, the hand which held her brush was trembling. It was impossible to work any longer. Guido's head danced before her sight, and the other head—the handsome one of Blair Leyton—came between her and the painted one.

How very far from guessing she had been that this, the young man she had called a savage, was the earl's nephew, Lord Blair Leyton!

What must he think of her? And yet he had taken her for a guest of the house, had asked her if she were not going in to dinner with him!

She sat, paint brush in hand, and stared musingly at the curtained doorway through which he had gone, and thought of him.

It is a dangerous thing for a young, impressionable girl to think of a young man. But how could she help it? Her grandmother's words were ringing in her ears; according to Mrs. Hale, nothing was too bad to be said of poor Blair Leyton. He was the wickedest of the wicked, bad beyond all description. And yet—and yet! How bravely he had fought a stronger and bigger man than himself on behalf of a helpless dog!

She pondered over this question for half an hour, looking dreamily in the direction he had gone, then, without having arrived at any answer to it, she jumped up and, putting her painting materials together, left the gallery.

"Grandma," she said, as she entered the room in which the old lady was seated, placidly knitting, for the dinner was in full swing, and Mrs. Hale's anxiety was over, "grandma, I have seen Lord Leyton."

The old lady almost jumped.

"Seen Lord Leyton, Madge?"

Margaret nodded.

"Yes; he came into the gallery——"

The old lady broke in with a groan.

"Margaret, no good will come of your going to the picture gallery! Mark my words! It isn't—isn't proper and right like! And you've seen him. Did he speak to you?"

"Very much," said Margaret, smiling, but pensively. "He asked me if I weren't going in to dinner with him!"

"You don't say so!" exclaimed Mrs. Hale, lifting her hands. "Took you for a lady! Dear, now!"

"Yes; isn't it strange?" said Margaret, with great irony.

"Well—I don't know that," said the old lady, eying the graceful figure and lovely, refined face. "But, Margaret——"

"Well, grandma?" said Margaret, as the old lady hesitated.

"Well, I was going to say that—that—you must be careful!"

"Careful? What of?" said Margaret smiling. "Does Lord Blair bite, as well as the earl? What am I to be careful of, grandma?"

The old lady frowned.

"My dear, it isn't right and proper that you and Lord Blair should be on speaking terms," she said at last. "He's the earl's nephew, and—and you are only my granddaughter, you know."

"Which I am quite content to be," said Margaret, busily engaged with her paint box. "But I don't see that I have done anything very wicked, grandma. I couldn't very well refuse to answer him when he spoke."

"No, no, certainly not," said the old lady; "but if he speaks again—but there, it isn't likely you'll see him again. He is only going to stop the night, and you're not likely to meet him again, that's one comfort."

"It is indeed," said Margaret, with a laugh. "Especially as he is the gentleman whom I saw fighting in the village, and whom I called a savage."

"You—you called him a savage!" gasped Mrs. Hale. "My dear Margaret, is it possible?"

"It is only too possible and certain," said Margaret lightly, "and his lordship remembered it, too. However, as he asked me to forgive him, I suppose he has forgiven me; and if he has not I don't care. He was like a savage, and I spoke the truth." Then after a pause, during which the old lady stared in a rapt kind of fashion—"Grandma, what a pity it is that so wicked a man should be so good-looking."

"Yes, he is handsome enough," sighed the old lady, shaking her head.

"Oh, handsome, yes! I didn't mean that exactly. I meant really *good* looking. He looks so frank and—yes!—gentle, and his eyes seem to shine with kindness and—and—boyishness. Nobody would believe that he was a bad young man."

"They'd soon learn the truth when they knew him," said the old lady, rather shrewdly.

"I dare say. What a good thing it would be if all the good men were handsome, and all the bad ugly. You would tell at a glance, then, how the case lay. As it is, the man who looks like a villain may be as good as a saint, while the other who looks like a hero and an angel, is probably as bad as—as——"

"Lord Blair," broke in the old lady.

"Exactly—as Lord Blair," laughed Margaret. "And now I am going out to hear the nightingales, grandma. We haven't any nightingales in London—not of your sort, I mean. Ours haven't nice voices at all, and they mostly sing 'We won't go home till morning,' or 'He's a jolly good fellow,' and their voices sound rather unsteady as they go along the pavement. Those are the London kind of nightingale! Oh, what a lovely night——"

"Put a shawl on, Madge!" called the old lady. "Come back now; I can't have you catching cold the very first night!"

"Shawl? I haven't such a thing!" laughed Margaret. "This will do, won't it?" and catching up an antimacassar she threw it round her shoulders and ran out.

Dinner at Leyton Court was a stately function. Very often the earl, as Mrs. Hale had said, would make his meal of a morsel of fish or a tiny slice of mutton, but all the same an elaborate *menu* was prepared, and the courses were served with due state and ceremony by the butler and two footmen.

This night, in honor of Lord Blair, the dinner was more elaborate than usual; Mr. Stibbings had selected his choicest claret, and a bottle of '73 Pommery, and had himself superintended its icing. Already, although he had only been in the house a few hours, the young man had won the hearts of the servants!

But notwithstanding the choice character of the wines and the elaborate *menu*, Lord Blair seemed rather absent-minded and preoccupied. The earl was silent, almost grimly so, but the young man seemed not grim by any means, but dreamy. The fact was that the face of the young girl who had called him a savage yesterday, and whom he had seen again in the gallery this evening, was haunting him.

And—he wondered when and how he could see her again.

Of course he knew, as well as did Mrs. Hale, that there should be no acquaintanceship between Viscount Leyton and the granddaughter of his uncle's housekeeper, but he did not think of that, and, if he had, the reflection would not have stifled the desire to find her out and get a few more words from those sweet lips, one more smile or glance from the lovely eyes.

So that, what with Lord Blair being Margaret-haunted, and the earl being possessed by the fact of his nephew's wickedness, the grand dinner was anything but hilarious.

They talked now and again, but long before the dessert appeared they had dropped into a mutual silence. Then Mr. Stibbings carried in, daintily and carefully, a bottle of the famous Leyton port, and, with the air of one bestowing a farewell benediction, glided out and left the two gentlemen alone.

"Do you drink port, Blair?" said the earl, with his hand on the decanter.

"Yes, sir; I drink anything," replied the young man, awaking with a little start.

"You have a good digestion—good constitution?" said the earl.

"Oh, yes," assented Lord Blair, cheerfully; "I suppose so. Never had a day's illness in my life that I can remember, and can eat anything."

The earl looked at him musingly.

"And yet——" he paused, "your habits are not regular; you keep late hours?"

Lord Blair laughed.

"I'm seldom in bed before ten," he said. "Yes," he added, "I'm afraid I don't keep very good hours; it's generally daylight before I am in my little cot. What capital port, sir!"

"Yes? I do not drink it," said the earl.

There was silence for a moment, during which the elder man looked at the handsome face and graceful, stalwart figure of the younger one. Lord Blair was one of those men who look at their best in evening dress, and the earl could not help admiring him. Then he sighed.

"Have you thought over the words that passed between us this afternoon, Blair?" he asked.

"Well—I'm afraid I haven't," he admitted, frankly.

The earl frowned.

"And yet they were important ones—especially those which referred to your future, Blair. We have not seen much of each other—perhaps wisely——"

"I dare say," said Lord Blair, cheerfully. "People who can't agree are better apart, sir."

"But," continued the earl grimly, and not relishing the interruption, "but I would wish you to believe that I have your best interests at heart."

"Thank you, sir. I will take another glass of port."

"And in no surer way can these interests be promoted than by your marriage with Violet Graham."

Lord Blair frowned slightly, then he smiled.

"'Pon my word, sir, I'm sorry to refuse you anything, especially after all your liberality; but it isn't to be done."

"Why not?" demanded the earl coldly.

Lord Blair hesitated, then he laughed grimly.

"Well, I suppose we can't hit it off; we don't care for each other."

The earl frowned.

"I have every reason to believe that Violet would be willing——"

"Oh, it's all a mistake, sir!" broke in Lord Blair quickly. "Nothing of the kind! Violet doesn't care a straw for me! And as to breaking her heart, as you said this afternoon, why"—he laughed—"she's the last girl in the world for that sort of thing! No, we thought we could manage it, but we found pretty soon that it wouldn't work, and so—and so—well, we just broke it off!"

"I can understand!" said the earl, grimly. "You wearied her with your dissipation, and stung her by your neglect."

Lord Blair flushed.

"Put it so, if you like, sir," he said, thinking what a good thing it was that they did *not* see much of each other.

"And so lost the chance of restoring your ruined fortunes," said the earl. "Violet's fortune is a large one. I am one of the trustees, and can speak with authority. It is large enough to repair all the mischief your wild, spendthrift course has produced. And you have lost, not only the means of your salvation, but one of the best girls in England. Great Heaven"—he spoke quite quietly—"how can a man be so great a fool, and so blind!"

At another time the young man might have retorted, but he had had a good dinner and two glasses of the wonderful port, and so he only laughed.

"I suppose I am a fool, sir," he said good-temperedly. "Perhaps it's part of my constitution. But don't let us quarrel. It isn't worth while."

"You are right. It isn't worth while," said the earl, sinking back in his chair. "After all, I ought to be thankful that Violet has escaped; but blood is thicker than—water and I have thought of you more than of her. But let it pass. You are bent on following the road you have set out upon, and not even she nor I can stay you. As to Ketton, you refuse to accept my offer——"

"Yes, sir," said Lord Blair, gently but firmly. "I shall mortgage Ketton. I can't take any more money from you. If we were—well, better friends, it would be different, but——It's a pity you can't touch this port! The best wine I ever tasted!"

The earl sat in silence for a few minutes, then he rose.

"Coffee will be served in the drawing-room," he said. "You will excuse me?"

"Oh, certainly," said Lord Blair, jumping up. "I don't care about the coffee, I will go and get a cigar on the terrace. Perhaps I sha'n't see you again, sir, I start early in the morning. If I should not, I'll say good-bye," and he held out his hand.

The earl touched it with his thin white fingers.

"Good-bye," he said, and with a sigh he passed down the corridor to his own apartments.

Lord Blair took out his cigar-case and stepped through the open window on to the terrace.

"Yes, I'm on the road to ruin, as mine uncle says," he mused, "and going along at a rattling good pace, too! Sha'n't be long before I reach the terminus, I expect. Hartwell gone, Parkfield gone, and now Ketton. I'm sorry about Ketton! But I'd rather pawn everything that's left than take any more money from him! Heigho! I wonder whether any of the fellows who are so thick now will cut me when I can't come up on settling day and my name's on the black list! And I could put it all right by marrying Violet Graham. Just by marrying Violet. But I can't do that. I suppose I *am* a fool, as the old gentleman politely remarked. It's wonderful that I'm the only man he is ever rude to. They say he is the pink of courtesy and politeness to the rest of the world. 'Courtly Ferrers,' they used to call him. Ah, well, what does it matter? All the same in a hundred years. I've had my fling, or nearly had it, and after me——"

Before he could conclude with "the deluge," a girl's voice rose softly and sweetly in the distance, and seemed to float in and harmonize with the rather melancholy strain of his musings; and yet the voice was blithe and joyous enough, too.

Lord Blair leaned over the stone rail of the balustrade and listened.

A spell fell upon the wild young man, and for a few minutes a strange feeling—was it of remorse for his wasted life?—possessed him. Then there rose the desire to see the singer, and as such desires were far stronger in Lord Blair's breast than remorse, he moved quickly along the terrace in the direction of the voice.

It did not occur to him that it might be Margaret Hale, and he experienced a sudden thrill of gratification as he saw the dove-colored dress shining, a soft patch of light against the shrubbery of the small garden.

At the same moment Margaret saw his shadow cast upon the smooth lawn, and the song died on her lips.

He stopped short, and stood on top of the steps leading to the little garden, looking down at her.

"May I come?" he said quietly.

Margaret inclined her head gravely and rose. It was quite unnecessary to tell the Viscount Leyton that he was at liberty to step into a part of the garden that would belong to him some day.

"I'm awfully unlucky, Miss Hale," he said, flinging his cigar away and coming up to the seat where she had been sitting. "This is the second time to-day I have disturbed you; and yesterday—oh, yesterday won't bear thinking of! You were singing, weren't you?"

"Yes, my lord," said Margaret gravely, for her grandmother's words had suddenly occurred to her, and she moved away.

"Are you going?" he said. "Now, I have driven you away! Please, don't go. I'll take myself off at once."

"I was going, my lord," said Margaret.

"Oh, come," he retorted pleadingly; "it's almost as wicked to tell stories as it is to fight; and you know you were sitting here comfortably enough until I intruded upon you."

His voice, his manner were irresistible, and produced a smile on Margaret's face.

"It is getting late," she said, "and Mrs. Hale may want me."

"I don't think she will. It isn't late—" he looked at his watch—"I can't see. Your eyes are better than mine, I'll be bound. I've spoilt them sitting up studying at night. Will you look? But upon this condition," he added, covering the face of the watch with his hand, "that if it isn't ten o'clock, you will stay a little while longer; of course I'll go—if you want me to!"

His eagerness was so palpable, almost so boyish, that Margaret could not repress a soft laugh. Rather gingerly she came back a step, and he held out his watch.

"It is half-past nine," she said.

"There you are, you see; it isn't late at all! Now you stop out till ten, and I'll take myself off"—and with a nod he walked toward the steps, with Margaret's antimacassar shawl in his hand.

"My lord!" she said, in a tone of annoyance, for it seemed as if he had done it on purpose.

"Yes," he responded, turning back very promptly.

"Will you give me my anti—my shawl, please?"

"Eh? Oh, of course, I beg your pardon," he said, "I took it up intending to ask you to put it on—nights are chilly sometimes. Here you are. Let me put it on for you."

"No, no, thank you," said Margaret, taking it from him.

"Well, it is warm," he said, looking up at the sky, and then quickly returning his gaze to her face. "It's a pity you can't paint this; but you artists get rather handicapped on these night scenes, don't you? Want a big moon and a waterfall, and all that kind of thing?"

Margaret smiled. Certainly, in matters pertaining to art he was a perfect savage.

"To-night could be painted, my lord," she said, just stopping to say it, then moving away again.

"You think so?" he said, displaying, with boyish ingenuousness, his desire to engage her in conversation. "Well, I don't know much about it; rather out of my line, you know. But I like seeing pictures, and I think you must be awfully clever——"

"Thanks, my lord!" said Margaret, with admirable gravity. "But your avowed ignorance rather detracts on the value of your expressed approval, does it not?"

He looked at her.

"That's rather hot and peppery, isn't it?" he said, ruefully. "Look here, you know, if I'm not up in painting, I know a little of other things. There are three things you might put me through a regular exam. in, and I shouldn't come out badly."

"For instance, my lord?" said Margaret, dangerously interested, and slowly stopping.

"For instance. Well, I know a horse when I see it."

"Very few people take it for a cow," retorted Margaret.

He laughed.

"Oh, *you* know what I mean. Many flats take a screw for a horse, though. Well, I know what a horse is worth pretty well, and I know a good dog when I see him, and I can tell you the proper kind of fly for most of the rivers in England and Scotland; and I know the quickest and surest way of stalking a stag; and—I can play a decent hand at ecarte—that is, if it's not *too* late in the evening; and—and——" he paused and looked rather at a loss.

"Is that all, my lord?"

"That's—that's all. It seemed rather a long lot, too, while I was running it over," he responded.

"And what use is your knowledge to you, my lord, unless you intend turning horse-dealer or gamekeeper?—but perhaps you do."

He laughed.

"By George, you're hard upon me! Won't you sit down?" Insensibly, Margaret sank into the seat, and he dropped carelessly on to the arm. "Well, I might do worse!"

"Much worse!" assented Margaret, severely.

He looked at her rather curiously.

"How strangely you said that," he remarked. "Meant for me from the shoulder, I expect; now wasn't it?"

Margaret was silent. She *had* meant it as a rebuke, but she would not have admitted it for the world.

He regarded her silently for a second, then he said:

"Miss Hale, they have been telling you something about me. They have, haven't they?"

A faint flush rose to her face.

"Would that matter in the slightest, my lord?"

"By George, yes!" he said. "Look here! there is an old proverb that says: 'Don't believe more than half you see, and less than half you hear.' I should like to know what they have been telling you about me!"

"What should 'they' say, my lord?" said Margaret. "Except that you are a very high-principled and serious-minded gentleman, doing all the good you could find to do, and setting a high example to your friends and companions?"

He leaned forward so that he might see her face, then broke into the musical and contagious laugh.

"It's too bad!" he said. "Miss Hale, I give you my word that the dev—, that nobody is quite as bad as he is painted——"

"It is to be hoped not, or, judging from the portraits one sees at the Academy, there must be a great many ugly people in the world," she said, quietly.

Lord Blair stared at her with unconcealed delight.

Pretty women he had met by the hundred, but a girl who was lovely as a flower, and witty as well, was a rarity that set his heart throbbing.

"All right!" he said. "I see you have made up your mind about me, and that you won't let me say a word in my own defense. But every poor beggar of a convict is allowed to say something before they pass sentence, don't you know, and you'll let me say my word before you send me away, painted black right through. Miss Hale, I'm in one of my unlucky months! Everything I've touched this June has gone wrong! My horse—but I don't want to trouble you about that—and to put the finishing touch to the catalogue, I had the bad luck to have you looking on while I'm having a set-to with a country yokel. Of course, you think the worst of me, and yet— —" He stopped. "Well, I'm bad enough, I dare say," he said, with a sort of groan; "but I haven't had much chance; I haven't, indeed. They don't make many saints out of the kind of life that has fallen to me. What can you expect of a fellow who is thrown upon the world at nineteen without a friend to keep him straight or say a word of warning? And that was just the way of it with me; my father died when I was nineteen and I was let loose with plenty of money, and not a soul to show me the right road."

"Your mother?" said Margaret, and the next instant regretted it, for across his handsome face came a spasm, as if she had touched a wound across his heart.

"My mother died two years before my father; her death killed him. I wish that it had killed me. Don't let's speak of her."

"I am very sorry, my lord," murmured Margaret.

"All right," he said cheerfully. "If she had been living—but then! Well, I had no one. My uncle—the earl, here—would have nothing to say to me; I reminded him too much that he had lost his own boy and that I must come into the property. As if I wouldn't rather have died instead of the lad! He was as nice a boy as ever you saw—poor little chap! Well, where was I? Oh, on the road to ruin as my uncle said this afternoon, and, by George, he was right!" and he laughed. "But there—once you make the first false step, the rest is easy; it's all down hill, you see, and nobody to put the skid on—nobody! But never mind any more about me; I can see you've passed sentence. Are you living here altogether, Miss Hale?"

"No," said Margaret with a little start, and very quietly. She was thinking of the wasted life, the friendless, guardless youth which his wild, incoherent statement revealed, and something like pity for him was creeping into her heart.

Pity! It is a dangerous sentiment for one like Margaret to harbor for one like Blair Leyton!

"No; I am here on a visit, my lord."

"How jolly!" he said. "I hope you are enjoying yourself. But, perhaps you always live in the country?"

"I am enjoying myself very much. No, I live in London, my lord."

"In London!" he said, quickly. "But I say——" he broke off appealingly, "I wish you wouldn't 'my lord' me, you know."

Margaret laughed.

"My circle of acquaintances does not include any noblemen, Lord Leyton, and I am not quite sure of the way to address one of your rank," she said, faltering a little.

"How well she said that!" he thought. "Most girls would have giggled and blushed, but she took it as quietly as a duchess would have done!"

Then aloud he said:

"Well, it's usual to address us by our surname; I wish you would call me Leyton."

Margaret was silent a moment, while he scanned her face with suppressed eagerness.

"If it is quite usual," she said in her blissful ignorance. "It sounds rather abrupt."

"Why, of course!" he said. "Abrupt, not a bit. And you live in London! Now, shall I guess what part? Let me see. You are an artist. Yes. Well, Chelsea——"

"Wrong; but Kensington is not so far away," she said, with a smile.

"Kensington," he said. "The Art School, of course. How jolly! I've got rooms not very far from there. Perhaps we shall—" he hesitated and watched her rather fearfully—"we might meet, you know."

"I should say that there was nothing more improbable, my—Lord Leyton. We don't know the same people, and never shall, and——" she stopped, her own words had recalled Mrs. Hale's warning. "I must go now," she said, rising suddenly.

"Oh, it's not ten," he pleaded. "You feel chilly? Let me put your shawl on. It has slipped down. Why, what a funny shawl it is!"

"It's an antimacassar," she said laughing.

"So it is!" he said. "And look here, it has got entangled in my watch-chain; but they are built to get entangled in things, aren't they?" he added, fumbling with all a man's awkwardness at the tangled threads.

"Oh, you'll never get it off like that," said Margaret impatiently, and innocently enough her small supple fingers flew at it.

His own hand and hers touched, and with a feeling of surprise he felt the blood tingling at her touch. He looked at the lovely face so close to his own, so gravely, unconsciously beautiful, and a wild desire to lift the hand to his lips seized him, but with a mighty effort he forced it down.

"There it is!" he said. "And now to reward me for—not getting it undone, will you let me give you this flower?" and he stooped and picked a red rose.

Margaret started slightly and looked at him; but the handsome face wore its frankest, "goodest" look, and with a laugh she held out her hand. He drew it back with an answering laugh.

"Before I give it to you, will you tell me one thing, Miss Hale?"

"That depends," she said, "upon what the thing is."

"It's not much," he said. "Only this: will you tell me that you don't think I am quite the savage you accused me of being yesterday?"

She looked up at him with a faint color in her face.

"Yes, I will do that," she said. "But I think you should keep the rose, Lord Leyton."

"No," he said, laughingly, but with an intent look in his eyes, fixed upon her. "No, I've got a fancy for leaving something behind me that you may remember me by. I'm going to-morrow, you know."

"I did not know," said Margaret.

"Yes," with a sigh. "My welcome to the Court is soon outworn, and I'm back to London and the old road," with a laugh.

Margaret stood with averted face.

"Is—is it so inevitable, that same road? Is there no other, my lord?" she said.

"No, I'm afraid not, my lady," he said, smiling, but rather gravely.

"I think there must be, that there might be if you cared to take it," she said, gravely.

"If you cared that I should take it—I mean"—he broke off quickly, for she had looked alarmed at his words and their tone—"I mean that it's very good of you to care what becomes of a useless fellow like me, and——"

"Margaret!" called Mrs. Hale's voice from the open window.

Margaret started.

"Good-night, my lord," she said, hurriedly, and yet with simple dignity.

"Stop," he said, in a low voice; "you have forgotten your rose," and, following her a step or two, he touched her arm. "It is not a very grand one; there was a bowl of beauties in my room: some good soul had pick—" he stopped, for the color rose to Margaret's face. "*You* put them there!" he exclaimed, his eyes lighting up. "*You!*"

"I—I did not know——" she said, faltering, and trying to speak proudly.

"Oh, don't destroy my pleasure by explaining that you did not mean them for me!" he pleaded. "You put them there at any rate. Will you let me, in return, fix this rose in your shawl? We shall be more than quits then on my side!"

Oh, Margaret, put back the proffered flower! Red stands in the language of magic for all that is evil, for a passion that will burn into ashes of pain; put back the hand that offers it to you!

But he was too quick. Gently, reverently he fixed the rose in the meshes of the antimacassar, and, as he put it straight with a caressing touch, he murmured:

"Good-night! Try and remember me, Miss—Margaret, at any rate as long as the rose lives!"

Red as the flower itself, trembling with a feeling that was painfully like the stab of conscience, Margaret glanced up at him, and without a word, sped from his side.

Lord Leyton stood looking after her, as strange an expression in his face as her own had worn.

Then with a long sigh he went back to the seat and threw himself down into it, in the place where she had sat.

Half an hour passed; the nightingale for which Margaret had been waiting came out and sang for him; but the song gave him no delight, for in his whirling brain its notes seemed to take the shape of words: words of such sad, strange import! "Spare her!—spare her!" the bird seemed to sing; and as if he could not endure the appeal any longer, he rose impatiently and walked toward the terrace.

As he did so, a tall, skulking figure moved snake-like after him.

Lord Blair stopped at the bottom of the steps, and the shadow pursuing him stopped also, and raised a heavy stick.

For a moment it hovered evilly over Lord Blair's head, then, as if smitten by a sudden remorse or a desire for a still deeper revenge, Pyke let the stick fall, and, slinking back, disappeared amongst the shrubs.

CHAPTER VI

Margaret ran into the house, her heart beating fast, the color coming and going in her cheeks. To her amazement and annoyance, she felt that she was actually trembling! Well, if not trembling, quivering, as a leaf quivers when the summer wind passes over its bosom.

What was this that she had done? Notwithstanding her grandmother's warning and her own good resolutions, she had spent—how long!—nearly an hour talking alone with Lord Blair Leyton. And he had given her a rose! Not only given it to her, but fastened it in the antimacassar.

She could feel his fingers touching her still, as it seemed to her! She looked down at the rose, gleaming like a spot of blood on the white cotton of the antimacassar, then, with a sudden gesture, she went to pull it out and fling it through the window; but she averted her hand even as it touched the velvet leaves. Yes, she had done wrong; she ought not to have spoken to him, ought not to have remained with him, and most certainly ought not to have taken the rose from him.

She saw now how wrong she had been. They used to call her "Wild Margaret," "Mad Madge," when she was a child, but she had been trying to become quiet, and dignified, and discreet, and, as it seemed to her, had succeeded, until this wicked young man had tempted her into flirting—was it flirting?—in the starlight.

"You look flushed, my dear," said Mrs. Hale. "Are you tired?"

"I think I am a little," said Margaret, longing to get to the solitude of her own room.

"It's the country air," said the old lady, nodding. "It always makes people from London sleepy. Was it pleasant in the garden?" she added, innocently.

Margaret's face flushed.

"Y—es, very," she replied; then she was going on to tell the old lady of her meeting with Lord Blair, but stopped short.

"I think I will go up to bed now," she said, and giving the old lady a kiss, she went up-stairs to her own room. There she thought over every word that the young lord said, and that she herself had spoken. There had been no harm in any of it, surely! He had spoken respectfully, almost reverentially, and even when he had given her the rose he had done it with as much diffidence and high bred courtesy as if she had been a countess. Surely there had been no harm in it.

It was a lovely morning when she woke, and dressing herself she went straight to the picture gallery. As she left the room Lord Blair's red rose seemed to smile at her from the dressing table, and she took it up and carried it in her hand. It was just possible that she might meet him; if so, it would be as well to have the rose with her, for give it back she meant to, if a chance afforded. The light in the gallery could not have been better, and she set to work at first languidly, but presently with more spirit, and was becoming perfectly absorbed, when she heard a voice singing the refrain of the last popular London song.

It was a man's voice, it could be no other than Lord Blair's, and in a minute or two afterward she heard him enter the gallery.

She heard him coming toward her with a quick step, and looking up with his eyes fixed upon her with eager pleasure. He was dressed in the suit of tweeds in which he had looked so picturesque on the morning of the fight, and in his buttonhole he wore a white rose. It drew her eyes toward it, and she knew it at once—it was the finest of the roses she had placed in his room.

"Miss Hale!" he exclaimed, holding out his hand, while his eyes beamed with the frank, glad light of youth when it is pleased. "This is luck! I only strolled in here by mere chance—and—and to think of my finding you here! How early you are! And what a lot you have done!" staring admiringly at the canvas. "I hope you didn't catch cold last night?"

"No, my lord," said Margaret, as coldly as if her voice were frozen.

He looked at her with a quick questioning.

"I'm off almost directly," he said, with something like a sigh. "It's a bore having to go back to London and leave this place a morning like this. I had no idea it was so—so jolly, until——" he stopped; he was going to add: "until last night."

Margaret remained silent, dabbing on little spots of color delicately.

"I quite envy you your stay here," he went on, looking in her grave face, which had become somewhat pale since his arrival. "That jolly little garden, and—and this grand gallery. I hope you will be happy, and—and enjoy yourself."

"Thank you my lord," coldly as before.

He looked at her with a slightly puzzled frown.

"Yes, I should like to stay; but I can't—for the best of all reasons, I haven't been invited, don't you know."

Margaret said nothing, but carefully mixed some colors on her palette.

"And so—and so I'm off," he said, with a sudden sigh. "Perhaps we shall meet in London, Miss Hale."

"It is not likely," said Margaret gravely.

"So you said last night," he responded; "but I shall live in hopes. Yes. London's only a little place, after all, you know, and—and we may meet. Well, I'll say good-bye!"

"Good-bye, my lord," she said, affecting not to see his outstretched hand.

"Won't you shake hands?" he said with a laugh, which died away as she took up the rose and placed it in his extended palm.

"Will you take back this flower, my lord?" she said quietly, but with a trembling quiver on her lips.

"Take back?" he stammered. "Take back the rose I gave you last night!" he went on with astonishment. "Why? what have I done to offend you?" and he stared from the rose to her face.

"You have done nothing to offend me, my lord," said Margaret quickly, and with a vivid blush, which angered her beyond expression. "Nothing whatever, but— —"

"But—well?" he said as she paused.

"But," she went on, lifting her eyes to his bravely—"but I do not think I ought to take a flower from you, my lord."

"Good lord, why not?" he demanded, with not unreasonable astonishment.

Margaret looked down. But she was no coward.

"I will say more than that," she said in a low but steady voice. "I ought not to have remained in the garden with you last night, Lord Leyton. I thought so last night, I am sure of it now. And if I ought not to have stayed talking with you, I certainly ought not to have accepted a flower from you! I beg your pardon, and—there is your rose!"

A look of pain crossed his handsome face.

"You haven't told me why yet," he said, after a pause.

Margaret bit her lip, and was silent for a second or two, then she said:

"Lord Leyton, there should be, can be, no acquaintance between you and me— —"

"Now stop!" he said. "I know what you are going to say; you are going to talk some nonsense about my being a viscount and you being something different, and all that! As if you were not a lady, and as if any one could be better than that! Yes, they can, by George! and you *are* better, for you are an artist! A difference between us—yes, yes, I should think there was, between a useless fellow like myself and a clever, beautiful— —"

"My lord!" said Margaret, flushing, then looking at him with her brows drawn together.

"I beg your pardon, I beg your pardon; I do indeed! But, all the same," he said, defiantly, "it's true! You are beautiful, but I don't rely on that. I say an artist and a lady is the equal of any man or woman alive, and if that's the reason you fling my flower back to me— —"

"I didn't fling it, my lord," said Margaret, gravely.

"I'm a brute!" he said, penitently. "The difference between a brute and—and an angel! That's it. No, you didn't fling it, but it's just as if you had, isn't it now?"

"You will take back the flower, Lord Leyton, please?" she almost pleaded. "I don't want to fling it, as you say, out of the window."

He stood looking at her.

"How—how you must hate and despise me, by Jove!" he said.

Margaret flushed.

"You have no right to say that, my lord, because I see that I acted unwisely last night. How can I hate or despise one who is a stranger to me?"

"Yes, that's it; I'm a stranger, and you mean to keep me one!" he said, half bitterly, half sorrowfully. "Well, I can't complain; I'm not fit for you to know. Why, even my own flesh and blood are anxious to see the back of me! Yes, you are right, Miss Margaret."

He dwelt on the name sadly, using it unconsciously.

"Oh, no, no!" she said, wrung to the heart at the thought of wounding him so mercilessly. "It's not that! It's not of you I thought, but of myself."

"Of yourself yes," he said. "Communication with me is a kind of pollution; you cannot touch tar, you know! Oh, I understand! Well"—he hung his head—"I'll do as you tell me; I can't do less. I'll take my poor rose——" He stopped short, and something seemed to strike him. "But if I do, I must return you this," and he gently unfastened the white one from his coat, and held it out to her.

Margaret put out her hand irresolutely.

"Oh, take it!" he said recklessly. "It is one out of the bowl you gave me."

"I gave you?" she said.

"Yes," he said; "you picked them yourself, the girl told me so. I asked her. And you put them in my room. If I take your rose back you must take mine."

"Well," she said, and she took it slowly, and laid it on the table beside her.

He drew a long breath, then the color came into his face and the wild, daring Ferrers' spirit shone in his eyes.

"That's an exchange," he said. "It's a challenge and an acceptance. Don't you see what you have done in cutting me off and flinging me aside, Miss Margaret?"

"What have I done?" said Margaret.

"Yes! You have given me back my rose, but you forget that you have worn it, that it has been in your dress, that you have touched it, that it's like a part of yourself. And you have taken *my* rose, which has been in my room all night, while I dreamt of you——"

"Lord Leyton!" she panted, half rising.

"Yes!" he said, confronting her with the sudden passion which lay dormant in him and always, like a tiger, ready to spring to the surface. "You can throw my offer of friendship in my face, you can put me coldly aside, and—and wipe out last night as if it had never been, as if you had done some great wrong in talking to such a man as I am; but you can't rob me of the rose you have touched, ah! and worn."

"Give—give it me back!" she exclaimed, with a trepidation which was not altogether anger or fear. "Give it me back, my lord. You have no right——"

"To keep it! Haven't I?" he retorted. "What! when you forced it back on me! No, I will not give it you back! You may do what you like with the white one. You will fling it on the fire, I've no doubt. I can't help it. But this one, *yours*, I keep! It is mine. I will never part with it. And whenever I look at it I will remember how—until you discovered that I was not fit to associate with you, such a bad lot that you couldn't even keep a flower I gave you!—I'll remember that you have worn it near your heart."

White as herself, with a passion which had carried him beyond all bounds, he raised the red rose to his lips and kissed it, not once only but thrice.

Then, as he saw her face change, her lips tremble, his passion melted away, and all penitent and remorseful, he bent toward her.

"Forgive me!" he said, as if half bewildered; "I—I didn't know what I was saying. I—I am a savage! Yes, that's the name for me! Forgive me, and—good-bye!"

He lingered on the words till they seemed to fill the room with their music, low as they had been spoken. Then he turned.

Margaret found her voice.

"My lord—Lord Leyton. Stop!"

He stopped and turned.

"Give me back the rose, please," she said, firmly.

"No!" he said, his eyes flashing again. "Nothing in this world would induce me to give it to you, or to any one else. I'll keep it till I die! I'll keep it to remind me of last night—and of you!"

He stood for a moment looking at her steadily—if the passionate glance could be called steady; then the thick folds of the velvet curtain fell and hid him from her sight.

Margaret stood for a moment motionless.

Lord Leyton strode through the corridor into the hall. He scarcely knew where he was going, or saw the objects before him.

"The dog-cart is ready, my lord," said a footman.

Mr. Stibbings stood with respectful attention beside the door.

"Good-morning, my lord; the portmanteau is in——" he glanced at the rose which Lord Blair still held in his hand. "If your lordship would like to take some flowers with you, I will get some: there is time——"

"Flowers? Flowers?" said Lord Blair, confusedly; then, with an exclamation, he hid the rose in his breast and sprung into the cart.

The horse bounded forward and dashed down the avenue, Lord Blair looking straight before him like a man only half awakened.

Suddenly, seeing and yet scarcely seeing, he noticed a tall, wiry figure lounging against the sign-post in the center of the village green.

"Stop!" he said to the groom.

He pulled up and Lord Blair beckoned to the man.

Pyke resisted the summons for a second or two, then he slouched up to the dog-cart with his hands in his pockets.

"Good-morning, my man," said Lord Blair. "I hope you're none the worse for our little set-to?"

"*I'm* not the worse, and I sha'n't be," retorted Pyke, lifting his evil eyes for a moment to the handsome face then fixing them on the last button of Lord Blair's waistcoat.

"That's all right," said Lord Blair. "I see you've got a bruise or two still left," and he laughed. "And I dare say I have. Well, here is some ointment for yours," and he held out some silver.

Pyke opened his hand, and his fingers closed over it.

"That's all right," said Blair again, cheerfully. "We part friends, I hope?"

"Yes, we part friends," said Pyke, but the expression of his face would have suited "We part enemies" equally well.

"Well, we shall meet again, I dare say," said Blair. "Good-morning."

"Yes, we shall meet again," said the man, and as he spoke he shot a vindictive glance at Blair's face. "Oh, yes, my lord, we shall meet again," he snarled as the dog-cart drove on. "And it will be my turn then. Ointment, eh! It will be a powerful ointment as 'ud do you any good when I've done with you!"

CHAPTER VII

About four o'clock the same evening a group of people was gathered round a young lady who sat on a magnificent and strong-looking horse, standing with well-bred patience near the rails of the Mile.

The park was crammed, carriages, riders, and pedestrians all massed and hot, in the lovely June air, which seemed laden with the scent of the flowers, and heavy with the sound of wheels and voices.

The lady was young, but certainly not beautiful. That you decided at once, immediately you saw her. After a time, when you got to know her, your decision became somewhat shaken, and you would very likely admit that if she were not beautiful, she was, well—taking. She was not tall—short indeed, one of those small women who make us inclined to believe that all women should be small; one of those little women who twist great men— and great in all senses of the word—round their very diminutive little fingers. She had a beautiful figure, *petite*, fairy-like, lithesome and graceful, and it looked at its very best in the brown habit of Redfern's make. Her hair was black, her eyes gray, and her mouth—well, it was not small, but it was wonderfully expressive.

She was the center of a group. There were other young ladies with her, but she was distinctly the center, and the men who crowded round bent their eyes upon her, addressed most of their remarks to her, and, in fact, paid her the most attention: the other ladies did not seem to complain even silently; they took it as a matter of course.

For this little lady, with the not small but expressive mouth, was Miss Violet Graham, and she was, perhaps, the richest heiress in London.

There were several well-known men in the circle round her. There was the young Marquis of Aldmere, with the pink eyes and the receding chin of his race, his pink eyes fixed admiringly upon the small, alert face as he fingered the beginning of a very pale mustache.

Next him, and leaning on the rails so that he nearly touched her skirt, was Captain Floyd, otherwise the Mad Dragoon, as handsome as Apollo, as reckless as only an Irish dragoon can be, and as cool as a cucumber till the red pepper is applied.

Near to him was young Lord Chichester, who had just married a very charming young woman, but who still found it impossible to pass any group of which Violet Graham was the center. There was several others—a Member of Parliament, a well-known barrister, and a curate who happened just then to be the fashion—and, although there were a great many of them "all at once," Violet Graham seemed quite able to keep the whole team in hand. And while she talked, the small, keen eyes were taking in the features of the procession which passed and repulsed her.

"There goes the duchess," said Captain Floyd, raising his hat, as a stout lady, in a handsome equipage, inclined her head toward them. "Looks very jolly, considering that she has lost so much money, and that the duke is supposed to have left her."

"She puts her gain against her loss, don't you see," said Violet Graham quickly.

There was an applausive laugh, of course.

"And here comes the new bishop. Why do bishops always have such awfully plain wives, Miss Graham?" murmured Lord Chichester.

"That they may not be too proud, like some of us," she said, promptly.

Charlie Chichester's wife was good looking. He blushed.

"You are harder than ever, this afternoon, Miss Graham," he said.

"Or is it that you are softer?" she retorted.

The ready laugh rang out.

"Tremendous lot of people," said the dragoon, languidly; "it makes one long for a desert island all to one's self."

"Any island would be a desert which contained Captain Floyd," she said.

"I don't see the point," he said, looking up at her languidly.

"Because you would soon quarrel with and kill anyone else who happened to be living there," she retorted.

"That's right, Miss Graham," exclaimed Lord Chichester, cheering up. "Give him one or two lunges; he's far too conceited, and wants taking down."

"I wonder where Blair is?" said the captain, and he looked at Miss Violet, but whether intentionally or not could not be said. If there was any significance in his glance she did not betray herself by the movement of an eyelash.

"Oh, Blair?" said the marquis; "he's off into the country somewhere. Come a dreadful cropper over Daylight, you know. Think he's gone to raise the tin; don't know, of course."

"Of course!" assented Miss Graham, smiling down upon him.

He was known as "Sublime Ignorance."

"One for you, Aldy," chorused Chichester. "But, seriously, where is Blair? He went off without a word, don't you know, let me see, two days ago. Perhaps he's bolted! Shouldn't wonder! He has been going it awfully rapidly lately, don't you know. Poor old Blair!"

For once Miss Graham seemed to have no repartee ready. She sat looking straight between her horse's ears, her eyes still and placid, her lips set.

Then she looked round them with a smile.

"Well, I can't stay chattering with you any longer."

"Oh, give us another minute," pleaded Lord Chichester. "It's too hot for riding."

"And far too hot for talking," she put in. "I must be off! Are you coming, girls?"

As she spoke the two girls who were with her, and who had been talking with some of the men, obediently—everybody obeyed Violet Graham—gathered up their reins, a horseman rode slowly up, and bringing his horse to a stand close beside Violet Graham's, raised his hat.

He was a tall, fine-looking man, thin and not badly made, but there was something in his face which did not prepossess one. Perhaps it was because the lips were too thin and under control, or the eyes too close together, or perhaps it was the expression of steadfast determination which lent a certain coldness and hardness to the clear-cut features.

"Ah, Austin, how do you do?" said Miss Graham, with the easy carelessness of an intimate friend, but as she spoke her eyes seemed to seek his face, and finding something there, dropped to her horse's ears.

He answered her salutation in a low, clear voice—almost too cold and grave for so young and handsome a man, and exchanged greetings with the rest. Then, without looking at her, he said:

"Are you riding on?"

"Yes," she said. "We were just starting. Good-bye!" and with a wave of her hand to her circle of courtiers, she rode on, Austin Ambrose close by her side.

"How I hate that fellow!" murmured the dragoon, languidly, looking after them.

"Hear, hear," said Lord Chichester.

"And yet he isn't a bad fellow—what's the matter with him?" stammered the marquis.

"Don't know," murmured Captain Floyd. "'I do not like thee, Dr. Fell, the reason why I cannot tell——'"

"Who's Dr. Fell?" asked the marquis, with a bewildered stare.

A shout of laughter greeted his question.

"Look here, Sublime Ignorance," said the dragoon, with a wearied smile, "you are too good for this world. Such a complete lack of brains and ordinary intelligence are utterly wasted on this sublunary sphere."

"Oh, bother!" grunted the peer. "I never heard of any Dr. Fell, how should I? But what's the matter with Ambrose?"

"I don't know," said Lord Chichester, thoughtfully. "I think it's that smile of his, that superior smile, that makes you long to kick him; or is it the way in which he looks just over the top of your head?"

"Or is it because Miss Graham is such a special friend of his that he can take her away from all the rest of us put together?" murmured the captain.

"Oh, there is nothing on there," said Lord Chichester. "My wife—and she ought to know, don't you know—stoutly denies it."

"I didn't say there was anything between them. If there was, that would be sufficient reason for all of us hating him—barring you, Charlie, who are out of the hunt now."

"You don't hate Blair?" said Chichester, thoughtfully.

"Well, there is nothing between him and her; now, at any rate; and if there were we shouldn't hate him."

"Fancy hating old Blair!" exclaimed the marquis.

There was a general smile of assent at the exclamation.

"Best fellow alive!" said Chichester. "Poor old chappie; he's dreadfully down on his luck just at present."

"Oh, he'll come up to time all right!" broke in the dragoon. "You never find Blair knocked under for long. He'll come up smiling presently. Always falls on his legs, thank goodness. By the way," he said, more thoughtfully than was his wont, "it's rather rum how he and that fellow Ambrose get on so well together."

"Oh, Blair could get on with any one—Old Nick himself!" exclaimed Chichester, and amidst the general laugh the group melted and passed on with the crowd.

Miss Violet Graham rode on in silence for a moment or two, then she said, in an undertone:

"Have you seen him? Where is he?"

Austin Ambrose cast a cold glance of warning toward the others, and with a little gesture of impatience Violet Graham answered it.

"You are right. Come in to tea, will you?"

"Thanks," he said aloud. "I will leave you now," he added, as they reached the gates; "I will be round as soon as I have put the horse in."

Violet Graham nodded, and immediately joined in conversation with the people near her, and with her usual vivacity exchanged greetings and rapid exclamations with the people who rode or drove by. It seemed as if she knew and was known of everybody!

But presently she pulled up.

"Well, girls, I'm tired out. It really is too hot for any more of it. Any of you come home to tea with me?"

They knew by the way the invitation was given that they were not wanted, and of course declined, and Miss Graham, turning her horse, rode pretty smartly, hot as it was, toward the gate.

In a few minutes she was in her house in Park Lane.

It was one of the largest houses in the lane, and the appointments were of a magnificence suitable to the richest lady in London.

The hall she entered, though not so large as those in country mansions, was superbly decorated and lined with choice exotics. Statuary, white as the driven snow, gleamed against the mosaic walls. Plush had given place to Indian muslin for the summer months, and the white place looked like an Oriental or a Grecian dream.

"I am out to everyone but Mr. Ambrose," she said to the footman who attended her, and passing by the drawing-room, she ascended the stairs and entered a really beautiful apartment, which, as she reserved it for herself, might be called her boudoir.

She shut the door and dropped on a couch, flinging her hat on a table and feverishly tugging at her gauntlets. Then she rose and began pacing the room. And all the time she looked as anxious as a woman could look.

Presently the door opened, and a servant announced Mr. Ambrose.

"Bring some tea," she said, "and show Mr. Ambrose in."

He came in, cool, self-possessed, bringing with him, as it seemed, a breath of cold air.

Just glancing at her, he put down his hat and whip, and seating himself in one of the delightfully easy chairs, leant back and looked at her from under his lids.

It was a peculiar look, critical, analytical; it was the look a surgeon bends on a patient who is a curious and, perhaps, difficult case.

"Well?" she said, sinking into a chair and fidgeting with the handle of her whip.

The footman entered with the tea-tray, and Austin Ambrose, instead of answering, said:

"No sugar in mine, please."

She poured him out a cup with not too carefully concealed impatience, and as he rose and fetched it, taking it leisurely back to his chair, she beat a tattoo on the ground with her small feet.

"How tiresomely slow you can be when you like," she said. "I believe you do it to—to exasperate me."

"Why should I exasperate you?" he responded calmly, coolly. "Are you angry with me because I would not speak before the women who were with us in the park, or before the servant here; it is a question which of them would chatter most."

"Oh, you are right, of course. You always are," she said. "That makes it so annoying. But there are no women or servants here now, and you can speak freely, and—and at once. Did you see Blair?"

"I had just left him when I met you," he answered.

"Well?" she said, and her eyes sought his face eagerly, impatiently. "Where has he been?"

"To Leyton Court," he replied.

"To the earl's," she said. "I thought so."

"Yes," he said slowly; "he has been to the earl."

"Well, has he done anything for him?"

"No; nothing."

A look of relief shone in her eyes.

"I am glad, glad!" she murmured.

"He offered to lend him—or give him—the money he wanted, but Blair refused."

"He refused? That was like him!" she said, with a touch of pride and satisfaction. "Yes, that was just like him. They quarreled, of course?"

"Oh, yes, they quarreled!" assented Austin Ambrose quietly. "There were the materials for a quarrel. It seems that, finding the journey tedious, Blair enlivened it by fighting with one of the rustics."

She smiled, and a strange look came into her eyes.

"Yes, that is Blair all over! And the earl heard of it?"

"Yes," he said, slowly, "he heard of it; and, as the combat took place just outside the Court gates, he was not altogether pleased. Blair's account is amusing."

"He shall tell me! He shall tell me!" she said, looking into vacancy, her cheeks mantling, her eyes glowing. "I—I have never seen him fight——"

"I dare say he would gratify any desire you may have in that direction. He is always ready to fight, and on the smallest provocation," remarked Austin Ambrose, with icy coldness.

"No," she said, "he is not! He is not easily provoked, but when he is— but what does it matter? We don't want to waste time quarreling about him. I want to hear all—all that occurred!"

"I came to tell you," he said, slowly. "The earl, notwithstanding his anger at the brawl outside the Court gates, offered to lend Blair the money to help him out of this difficulty, but Blair refused."

"And—and Ketton must go?" she said, in a tone of satisfaction.

"Ketton must go the way of the rest," he assented.

She nodded, her small eyes shining brightly—too brightly.

"Ketton gone; there is not much left to fall back upon, is there?"

"No, not much," he replied.

"And—and he will not pull up; will not retrench? You will prevent that?" and she looked at him anxiously.

He did not reply, but his silence was significant enough.

"And he thinks you his best friend, his Fides Achates. Poor Blair!" and she laughed. "All his money gone, and his estates; Ketton is the last! Yes, he cannot keep the pace much longer. He will be—what do you men call it?—'stone broke,' and then—and then!" She drew a long breath, and her lips closed and opened. "And then he will come to me! He *must* come!" she exclaimed, her hand trembling. "He will come back to me, and——" She stopped suddenly, arrested by a look in his cold secretive eyes. "Is there anything else? Have you told me all?"

He was silent a moment, and she accosted him with an exclamation of impatient impetuosity.

"What else is there? Why do you sit there silent, if there is anything else to tell? Do you remember our bargain?"

"Yes, I remember it," he said, after a moment's pause, during which he looked, not at her, but just over her head, in the manner which Captain Floyd found so objectionable. "It is not so long ago that I should forget it. It was made in this room. I had the presumption to offer you——"

"Never mind that!" she broke in, but as if she had not spoken he went on in his cold, impassive manner.

"I had the presumption to offer you my hand, to beg yours! I was fool enough to imagine that your smiles and your sweet words were intended to signify that such an offer would not meet with a refusal. It was a mistake! I had forgotten that I was poor, and that you were rich. You recalled me to my senses by a laugh, which I hear still——"

"What is the use——" she tried to break in with, but he went on.

"Most men, I believe, placed in a like position, that of a rejected suitor, implore the lady who refuses them her love to grant them her friendship. I did so. But while most men mean nothing by it, I meant a great deal. If I could not have you for myself, I was ready to serve you as a grand vizier serves his sultan, or a slave its master. You accepted my offer. It was not I you wanted, but another man; that man was Blair Leyton."

"You—you put it plainly," she murmured, biting her lip.

He looked over her head.

"Yes. Truth is natural, always," he said. "I undertook to help you to gain him, asking for no definite reward, but trusting to your generosity."

"You shall ask for what you like. I will grant it," she said, "you know that."

"Yes," he said, "I know that," but his response was uttered with a significance which she did not appreciate. "You and he were engaged, the engagement is broken off; it is my task to see that it is renewed. I am engaged in that task now. Between us, it is understood there should be no concealment. Concealments would be fatal. You ask me to tell you all concerning this visit of Blair to the Court. I intend doing so. There is not much difficulty, for I have just left Blair, who has found out his heart after his fashion."

"His heart! About what?" she demanded, taking up her tea cup.

"About a girl he met there," he said, quietly and coldly.

The fragile and priceless piece of porcelain fell crushed by her fingers.

He rose courteously and picked up the fragments.

"It will spoil the set," he remarked, coolly.

"Girl—girl! What girl?" she demanded.

She was white to the lips, and her gray eyes seemed to have grown dark, almost black.

"A girl whom he found staying in the house," he rejoined, with a cool ease that maddened her. "I can describe her, for Blair was minute to weariness. She is tall, graceful, has auburn hair, large and expressive eyes, a small mouth, a clear, musical voice, an angelic smile——"

She put up her hand.

"Are—are you saying all this to—to play with me?" she said, and her voice was almost hoarse.

He raised his brows and looked above her head with an air of surprise.

"No. They are his own words," he said.

"And—and you think he is in"—she paused; something seemed to stop her utterance for a moment—"he is in love with this girl?"

He sat silent for a moment.

"If he is to be believed, he is most certainly," he responded, coldly; "very much in love—head over heels! He raved about her for nearly an hour by the clock; I timed him."

She sprung to her feet and moved to and fro, her tiny hand clutching the riding-whip until the nails ran into her soft, pink palm. Then she stopped suddenly and looked at him.

"And this—this girl?" she said. "Who is she?"

"The daughter—no, to be exact, the granddaughter of the earl's housekeeper," he said slowly, as if he enjoyed it.

She panted and drew her breath heavily.

"A servant!" she exclaimed, and she laughed, a cruel unwomanly laugh.

"By no means," he said. "She is, according to Blair, and he is a fair judge, a lady. She is an artist, and is copying the pictures in the Court gallery."

Her face grew white and anxious again.

"What—what is her name?" she demanded, and her voice was hard and hoarse.

He took an ivory tablet from his pocket and consulted it.

"Her name is Margaret—a pretty name; reminds one of Faust, doesn't it? Margaret Hale."

"Margaret Hale," she repeated slowly; then she came and stood in front of him, her gray eyes as hard as steel, her lips drawn across her white, even teeth. "And he—you say—he is in love with her?"

He shrugged his shoulders.

"He says so," he said coldly.

"And—and he speaks of marrying her?"

"Apparently it is the one and absorbing desire of his life," he responded in exactly the same manner.

She opened her lips as if about to speak again, then sank on to a couch in silence.

He rose.

"I'll go," he said.

"Wait!" she said, and she stretched out her hand with the whip in it. "Austin, this—this, must be stopped, prevented——" she spoke with a panting breathlessness. "You—you understand. It *must* be prevented, at *all* costs, at any risks! You will do it! Promise me! Remember our bargain! Ask what you please, I will grant it. Half—every penny I possess—anything! You will prevent it!"

He stood looking at her without an atom of expression on his clean-cut face, which might have been a marble mask.

"I understand," he said, after the pause. "At any cost? You will not upbraid, reproach me in the future, whatever may happen?"

"No. I shall not! At any cost!" she repeated, meeting his cold glance.

He stood regarding the wall above her head for a moment, then, without a word, went out and left her.

Slowly, impassively, he paced down the stairs, his eyes fixed on the open doorway and the street beyond, but reaching the hall, which happened to be empty, he paused, and with his foot on the doorstep, he turned round and smiled.

It was a peculiar smile and difficult to analyze, but supposing a man had caught a wild animal in a trap and had left it hard and fast, to be killed at his leisure, that man might smile as Austin Ambrose smiled as he looked round the hall of Violet Graham's house in Park Lane.

CHAPTER VIII

Margaret had never been in love. If any one had asked her why not, she would have said that she was too busy, and hadn't time. Young men had admired her, and some few, the artists whom she met now and again, had fallen in love with her, but no one had ever spoken of the great mystery to her, for there was something about Margaret, with all her wildness, an indescribable maiden dignity which kept men silent.

Lord Blair had been the first to speak to her in tones hinting at passion, and it is little wonder that his words clung to her, and utterly refused to be dismissed from her mind, though she tried hard and honestly to forget them; even endeavored to laugh at them, as the wild words of a wild young man, who would probably forget that he had ever spoken them, and forget her, too, an hour or two after he had got to London.

But she could not. She said not a word of what had occurred to old Mrs. Hale, for she felt that she could not have borne the flow of talk, and comment, and rebuke which the old lady would pour out. It would have been better if she had spoken and told her all; a thing divided becomes halved, a thing dwelt upon grows and gets magnified.

Margaret brooded over the wild words Lord Blair had said until every sentence was engraved on her mind; even the expression of his face as he stood before her, defiant as a Greek god, got impressed upon her memory so that she could call it up whenever she pleased, and, indeed, it rose before her when she did not even wish it.

"This is absurd and—and nonsensical!" she exclaimed on the second day after his departure, when she suddenly awoke to the fact that she had been sitting, brush in hand, staring before her and recalling Lord Blair's handsome, dare-devil eyes, as they had looked into hers. "I am behaving like a foolish, sentimental idiot!" she told herself, dabbing some color on her canvas with angry self-reproach. "What on earth can it matter to me what such a person as Viscount Leyton said to me? I shall never see him again, and he has probably forgotten, by this time, that such a person as myself exists! I am an idiot not to be able to forget him as easily. He behaved like a savage to the very last, and I would not speak to him again if—if we were cast alone on a desert island!"

She sprung to her feet with an exclamation of annoyance, and began bundling her painting materials together, and was in the midst of clearing up, when she heard a step behind her, and saw the earl.

It was near the dinner hour, and he was in evening dress, for, though he dined alone, he always assumed the regulation attire; and Margaret, as she looked at him, could not help noticing the vague likeness between him and Lord Blair.

"Do I disturb you?" he said, in his low, grave voice, and he paused with the knightly courtesy for which he was famous.

"No, my lord. I have just finished for to-day," said Margaret, rather shyly, for she felt his greatness, which spoke in the tone of his voice, and proclaimed itself even in his gait, and the way he held himself.

With a slight inclination of his head he came and stood before the canvas.

A slight expression of surprise came over his face.

"You have made an excellent copy," he said. "I think you are capable of higher work—original work."

Margaret's face flushed with pleasure, but she said nothing. It was not for so humble an individual as herself to bandy compliments with so great a personage as the Earl of Ferrers.

"You have worked hard," he said, looking at her; "not too hard, I hope."

Now Margaret had grown rather pale during these last two days. It had been one of the results of Lord Blair's passionate words. She did not sleep much at night, and what with this and dwelling upon the scene that had passed between them, the roses which Mrs. Hale wished to see had vanished from her face.

"You are looking tired and pale," said the earl, in a gravely kind fashion.

"I am quite well, my lord," she said, standing with lowered lids under the piercing gaze of the dark-gray eyes.

"Yes, it is a very good copy," he said, returning to the picture. "I should have paid you a visit before; I have not lost my interest in art, but I have been engaged and indisposed. I have had my nephew with me," he continued, more to himself than to her—"Lord Leyton." He sighed. "You may not have seen him?"

"I have seen him, my lord," said Margaret, and for the life of her she could not help the tell-tale flush rising to her face.

His eyes rested on hers, and seemed to sink to the innermost depths of her soul.

"Have you spoken to him?" he asked, not angrily, but in the tones a judge might use.

Margaret's face grew pale again.

"I have spoken to him, my lord," she said.

The earl's face grew stern and he stood perfectly motionless, with his eyes fixed on her face.

"I am sorry for that."

"Sorry, my lord?" faltered Margaret.

"I am sorry," he repeated. "My nephew, Lord Leyton, is a wicked and unprincipled young man. He is not fit— —"

"Oh, my lord!" said Margaret, all her womanly chivalry rising on behalf of the absent.

The earl looked at her, his eyes dark and severe.

"He is not fit to hold converse with such as you." Then the look of grief and surprise seemed to recall him to himself. "No matter. He has gone. It is not likely that you will see him again— —"

"No, my lord," assented Margaret, with simple dignity.

"Let us say no more about him. He has nearly broken my heart; he is the one thorn in my side," he went on, notwithstanding that he had said no more should be spoken of the wicked young man. "He is a spendthrift and a gambler, and— —" he stopped, suddenly. "If your work is done, permit me to walk with you on the terrace; the air is cool and inviting."

"I have finished for to-day, my lord," she said.

He went to the window and opened it wide for her, and held it open until she had passed out.

It was only to Lord Blair that he was rough and fierce.

"It is a lovely evening," he said, looking out upon the far-stretching lawns.

Margaret stood beside him in silence.

"What will you do with your Guido when you have finished it, Miss Hale?" he said, after a moment or two.

Margaret laughed softly.

"I don't know, my lord," she said at last.

"If you will sell it, I will buy it," he said.

Margaret flushed with gratification.

"I do not know its worth, but I will venture to offer you fifty pounds."

"That's a great deal too much, my lord," she said, decidedly.

"I think not," he responded, so quietly that she could say nothing else beyond "Thank you, my lord!"

"You shall paint another picture for me," he said; "not a copy this time." He paused a moment, then went on, "Choose some small piece of woodland scenery and paint it for me, if you will, Miss Hale."

"I will, my lord," said Margaret, gratefully.

Her simple response seemed to please him, and he looked at her thoughtfully, and with a sad regret. Why had not Heaven blessed him with a daughter like to this beautiful girl? was passing through his mind.

Then he said suddenly:

"You have no parents, Miss Hale?"

"No, my lord," said Margaret sadly.

"And you rely upon your own efforts?" he said gently.

"Yes," replied Margaret, "I depend entirely upon my painting, Lord Ferrers."

"It is not an ignoble dependence," said the stately old man. "You are happy in being able to rely upon yourself. And you delight in your work?"

"I am fonder of it than anything else, my lord," said Margaret, with a smile.

The earl paced toward the broad steps that lead from the terrace to the gardens, and Margaret, feeling that she must not go until she was dismissed, walked by his side.

At a turn in the path he stopped short.

"I must leave you now," he said. "Good-bye! Perhaps, some day, you will be kind enough to give me your company in another stroll. You will not forget the picture?"

"Oh, no, my lord," said Margaret, dropping a courtesy.

The earl paced slowly to his own apartments, and entering the library, sat down before the great carved writing-table.

For half an hour he sat musing.

"So young, so innocent, so much at the mercy of the cold, cruel world. Depends upon her art! Poor child, a frail dependence! Why should I not? I am rich beyond calculation, as they tell me. Why should I not do one act of common kindness, and make my money of some use to one deserving it? Hitherto it has passed, through Blair's hands to blacklegs and scoundrels."

He drew the paper toward him and took up the pen with an air of resolution and wrote a note to Messrs. Tyler & Driver, the family solicitors.

> "Gentlemen," he wrote, "add a codicil to my will, bequeathing five thousand pounds to Margaret Hale, the granddaughter of Mrs. Hale, who acts as the Court housekeeper.
>
> Very truly yours,
>
> Ferrers."

It was an important letter for Margaret, but it bore upon her future to an extent far greater than would be inferred even by the gift of so large a sum of money.

CHAPTER IX

It was only when she had left the earl that Margaret noticed how kind and gracious he had been. He had not only bought the copy of the Guido, and commissioned another picture of her, but had walked by her side and smiled upon her, treating her almost as an equal, with a gentleness and deference indeed which seemed to indicate that he thought her a superior.

"I'll go into the woods and find a subject at once," she said to herself. "And it shall be my very best picture, or—I'll know the reason why. No wonder people are fond of lords and ladies, if they are all like the great Earl of Ferrers."

No doubt, if she had known the contents of the letter he had just written to Messrs. Tyler & Driver, she would have thought still more highly of him.

She had a sketch-block and pencil in her hand, and she went through to the woods that fringed the Court lawns on three sides.

They were lovely woods: there was no more beautiful place in England than Leyton Court, and Margaret almost forgot the purpose for which she had come, as she sat in a little bushy dell, through which ran a tiny stream, tumbling in silvery cascades over the bowlders rounded by the hand of Time.

But presently, when she had drank deep of its beauty, she began to make a sketch of the dell.

What a lucky girl she was! The possessor of the silver medal, an exhibitor in the Academy, and now commissioned by no less a personage than the Earl of Ferrers.

"I shall be really famous if I go on like this," she said to herself, with a soft laugh.

Then the laugh died out on her lips, for, with a sudden spring, a young man reached the rock she was at that moment sketching, and from it dropped to her side.

It was Lord Leyton.

Margaret was so startled that she let the sketch-block fall from her hand, and sat looking at him, with the color slowly fading from her face. She had succeeded in forgetting him for a short hour or two, and here he was at her side again.

And Lord Blair assuredly looked, if not startled, pale and haggard.

For the last two days, since he had left Margaret, overwhelmed by his passionate outburst, he had been living after his wildest and most reckless fashion, and two days of such dissipation and sleeplessness, added to passion, tell even upon such perfect physical specimens of humanity as Blair Leyton.

"Lord Leyton!" she said at last.

He picked up her sketch-block, but held it, still looking at her.

"I've frightened you," he said, remorsefully; "I—I am a brute. I did not know you were here until I jumped upon that stone, when I was close upon you."

Margaret tried to smile.

"It does not matter," she said. "Give me my block, please," and she held out her hand.

He drew a little nearer, and gave her the block.

"You are sketching?" he said, his eyes fixed on her face with a wistful eagerness.

She inclined her head.

"Yes; I am painting a picture for the earl."

"For the earl!" he repeated dully, as if her voice, and not the words she said, were of importance to him.

"Yes; if you wish to see him, you will find him at home; he has just left me."

"Just left you!" he repeated as before. "No; I don't want to see him."

Margaret raised her eyes and looked at him.

"You have not come down to see him?" she said with faint surprise.

"No!" he responded. "He wouldn't see me if I had. But I didn't come to see him; I came——" then he stopped for a second. "Miss Margaret, I am afraid to tell you *why* I came."

"Then don't tell me," said Margaret, trying to force a smile. "It sounds as if you had come for no good purpose, my lord."

He stood silent for a second, then he flung himself at her feet, and leaning on his elbow, looked up at her with the same eager wistfulness in his handsome eyes.

"Yes, I will tell you," he said; "I came to see you!"

"To see me?" said Margaret, flushing. Then the straight brows came together. "Lord Leyton, you should not have said that!"

"Why should I not?" he demanded, "if it's true—and it is true! Miss Margaret, I have been the wretchedest man in London these last two days."

"I doubt that," said Margaret quietly, and going on with her sketch.

"It's the truth. If there was a man condemned to be hanged, I'll wager he wasn't more wretched than I have been."

"Wicked people are always wretched—or should be, my lord," said Margaret coolly.

"And I am wicked. Yes, I know," he said; "I am the vilest of the vile, in your eyes. But it isn't for what I've done in the past that I'm so miserable, it is for what I said to you in the picture gallery the other morning. Miss Margaret, I behaved like a brute! I—I—said words that—that have made me wish I were dead——"

"That will do, Lord Leyton," said Margaret, interrupting him. "If you are so sorry there need be no more said excepting that I forgive you, and will forget them. I knew that you did not mean them at the time."

His face crimsoned, and his eyes grew almost fierce.

"Stop," he said; "I don't say that. I won't. I'm sorry I was rough; I'm sorry I behaved like a bear and blared and shouted, but I did mean what I said, and mean it still."

"I don't care whether you meant it or not, it is not of the least consequence, Lord Leyton," said Margaret, and she put her pencil in its case, and closed her sketch-block.

"Wait—do wait!" he explained. "Don't go yet. I have so much to say to you, so much, and I don't know how to say it! Miss Margaret, I came down on the chance of seeing you, and all the way down I prepared a speech, but the sight of you so suddenly has driven it all out of my head, and I can think of nothing but three words of it, and—and those I dare not say."

"I must go, my lord," said Margaret, trying to speak calmly and indifferently, but feeling her heart beginning to throb and quiver under the sound of his voice and the passionate regard of his dark eyes.

"Wait—wait five minutes," he implored. "Miss Margaret, don't send me back to London feeling that you despise me. Don't do that! I'm bad enough as it is, but I shall be worse if you do that."

Margaret sank down on the stones again, and listened with her eyes guarded by their long lashes; but she still could see his face.

He drew himself a little nearer.

"Miss Margaret, are you a witch?"

"A witch?" she faltered.

"Yes," he said. "I think you must be one, for you have bewitched me."

"Lord Leyton——"

"Am I not bewitched?" he said, holding out his hands appealingly; "isn't a man bewitched when he can only think of one thing, day and night, and can get no rest or sleep from thinking of it? And that is how it is with me. I can think of nothing but you."

Margaret made a motion to get up, but he laid his hand on the edge of her skirt imploringly.

"That is how it is with me," he went on. "I tell you the simple truth. I—I have never felt like it before. None of the women I ever met made me feel like this! What is it you have done to me to steal the heart out of my body? for I feel that it is gone—gone!" and he touched his breast with his finger.

Margaret tried to smile, but there is a tragedy in real passion which, however wild the language, forbids laughter, and Lord Leyton's passion was real.

"I see your face all day, I hear your voice. I go over every word you said to me—and some of them were hard words!—and—and to-day I felt that I must get near to you, that I must come down to Leyton if I died for it. Do you believe what I say?"

"I know that I should not listen to you, my lord," she said, in a low voice.

"Why not?" he said. "It is true. Miss Margaret, you have stolen my heart; what is there left to me? I have come because I must, and now I am here I am no better, for I feel that I must tell you more, all that there is to tell, even if you send me away. But don't do that if you can help it, for Heaven's sake don't do that!" and she saw that his lips were quivering. "Margaret, you know what I would say," he went on, in the low, thrilling tones of a young and strong man's passion. "I love you!"

Margaret did not start, but a red flush rose and covered her face, then left it pale even to whiteness, and she sat as if turned to stone.

"I love you! Dear, I love you!" he murmured. "Do you—will you not believe me?"

She opened her lips, but he put up his hand.

"No, don't speak—not yet. I know what you were going to say. You were going to say that it is impossible, that we only met a few days ago, that we are strangers. Yes, I know that is what you would say. But it is of no use to say that. Do you think people can get to love by knowing each other a certain number of months—years? Margaret, I think I loved you when I saw you in the village the first time; I know I loved you when you sat by my side in the garden and let me put the rose in your dress! Only a few days ago! Why, it seems years to me—it *is* years! Oh, Margaret, don't be hard and cruel, and you can be so hard, so cruel! See here; I lay all my life at your feet! It's a bad lot, I know! Why, I told you so, didn't I? But—but I'll change all that! You shall see! Let me go on loving you; let me hope that, some day, you'll try and love me a little in return, and I'll turn over a new leaf! I can never be worthy of you. Oh, I know that. Why, where is there a man in all the world who could be worthy to touch the edge of your dress?" and as he spoke he raised her skirt to his lips, and far from touching herself as his lips were, she seemed to feel them. "But every day, every hour, if you will let me love you, I'll tell myself that I'm of some consequence to someone in the world, and that will keep me straight! Margaret—" he paused and crept a little nearer—"Margaret, you are an angel, and I am a—well, just the other thing; but I ask you to be my guardian angel! Dear, if you knew how I love you! I cannot get your face from before my eyes; every word you have uttered sings in my heart! I am bewitched, bewitched! And—and all I can say is, let me love you all my life, and try and love me a little!"

Pale, trembling, Margaret listened, her eyes downcast, her hands clasped tightly in her lap.

It was all so new, so strange, so unexpected that her heart throbbed and her brain whirled. His words, in their passionate assertion and entreaty, seemed to penetrate to her soul, and with it all a sense of ineffable joy and delight suffused her whole being and ran through every vein.

"You won't speak to me?" he said, with a quick sigh that was almost like a sob. "I see how it is! I am not fit; yes, I know! And I have offended you worse than I did the other morning. I—I am a fool, and I have destroyed my only chance! I meant to be so quiet and—and gentle with you, but I can't teach myself to keep quiet and soft-spoken when my heart is all on fire, and I long to clasp you in my arms and hear you tell me that you love me! Margaret, my good angel! Margaret, won't you say one little word to me? Not to send me away, but to tell me that, bad as I am, you will—well, think a little kindly of me!"

He had drawn himself still closer, so that his face almost touched the lace of her sleeves, and she could see the quiver of his lips under the thick mustache.

He waited a moment, then his head drooped.

"All right," he said; "don't speak. I see how it is. No, I'd rather you didn't speak. I might have known that you wouldn't listen to me, that you wouldn't give me any kind of hope. Good Lord, why should you? Well, I'll take myself off; I'll get out of your sight."

He had raised himself, but Margaret's hand stole out and fell, light as a feather, on his arm.

He seized it as a man dying of thirst in the desert seizes the cup of water that will save him, and covered it with hot passionate kisses.

"No, no!" she breathed, trying to draw it away. "You—you have unnerved me, Lord Leyton!"

"Go on!" he said. "I can bear it better if you will let me keep your hand!" and he pressed it to his lips again "What are you going to say, Margaret? Don't be hard upon me."

"Hard!—how can I be hard?" she faltered, and the tears came thickly into her sweet eyes. "How could anybody be hard, after such—such things as you have said? But—but—oh, my lord—isn't it all a mistake? You—you cannot lov——it is impossible!"

"Just what I told myself!" he exclaimed almost triumphantly. "I said it was impossible! But a starving man won't persuade himself that he isn't hungry by telling himself that he had something to eat a week ago. Margaret, I love you—I *do* love you!" and he pressed her hand against his heart, which throbbed passionately under her fingers like an imprisoned bird. "You know that it is true—do you not?"

"I—I think it is true!" she faltered in all modesty, in all honesty, but with a strange look in her face; "I do not know! No one has ever spoken to me as you have spoken; no one—no one!"

"Thank God for it!" he exclaimed. "I couldn't bear to think that any other man had been before me, Margaret! And will you try—oh, my dear, be good to me!—will you try and love me——"

She turned her eyes upon him with a grave, touching appeal which rendered her face angelic in its perfect maidenly innocence and trustfulness.

"I—I will try," she murmured in so low a voice that it is wonderful that he should have heard it.

But he did hear it, and leaning forward, caught her in his arms and drew her to him until her head rested on his shoulders, her face against his.

Then, as his lips clung to hers in the first love kiss that man had ever imprinted there, she drew back, startled and trembling.

"Margaret, dearest!" he exclaimed, in tender reproach, attempting to take her in his embrace again.

"No, no!" she panted. "Not yet—not yet! I am not sure——"

"Of me, of my love, dearest? Not sure?" he murmured reproachfully.

"Not sure of myself!" she said, locking her hands together. "I—I must think, I cannot think now. Ah, you have bewitched *me*——" and she put her hand to her brow, and looked down at him with a far-away, puzzled look. "I want to be alone, to think it all over. It seems too—too wild and improbable——"

"Think now, dearest. Give me your hand. I will not speak, I will not look at you!" he said, soothingly.

"No, no!" she said, almost fearfully, drawing her hand from him; and rising, she stood as if half giddy.

"You will leave me," he said, piteously, "with only——"

"I have said I—I will try!" she answered. "I will go now."

He sprung to his feet.

"Let me come with you—to the house, my dearest," he pleaded.

But she put up her hand.

"No; go now! We shall meet again—perhaps—soon."

"Yes, yes!" he responded, catching at the slightest straw of encouragement, like a drowning man. "I won't hurry you, or harass you, Margaret! I will try and be gentle with you. I will be a changed man from now. You shall see. But you will let me come again soon? You will meet me here to-morrow, Margaret?" he added, anxiously.

"The—the day after," she faltered. "Good-bye!"

He took her hand and held it to his lips, then she drew it away, and seemed to vanish from his sight.

At twenty paces she stopped, however, and holding up the hand he had kissed and pressed against his heart, she looked at it with a curious look, then laid her lips where his had touched it.

Poor Margaret!

CHAPTER X

Austin Ambrose had chambers in the Albany. He was not a rich man, as he had remarked, but the rooms were comfortably, even luxuriously furnished, and the taste displayed in their ornamentation and decoration was of the best. There were good pictures, rare china, and bronzes, that, if not priceless, were curious enough to be reckoned as valuable.

How Mr. Austin Ambrose lived was a mystery, just as he himself was somewhat of a mystery. He was supposed to have a small income, and he was known to play an admirable hand at whist, and to wield a remarkably good cue at billiards.

He was also a capital judge of a horse, and it was conjectured that he added to his certain income by these usually uncertain adjuncts.

On the evening of Blair's avowal in the Leyton Woods, Austin Ambrose sat over the dessert which followed his modest dinner.

A bottle of very fine claret was on the table, and he was sipping this in silent abstraction, when the door burst open, and Lord Blair rushed in.

Austin Ambrose looked up without a particle of surprise, but with a faint smile of irony.

"House on fire?" he said.

"My dear old chappie!" exclaimed Blair, laying his strong hand on Austin's shoulder, "I've such a lot to tell you! Austin, I've seen her!"

"Seen her? Seen whom?" said Austin raising his brows as if trying to recollect, whereas he had been thinking of the "her" as Blair rushed in. "Oh, the young lady, Miss—Miss Hale."

"Of course, of course!" exclaimed Blair, pacing up and down the room. "Austin, old fellow, I don't know where to begin. I've only just come back from Leyton and from her! Austin, she is an angel!"

"I dare say," was the cool comment. "And so you have been to Leyton. Another fight, Blair?"

"Pshaw!" exclaimed Lord Blair. "Be serious, old fellow. My heart is bursting with it all."

"Perhaps it will burst all the easier—at any rate you will be more comfortable—if you sit down," said Austin Ambrose, dragging a chair forward without rising. "Sit down, man, and don't wear my carpet out. I'm not rich enough to afford another, you know."

Lord Blair sank into the chair and took the wine which the other man poured out for him.

"And so you have been down to Leyton, Blair, have you? 'Pon my word, I didn't think you were so hard hit!"

Lord Blair made a gesture of impatience.

"I told you that I loved her!" he said, almost savagely.

Austin Ambrose shrugged his shoulders and raised his eyebrows.

"My dear fellow, you have made the same interesting remark about so many women!"

"No!" said Blair, vehemently. "I have never spoken about any other woman as I have spoken to you about her, because I have never felt for any other woman as I feel for her. Austin, if you could see her! She is the most beautiful creature you ever saw, and so modest, so sweet, so refined, so— there, if I were to rave about her from now till midnight I should not give you an idea of what she is like. Do you know that picture of Gainsborough, the girl gathering flowers—but there, what is the use of trying to describe her!"

"There is no use," said Austin, sipping his wine critically and lighting a cigar.

"No, and to you, especially!" said Lord Blair. "As well talk to a stone image. *You* know nothing of love or women."

Austin Ambrose smiled, a peculiar smile.

"Not the least," he said, cheerfully and placidly. "Love and women are not in my line. Wine and weeds and a good suit of trumps now—but tell me about her, for I know you are dying to. You saw her?"

"Yes, I saw her," assented Lord Blair, with a long sigh.

"And is that all?" asked Ambrose carelessly, but with a certain quick, attentive look in the corner of his cold gray eye. "Simply raised your hat and said 'good-day!'"

"No, by the Lord, no! I spent an hour with her—I think—I don't know—I lost all count of time, of everything."

"You talked to her? Did you mention that you had lost your senses—I mean your heart?"

"No chaffing about her, Austin," said Lord Blair, almost sternly, and with the look of passion that came so readily to his frank eyes. "Yes, I *did* tell her that I loved her!" he said, after a moment's pause.

Austin Ambrose looked over Blair's head without a particle of expression in his eyes.

"And may one ask how she took it?" he said, as carelessly as politeness would permit, but with his attention acutely on the alert. "What did she say?"

"I can't tell you all she said. I wouldn't if I could," said Blair, the color coming to his face, his eyes glowing with a rapt look. "She gave me no direct answer. I—I have to wait, Austin. Oh, how can I wait! The hours will seem years. Don't laugh, or I shall get up and kill you," he broke off blushing, but half in earnest. "Austin, if ever a man loved with all his heart, and mind, and body, and soul, I love her!"

"Yes," said Austin, slowly, almost gravely, "I think you do."

There was a moment's silence.

"And you propose—what do you propose?" he said, quietly; "do you mean to marry her?"

Blair sprung to his feet and his face turned white.

"Tut, tut, man," remarked Austin Ambrose, with perfect coolness, "you don't always marry them!"

Lord Blair sank back into his chair with a look of remorse and shame that was of more credit to him than any other expression could have been.

"You hit me fairly, Austin," he said, almost hoarsely. "But—but—all that has gone forever, I hope! I—I turn over a new leaf from to-day, please Heaven! Do I mean to marry her? Yes, yes! If she will have me! If she will stoop, the angel, to pick me out of the mud with her pure white hand, I mean to go to the earl and say—'My lord, this is my future wife!'" and he sprung up and began to pace the floor.

Austin Ambrose sipped his wine.

"Hem!" he said, slowly. "I don't think I should do that, if I were in your place, Blair."

Lord Blair stopped.

"You wouldn't—why not?"

Austin Ambrose was silent for a moment, then he set down his glass and leant back in his chair, but still looked just over Blair's head, instead of into his eyes.

"Look here, Blair," he said; "I don't know that I have any right to intrude my advice, or even my opinion, upon you, but I am, as you know, your friend."

"I should think so!" exclaimed Lord Blair.

"Yes, I am your friend! I owe you my life! Ever since you picked me out of the Thames that August morning— —"

"Oh, nonsense!" broke in Blair. "Any fellow would have done the same! You'd have picked me out if I'd had the cramp, and was going down instead of you."

"Well, we won't talk of it then," said Austin Ambrose; "but, of course, I don't forget it. When I look in the glass in the morning, I say to the not particularly handsome gentleman who regards me, 'My friend, but for Lord Blair's strong arm and good wind, *you* would not be outside the world's crust this morning.' Of course, I can't forget it, and as I owe you my life, I will continue to be a nuisance to you by offering my advice, and that is, 'Don't go to the earl and tell him you are going to make his housekeeper's granddaughter his future niece and the Countess of Ferrers!'"

CHAPTER XI

"What do you say?" said Lord Blair, staring at Austin Ambrose with astonishment. "You wouldn't tell the earl?"

"No," said Ambrose, lighting a cigarette and stretching out his legs with comfortable indolence. "I certainly should not."

"But—but why not?" demanded Lord Blair.

"Well," said Ambrose slowly, "you are awkwardly placed, you see. I imagined from all you have told me that you and the earl do not get on very well together as it is."

"You are right, we don't," admitted Lord Blair shortly.

"Just so. You have led—well, not to put it too plainly—you have been engaged in that branch of agriculture which is called sowing wild oats for a considerable period, and with a great deal of energy. You have had, I believe, rather a large sum of money from the earl?"

"Yes, I have," admitted Blair with a sigh and a frown.

"Not a penny of which he would regret, if you would only oblige him by marrying the woman he has chosen for you."

"Violet Graham?"

"Exactly; Violet Graham," assented Austin Ambrose, knocking the ash off his cigarette and keeping his eyes fixed upon it. "And that, I take it, you don't care to do?"

"You know I don't. And Violet doesn't either. Why, you yourself advised me to release her, you know that she doesn't care a brass farthing for me!" exclaimed Blair, pacing to and fro.

"Oh, as to knowing, I don't go so far as that. You asked me for my opinion, and I gave it to you. I don't think she cares for you. I don't think Miss Graham is the kind of woman to care very much for any one."

"Very well, then, how the deuce could I marry her?" said Blair. "But what's the use of talking about that? Whatever I might have done before I saw Margaret, I certainly couldn't marry any one but her now, not to save a dukedom!"

"All right," assented Austin Ambrose, without permitting the slightest expression of the thrill of satisfaction that ran through him. "I quite understand, and I must say I think you are acting wisely. The man who marries one girl while he loves another is worse than wicked—he is foolish. But, all the same, the earl remains disappointed and displeased. Do you think, Blair, that his disappointment and displeasure would be lessened if you were to go to him and say, 'I can't marry Violet Graham, the woman you have chosen for me, and whose money would set me straight; but behold the girl I intend to make my wife and the future Countess of Ferrers!—she is your housekeeper's niece!'"

"Grand-daughter," said Blair. "And what if she is? I tell you, Austin, Margaret is a lady, from the crown of her head to the soles of her feet!"

"I dare say. I am sure she is, if you say so. You are a very good judge. But, my dear Blair, you can't expect everybody to see her with your eyes, especially an old man who has outlived the age of romance! Miss Margaret, with all her beauty, and grace, and refinement, will be his housekeeper's granddaughter—and nothing more to him. He will, to put it plainly, be very mad, my dear Blair."

"Well!" said Blair, with the Leyton frown on his handsome face, and the firm look about his lips which when seen by his friends was understood by them to mean that he had made up his mind—"what then?"

Austin Ambrose raised his eyebrows and looked just over Blair's head with a smile.

"What then? Well, you ought to know better than I whether you can afford to quarrel right out with your uncle, the great earl."

Blair flushed.

"What can he do to me—or her?" he asked.

"He can't order you off to instant execution, as he would no doubt like to do," said Ambrose, "but he can injure your prospects very materially, my dear Blair. Oh, I know about the title and estate," he went on, as Blair opened his lips. "Those *must* come to you—lucky beggar that you are! But there is something more and beyond those. The earl has a large personal property, a vast sum of money, that he can leave as he pleases— —"

"How do you know that?" demanded Blair, with a faint surprise.

The slightest flush rose to Austin Ambrose's face.

"Well," he replied, "I only imagine so. Like most people, I know that the earl has not lived up to a half, or a quarter of his income for years. And what an income it is! He must have saved an enormous sum of money— —"

"Let him do what he likes with it!" exclaimed Blair, bluntly. "I have had more than my share already. Let him leave it to anybody he likes. It is his own."

"Whom is he to leave it to?" said Ambrose. "The Home for Lost Dogs?"

"Or Sick Cats. I don't care!" said Blair, impetuously.

"That is all very well, and very noble, and all that, my dear Blair," said the cool, quiet voice. "But—pardon me—you haven't only yourself to think about, you know. There is your wife—the fair Margaret——"

"Heaven bless her, my darling!" murmured Blair.

"Just so," retorted Ambrose, with a cynical smile. "But when you say Heaven bless her, you mean that you wish Providence to pour out the good things of this life upon her with a liberal hand, but at the same moment you declare your intention of depriving her and her children of a large sum of money. Rather inconsistent, isn't it?"

Blair stood and looked down at him.

"What a head you have, Austin!" he said. "You ought to have been a lawyer. All this never struck me. I—I—never look forward to the future."

Austin Ambrose shrugged his shoulders.

"If we don't look forward to the future, the future has an awkward knack of looking back upon us!" he said indolently. "Depend upon it, my friend, that if you let the earl's money slip, you'll live to be sorry for it, not for your own sake, I dare say; you don't care about money, but for your wife and children's!"

"We shouldn't be paupers exactly!" said Blair, with a laugh.

"No!" assented Ambrose; and he shot a glance of envy, hatred, and all uncharitableness at the frank, handsome face. "No, you will be one of the richest men in England, but all the same——"

"And—and I hate anything like concealment and deceit," Blair broke in impatiently; "especially in connection with *her*."

Austin Ambrose nodded.

"Well, you asked for my opinion, and you are quite at liberty to reject it as per usual," he said carelessly. "But though I am not a rich man, I don't mind betting you fifty to one—in farthings—that if you declare your purpose of marrying this young lady to the earl, that before many years are over you will come to me and wish to Heaven you had taken my advice."

Blair bit at his cigar and fidgeted in the chair he had thrown himself into.

"I hate the idea of secrecy, Austin," he said at last; "and yet—but there! ten to one Margaret would refuse a clandestine marriage."

Austin Ambrose did not sneer, but he lowered his lids till they covered the cold gray eyes.

"Yes? I think not. Not if you told her all that you would lose by an open declaration. Women—forgive me, my dear fellow, but I know a little about them, though you think I don't—women have a better idea of the value of money than we men have. I think Miss Hale will consent to a quiet wedding when she knows that by so doing she will save several score of thousands to her husband, and to her future children."

There was silence for a moment, then Blair spoke. His fate and Margaret's, and more than theirs, had hung in the balance while he had hesitated.

"I think you're right, Austin," he said. "You always are, I know, and though I hate doing it, I'll take your advice. It—it will be only for a short time."

"Yes, the earl is quite an old man——"

"I didn't mean that," said Blair, quickly, "I don't want him to die, Heaven knows! I am not at all anxious to be the Earl of Ferrers. I shouldn't make half as fine an earl as he does."

"Just so," said Austin Ambrose. "But I am glad you intend to take my advice."

"Of course it all depends upon what Margaret says," said Lord Blair, gravely. "She may tell me that she—she will not marry me"—Austin Ambrose smoothed away a smile that was more than half a sneer—"but if she should say 'Yes,' then I will ask her to marry me quietly, though I hate the idea of any secrecy."

There was silence for a moment, then Austin Ambrose said, with a meditative smile:

"And are you going to turn over a new leaf, eh, Blair? What will the gay world do without you? What will they all say?—Lottie Belvoir, for instance."

Lord Blair colored and frowned.

"What has my marriage to do with Lottie Belvoir?" he said. "I have not seen her for months."

"Oh, nothing," assented Ambrose. "But you and she were so very thick, that I expect she will be a little heart-broken, you know."

Lord Blair made an impatient movement.

"I wish to Heaven I had never seen her or any of her kind," he said, remorsefully. "What fools men are, Austin! If we could only live our lives over again—but there, I mean to begin afresh now. And you will help me, old fellow!" and he laid his hand on the other man's shoulder. "You have always been the best friend I ever had, and you will help me now!"

"Of course, I'll help you; but I don't see what I can do," said Austin Ambrose, quietly. "If Miss Hale says 'Yes,' I should beg her to marry me as soon as possible. All you have to do then is to go down to some out-of-the-way place where there is a church—and there are churches everywhere—get the bans put up, or, better still, get a special license. You can be married as snugly as possible, and no one will be any the wiser. Such marriages are managed every day. Who knew that old Fortesque was married? We all thought him a bachelor, and yet he'd had a wife seven years! I'll help you all I can. I can't do less, having given you my advice to keep the thing a secret from the earl. Of course, I'd rather not have anything to do with it, but"—he shrugged his shoulders—"you can't refuse anything to a man who saved your life, you know! Have some more wine?"

"No, thanks; no more," said Lord Blair, jumping up; "I'll take a stroll in the park. I want to think it all over. I am to see her the day after to-morrow, to know if I am to be the happiest or the most miserable of men. Ah, Austin, if you could only see her!"

"I hope I may have the honor soon," he returned. "They say that when a man marries, his wife always hates his most intimate friend. I hope it won't be so with your wife, Blair, I must confess."

"Margaret is incapable of hating any one," said Blair; "she is an angel, and angels can't hate if they try! Austin, old fellow cynic and woman-hater as you are, you will admit that I have some reason in my madness when you see the girl I love."

"I dare say," said Ambrose. "Well, good-bye! Come and tell me how it all goes."

"Of course," said Blair, getting his hat and stick.

"By the way," said Ambrose indolently; "this is quite a secret at present, isn't it? You have not told any one but me that you have ever seen this young lady?"

"It is quite a secret if you like to call it so," said Blair. "I have told no one."

"I can't help thinking you were right," said Ambrose. "If I were you I would not open my lips to any one."

Lord Blair nodded, but his face grew overcast.

"I do hate all this mystery," he said; "but I suppose you are right. What I want to do is to take her hand and stand before the world and say, 'Look here, what a prize I have got!'"

"Yes; very nice of you," said Austin Ambrose, "but as we concluded that it is your duty and policy to keep the world in the dark for the present, the best thing you can do is to say nothing to anybody."

"Yes," said Blair; "very well," and he strode out of the room.

Austin Ambrose sat and listened to the firm, decided step as it died away on the stairs, then he rose and paced the room with slow and measured tread, his hard, cold face set like stone.

"It's risky!" he muttered at last. "It may fail, and then——But it will not fail! Blair is easy enough to manage, and the girl—well, she is like the rest, I suppose and, Heaven knows, they are easy enough to deceive! I'll chance it!"

He sat down and remained in thought for another quarter of an hour, then he rose, and putting a light overcoat over his dress clothes, he took his hat and went out.

Passing up one of the small streets, he reached a short row of houses, quiet, miniature boxes of residences, called Anglesea Terrace, and knocking at No. 9, inquired if Miss Belvoir were at home.

Before the maidservant could reply, a feminine voice called out through the open door in the narrow passage:

"Yes, she is. Is that you, Mr. Ambrose? Come in," and Austin Ambrose, passing through the little passage, which was lined with large photographs of Miss Belvoir in various costumes, entered the room from which the voice proceeded.

The room was a very small one—far too small to permit of that oft-mentioned performance—swinging a cat—and it was rather shabbily, though gaudily furnished. The furniture was old and palpably rickety, the carpet was threadbare, but there was a brilliant wall paper, and a pair of gay-colored cushions. An opera cloak, lined with scarlet, lay on one of the chairs, and on the sofa were a hat and a pair of sixteen-button kid gloves.

The owner of the hat, opera cloak, and gloves, sat at the table "discussing," as the old authors say, a lobster and a bottle of stout.

She was a girl of about two-and-twenty, neither pretty nor plain, but with a sharp, intelligent face—the sort of face one sees amongst the London street boys—and a pair of dark and wide-awake eyes, which were by far her best features. She wore a light-blue dressing grown—rather frayed at the sleeves, by the way, and trimmed with a cheap and—by no means slightly—dirty lace. But for all its sharpness and the vulgarity of its surroundings, it was not altogether a bad face.

This was Miss Lottie Belvoir. She was an actress. Not a famous one by any means—only a fifth-rate one at present; but she was waiting for a favorable opportunity to become a first-rate one. Perhaps the opportunity might come, perhaps it mightn't; meanwhile, Lottie Belvoir was content to work hard and wait. Some day, perchance, she would "fetch" the town, and then she would exchange the grimy back room in Anglesea Terrace for a house at St. John's Wood, the old satin dressing-gown for a costume of Worth, and the lobster and stout for *pate de foie gras* and champagne. Until that happy time arrived, she was perfectly content with minor parts in the burlesques at the Frivolity Theater.

"Oh, it is you, is it?" she said, without rising or stopping at the manipulation of one of the lobster claws; "I thought I recognized your voice. Who was it said that he never forgot a voice or a face? Some great man. Well, I'm like him. You have come just in time. Have some lobster?"

"No, thank you, Lottie," said Ambrose Austin; "I have only just dined."

"Of course, you swells dine later than ever, now, and that's why you can't turn up at the theater until we have got half through the piece. Well, sit down. Make yourself at home. Take care!" she exclaimed, as he sank into an arm-chair; "that chair's got a castor off. Here, take this," and she kicked and pushed another one toward him. "Don't put your cigar out; I'm just going to have a cigarette. Have some stout? No? Too heavy, I suppose? Well, here's some whisky. And how's the world treating you? You look very flourishing; but you always do."

"I might return the compliment," he said. "You are still on the Frivolity, Lottie?"

"Still at the Friv.," she assented, lighting a cigarette and throwing herself not ungracefully on the sofa. "Why don't you drop in some evening and give me a hand? You are too busy at your club with another kind of hand—a hand at cards, I suppose?" she added with charming candor.

He smiled.

"I'll look in some night," he said; "but I suppose they will soon be going on tour."

"Yes, in another fortnight," she said with a yawn, "and precious glad I shall be. London's getting too warm even for this child."

"And yet I want you to stay in London," he said quietly.

She looked across at him and blew out a ring of smoke scientifically.

"You do, do you? What for? Are you going to take a theatre and engage me as leading lady?"

"Do I look like it?" he retorted with a smile.

"Well, not much," she said, surveying him critically. "People might take you for a good many things, Mr. Ambrose, but they wouldn't take you for a fool, or if they did they would be taken in."

"Thanks, Lottie," he said. "That is something like a compliment."

"No, I don't think you are such an idiot as to take a theater," she said, "but what do you want me to stay in London for?"

"To assist me in a little business I'm engaged in," he said.

She regarded him with sharp scrutiny as she leant back and smoked her cigarette.

"You seem rather shy in mentioning it and coming to the point," she said dryly; "is it anything very bad?"

He laughed.

"Oh, no, something quite in your line. You know, Lottie, I always said you would turn out a great actress."

"You have said so a dozen of times," she said, "but whether you meant it— —"

"I was quite serious, I assure you," he responded, "and in proof of my sincerity I am going to ask you to play a very difficult part."

"Oh, you've written a play!" she said coolly; "well, that's more in your line. And when are you going to produce it? And I'm to have a big part, am I, or is it a little one as usual? The authors always try and persuade you when they are giving you a part with about five lines in it, that it's the most important in the cast."

"I haven't written a play, and yet I have, so to speak," he said. "And you have the best part, far and away, Lottie. By the way, I have a piece of news for you. Lord Blair is going to be married!"

He burst it upon her purposely to see how she would like it, and for a moment Lottie turned crimson and then white, and her eyes blazed; then the actress asserted herself over the mere woman, and taking up another cigarette she lit it before she gave vent to a cool— —

"Oh, really!"

But Austin Ambrose had seen the deep red and the quick flash of the eyes and was not taken in by the nonchalant "Oh, really!"

"Yes," he said; "but it is a profound secret at present."

"And so you want me to tell everybody! I understand."

"No," he said, "I do not want you to tell anyone this time. I want it to be really kept quiet. You will see why directly."

"And the happy young lady is Miss Violet Graham, I suppose?" said Lottie, after a moment's pause. "What a funny thing it is that Fortune showers all her gifts on some persons and bestows only slaps on the face on others. Now, there's Miss Graham, the richest woman in England, and Fortune goes and gives her the nicest and handsomest young man for a husband, while I, poor Lottie Belvoir, have to struggle and struggle, and work like a nigger, and all I get is some small part in a frivolity burlesque. It *is* funny, isn't it?"

"Very funny," assented Austin Ambrose; "but you are a little wrong in your guess. It is not Miss Graham."

"Not Miss Graham! Who then?"

Austin Ambrose did not hesitate a moment. He had well calculated his plans, and he knew that if he meant to tell anything to the sharp Miss Lottie he must tell all. Half confidences could be of no use.

"Look here, Lottie," he said, "I am going to confide in you because I know that you are unlike most women, inasmuch as you can, if you like, hold your tongue."

"Thanks," she said, watching him closely; "that's a compliment for me. I really think you do mean business, you are so very polite."

"I told you I wanted you to help me, and you can't help me unless you know all I know. Blair is not going to marry Miss Graham, but a young woman whom I have not seen, whom I never heard of—nor any one else. She is, I believe, a kind of servant— —"

Lottie sat up, open-eyed.

"What!" she exclaimed and the color came into her face again. If Lord Blair had been going to marry Miss Graham, she would have regarded it as a matter of course, but that he should be going to throw himself away upon a "kind of servant" was more than she could bear with equanimity.

"It is true," said Austin Ambrose.

"Blair—*Blair*, of all people!—going to make such a fool of himself as that! Why, he must be out of his mind!"

Austin Ambrose shrugged his shoulders.

"I think he is," he said, coolly. "I never saw him so mad. He simply raves about her like a schoolboy. She's everything that is beautiful and angelic. Oh! he is most completely gone, my dear Lottie."

Lottie bit her lip.

"The nicest and handsomest fellow in London," she murmured. "To be picked up by a—a slavey! What a beastly shame it is! What a fool he must be! What's her name?"

"Margaret Hale," said Austin Ambrose, instantly. "You understand, Lottie, that I am telling you what I would tell to no one else."

She nodded.

"And it's about this you came to see me?" she said.

"Yes," he said; "I want you to help me save Blair from this folly. Of course it would ruin him. He would never be able to hold up his head again."

"He'd get tired of her in a week. I know him so well," she said, in a low voice.

"Exactly. In less than a week, perhaps, and then——" he shrugged his shoulders.

"And she would be the Viscountess Leyton, and, of course, the Countess Ferrers when the old man died?" for Lottie knew her peerage pretty well.

"Yes, and we must prevent that," he said, looking at her.

She made an impatient gesture.

"I don't care about the title, and all that," she said; "why should I? If he had been going to marry Miss Graham, or any other of the swells, why—why it would be all right, and I shouldn't complain; but a servant! Blair, too! Why, he's as proud as Lucifer, really, though people wouldn't think it! He'd be wretched for life! He'd be fit to cut his throat a week afterward, and he's too good for that sort of thing."

There was a pause. She drank some of the stout, for her lips felt dry, then she said, more to herself than him:

"Yes, he's far too good! Poor Blair! Why, the very first diamonds I ever had he gave me. He'd have given me the top brick off the chimney if I'd asked for it! You won't believe it, because you don't believe anything, Mr.

Ambrose, but I tell you I'd do anything for Lord Blair! I never told you when I first met him?"

"No," said Austin Ambrose.

Lottie took another draught of the stout, and her color came and went.

"It was when I was singing at the South Audley Music Hall. I wasn't much of a singer, then, and one night I sang worse than usual; I was ill too, and out of sorts, and the people—they aren't the most refined at the South Audley, you know—they cut up rough, and began to hiss and shout. I was only a slip of a girl, and I got frightened—too frightened to run off, and one brute of a fellow took up a wineglass from one of the tables, and flung it at me. I suppose I must have fainted, for the next thing I remember was finding myself in a young gentleman's arms. It was Lord Blair. He'd sprung on the stage, and caught me, and I shall never forget, till the day of my death, the look on his face as he looked down at them. 'I'll give a sovereign to anyone who'll keep that fellow in the hall till I come back!' he said, and though he didn't shout it, you could hear his voice all over the hall. Then he carried me into the greenroom, and got me some wine, and put me into a cab, as if I was a lady! Just as if I was a lady, mind! Then he went back to the hall, and it was a bad time for that brute with the glass, I expect."

She paused a minute and caught her lip between her teeth.

"We didn't meet again for three or four years, and he didn't know me. I was a woman, then, and he had grown into a man. I dare say he'd forgotten all about the girl he protected at the South Audley, and I didn't remind him. But I haven't forgotten it. No!" and she made an impatient dash at her eyes, as if ashamed of the moisture which had made them suddenly dim.

Austin Ambrose listened and watched.

"That's like Blair," he said. "He's a good fellow."

"A good fellow!" she exclaimed, almost fiercely; "that's what you say of any man who is free with his money and can make himself pleasant. Blair is more than that; he's—he's—" she paused for want of a word, then wound up emphatically, "he's a gentleman!"

"Too good a gentleman to be wasted on Miss Margaret Hale!" said Austin Ambrose, insidiously.

"Yes!" she assented, as fiercely as before. "What is to be done? I suppose you have got some plan? You generally have your wits about you." She paused a moment. "But why are you so keen about this business?" she inquired, suspiciously.

"Simply out of pure good nature," he said. "Don't look so incredulous, my dear Lottie. Permit me to possess some good nature as well as yourself.

Blair and I are old and fast friends. I don't think I ever told you, but one confidence deserves another, and I will tell you now. Blair once saved my life. If it had not been for him I should have been lying at the bottom of the Thames."

Lottie nodded.

"They say it's the worst thing you can do for yourself is to save another person's life. I don't say he saved mine, but he did me a good turn, and—and—well, I expect now he wishes he had never seen me, and I dare say he'd have been all the better off if he hadn't. And as for you—well, Mr. Ambrose, I don't see why you shouldn't want to do him a good turn."

"I do," he said. "And I couldn't do him a better than by preventing this marriage. And now, Lottie, I will tell you plainly that this marriage can be prevented if you will lend me a hand."

"How?" she said.

"Lottie, you are a good actress," he said, slowly; "I always said so, and I always thought so. I want you to prove it. I have a little plot, as you surmised, and I want you to play a part in it. It's a difficult one, but you can play it if you like. And, Lottie, if you *do* play it well, why, I'll see what I can do in getting you an engagement at the Coronet."

Lottie's face flushed. An engagement at the Coronet was one of the dramatic prizes.

"You will? But you needn't take the trouble to bribe me. I don't want anything for helping Blair out of this mess," she said; "I'll do it for—for auld lang syne!"

"That's right, Lottie," he said; "but you shall get your engagement at the Coronet all the same. And now I'll tell you what I mean to do."

He leant forward and began to speak in a low, impressive voice, and Lottie Belvoir listened, her eyes fixed on his face. Suddenly she started, and turned pale.

"I say! Isn't that rather—rather strong?" she said.

"Rather strong?" he murmured, blandly.

"Rather risky?" she responded. "I—I don't much like it. Seems to me that it's a part which might land me—well, I don't know where."

"My dear Lottie, there is no risk, or very little," he said, with a cool laugh. "What can happen to you?"

"I don't know; a good many things if I were to be found out," she retorted. "Especially if Blair found it out!" and her face grew paler. "You don't know what Blair is when his temper is up. I've seen him, and probably you haven't."

"But there will be no need to get in his way," said Austin Ambrose. "Directly the thing is done, and your part is played, you can get away for awhile, go to Paris, or where you like. I'll find the money. You may look upon yourself as engaged to me for a term, just as if I were manager of a theater."

Still she hesitated, biting her lip softly and looking at him with evident apprehension.

"I don't like it," she said in a low voice. "It—it seems like playing it very low down on her—and him, too! And if it failed! Good Lord, Mr. Ambrose!"

"It will not fail," he said calmly and confidently. "I will take care that it shall not fail. I'm responsible for this little plot, and from mere pride in it I shall see that it comes off all right. Where is the difficulty? You have hardly a dozen lines to speak and a few others to make up, as the occasion may demand, and your woman's wit, Lottie, will supply you with those."

"Oh, that is easy enough," she said, with a wave of her hand. "I could play the part well enough! I see myself at it now!" and her face took color and her eyes began to glow. "It is a part I could do to perfection. And shouldn't be at a loss for gagging if it were needed, but——"

"But what?" he said, softly.

"But I don't fancy it all the same. It's risky and dangerous and——" she stopped for a moment and looked at his cool, set face keenly. "Mr. Ambrose, I suppose if I got found out, they could send me to prison?"

His face did not alter in the slightest.

"Nonsense!" he said. "Prison! What an absurd notion! Besides, who could find you out? I'm surprised, Lottie, you should hesitate. I thought you were a girl of spirit!"

"I've spirit enough," she said, grimly. "I've spirit enough for most things. For instance, if a man were to throw a glass at me now, I shouldn't faint, but I should throw it back at him. But this—well, this is quite a different thing."

"It is all in your line," he argued.

She remained silent, and he leaned back and shrugged his shoulders.

"Well, I suppose poor Blair will have to drift to the dogs, then? I am surprised; I must say I am surprised, Lottie. I did think that you were as good and stanch a friend of his as I am, and I thought I'd only to tell you the plight in which he stood, and show you how to help one to save him.

I thought you'd jump at it. But never mind. I don't want to persuade you against your will; but I tell you plainly that if you won't help me, I shall go to no one else—I shall let things slide. I'm sorry for Blair; I am, indeed, very sorry, but——" he reached for his hat.

"Wait," she said, and her voice sounded dry and troubled, "give me a minute."

He leant back and watched her from under his lowered lids, while she leant her head on her hands, her intelligent face all puckered with thought.

Then she looked up suddenly.

"I'll do it," she said, with sharp decision.

Austin Ambrose's eyes flashed, then he smiled coolly.

"Of course you will. I can't think why you should hesitate. Why, my dear Lottie, no woman of spirit could sit down idly and see an old flame picked up by a mere nobody of a girl, a kind of servant——"

"That will do," she broke in, his words affecting her as he intended. "I've said I'll do it, and I will, let the consequences be what they may. But mind, you have promised to stand by me?"

"Certainly I will," he said, promptly, "and you shall have the engagement at the Coronet, as well as the satisfaction of feeling that you have saved Blair from ruining his life, and an old title from disgrace."

"Hang the title!" she exclaimed, carelessly, "it's Blair I'm thinking of. And—and when will you want me?"

"I can't tell you now," he said. "I may want you at any moment, so that you must hold yourself in readiness. I suppose you will dress the part carefully?"

She looked up and smiled.

"You can trust me to do that," she said. "Wait! Take another cigar; there's some more whisky there. I won't keep you ten minutes," and she got up and ran from the room.

She was scarcely gone more than ten minutes when there came a knock at the door.

"Come in," he said, and a fair-haired lady, dressed in black, with a pale face and dark hollows under her eyes, with quivering lips and shaking hands, nervously and timidly entered the room.

Austin Ambrose rose with some surprise and embarrassment.

"Do you wish to see Miss Belvoir?" he said quietly.

The lady threw up her hands to her face and broke into passionate sobs; then suddenly they changed to peals of laughter, and, whipping off her bonnet and wig, Lottie herself stood before him.

"Will that do?" she demanded.

Austin Ambrose nodded emphatic approval.

"Excellent! You nearly took me in, my dear Lottie, and I was prepared for you. Capital!"

"Oh, I can do better than that!" she said, half contemptuously, as she wiped the paint and powder from her face with her handkerchief. "But it isn't the make-up I shall rely on so much as the acting. I flatter myself that I can play the part to a nicety. It mustn't be overdone, you know; and it mustn't be taken too slowly. Oh, I know! You leave it to me, Mr. Ambrose!"

"That's just what I meant to do!" he said. "I place every confidence in you, my dear Lottie!"

"And you'll come and see me in prison on visiting days?" she said, with a smile that was rather serious.

"Yes," he said, laughing lightly, "I'll come and see you, and bring you a tract. But all that is nonsense! There is not the slightest risk of such a thing. Once you have played your part, you shall be off to Paris and take your fling for a month or two."

"All this will cost you something," she said, thoughtfully.

He shrugged his shoulders.

"It isn't a question of pounds, shillings and pence on such an occasion as this," he said; "and as to money, I dare say Blair will be only too glad to pay all the expenses when he comes to his senses, and finds who it is that has saved him from committing social suicide. He will owe us a deep debt of gratitude, Lottie."

"I hope he'll think so," she said, rather doubtfully, and with a little shudder; "if he shouldn't—well, I don't think Paris will be far enough off for me, and as for you" —and she smiled strangely and significantly—"well, I wouldn't care to insure your life, Mr. Austin Ambrose."

He laughed as he shook hands with her.

"My dear Lottie, Blair will know that we have been his best friends, and will be grateful accordingly. Good-night. Mind, not a word to a soul!"

"No," said Lottie, grimly; "I'm not likely to proclaim this business from the housetops. This is a play that it will be best *not* to advertise. Good-night!"

CHAPTER XII

Margaret had read those lines of Swinburne's:

"Nothing is better, I well think,
Than love; the hidden well-water
Is not so delicate to drink.

"Nothing so bitter, I well know,
Than love; no amber in cold sea,
Or gathered berries under snow,"

and she remembered them; they came floating up through her memory during the still hours of the night following Lord Blair's passionate avowal.

It had taken her so completely by surprise that even yet she had scarcely realized what this was that had happened to her.

She had read of love, had painted it, but hitherto she and it had been perfect strangers; and now—and now all wonderful mysterious sweetness of it suffused her whole being. "He loves me! he loves me!" she found herself repeating over and over again in a species of half-unconscious rapture; and as she murmured the significant words she hid her face in her hands, and the words he had spoken came surging back on her ears and in her heart, and she could still feel his hot, passionate kisses on her hands and hair.

All the next day she lived like one in a dream.

She never asked herself whether she had acted wisely or even rightly in listening to him, or promising to meet him again. Wisdom and propriety were swamped and overwhelmed by the full tide of love which had taken possession of her.

Once there flashed upon her the thought that she ought to tell her grandmother, but the same instant she felt that it would be impossible. It would be like sacrilege to utter a word of this new mystery which she had discovered. Besides, she had not yet given him his answer. It would be time enough to tell Mrs. Hale after then.

In the evening she wandered slowly to the glade, and rested on the spot where she had sat the day before; and there she re-enacted the whole scene so vividly that she could almost believe that he was really present, kneeling at her side, and holding her hand.

With a sigh, she leaned her head on her hand, and tried to think it out, but she could not think. A great joy, like a great pain, makes thought impossible.

The day passed, she scarcely knew how, and the night. She slept some hours, but her sleep was full of dreams, in which Lord Leyton was the predominant figure; the handsome face may be said to have hovered about her pillow; and when she awoke, flushed and quivering, it was to have the sense of her great joy sweeping over her anew like an overwhelming flood.

"Margaret, my dear, you look pale," said Mrs. Hale, at breakfast. "It's the heat. I wouldn't go painting in the gallery to-day. It's hot there, and the colors must give you a headache, I should think. If I were you, I'd go and sit in the woods; there is some shade there, and it's cool, especially near the cascade."

Margaret colored furiously. It almost seemed as if Mrs. Hale had got an inkling of her appointment with Lord Blair.

"I will go to the woods, grandma," she said; and she put her arm round the old lady's neck, and laid her soft cheek against the withered one.

"Yes, my dear," said Mrs. Hale, "you can go there quite safely, for the earl never walks there even when he does go out, and Lord Leyton's gone. But you won't disturb the birds, Margaret, will you? Mr. Simpson, the head keeper, is so particular."

"No, I will do no harm, grandma," Margaret said, and she got her hat and went to the woods.

It was a lovely morning; the birds were singing in full note; the butterflies were flitting from wild flower to wild flower; the miniature cascade made a delicious music. But it and the birds seemed to sing the same song for Margaret. "I love you! I love you!"

Surely, if she lived to be a hundred, whatever happened in her life, she should never forget this spot sacred to her in the first passion that had ever stirred her maiden heart. Always before her eyes in the future would rise this glade at Leyton woods; always would she hear the ceaseless babble of the brook, the song of the linnets!

She had not long to wait. There came a quick, firm step—she knew it so well, although it had come into her life so recently—and with a spring like a boy's, Lord Blair was beside her; not only beside her, but on one knee.

For a moment he seemed unable to speak, and the color came and went on his tanned cheek.

"Do you know," he said with a smile, and in that hushed, lingering voice which love takes to itself, "all the way I have been tormenting myself with the dread that you wouldn't come!"

"I said that I would come!" she said, with downcast eyes.

"I know! And I ought to have known that you would rather die than break your word. But I thought that perhaps you would be prevented, that you might have told some one—Mrs. Hale——"

"I have told no one," said Margaret, with a sudden feeling of gratitude.

"That is right," he said; then, as the shadow swept over her face, he went on quickly—"Not that I should have cared for myself. No! I would like all the world to know how I love you; not that they could possibly know that. Not even you can guess at that, Margaret. But I should like to tell everybody that I love you, and that——But, ah, Margaret, you haven't told me yet! Are you going to let me stay? Are you going to let me go on loving you? Dearest, you have not come to be hard and cruel to me! You will say 'yes?'" and he held out his arms to her.

Margaret sat silent for a moment, then she raised her eyes; they seemed heavy with love's mysterious shyness, and she breathed the word that gave her to him.

His arms closed round her, and he held her to him with one passionate kiss until, half frightened, she drew away from him.

There was silence between them then, and they sat hand in hand in that communion of spirit which is only permitted to us poor mortals once in a life. To him she was the embodiment of all that was beautiful and good! To her he was the epitome of all that was handsome and brave; and he was to be good also now, for had he not said that her love should be his salvation?

After a time they began to talk, as newly-made lovers do talk. Short little sentences, full of delicious meaning; small nothings, which represented the sum of all things to them.

Then Blair said, suddenly:

"Dearest, you said you had told no one: Mrs. Hale, or any one, about our meeting?"

"No," she assented.

"That was right, Margaret," he said. "I don't want you to tell any one."

She looked at him trustingly, but with a vague surprise.

"Do you mind, dear?" he asked. "If so, if you would rather this were told, we will go together, you and I, and then we will go to the earl——"

"No, no," said Margaret, shrinking from such an ordeal, and longing—girl-like—to keep her delicious secret to herself for a little longer.

"It shall be as you wish, dearest," he said, frankly; "but there are reasons why it would be better for us to say nothing about our engagement. Look here, Margaret," he went on, earnestly, "I spoke the truth just now, when I said that I would like to proclaim my happiness to all the world, but I'm afraid it wouldn't be a good thing to do. It would be better not to do so, for your sake."

"For mine?" she said, looking into his dark eyes with a tender questioning.

"Yes. I don't want you to lose anything by your goodness to me, dear; that's natural enough, isn't it? And I am afraid you would lose a great deal if we declared our engagement."

"What should I lose?" she asked.

"You know, dear," he answered, "that I am the heir to my uncle's title and estates."

"I know," said Margaret.

She would not wound him by reminding him that she was the granddaughter of the earl's housekeeper, and penniless.

"Well, that's very good; and I wish I were the King of England, that I could make you the queen, Madge," he said, with a smile. "But in addition to the title and estates, mine uncle has a great deal of money, and if he likes he can leave that to us, or to anybody else."

"To us?" said Margaret. "To you."

"I and you are one, dear," he said, simply. "Now, so far as I am concerned, I don't care a fig for the money; but I don't think I ought to rob you of it."

"And I care less than a fig!" she said, smiling.

His face cleared from the faint shadow which had dwelt upon it while he had been speaking.

"You don't! Madge, you don't know how glad you make me! I might have known that you would not care about it! Let it go! I would rather let a million slip than there should be any concealment! We'll go and tell him at once—or I'll go, and fetch you afterward. I knew you'd say so, even while Austin was advising me!"

"Austin? Who is Austin?" she asked.

"What an idiot I am!" he exclaimed, with a laugh. "I am talking as if you knew everybody I know, and everything I know! You see, it seems as if I had known you for years, and that we had been one since we were boy and girl!"

She laid her hand timidly on his head, and lovingly smoothed the black, clustered hair.

"Austin is Austin Ambrose," he went on; "the best fellow in the world. He is the greatest friend I have, Madge, and I want you to like him awfully."

"I like him already if he is a friend of yours—Blair," she said.

His face flushed as she let his name fall from her lips for the first time.

"He is a great, a true friend," he said. "I was lucky enough to be on the spot when he got the cramp, bathing, and I lugged him out, and the foolish fellow can't forget it."

"How very foolish," said Margaret. "You saved his life, Blair?"

"So he says; but he makes the most of it. Anyway, we have been fast friends ever since, and—you won't mind, Madge?—I told him how I had met and fallen in love with you. I was bound to tell some one or go mad, and I have always told him everything."

"I do not mind—why should I?" said Margaret, smiling. "And I had no one to tell."

"Poor Margaret!" he murmured, smiling up at her tenderly.

"And what did Mr. Austin Ambrose say? What a pretty name it is—almost as pretty as Blair Leyton."

"Well, he was awfully pleased, of course," said Blair. "Anything that pleases me pleases him."

"I shall be a little jealous," murmured Margaret.

He laughed.

"You needn't be. Not even Austin could come between you and me, dearest," he said. "He was awfully pleased, and—and all that, but he thought of this property. He is one of those cute, long-headed fellows, you know, darling, who are always looking to the future, and it was he who wanted us to keep it secret."

"He knows that I am so unfit, so unworthy," said Margaret, in a low voice, and with a sudden pang.

Blair's face flushed, and he looked up at her reproachfully.

"Don't ever say that, Madge," he pleaded; "it hurts me."

"Forgive me, Blair," she whispered. "But he did think so, did he not?"

"I don't care what he thought," he said, firmly. "And whatever he thought, he will have only one idea when he sees you, and that is that you are a thousand, a million times too good for me."

"Poor Blair," she murmured.

"And, Margaret, I want you to see him very soon. I want you to feel that he is your friend as well as mine." He paused for a moment, then went on—"Madge, he is down at Leyton now."

"At Leyton now—here?" said Margaret with momentary surprise.

Blair nodded.

"Yes. He was so anxious to see you, that I asked him to come down with me. Shall I tell you why I did so?"

"Yes," said Margaret. A strange feeling, scarcely of dread—how could it be?—had crept over her. "Tell me everything."

"Everything!" he repeated emphatically. "From this moment I will not have a thought you shall not share, dearest. Well, then, I didn't know what your answer would be, Madge, and I felt so afraid of myself; I know what a stupid idiot I am when I want to say anything and can't, that I brought him to plead for me if it should be necessary."

"It was not necessary," she murmured, and he kissed her hand.

"He held out at first, and wouldn't hear of coming, but I persuaded him at last; poor old Austin can't refuse me anything, and so he came with me. He is waiting at the stile, in case you will condescend to see him."

Margaret shrank a little. She could not guess that though Lord Blair fully believed that it was he who had persuaded Austin Ambrose to come against his will, it had really been Austin's own suggestion artfully made.

"I will do as you wish, Blair," she said. "Yes," she added quickly, "I will see him."

After all, she could not even seem to be cold to her lover's closest friend!

Blair sprung to his feet.

"He will be so glad, Margaret!" he said. "He is the best fellow in the world, and the wisest; and he is dreadfully afraid that you may not like him."

"Bring him, and I will put him out of his misery," said Margaret with her divine smile. "Do you think that I should not love all you love, and hate all you hate, Blair?"

"You are an angel!" he said, looking at her; "yes, that is what you are!"

She put her hands against his breast and pushed him gently away from her.

"Go and fetch him," she said, and he strode away.

Austin Ambrose was seated on the stile, smoking a cigarette. He greeted Blair with a nod and a smile.

"Well, my Adonis! Well, my Corydon! Have you come to tell me that the beloved mistress declines to see the intruder?"

"Ah, you don't know her yet, old fellow!" said Lord Blair, with all a lover's pride. "She has sent me to bring you to her at once! My friends shall be her friends, and you, Austin, shall rank first."

Austin Ambrose flung his cigarette away and smiled.

"Then she has made you a happy man, Blair? All doubts dispelled, eh?"

"She has made me the happiest man in all the world," said Blair, almost solemnly.

"At any rate, she is good-natured," said Ambrose. "Most women would have sent me to the right-about— —"

"Not Margaret! not Margaret!" broke in Blair. "Wait till you see her and hear her talk, old fellow!"

"Well, I sha'n't have to wait long," he said, as he caught sight of Margaret's dress.

The next moment he stood before her.

Mr. Austin Ambrose was a man who had raised the art of concealing his emotions and his thoughts to a positive science; therefore he neither started nor uttered an exclamation as his eye fell upon Margaret Hale; but a swift and sharp surprise and astonishment went through him like the stab of a dagger.

She had risen at the sound of their footsteps, and stood upright before him in all her beauty, and with all her infinite grace; and instead of the pretty, hoidenish, middle-class young woman he had pictured, Austin

Ambrose found himself confronted by a girl who was not only lovely, but refined, and, in short—a lady!

And Margaret? For a moment she was conscious of a feeling of repulsion, of dread, and almost of dislike, but she fought it down, and instead of responding to his respectful and almost reverential inclination with a formal bow, she held out her hand.

"This is very good, very gracious of you, Miss Hale! To accept the acquaintance of a stranger so suddenly——"

"No friend of Lord Blair's must be a stranger to me," she said, with a blush.

Blair took her hand and kissed it, and he looked at Austin Ambrose triumphantly.

"Thank you, thank you," murmured Austin, as if deeply touched. Then after a pause, with a look of respectful admiration, "Miss Hale, I can understand Blair's fascination, he should indeed be the happiest man in England this June morning!"

Margaret blushed still more vividly, and Blair colored, too, but with pleasure.

"I forgot to tell you, Madge," he said, "that Austin is a perfect dab at fine speeches."

"And a martyr to truth," said Austin Ambrose. "And are you sure that you can quite forgive me for intruding this morning?"

"There is nothing to forgive, I am very glad," Margaret said, simply.

Blair drew her gently to her old seat, and then threw himself at her feet. Austin Ambrose seated himself on the bank a little above and in front of them.

"Lord Blair and I are such old friends, Miss Hale," he said, "that I suppose neither of us would think of doing anything important without consulting each other. Not that Blair has consulted me," he added, quickly. "He had made up his mind before he spoke to me, and would not have dreamed of consulting Solomon himself if he had been alive. And I think he was right!"

"Two very outspoken compliments," said Blair laughing with pleasure. "And it's a poor return, old fellow, to tell you that we have made up our minds not to take your advice. I am going to send an announcement of our engagement to the society papers to-night—after I have seen my uncle."

Austin Ambrose nodded and smiled as if he were rather pleased than otherwise.

"That is delightful!" he said, genially. "Lovers should always be imprudent. Yes, I like the idea very much."

Margaret glanced from the clear-cut, self-possessed face to Blair's handsome, careless one, and her eyes grew troubled.

"Is it so imprudent?" she said softly.

"Very, deliciously so!" said Austin, laughing. "And that is why I like it. Lovers should always be unwise and reckless. It is, as Doctor Watts observed, 'their nature to!' Miss Hale, I have one weak spot, amongst many, and you will discover it presently, I dare say. I am foolishly romantic. Anything in the shape of sentiment conquers me directly. I assure you that when Blair came and told me that he had met and lost his heart to the most beautiful young lady in the world, I felt as if I had lost mine, and I was as anxious—well, *nearly* as anxious, as he was to learn whether he was to be the happiest or the most miserable of men."

Blair laughed, Margaret smiled, but she was fighting against the strange repulsion which grew more distinct with every word the supple lips uttered.

"Yes," he went on. "And the idea of your going hand in hand to the earl and saying, 'My lord, we mean to be married. We don't care whether you like it or not, we defy you. You may leave us your immense wealth or you may bequeath it to the Home for Lost Dogs, we don't care. We love each other, and that is enough. My lord, good-morning!' Now, that is delightful! It is imprudent, it is reckless, and—and—well, yes—foolish; but it is so charming, so perfectly romantic, that I can't help admiring it."

Margaret's eyes grew more troubled. Blair smiled no longer.

"I say, Austin!" he expostulated.

Austin Ambrose held up his finger.

"No, no! I won't hear a word said against it. I have a distinct conviction that the whole romance—and what a charming romance it is!—would be completely spoiled by one word of wisdom, and I am very sorry that I ever uttered one! Here, in Miss Hale's presence, I make full recantation, and implore her forgiveness for ever having harbored one sordid thought concerning her. Let the earl's fortune go to the winds!" and he waved his hand dramatically. "With Miss Hale's love, my dear Blair, you will be the richest man in England, although you should be the poorest peer."

"You are right," exclaimed Blair, pressing Margaret's hand. "Those are the truest words you ever spoke, old fellow! Eh, Margaret?" he whispered.

She sat silently looking at Austin Ambrose's face.

Though he had not said so in so many words, he had as good as told her that by marrying Lord Blair she would deprive him of his uncle's fortune.

The color came and went in her face, her eyes grew downcast, while both men looked at her; Blair with loving adoration, Austin Ambrose with a covert and concealed intentness.

At last she looked up—at Blair, not at Austin Ambrose.

"It must not be known," she said in a low voice.

"Margaret!" exclaimed Blair, astonished; but Austin Ambrose, watching her eyes, gave a slight, a very slight, nod of approval.

"No," she said. "Mr. Ambrose is—is right! You shall not make such a sacrifice for me, Blair." Her face flushed, her eyes shone with the fire of a woman's resolution to sacrifice herself rather than injure the man she loves. "We—we will not tell any one!"

Austin Ambrose raised his hat, and looked at her with a fine assumption of admiration.

"That was nobly spoken, Miss Hale," he said gravely, "nobly and wisely. I am too much Blair's friend, and yours, if you will permit me, to conceal my anxiety on your account. You would sacrifice not his future alone, but yours, for it would be yours, you know, by doing anything rash. The earl is an eccentric old gentleman, and easily offended. It would be worse than folly to do so. You have made a wise decision, Miss Hale, and you have added respect to my admiration!" and he bowed.

"Well!" exclaimed Blair, half amused, half annoyed. "You two are beyond me! Why, half an hour ago, Madge, you were aghast at our keeping our engagement secret, and now——"

"Miss Hale had not considered the matter in all its bearings," broke in Austin Ambrose, gently and smoothly. "Trust me, Blair, she has more sense in her little finger than you have in all your great, hulking body."

"I know that," said Blair, with a good-humored laugh. "You've found it out already, have you? Didn't I tell you that she was as clever as she was beautiful? My Margaret!"

"Your Margaret is far too clever to let you say such silly things!" murmured Margaret, blushing.

Austin Ambrose rose and smiled down upon them, and his cold eyes seemed to grow really benevolent, as if he were blessing them.

"I will go now," he said. "Miss Hale, this has been a happy day for me, as well as for Blair. He has found a sweetheart, and I have found, I trust, a friend. May I say that?" he asked, as he held out his hand.

"Yes," said Margaret, trying to speak heartily.

He took her hand and raised it to his lips.

"Then you must let me prove myself one. You are both young, and perfectly imprudent. You must promise to do nothing without coming to me first. This is all I ask. Is it too much?"

"Not a bit, old fellow!" said Blair, promptly, showing his delight at the impression Margaret had made upon the wise and critical Austin Ambrose. "We are a couple of spoons, you know, and not fit to be trusted to act alone, eh?"

"Honestly, I don't think you are," said Austin Ambrose, smilingly.

"All right!" said Blair. "We've taken your advice—at least Margaret has—and the least you can do, having accepted the responsibility, is to see us squarely through, eh?"

Austin Ambrose nodded.

"Yes," he said, simply. "I'll go and see if the dog-cart is ready, and drive it to the end of the lane. You will find me there. You have no idea the precautions we have taken, Miss Margaret," he added, with a smile. "We just drew the line at coming down in disguise! Good-bye!" and with a wave of his hand he pushed through the underwood and left them.

He stopped at a distance of a hundred yards to get a cigarette, and was putting it to his mouth with a smile of cynical satisfaction, as he thought of the way in which he had gained his point, when his quick eyes saw something moving at a little distance between him and the spot where he had left the lovers.

He thought it was a rabbit at first, but looking intently he saw it was a man's fur cap.

"A cap doesn't move without a head in it," he murmured, and putting his cigarette in his pocket, he made a detour round some trees and crept close to the object.

As he did so he saw a man was lying full length in the long bracken, through which he had made a clearing just before his face, so that he could watch Blair and Margaret. Austin Ambrose grew interested, and crept a little nearer.

Poachers do not work in the daytime, and besides, this man had no gun, but a thick stick lay near his hand.

Austin Ambrose watched him thoughtfully, then a look of intelligence flashed into his face. Blair had described the man he had thrashed on Leyton Green; this was he, this was Jem Pyke! Amongst Austin Ambrose's great gifts was a faculty of never forgetting a face or a name.

Lowering himself noiselessly, he sat down just behind the man, and after waiting a minute or two, coughed slightly.

The man looked round with a start, then sprung to his feet and grasped his stick.

Mr. Ambrose looked him squarely in the face.

"Don't speak a word, my friend, or I shall call," he said.

Pyke looked uncertain, and then made ready for a spring; but the cold eyes—and they were like glittering steel now—held him fascinated.

"Not a word," said Austin, in a low, distinct voice, "unless you want another thrashing, Mr. Pyke!"

Jem Pyke started, and he lowered the stick.

For a moment the two men looked into each other's faces, then, with a smile, Austin got up leisurely and sauntered off, beckoning him to follow.

Austin Ambrose led the way until they had gone out of hearing of Blair and Margaret, then he sat down on a fallen tree, and lighting a cigarette, coolly and critically surveyed the captive.

"I'm rather curious to know what you were doing just now, my man," he said, when he had finished his examination.

"I was watching for a rabbit," replied Pyke, promptly but sullenly, and without looking up.

Austin Ambrose smiled.

"Oblige me by looking at me," he said.

Pyke raised his eyes slowly.

"Thanks. Do I look like a fool?" demanded Austin Ambrose, politely.

"No," replied Pyke, reluctantly, and with an oath.

"Thanks again, though your language is unnecessarily emphatic. Then, not being a fool, how do you expect me to believe you? Shall I tell you what you were doing?"

No reply, but Pyke shifted one leg uneasily.

"You were watching my friend, Lord Blair. I am right, I think? Silence denotes assent. Thanks," suavely; "and why were you watching him?"

Pyke, tortured as much by the tone as the question, growled out an imprecation under his breath.

"Shall I tell you? Because you are anxious to get a little revenge for that beating he gave you. Am I right? Thanks again. I am good at guessing, you see. And as you can't pay him back in a fair stand-up fight you are hoping later for an opportunity to give him one in the back. Y—es," slowly and suavely, "I think that is the whole case in a nutshell. Now, my friend, you *are* a fool."

Pyke raised his eyes and scowled evilly, and Austin Ambrose shook his head and smiled.

"No use scowling, my friend. I know what you are feeling, and I can sympathize with you; I can indeed. It is so unpleasant to be caught, isn't it? And it is so tempting to see me sitting here without even a stick, and to know that you could dispose of me so easily, if my friend with the big fists that you felt so lately were not within call."

Pyke's face grew livid, and he grasped his stick till the veins started out like string in his wiry and sunburnt hands.

"Curse you!" he snarled at last. "Who are you, and what do you want?"

"Gently," said his tormentor. "One question at a time, and though you don't put them politely, I'll give you a true answer. My name is Ambrose—Austin Ambrose. Say it over to yourself once or twice, and you won't forget it. And what do I want? Well, I want a strong, active young ruffian like you, a man who has pluck enough to remember an injury and burns to pay it back. And that's your case again, isn't it?"

He lit his cigarette, and blew a ring in the air, and watched it until it had faded away.

"And now I'll explain why you are a fool. You are a fool because you lay in wait with a big stick to bang your enemy about the head. No one but a fool would do that, my dear Pyke; firstly, because he might not hurt his enemy——"

Jem Pyke scowled fearfully.

"Well, yes, you might hurt him, but—and that brings me to my secondly—you couldn't do it without its being traced to you. There might be a struggle, there would be blood and other unpleasant traces, and, all Lombard Street to a china orange, the police would have you by the heels before an hour was passed, and then— —!" The speaker wound up the sentence by a playful gesture indicative of strangulation.

Pyke's face was a study. At first, from hate and the desire to crush his tormentor it displayed the emotion of murder, and then a reluctant admiration; and at last he stood, the stick hanging loosely in his hand, his small, evil eyes fixed with a fascinated stare on his companion's face.

"I am right, you see," said Austin Ambrose. "Now, if I owed a man a grudge—I don't, I am happy to say, for I have not an enemy in the world, my dear Pyke—but if I owed a man a grudge, I shouldn't set to work in your clumsy fashion. No; I shouldn't dog him and knock him about the head just outside my own door, because I should feel assured that the police would track me down. No; I should wait until he had got some distance off—to London, for instance, or another part of the country—and then, some dull evening, I should bring him down with a gun or a pistol from a safe distance, and then quietly"—he blew a cloud of smoke into the air and pointed to it—"vanish!"

The man stood and listened with every sense on the alert, absorbed and rapt.

Then he drew a long breath.

"That's what you'd do, guv'nor, is it?" he said at last, hoarsely.

Austin Ambrose nodded.

"Yes. And if I had a friend who could point out to me my best way of doing it, and help me to choose the time and place, why, I should feel very grateful to that friend."

Pyke looked somewhat mystified for a moment, then he started, and a look of cunning flashed from his eyes.

"Why, you hate him, too, guv'nor!" he exclaimed, hoarsely, with an oath.

Austin Ambrose looked at him and smiled.

"After all, you are *not* such a fool as you looked, my friend," he said.

Pyke stood eying him stealthily and curiously, then he slapped his knee cautiously.

"I've got it!" he said with a leer. "He's after your girl, guv'nor!"

Austin Ambrose smiled again.

"You are really an intelligent person, Mr. Pyke," he said, suavely. "And now that we understand each other—and we do, I think?"

Pyke swore horribly for assent.

"Exactly. Then I think we had better part. Take my advice, and don't— watch for rabbits any more! Go home and rest until your friend sends you word that the time has come to pay back old scores. When he does so, well— be ready, *and strike home!*"

"I will!" Pyke declared, setting his teeth.

Austin Ambrose flung his cigarette away.

"Poaching is a hard trade," he murmured, looking up at the sky, which shone blue as a turquois through the trees. "One should pity the poor fellow who is driven to it, rather than condemn him. There, my poor man, take this small coin and find some honest work. You are strong and able, get some employment. Believe me, honesty is the best policy!" And he held out a sovereign.

Pyke took it, examined it, and put it in his pocket. But he stood still, waiting like a well-trained hound, for further orders.

Suddenly Austin Ambrose raised his hand and pointed to the road.

"Go!" he said sternly.

Pyke started, just as a dog would start, fingered his fur cap, and muttering, "Yes, guv'nor, yes," disappeared.

Austin Ambrose remained seated for some minutes, his brows knitted, his eyes fixed on the ground, then he murmured:

"Yes, I shall win this! Everything goes with me! Everything! It is a bold game, but I shall win it! A man gets all the trump cards dealt him, or breaks the bank at faro, once in a lifetime; it is his one chance! This is mine! Even this country clown makes one. Yes, I shall win, and then, Violet! and then— —"

He walked quickly through the wood. The dog cart he and Blair had engaged was waiting, and he dismissed the boy who was holding the horse. They had driven from Harefield, the nearest large town, to which they had come by rail, and were going to drive back and take the return train there.

As he had said, they had taken every precaution to keep their visit a secret.

After he had been waiting five or ten minutes, Blair came striding toward him. He was rather pale and very quiet, and signed to Austin to drive.

"I should drive you into a ditch," he said; "my hands are all shaky! Austin, she is an angel!" and his voice was shaky, whatever his hands may have been.

"Meaning Miss Margaret? She is better than an angel! She is a lovely and a charming lady," said Austin Ambrose.

"Isn't she?" exclaimed Lord Blair. "Austin, I did not exaggerate?"

"No; you did not even do her justice! I never saw a more beautiful and bewitching young creature! I don't wonder at your infatuation."

"Infatuation! I don't like the word. Infatuation is not love, and I love her more than ever a man loved yet, I think."

"And you are right," said Austin Ambrose, emphatically. "Blair, my boy, you are in luck. I'm not given to raving about women, but, upon my word, I could do a little raving about Miss Margaret!"

"Rave away, then!" said Blair, bluntly. "You won't bore me. Ah, Austin! if you knew how I hate all this secrecy and deception! I tell you I hate it! Why should not I declare my love for her to all the world? I tried to persuade her to let me go to the earl after you had left us, but she wouldn't let me."

"You are a fool!" burst from Austin Ambrose's lips; then, as Blair looked at him with astonishment, he added quickly, "I beg your pardon, Blair; but it does make me mad to see you so bent upon destroying that sweet girl's future in the way that you propose to do. Why, man, what harm does it do her or you keeping it quiet for awhile? The earl is an old man, any year—a month, a day—he may die, and then—why, then you may tell all the world, when you have got his money safe at your banker's for you and your wife and children! Miss Margaret is more sensible than you."

"Yes, after she had heard you," said Blair, slowly. "Well, I suppose it's the best thing to do, but I hate it, all the same. Though, after all, I don't care; it's enough for me to know she loves me."

There was silence for a moment, then Austin Ambrose said smoothly:

"If I were you, Blair, I should secure that beautiful creature as soon as possible."

"What do you mean?" demanded Blair, awaking from a reverie.

"I should marry her."

The hot blood mounted to Lord Blair's face, then left it pale.

"If she would," he murmured, in a low voice.

"Oh, yes, she would," said Austin Ambrose, in a quiet tone of confidence. "I think I could help you to that, Blair. Honestly, I think her such a treasure that, if I were in your place, I should never rest easy for a day until she were mine! A prince might long to make her his consort! To tell you the truth, I am as bewitched as you are. I had expected to see—well, I won't tell you what, but I will tell you what I did see, a lovely girl, who was not only lovely, but a refined and gifted lady. Marry her, Blair, and at once!"

"I'd marry her to-morrow if she'd let me," said Blair hotly; then he relapsed into silence, and Austin Ambrose was content to let the seed he had dropped take root.

"Will you come to the club and dine with me?" he said, when they walked home. Lord Blair shook his head.

"No, thanks, old fellow," he said. "I want to be alone. Don't think me a bear."

"No, no, I understand," said Austin Ambrose, as he shook hands; "go and dream of Margaret, and remember what I say, my dear fellow. A prize like that is never too quickly secured."

Blair wandered to his rooms, to pace up and down his sitting-room, and think over every word Margaret had said. Austin Ambrose went to his chambers, and having dressed carefully and leisurely, dined luxuriously at his club, and at half-past ten called a cab and had himself driven to Lady Marabout's, who had an "evening" that night. Lady Marabout's rooms were filled to overflowing when he entered, and he had to make his way through a crush that extended as far as the hall and stairs; but in his cool and leisurely fashion he reached the principal saloon at last, and having shaken hands with the hostess, who greeted him with a brave though tired smile, he bent his steps toward a small crowd that surrounded some favored person at the end of the room.

The favored person was Violet Graham, the heiress. The dragoon, Colonel Floyd, the Marquis of Aldmere, and other well-known men were round her—one holding her fan, another proffering her an ice, and a third looking over her ball *carte* in the hope of finding a vacant space; and she leant back on the settee smiling absently, and listening, "with half an ear," to their compliments and flattery.

Austin Ambrose made his way to her slowly, his opera hat under his arm, his clean-cut face serene and perfectly self-possessed.

"Is the dancing all over, or just begun?" he said, as he inclined his head before her. "I am too late for anything, I suppose?"

Nothing could have been cooler or more matter-of-fact than his words, or the tone in which they were uttered; but she looked up with a sudden flush.

"I don't dance the next; it is a square dance," she said. "Take me to some cool place—if there is a cool place, Mr. Ambrose!"

He held out his arm, and to the mortification of her circle of courtiers, he led her away.

"Confound that fellow Ambrose!" muttered Colonel Floyd. "Why couldn't she ask me to take her into the conservatory?"

"Or me?" muttered two or three others, as they sauntered away ill-temperedly.

Austin Ambrose led her into the conservatory and placed her in a seat, then he broke off a palm-leaf and fanned her patiently, as if it were his sole mission on earth.

"Well?" she said, and it was the first word she had addressed to him since her greeting.

He smiled, a confident smile.

"Meaning our friend Blair?"

"Yes, yes," she said, impatiently. "Where is he? What is he doing? He was invited to-night. I came expecting him to be here."

He smiled again.

"Don't be impatient. At present our friend Blair shuns the revel and the dance——"

She flashed her eyes upon him angrily.

"You have seen him?"

"Yes," he said. "I have seen him. He is still infatuated over his dairymaid. But don't be alarmed. I have nipped that little affair in the bud, I think."

"You have?" she exclaimed, with a quick glance.

"Quite," he said, easily. "Before a week is passed you will find him at your feet again."

"Can I trust you?" she murmured.

He shrugged his shoulders.

"As much as one can trust another seeing that, according to the latest novelist, we are all Judases. But you can trust me. This affair of Blair's will end in smoke, believe me."

Violet Graham drew a long breath.

"Remember!" she panted. "Put a stop to this—this madness of his, and I will give you anything you can ask!"

"I shall not forget," he said. "Let me take you back now."

CHAPTER XIII

Margaret was living in an earthly paradise. Existence, indeed, was more like a beautiful dream to her than the gray and sober reality it is to most of us.

To be loved is a nice thing, a grand thing, a fact which gilds even the most prosaic life and makes it bright; but to be loved by such a man as Lord Blair—so handsome, so brave, so devoted, and so passionately and entirely hers! It passed all saying, as the Italians put it; and Margaret's days were full of sweetness and joy; for if he did not see her every day, he managed to come down three or four times a week, and they met in stolen interviews at the cascade, or in the deeper recesses of the woods.

And Blair—Blair, who had gained for himself the reputation of the most fickle young man in London—seemed more deeply in love every time they parted.

If Margaret had been the scheming girl, aiming at the Ferrers' coronet, which Austin Ambrose at first imagined her, she could not have gone more cleverly to work to secure Lord Blair Leyton.

Once or twice he had brought her down some presents, a ring at first, a bracelet the next time, but Margaret would not accept them.

"I will take nothing I cannot wear, Blair," she said. "Pick this bunch of honeysuckle for me, and I will put it in my hair; I like that better than all your jewels."

But the third time he brought her a locket. Its face was a mass of pearls, with one large and costly diamond sparkling in the center.

"You can wear this, dearest," he said pleadingly.

"Yes, I can wear that," she said in the soft, melting voice, which used to echo in his ears long after he had left her and was up in town. "I can wear that," and she tied it by her ribbon round her neck and hid it away in her bosom. "No one can see that, and I can take it out——"

"Off?" he said.

"No, sir," she corrected him, blushing; "I shall not take it off again, but I shall take it out whenever I am likely to forget you."

"Don't say that, even in fun, Madge," he said in a low voice, and with a sudden look of pain. "I can't bear to think of you forgetting me. Why, if I were dead, and you were walking near my grave— —" he stopped; and she murmured the well-known song:

"Were it ever so airy a tread,
My heart would hear her and beat,
Were it earth in an earthy bed;
My dust would hear her and beat,
Had I lain for a century dead;
Would start and tremble under her feet,
And blossom in purple and red."

"That's it!" he said, approvingly and admiringly. "What a memory you have got, Madge. Is it Shakespeare?"

"No; Tennyson," and she smiled. "What an ignorant boy it is!"

"Ain't I?" he said, with a laugh. "Austin often says that the things I know would go into half a sheet of note-paper, and the things I don't would more than fill the reading-room at the British Museum. But one thing I know, Madge, and that is that I love you with all my heart and soul."

"I'll forgive you all the rest!" she murmured.

She was painting the picture the earl had commissioned, and she took up her brush and palette and worked, while Blair sat at her side, watching her with an admiring wonder, as the skillful hand conveyed the little bushy dell to the canvas.

"What a fuss they'll make about you when we are married," he said, after a pause.

Margaret bent forward to hide the blush which the words had called up.

"Who are they? And why should they make a fuss?" she asked.

"They? Oh, all the people, you know. They'll make no end of you, Madge. You see, you are so good-looking— —"

She threatened him with her wet brush.

—"And then you are so clever, and this painting of yours will just finish them off. I shouldn't wonder if you are the leading item in the next season."

"The next season!" echoed Margaret, turning her eyes upon him.

He colored and looked rather guilty; then he raised his eyes to hers boldly.

"Yes, next season. You are going to marry me soon, you know, Madge!"

"Soon?" she repeated dreamily. "Two years, five years hence will be soon."

"Oh, will it?" he remarked, aghast. "Why, Madge, Austin says we ought to be married next month."

Margaret almost dropped her pencil, and stared at him; then her eyelids fell, and the warm color spread over her face and neck.

"And yet you are always boasting that Austin Ambrose never talks nonsense!" she said, with gentle irony.

"But is it such nonsense, dear?" he urged, putting his arm around her waist, and looking up at her downcast face. "I don't think it is nonsense at all! If you knew how long even a few weeks seem to me—but I don't put it that way. But, remember, my darling, that this is all very well down here; I can run down and spend some hours with you—how short they seem, heigh ho!—but you will be going to London directly— —"

"Directly I have finished this picture—next week," she put in gently.

"So soon?" he said, sadly. "Well then we sha'n't be able to see so much of each other; at least, Austin says we mustn't."

"Mr. Austin says so?"

He nodded.

"Yes; he is more anxious than ever that our engagement should be kept secret, and every time he sees me he talks and lectures me about it. 'He's such a careful man,' as the song says," and he laughed.

Margaret remained silent. What would the days be like in hot and dusty London if she were not to see Blair, not to hear the voice she loved murmuring its passionate devotion in her ears! Her bosom rose with a soft sigh.

"I suppose he is right—yes, he *is* right," she said. "And we shall meet, if we do meet, as strangers, Blair? But we sha'n't meet, shall we?"

"You are talking nonsense now," he chided her. "Of course we shall. I can take you up the river, up to Cookham and Pangbourne. How delightful it will be!"

"And some of your grand friends will see us, and then— —"

"Oh, we'll chance that!" he said, lightly.

"We must chance nothing that may do you an injury, Blair," she said, gravely.

"Oh, Austin will take care that we do nothing imprudent," he said. "He has taken our case in hand, as he says, and we can't do better than put ourselves under his charge. You must paint some of our Thames views, Madge. You must paint one for me. By George! my uncle has got more mother wit in his little finger than I have in the whole of my body! Why didn't I give you a commission for a picture the first moment I knew you were an artist!"

"I shouldn't have accepted it," she said, smiling down at him. "But I'll paint you a picture, Blair; I will do it after I have finished this. Business must be attended to, you know, my lord."

He laughed.

"I wonder what he'll give you for that, Madge?" he said. "He ought to give you a hundred pounds. It's worth it. I'd give you a thousand if you'd let me."

"You'd ruin yourself, we all know," she said lightly, scarcely paying any heed to what she said, then as she saw him wince she dropped her brush and put her arm round his neck penitently.

"Oh, Blair, I meant nothing!" she murmured.

"I know, I know, dearest!" he said gravely. "But your light words reminded me of the fool I have been. But that is all altered now. Do you know that I have not made a single bet since—since you gave yourself to me? No! And I'm living as steady an existence as that man who always went home to tea. Austin says it won't and can't last; but we shall see."

It was always Austin. Scarcely ten sentences without his name cropping up.

"I don't see why Mr. Ambrose should discourage you, Blair," she said, smiling. "But you can prove him in the wrong all the more triumphantly," she added.

He laughed as he kissed her, telling her that she was his good angel, and that while she would continue to love him he was all right; but when he had gone, and she sat listening to his departing footsteps, she pondered over Austin Ambrose's words.

The next two days she worked hard at her picture, and on the third day finished it.

"What shall I do, grandma?" she said to Mrs. Hale. "I am going to London to-morrow, you know. Shall I send the picture from there, or give it to Mr. Stibbings to take to his lordship?"

"Give it to Mr. Stibbings," said Mrs. Hale, "with your dutiful respects and compliments, my dear."

Margaret gave the picture to Mr. Stibbings, but with her compliments only, and presently that important functionary returned.

Would Miss Hale honor the earl by joining him in the picture gallery?

Margaret went at once, and found him standing before her picture, which he had caused to be placed on an easel in the best lighted part of the gallery.

He held out his hand, and bowed to her with a kindly smile.

"You have painted a beautiful little sketch for me, Miss Hale," he said. "One I shall often look upon with pleasure and delight. And you have done it quickly, too, but not carelessly—no, no!"

Margaret murmured a few words in acknowledgment of his graciousness, and he went on:

"There is a career before you, my dear Miss Hale! You are one of the fortunate ones of this earth! Great gifts—great gifts"—and he looked at her absently; then he sighed and roused himself again—"but don't waste them, my child! I hope you are enjoying yourself here?"

"Very much, my lord," said Margaret. "I leave to-morrow," and she sighed faintly.

"To-morrow! So soon?" he said. "And you go back to London? I hope you will pay the Court another visit soon! I must speak to Mrs. Hale concerning it! Will you wait a moment or two?" and he drew a chair forward before he left the gallery.

Margaret sat and waited. How happy she had been! and yet if he only knew the cause of her happiness! If he could but guess that it was because she had won the love of his nephew, the Viscount Leyton.

She felt guilty and ill at ease, and when he returned, and approaching her with a smile, pressed some bank-notes into her hand, she began to tremble, and the tears rushed to her eyes.

"No thanks, my dear," he said. "Tut, tut! You must not wear your heart upon your sleeve, or daws will peck at it. You have no cause for gratitude; it is I who should and do feel grateful to you. Good-bye. May Heaven watch over you and make you happy, my dear!" It was almost like a benediction, for he half raised his white hand over her head.

When Margaret looked up he had gone.

She turned away, and the tears were still in her eyes as she opened the folded notes and looked at them. They represented a hundred pounds.

Mrs. Hale was quite overwhelmed.

"Well!" she exclaimed. "Gracious goodness!—a hundred pounds! Well, Margaret, my dear, I don't think you have any cause to regret your visit to your poor old grandmother. It hasn't been altogether a waste of time, now, has it?"

"No," said Margaret; "no, indeed, dear!" but even as she kissed the old lady and hid her face on her ample bosom, the same guilty feeling assailed her as that which had come upon her under the earl's generosity.

On the morrow she returned to London, but she had not to walk as she had done in coming. The earl had given orders that a brougham should be in attendance, and she started with a footman to open the door, and another to place her modest portmanteau on the roof, while the coachman touched his hat.

"Good-bye, grandma!" she said brokenly, as she clung to the old lady.

"Good-bye, Margaret, my dear! You will come again, and as soon as you can?"

"Yes," said Margaret, a lump rising in her throat. "Yes, I will come again—and soon."

But man proposes, and Providence disposes!

It was hot in London, and Margaret found her fellow-lodgers were away in the country, so that she had the rooms to herself.

She was thankful for their absence, for she would have shrunk from their affectionately close questioning, and they might have worried some hint of her secret from her.

An hour after her return a telegram arrived.

"Will you meet me at Waterloo at two o'clock? We will go up the river."

It was not signed, but Margaret knew that it was from Blair. Should she go?

She lay awake a long time that night asking herself the question, but at two o'clock the next day she found herself at Waterloo, and Austin Ambrose came up and raised his hat.

"You did not expect me?" he said with a smile, as her color rose.

"I—I thought——"

"It would be Blair," he finished smoothly. "He is not far off. He will join us at Clapham Junction. He wanted to come and meet you here, but I persuaded him to let me come instead. You know how prudent I am. A dozen people on the platform might chance to see him and recognize him and talk, while I—well nobody feels enough interest in me to care where I went," and he laughed.

"It is better so, and it is very kind of you," said Margaret.

"I am all kindness," he said, smiling. He put her into a first-class carriage, and Margaret saw his hand in close contact with the guards, and heard the lock turned.

"May I say that you are looking very well, Miss Margaret?" he said, leaning forward and looking at her with respectful and friendly admiration.

Margaret laughed.

"Did you take all this trouble to pay me compliments, Mr. Ambrose?"

"No," he said, with sudden gravity, but still smiling, "I came for prudence' sake, and because I wanted to speak to you. And I have so few minutes that I must get to the point at once. Miss Margaret, are you going to be good to Blair and marry him?"

Margaret flushed, then grew pale.

"Some day," she said, trying to speak lightly.

"Some day is no day," he returned. "Miss Margaret, you know, I hope and trust, that I am your friend?"

Margaret inclined her head.

"It is as your friend and his that I venture to beg you to make him the happiest man in the world as soon as possible."

Margaret remained silent; her hand trembled as she touched the window-strap.

"Why—why should it be soon?" she faltered. "It seems only a few days since—since——"

"It is some weeks," he said, quietly and impressively. "But, indeed, if it were only a few days, I would say the same. Miss Margaret, I can scarcely tell you all the reasons I have for pressing this upon you, and I would not do it, but that I know Blair is too—well—shy to do it altogether for himself. A simple 'no' from you silenced him! He told me, you see, that he spoke to you when he was down at the Court last."

"He tells you everything!" Margaret could not help saying.

"Do not be jealous!" he said; "if he does, it is because he knows that all that interests him interests me, and that I have his welfare at heart."

"Forgive me," she said, in a low voice. "Yes, he did speak to me."

"And he did not tell you the reasons? His, of course, are that he cannot be completely happy until you give him the right to call you his. But mine are as strong, I think! Miss Margaret, my friend's love for you has changed him; has made a better and a nobler man of him! Will you run the risk of that change deteriorating? Can you not guess something of the temptations which assail a man in Blair's position? Don't you apprehend that shadows from the past may arise, that—I will say no more! Complete the good work you have begun! Place him beyond the weak and wicked past in the harbor of your love. If Blair asks you to marry him early next month, Miss Margaret, I beseech you do not refuse!"

Margaret sat pale and trembling.

"Do not answer now," he said. "You shall tell him. I will only say this, that, if you will let me, I will remain your friend all through. I will see that all the arrangements are made, and that the whole thing is kept perfectly secret. You shall please yourself how soon you declare the marriage, but I should advise, strongly advise that you wait for a favorable opportunity." He was too wise to say, "Till the earl is dead!"

The train stopped at Clapham, and as Blair came hurrying up to the window, Austin Ambrose jumped out.

"Go and enjoy yourselves," he said, with a pleasant smile, and shaking his head to a request that he would accompany them. "Two are company, and three are none. Good-bye, Miss Margaret—and remember," he added, in a low voice.

Margaret did remember. All the afternoon, the happy afternoon, as she sat opposite Blair as he rowed up the beautiful reaches of the Thames, she thought of Austin Ambrose's words, and so it happened that when, later on, they were sitting under the trees, on an island that glowed like an emerald in the middle of the silver stream, he bent over her and murmured:

"Madge, will you marry me next month?" she placed her hand in his and answered:

"Yes!"

CHAPTER XIV

Just at this period a singular change came over Mr. Austin Ambrose's mode of life. As a rule he rarely left London. At a certain hour of the day you would find him in his chambers, at another riding or walking in the park, at another he would be dining at his club, and every night you were sure of seeing him at the whist table at any rate for an hour or two. But immediately after Margaret's promise to marry Lord Blair, Mr. Austin Ambrose took to taking little excursions in the environs of London, and the special objects of attraction for him seemed to be, strangely enough, seeing that he could by no means be called a religious man, the various churches in the villages dotted about Kent and Surrey. The smaller and more out of the way the village, and the more dilapidated and neglected the church, the more Mr. Austin Ambrose seemed to be attracted by them.

He chose the churches where the congregation is small and the clergyman old and feeble, and he would sit and listen as the old parsons dribbled out their prosy sermons, and the scattered people in the great pews nodded and slept.

One church he appeared to have a special liking for. It was situated in one of the small villages in Surrey called Sefton. There were only a few cottages and a farm, and the church was in a very dilapidated condition, and the clergyman seemed almost as worn out.

He was a very old man and nearly blind, and how he got through the service only those who are acquainted with similar cases can understand or believe. So past his time and dead to everything did the old gentleman appear that one could easily understand the point of the poet's lines:

> "He lived but in a living sleep,
> Too old to laugh or smile or weep."

"If one were to be married or buried by him on Monday he would forget it on Tuesday," Austin Ambrose murmured to himself as he sat at the back of one of the high backed pews and watched the old gentleman.

There was a parish clerk, too, who droned out the responses, and slept through the sermon—and snored—who was almost as old as the clergyman, and Mr. Austin Ambrose waylaid him and got into conversation with him after the service. It could scarcely be called conversation, however, for the old man merely grunted a "Yes," or "No," and smiled a toothless smile to Austin Ambrose's questions and remarks.

He seemed to remember nothing—excepting that "It were forty-two years agone since the small bell were cracked, and that's why we doan't ring 'em at marriages; they do seem so like a tolling, sir."

"You don't have many weddings, I suppose?" asked Mr. Ambrose.

The old man shook his head.

"Not a main sight," he said without exhibiting the faintest trace of interest. "Moast of our folks is too old to marry, and the young 'uns goes to the big church at Belton—away over there."

"When was the last?" asked Mr. Ambrose.

The clerk took up his hat slowly and scratched his head.

"I do scarce remember, sir," he said; "my memory ain't what it were. I'm getting on in years, you see—nearly eighty, sir; me and the parson runs a closish race," and he chuckled. "When was the last? Lemme see! Well, I could tell 'ee by the book, but the parson keeps that. I dare say he could put his hand upon it."

Mr. Ambrose laughed softly.

"You seem half asleep here at Sefton," he said pleasantly.

The old clerk grunted.

"I think we be sometimes, sir," he said. "But, you see, it's a miserable place now the coach has given up running through. Them railways and steam indians have a'most ruined the country."

"How long ago is it since the last coach ran?" asked Mr. Ambrose.

The poor old man looked bored to death.

"Thirty—forty year," he said. "I can't call to mind exactly; my memory hain't what it were."

Mr. Ambrose wished him good-day, and without tipping him—he did not want to fix himself in the old man's feeble memory—and repaired to the inn.

He called for a glass of ale, which he took care not to drink, and asked for a paper.

The landlord brought him a local one.

"Could I see a London one?" asked Mr. Ambrose.

The landlord shook his head.

"All the news as we care about, such as the state of the crops, and the prices at Coving Garden Market, is in that there paper; we don't trouble about a Lunnon one," he said.

Mr. Ambrose nodded and smiled, paid for his ale, and went back to London.

"Sefton is the place," he said. "It is so out of the world that they never see a London newspaper; so asleep that the noise of the great world rushing onward never wakes it, and the parson and clerk are faster asleep than anything else in it!"

He described the place in glowing colors to Margaret and Blair, a few nights afterward, as they three were sitting in a cool corner of the Botanical Gardens.

"A most delightful nook, my dear Miss Margaret; quite a typical old English village. I could spend the rest of my days there, and if I were going to be married—alas! why should it be one's fate to assist at other people's happiness, and have none oneself?—it is the place of all others I should choose for the ceremony."

"What does it matter where the church is?" said Blair, in his blunt fashion, and with a point-blank look of love at the sweet, downcast face beside him.

"It matters a great deal, my dear Blair; but I'm addressing Miss Margaret, who can appreciate the beauties of a scene, being an artist. I assure you it is a most charming spot, and it is so quiet and out of the way that I really think one might commit bigamy three times running there in as many weeks, and no one would be any the wiser. Why did you start, Blair?"

Margaret looked up at Blair at the question, and he met both her and Austin Ambrose's gaze with astonishment.

"Why did I *what*? Start? I didn't start," he said. "Why should I? What were you saying? To tell you the truth, I was looking at Madge's foot at the moment, and wondering how anybody could walk with such a mite, and comparing it with my own elephant's hoof. I didn't hear what you said quite."

Margaret drew her foot in, and looked up at him rebukingly.

"You shouldn't be frivolous, sir," she said.

"You shouldn't have such a small foot, miss," he retorted, in the fashion which is so sweet to lovers, and so silly to other people. "Now, what was it you said, Austin?"

Austin Ambrose laughed.

"Oh, some joke about bigamy, not worth repeating. I thought I had said something funny, you started so."

"But I *didn't* start," replied Blair, with a laugh.

"All right," assented Austin Ambrose; "you didn't, then. But I was going to say that another advantage is that Sefton is on the main line, and that you start from the church to that place in Devonshire where you are to be happier than ever two mortals have ever yet been. What is the name of it?"

"Appleford," said Blair.

"You will be down there about five o'clock," continued Austin Ambrose. "Just in time for dinner."

"What do you say, Madge?" asked Lord Blair, in a low voice.

Austin Ambrose rose and strolled toward some flowers.

"I say as you say, dearest," she answered, with a little sigh.

He looked at her.

"Just give me half a hint that you don't like all this secrecy— —" he began; but she stopped him, raising her eyes to his with a trustful smile.

"We won't open all that again, Blair," she said. "Yes, Sefton will do."

"And you won't mind doing without the bridemaids and the white satin dress, and the bishop, and all that?" he asked, with half anxious but wholly loving regard.

Margaret returned his gaze steadily and unflinchingly.

"I care for none of them," she said, quietly. "If I could have had my choice I should have liked my grandmother; but we haven't our choice, and so nothing matters, Blair."

"You are the best-natured girl that ever breathed, Madge!" he said in a passionate whisper. "All my life through I shall remember what sacrifices you made for me. I shall never forget them! Never!"

"Have you made up your minds?" asked Austin, coming back.

"Yes; it is to be Sefton," said Madge herself.

"Very well, then," he answered. "Then, all the rest of the arrangements I can make easily."

And he was as good as his word.

He went down with Blair to get the special license; he engaged a sweet little cottage at Appleford; he saw the parson's clerk, and informed him of the date of the wedding; he even went with Blair to his tailor's to order some clothes.

The day approached. Margaret had made her preparations. They were simple enough, wonderfully and strangely simple, seeing that the man she was going to marry was a viscount, and heir to one of the oldest coronets in England.

"Don't buy a lot of dresses, Madge," Blair had said. "We shall be going to Paris and Italy after Appleford, and you can buy anything you want at Paris, don't you know."

She gave notice to quit to her landlady, and wrote a line or two to some of her companions. She did not say that she was going to be married, but that she was going for a long stay in the country, and she did not add what part.

The morning—the wedding morning—was as bright and even brilliant as a real summer morning in England can be—when it likes; and the sun shone on the new traveling dress—which was to be her wedding dress as well—as bravely as if it had been white satin itself.

All the way down to Sefton, Blair looked at her with the loving, wistful admiration of a bridegroom, and seemed never tired of telling her that she was all that was beautiful and lovable.

Austin Ambrose had gone into a smoking carriage and left them to themselves, but when the train pulled up at Sefton he came to the door.

"Are we going to walk?" inquired Blair.

"No, there is a fly," said Austin, and he led them to it quietly and got them inside.

Blair laughed.

"Poor old Austin! Upon my word, I think he enjoys all this mystery! He'd make a first-rate conspirator, wouldn't he? I say, he was right about the place, though, wasn't he? It is dead and alive!"

Margaret looked through the window. There were a few scattered cottages, one solitary farm, and at a little distance, half hidden amongst the trees, the old dilapidated church.

"It is quiet," she said; "but it is very pretty."

"Quiet!" and he laughed. "I'd no idea there were such spots near London. Austin must have had some trouble in finding such an out-of-the-way place."

And he spoke truly. Mr. Ambrose *had* taken a great deal of trouble.

The fly drove up to the church door, and Austin Ambrose got down from the box.

"You need not wait," he said to the flyman; "we are going to take a stroll through the church. It looks interesting."

The flyman pocketed his fare—the exact fare—and concluding that they were sight-seeing, drove sleepily off.

"Come along," said Austin Ambrose in a matter-of-fact fashion, and they followed him.

But the door was locked, and there was no sign of parson, or clerk, or pew-opener.

Austin Ambrose bit his lip, then laughed.

"I know where the old fellow lives," he said; "I'll rout him out."

He went to a little ivy-grown cottage just outside the churchyard, and presently returned with the ancient clerk.

"Mornin', miss; mornin', sir," he said, touching his battered old beaver. "I begs ten thousand pardons, but I quite forgot as how there was a wedding this mornin'; but I dessay the parson have recollected. Howsomever, I'll open the church," and he unlocked the door and signed for them to enter.

Margaret tremblingly clung a little closer to Blair's arm and he murmured a few words of encouragement.

"Hang it, Austin!" he said, aside; "it scarcely seems as if we were going to be married. It only wants a hearse——"

Austin laughed.

"Nonsense. It is just what you want. They have forgotten you are to be married, and they'll forget all about it half an hour after it is over. Here is the parson; I did his memory an injustice!"

The old gentleman came shuffling up the porch and blinked at them over his spectacles.

"Good-morning, Mr. Stanley," he said.

Blair stared, then, remembering that that was the name he had arranged to assume, returned the greeting.

The pew-opener, an ancient dame, with a "front" slipping down nearly to her nose, now made her appearance, and the party went into the church.

The clerk assisted the clergyman into his surplice, and got out the register, and Blair, pressing Margaret's hand, walked up to the altar.

Austin Ambrose paused a moment before accompanying, and whispered to Margaret:

"You will take care not to address either of us by name?"

She made a motion of assent, and, pale and trembling, followed with the pew-opener and clerk.

The service began. It was scarcely audible; at times the old clergyman was taken with a cough that threatened to shake him, and the book he held, and, indeed, the church itself, into pieces, but he struggled through it; and in a few minutes Margaret found herself leaning upon Blair's arm, and heard him murmur—with what intensity of love!—"My wife!"

"Now, if you'll sign the book," said the clerk. "Lemme see; what is the name?" and he peered at the license.

"Here is the name!" said Austin Ambrose. "It is rather a long one, and I've written it down," and he handed him a slip of paper.

Blair, to whom the remainder of the formalities was *caviare*, was bending over Margaret at a little distance, and buttoning her gloves.

"Ah! yes! ahem! thank you!" said the clerk. "Now, if you'll sign, please."

They signed, the old clergyman peering down at them with a benign and utterly senile smile.

He had never heard of Lord Ferrers or of Lord Leyton, and this string of names might belong to some young shopkeeper's assistant for all he knew or cared; but he did inquire for the license.

"I put it in the book," said Austin Ambrose. He had got it in his pocket.

"Oh, very well! Yes, thank you! Well, I trust you will be happy, young couple; yes, with all my heart. You have got a beautiful morning; and where are you going to spend your honeymoon?"

"In France," said Austin Ambrose, blandly. "So we must hurry away. Good-morning, sir," and slipping their fees into the hands of parson, clerk, and pew-opener, he made for the door.

"My wife!" said Blair again. "George! I can scarcely believe it is true!" and he looked round with a half-dazed glance; but it changed to one of triumph and happiness as he drew her arm within his and pressed it to his side.

"Yes, you are man and wife," said Austin Ambrose, "and I echo the good old clergyman's wish, 'May you be very happy,'" and he held out his hand.

Blair seized it and wrung it.

"Thank you, Austin," he said simply, but with a ring of deep feeling in his voice. "You have been a true friend to us both, eh, Madge?" and he passed the hand on to her.

She took it and looked at the owner. Then suddenly she started and drew back. For a moment—in his secret exultation—Mr. Austin Ambrose had been off his guard, and there shone a light in his eyes that almost betrayed him.

It was gone in an instant, however, and with the pleasant, friendly smile, he pressed Margaret's hand.

"We mustn't try her too much, my dear Blair," he said. "It has been an exciting morning. Would you like to rest, or will you go on, Lady Leyton? There is just time to catch the train."

Margaret started. Lady Leyton!

Blair laughed.

"Margaret doesn't know her own name!" he said. "Which will you do, my lady?"

"Let us go on," she murmured, a desire that was almost absorbing possessed her—the longing to get rid of Mr. Austin Ambrose. It was very ungrateful, but so it was.

"All right," said Blair.

They walked to the station. As Austin Ambrose had said, there was just time to catch the down train to Devon, and in a few minutes it came puffing up.

A faithful friend to the last, Austin Ambrose got them a carriage, and tipped the guard.

"Good-bye," he said, standing on the step and waving his hand; "good-bye, and Heaven bless you!" and there seemed to be something really like tears in his voice.

And, indeed, he was paler than usual as he walked up and down the platform, waiting for the train to London.

Sometimes our very success frightens us.

The train reached Waterloo pretty punctually, and Mr. Austin Ambrose sprung out and got into a cab.

"Drive to No. 9, Anglesea Terrace," he said.

CHAPTER XV

It was a week after Margaret's wedding in the moldy and dilapidated old church at Sefton, and she and Lord Blair—she and her husband!—were sitting on the cliff at Appleford looking out upon the sea, which lay at their feet like a level opal glistening in the rays of the morning sun.

The history of these seven days might be epitomized in the three words—They were happy!

Happy with the happiness that few mortals experience. Lord Blair had been in love before his marriage, but he was—and, believe me, dear reader, what I am going to state is not too common—he was more in love now, after these seven days, than before.

Margaret was not a girl of whom even the most fickle of mankind could tire easily, and Blair was not the most fickle.

He had often declared that his Madge, as he delighted to call her, was an angel; he married the angel, and discovered that she was a lovely and lovable woman, and I make bold to say—that for sublunary purposes—that is better, from a husband's point of view, than an angel.

"With each rising sun some fresh charm comes to view," says the poet; and Lord Blair found it so with Margaret.

Under the spell, the witchery of her presence, Lord Blair seemed to grow handsomer, younger, more taking, and to Margaret more charming. Oh, why cannot such epochs last forever, until they glide unconsciously into that eternity where all is love and happiness?

On this morning Blair lay stretched at her feet, near enough to be able to touch her hand, to put his arm round her waist. He was dressed in his flannels, she in a plain dress of some soft *comfortable* material which, while it showed the deliciously graceful outlines of her figure, enabled her to move about freely and without hindrance.

The light of love and happiness played like sunlight on her beautiful face, and glowed starlike in her eyes, which had rested on the glorious view, and now sought her husband's—and lover's—face.

"Madge," he said, after a long silence, during which he puffed at his pipe, "I am going to pay you a big and an awful compliment, and yet it's true—you are the only woman I ever met who didn't bore me!"

"In-deed!" she said, flashing a smile upon him which seemed like a sunbeam.

"It's true," he said with lazy emphasis. "Some women are pretty, and are content with that, and think it's good enough for you to sit and look at them; others are clever, and consider that if they talk and you listen it's all right. But you—why, you are the loveliest woman I know, and you are the cleverest. Madge, dear, I have no right to get the whole thing like this. There are so many better men who deserve it more than I do."

Margaret laughed.

"We don't get our deserts, Blair," she said. "*You*, for instance, might have married a dragon of propriety, who would keep you in order by the terror of her eye; or a plain heiress, who would bring you a large fortune to waste, anything but a foolish girl, who has no money and no family to bless herself with. There's that boat again! Where is it going?" she broke off.

He raised himself on his elbow indolently.

"That is the Days' boat," he said drowsily. "I don't know where it is going. Fishing, I suppose."

"They can't fish on this tide," said Margaret, who, though she had been only a week in Appleford, had learned more about its ways and habits than Blair would have gleaned in a year.

"No!" he said carelessly. "I can't quite make these Days out. They let us these lodgings, and they make us very comfortable, but I've a kind of feeling that they have some other way of getting their living that I don't understand. Now, why should he go out to sea this morning if he isn't going fishing?"

"The ways of Appleford are mysterious," said Margaret with a laugh, "and it would take a clever man to fathom them."

"Austin, for instance," he said, drawing a little nearer so that he could take her hand.

A slight cloud crossed Margaret's brow.

"I don't know that Mr. Ambrose even would fathom them," she said. "But I have discovered one thing, Blair," and she laughed softly.

"What's that, dear?" he asked.

"Why, that smuggling is not the extinct profession it is generally considered to be!"

"Smuggling!" he exclaimed incredulously.

"Yes," said Margaret. "I am certain that it is carried on here, and I have a shrewd suspicion that the landlord, Mr. Day, is engaged in it."

"Nonsense, Madge!" he said. "What a romantic child it is!"

"But my romance lies within reach of my hand," she murmured, touching his lips with her forefinger and receiving the inevitable kiss. "But I am sure of it. On Thursday night—do you remember how it blew?—no, you were fast asleep! Well, the wind woke me, and I went to the window to close it. And as I stood there I heard Day and his son talking outside. They, of course, thought themselves unheard, or they wouldn't have spoken 'so loudly."

"And what did they say?" Blair asked, smiling.

"I did not hear all of their talk, but I caught some of it. There were words spoken about 'kegs' and 'brandy' and 'tobacco.' That I am sure of."

Blair laughed.

"Nonsense, darling, you dreamt it!" he said.

Margaret smiled.

"Perhaps so, but it was a very lifelike dream then, and to put a touch of reality to it, I saw a keg of something—spirits or tobacco—in the kitchen the next morning. I asked Mrs. Day what it was, and she said, 'Water.' But there is a capital well just outside the door!"

"Upon my word you would make a first-class detective, Madge!" said Lord Blair, with a laugh, in which she joined.

"Should I not? I had a great mind to ask Mrs. Day to let me have a glass of the water, but I felt that if I were right, the consequences would be too embarrassing."

"I should think so," said Blair. "And you imagine that Day and his son are going on a smuggling expedition now?" and he looked at the boat dancing on the waves beneath them.

Margaret nodded.

"Yes, I do," she replied lightly. "I think that presently Mr. Day, with his little boat, will meet one of those rakish-looking craft in the offing there, and then the rakish-looking craft—isn't that the proper nautical phrase?"

"First rate!" he assented, languidly. "You would make your fortune as a novelist, Madge."

—"Will put a couple of small barrels on board of Day's boat," she said, pinching his ear tenderly. "Day will wait until the tide turns, and then, it being dark, will sail into Appleford harbor with a cargo of fish—and the two barrels. No one will suspect him, least of all the merry and comfortable coastguard; and those two barrels, after resting there for a night, will be sent off to Exeter—or somewhere else!"

Lord Blair laughed with indolent enjoyment.

"Bravo!" he said. "Well, Austin is better than his word. He said Appleford was pretty, but he didn't add that it possessed all the charms that you credit it with."

Once more the faint cloud crossed Margaret's happy face.

"Have you heard from him?" she asked, after a moment's pause.

Lord Blair pulled a letter from his pocket.

"Yes, this came this morning. I didn't read it through. Austin writes such awfully long letters. Read it yourself, darling, and tell me what it's all about."

Margaret read it.

"There is not much," she said. "He says that no one suspects what—what we did at Sefton, and that he has told every one that you have gone abroad."

Blair laughed.

"Trust Austin to keep a thing secret," he said. "He is the best man in the world at this sort of thing. Now, I should blare out the whole story to the first man I met; but Austin! Oh, Austin could keep his lips shut till he died!"

Margaret looked out to sea, and sighed.

"Now, what does that mean?" he demanded instantly. "Are you tired? Would you like to go in-doors? Are you—unhappy?"

She laughed slowly and softly.

"I think I am too happy!" she said in a low voice. "Blair, it seems to me sometimes as if there were something wicked in being so happy! We are told, you know, that there is no real happiness in this world, and that joy cannot last. If it is true, then—then——" she let her lovely eyes rest upon him doubtfully.

"Nonsense, my darling!" he retorted. "Don't believe it! We were all meant to be happy, but some of us have missed the way. I know what is the matter with you."

"What?" she demanded, her fingers clinging to his lovingly.

"Why, you feel strange without your work. You are an artist, don't you know; and you haven't touched a brush for—well, for seven days. That's bad for you. Oh, I know. I am a simple idiot, but I understand all about this sort of thing. You want to paint. Well, do it," and he threw himself back with a confident air.

Margaret laughed.

"If I wanted to paint ever so much," she said, "I couldn't; I haven't any materials. No colors, no canvas——"

He raised himself on his elbow.

"Oh, that's an easy matter; we can get all that at Ilfracombe. I'll go and get them; it's only a walk, or I can take the boat."

Margaret stopped him with a gesture of curiosity.

"Blair, there is that woman I spoke to you about last night," she said; "there, on that rock."

"What woman?" he asked, without moving.

"That young woman dressed in mourning," said Margaret. "I have seen her three times. I think she must be a widow."

"Oh," he said lazily; "I dare say. Well, about these said drawing materials. I'll walk into Ilfracombe, and get them. No; you sha'n't go. It is too hot, and you will get a headache."

"And do you think I will let you go all that way to gratify a whim which you have fastened upon me, you silly boy?" she said. "Seriously, Blair— don't trouble."

"But that is just what I mean to do," he said. "I don't want you to be bored, even for a moment; and I should feel happier myself if I could see you with your beloved paints and turpentine. You shall make a sketch of Appleford—and we'll hang it up wherever we go, and look at it when we are quite old, so that we may remember that we were 'too happy,' eh, Madge?" and he put his arm round her and kissed her.

At this moment the landlady, Mrs. Day, came from the cottage behind them. She was still a young woman, and her appearance was rather above that of the ordinary Appleford fisherwives. She had an intelligent face that rather impressed one.

Margaret had taken to her at once, and for Margaret Mrs. Day had a warm admiration, which expressed itself in her dark eyes and a smile which shone in them when Margaret spoke to her.

Mrs. Day generally had some knitting in her hands, and the needles were glistening in the sunlight as she approached. She had evidently not seen them, for while her hands were busy her eyes were fixed on the boat, which was gradually making its way across the bay.

Suddenly she lowered her eyes, and catching sight of her lodgers she started slightly, and, with a quick glance from them to the boat, turned to retrace her steps, when Blair called to her.

She came up to them with a little bow, that was almost a courtesy.

"Sorry to call you back, Mrs. Day," said Blair, in his genial manner, which won all hearts; "but I want to know the best way to get to Ilfracombe?"

Mrs. Day's needles stopped.

"The boat's out, sir," she said, "or you could have gone by that."

"Yes, I know that she is," said he, pointing to it; "Day's gone fishing, I suppose?"

"Yes, sir," said Mrs. Day, promptly and placidly. "There's no train now till the evening, and it's too far for Mrs. Stanley to walk."

"Mrs. Stanley isn't going," said Blair. "I'm going alone."

"Then you could ride, sir," said Mrs. Day: "I could borrow Farmer James' colt, if you cared— —"

"The very thing," said Blair, at once.

Mrs. Day inclined her head respectfully.

"I'll go and send for it, sir," she said, with the promptness which had struck Margaret as rather uncommon in a woman of Mrs. Day's class.

In about twenty minutes she came back to them.

"The colt is here, sir," she said, simply.

"Mrs. Day, you would make an excellent aid-de-camp," said Blair, with a laugh, as he jumped up. "Good-bye, Madge; I sha'n't be long. I can't bring all the things, but I'll bring some of them, and they shall manage to send the rest."

Margaret put her arm round his neck. Mrs. Day had retired.

"Don't go, Blair," she said, with sudden and unexpected earnestness. "I don't care about the painting; I would rather— —"

"No, no!" he said, steadfastly; "you only say that to save me a little trouble, and all the while I'm feeling glad to be able to do something for you, Madge! Trouble; the ride will be rather jolly. I'll tell you what Ilfracombe looks like, and, perhaps, you'll feel inclined to tear yourself away from your beloved Appleford, and make an excursion."

Margaret turned her face away. A strange and sudden presentiment had taken possession of her, and she was ashamed of it.

"Well, go then!" she said, forcing a laugh; "and if you do not come back, why I shall think Ilfracombe has proved too fascinating."

"All right," he said; "but I think you'll see me back by dinner time."

At the corner of the lane he turned in his saddle and looked round for a last glance at Madge—his wife, his darling—and was rewarded by a wave of her white hand.

"Now, my young friend," he said, addressing the colt, who was rather frisky, "have your little game by all means, but when it's over let us get on, for I'm anxious to get back to that young woman on the hill behind there."

Margaret stood until Blair had disappeared, then she sank onto the ground again.

After all, it had been foolish of her to let him go, or why had she not gone with him? She had had half an idea that the change would be good for him, it was not wise to keep a man tied to your petticoat though he love you ever so truly, and so she had given him his liberty. Well, he would come back at dinner time hungry and gay after his ride, and would love her all the more dearly for the short separation.

After a time she put on her hat and went down into the little fishing town, which clustered on the hill rising from the point where the sea and the two rivers met. It was a quaint old town, quite a hundred years behind the rest of the world, and the people, fishermen and sailors, were supposed to be rather rough; but they had never been rough to her, had never failed in that rustic courtesy which springs from the heart and is much better than the imitation which is manufactured so cleverly in towns.

She wandered to the beach and stood there for awhile, the women looking after her with a smile, the children gazing up at her, as they drew near, with that frank admiration for her beauty which did not always confine itself to looks, for she heard one child say to another:

"That be pretty maiden from London, that be."

An old man was seated on an upturned boat mending a net, and Margaret, feeling lonely, gave him good-evening.

"Good-evening, miss," said the old man, touching the wisp of white hair that shone like snow against his tanned face. "Be 'ee going out for a sail?"

"No," said Margaret, "I am only strolling about."

He nodded approvingly.

"Well, you be wise. Better on land, miss. We're goin' to have a shift in the weather."

Margaret looked at the cloudless sky and smiled down upon him with gentle incredulity; the old man shook his head.

"Oh, it be bright as a new penny now, miss, surely," he said, smiling back, "but it bean't going to last. There's a wisp in the wind as threatens a storm. It 'ull come before night; a tough un, too."

"Oh, I am so sorry," said Margaret. "There are some boats out at sea. Will they be safe?"

"There bean't many," said the old man.

"Mr. Day's boat has gone," said Margaret.

"Ay," he returned, slowly, and he looked steadily at his net. "She'll be safe enow. She's a stiff un, and used to rough weather, miss," and he laughed. "We always have it rough a'most when there's a high, strong tide, and it's very high to-night. You see that rock, miss?" and he pointed to a dark mass that rose on the black line at a little distance from them. "Well, the tide will cover that rock to-night. People won't allus believe it. There was a gentleman and a lady washed off that rock two year agone; they thought themselves safe enow, and was up there to watch the tide come in; they never saw it go out!" and he chuckled grimly.

Margaret shuddered.

"Do you mean that they were drowned?" she said.

"I 'spect," he replied; "leastways, they were never seen again."

"But I thought people who were drowned always came back?" said Margaret.

He shook his head.

"Not hereabouts, miss. There's sands here, miss, as is onreliable and hungry as a wild beastie; things they gets hold of they sticks to."

Margaret, not being desirous of continuing this cheerful conversation, wished him good-day and turned toward the cottage on the cliff.

Luncheon was laid in the neat little room, and she took off her hat and light jersey jacket and sat down with a wee little sadness. It was the first time she had sat down to a meal without Blair since their marriage; and Blair was a person likely to make his loss felt. The little room seemed desolate without his light, musical voice and his quick, ready laugh. Margaret looked round cheerlessly, and thought she wouldn't have any lunch, then she felt ashamed of her weakness, and dreading the look of surprise and astonishment with which Mrs. Day would be sure to view the untouched sole, forced herself to make a "pretending" lunch.

And as she chased a minute piece of fish round her plate with a fork and slice of bread, she fell to thinking of her great happiness, and the difference it had and would make in her life.

She was Blair's wife! Soon all the world would know it, and they would be drawn away from this quiet spot, which was like a placid pool in the whirling river—they would be drawn into the vortex, and be one of the giddy, rushing throng. If they could only always remain serene and happy outside the tumult of the great world!

How surprised everybody would be. The earl, her grandmother, her old companions at the art school! She could almost see her grandmother weeping and laughing over her with loving pride. Then she sighed. With all Blair's flattery she felt so unfit to be a grand lady, a viscountess who would some day wear the Ferrers' coronet!

"If we could only stay as we are," she thought, girl-like. "It is Blair I want, not the title or the money. I would rather live with him here until we die, than be the mistress of Leyton Court. What a pity it is he is not a fisherman! I could have mended nets, and knitted his jerseys, and stockings, and cooked his dinner in time, but to learn to play the part of viscountess!— oh, it frightens me a little!"

But she laughed even as she sighed. For, after all, would not Blair be at her side to guide and protect her, and envelop her with his great, strong love?

She got up and went to the window, and as she did so she picked up a pipe of Blair's and kissed it, though the caress was followed by a grimace.

There were still some long hours to be got through before Blair and happiness came home to dinner, and she was thinking rather disconsolately of another walk when the door opened and Mrs. Day entered.

"There is a lady to see you, ma'am," she said, hesitatingly.

"A lady to see me!" said Margaret, with surprise; then thinking that it might be one of the residents, who had come to pay her the compliment of a call she said, quickly:

"Oh, I am very sorry. Will you say I am not at home, please, Mrs. Day? But are you sure she wishes to see me?—it is so unlikely."

"Yes, she wants to see you, ma'am. She said Mrs. Stanley quite distinctly. And it's no use saying not at home, because she saw you at the window."

Margaret smiled at the unsophistication which was not familiar with the conventional white lie.

"By not at home I mean that I don't want to see her," she said. "She will understand, I think, Mrs. Day."

"Very well, ma'am," said Mrs. Day, and she went out. She was back again in a couple of minutes, however.

"The lady says she has come a great distance on purpose to see you, and begs that you will see her, if only for five minutes, ma'am," she said.

Margaret changed color. Could it be her grandmother?

"Is—is it an old lady?" she asked.

"No, ma'am, quite young, I should think; she has kept her veil down. I'll send her away if you like, ma'am; after all, she sha'n't bother you if you don't want to see her, though she be so pleading."

The last words decided Margaret—and sealed her fate.

"Oh—well—then, I will see her," she said, reluctantly.

"She's in the parlor, ma'am," said Mrs. Day, still hesitating; and Margaret, after that glance in the glass without which no woman ever goes to meet another, passed into the little passage. But she paused, even with her hand on the handle of the door.

After all it was only some stranger come to beg a subscription to one of the local charities; and yet she had come from a distance! Determining to get rid of her as soon as possible—for she knew that Blair would not wish her to see any one—she opened the door and entered the room.

A woman—Margaret's quick eyes saw at a glance that she was young—was seated with her back to the window. She was dressed very simply, and yet tastefully, in clothes that were almost, if not quite, mourning, and she wore a veil.

As Margaret entered, a faint color mounting in her lovely face, the visitor gave a scarcely perceptible start, either of surprise or admiration, and the hand that held her sunshade trembled.

"Do you wish to see me?" said Margaret, in her musical voice, which seemed to affect the visitor as her face had done.

"Yes," she said in a low voice, which she appeared to keep steady by a palpable effort, "You are—Mrs. Stanley?"

The color grew a little deeper in Margaret's cheeks, and her lids fell a little; but she said quietly:

"Yes, I am Mrs. Stanley."

Thereupon the visitor raised her veil, and Margaret saw a face that was pretty, and would have been girlish, but for its pallor and the lines which had been impressed upon it either by sorrow or sickness.

When she raised her veil she let her hands drop into her lap, and clasped them tightly and nervously, and her lips quivered.

Margaret remained standing, but the visitor sank into the seat from which she had risen, as if unable to stand.

"You—you will wonder—you will be surprised at my—my presence," she began, then she broke off and clutched at her dress nervously. "Oh, how can I go on? Bear with me, I beseech you! Be patient with me, I implore!"

Margaret looked down at her with surprise, that slowly melted to pity.

"I am afraid you are in some trouble," she said, gently, and Margaret's voice, when it was gentle, was compounded of the music which is said to disarm savage beasts.

It seemed to move the pale-faced girl strangely. She caught her breath and appeared to wince.

"I am in great trouble," she said. "You cannot tell, you will never know what it has cost me to come to you. But—but it is my only chance!"

She paused to gain breath, and Margaret sank into a chair, and wondered how much she might venture to offer her. She had all the money the earl had given her for her pictures, and some other savings besides. Of course it was pecuniary trouble.

"I am very, very sorry," she said, "and if I can help you——"

"You can, and you only!" said the girl.

"Will you tell me——" murmured Margaret.

"Yes, yes, I will!" she broke in; "but give me a minute, give me time, Mrs. Stanley. I will tell you my story. If it should fail to touch your heart— but it will not; I see by your face that you have a kind heart, that, though it might be led astray, would not do a fellow-creature, a helpless woman like yourself, a deadly wrong!"

Margaret stared at her, then turned pale. That the woman was mad she had now not a shadow of a doubt; and she, not unnaturally, glanced at the door.

The girl seemed to divine her suspicions and intentions, for she put out her hand pleadingly.

"No, I am not mad! You think so now! But you will see presently that I am not! It would be better for me—yes, and for you—if I were! Heaven help us both!"

She panted so and looked so faint that Margaret half rose. There was a carafe of water and a glass on a small table near her, and the girl caught at it and filled the glass, but in lifting it to her lips she spilt some, her hand shaking like an aspen leaf.

"I will try to be calm!" she said, pleadingly, as Margaret took the glass from her. "Mrs. Stanley, I am a poor and friendless girl. I was a governess in a gentleman's family—I am not a lady by birth, but I had struggled hard to qualify myself—and I did my duty, and was"—her voice broke—"happy! One day a gentleman came to visit the family. He was young and handsome; he was more than that, he was gentle and kind to the girl who felt herself so much alone in the world. He used to come to the schoolroom, and sit and talk at the children's tea, with them, and with me. I thought there was no harm in it. I did not guess that it was me he came to see until one day he told me—all suddenly—that he loved me!"

She panted and paused, and moistened her lips, keeping her dark eyes fixed on Margaret's face.

Margaret listened with gentle patience and sympathy, feeling, however, that there was some dreadful mistake, and that the girl had mistaken her for some one else.

"I did not know how it was with me until he spoke those words, but when he said them they seemed to show me my own heart, and I knew I loved him in return. Mrs. Stanley, I was not a wicked girl. No! I did not wish to do wrong, and I told him that he must go, and never see me, or speak to me so again, or that I must leave the place that had become a home to me."

"Poor girl!" murmured Margaret unconsciously.

The girl started, looked slightly—very slightly—confused, as a child does when it is interrupted in the middle of its lesson, then, with a heavy sigh, went on:

"But he would not listen to me; he said that he loved me as an honest girl should be loved. I fought against him and my own heart day after day, but he was too strong, and my love made me weak, and though he was rich and powerful, and I knew I was not fit to be his wife, I consented to marry him."

She stopped and eyed her listener.

Margaret, a little pale, but still wondering, gently opened the window to give her some air.

"Would you like to wait—let me get you some wine?" she murmured.

"No, no! I must go on while I have strength—while you will consent to listen," said the girl. "We were married secretly because he did not wish his powerful relatives to know anything of the marriage for awhile, and his prospects might be brighter. We were married"—she sighed—"and I was happy—oh, so happy!" and the tears coursed down her cheeks, and she hid her face in her handkerchief. "We had a pretty little cottage near London, and my husband seemed as happy as I was. He never wanted to leave my side; and so it went on for months, until—until"—she paused and panted—"until one day my husband left me—he said to see his relatives and find out if he could break it to them. He came back silent and moody, and he went away again all next day. Soon he stayed away for days, then weeks, and at last he left me altogether."

Margaret uttered an inarticulate cry of pity and sympathy and indignation.

"No, no, do not blame him," said the girl. "It was not altogether his fault. He was light-hearted and—and fickle by nature, and it was her fault as much as his."

"Hers?" said Margaret.

The girl looked at her with a vague wonder.

"Yes. Have you not guessed? The other woman!"

Margaret's face flushed.

"No!" she said.

"Yes, there was another woman. I discovered it by accident. I saw them together, and knew in an instant why he had left me. She was beautiful, more beautiful than I, and looked a lady, which I never was. And—and it was not wonderful that he should leave me—a poor, simple girl——"

"It was wicked, cruelly wicked!" exclaimed Margaret, hotly.

The girl sobbed.

"I did not know who she was! She looked good—and yet it was her fault! I went home—after seeing them—and waited for him to come that I might tax him with it! But he never came back! He sent me money—but I would not touch it! I—I had my savings, and I lived on them——"

"That was right!—that was right!" murmured Margaret, her womanly heart aglow.

"And—and I thought that I could learn to let him go, and live without him! But—but it was too hard a lesson! I could not! You see, I loved him so!"

"Poor girl, poor girl! Oh, he was a villain! You should have——" she stopped.

"What should I have done? Gone to him and reproached him? Oh, you do not know him! It would have made him hate me, and parted us forever and ever!"

"The law—there is justice," said Margaret.

The girl shook her head in dull misery.

"No, my pride was too great for that. Besides, I did not want my friends to know how I was treated. There was only one thing to do"—she paused, and her dark, restless eyes fixed themselves covertly on Margaret's face as if she were waiting for a cue.

"What was that?" breathed Margaret, bending forward.

"To go to the girl he had deserted me for, to go to her and pray her to let him come back to me. He was deceiving her, leading her astray, and she might turn on me and laugh at me. But she looked good, and perhaps, who knew, she might listen to my prayer! She could not love him better than I do, and if she did, she might not be so lost to all shame as to keep him from his wife!"

"No, no! you were right!" said Margaret. "Why do you not go to her?"

"I have come to her!" panted the girl. "Oh, Mrs. Stanley!——" but she stopped perforce, for Margaret's open-eyed bewilderment showed that the words were lost upon her.

"You have come?" she said. "Come where—to whom?"

"I have come here, to *you*!" exclaimed the girl, stretching out her hands. "Oh, dear lady, you are beautiful, ten times more beautiful than I am; but you look good and kind. Have mercy on me, and give me back my husband!"

Margaret shrank back, paling a little, but once again convinced that she was in the presence of a mad woman.

Yes, that was the key to the whole scene. The woman was one of those monomaniacs who are possessed by the shadow of an imagined wrong, and had pitched upon her as the person who had injured her! She looked toward the door and half rose, but before she could rise from her chair, the girl threw herself on her knees before her, and caught at her dress.

"You do not believe me! You would spurn me! Oh, my dear lady, in Heaven's name, listen to me! Do not turn from me! Think of my great wrong, my broken heart. You think you love him, but remember me! I am his wife—his wife; while you—ah, you have no claim on him! Besides, he has wronged you as cruelly almost as he has wronged me! Do not hesitate, dear, dear lady; have pity on me, and let him come back to me!" she cried, sobbing now bitterly.

Margaret tried to jerk her dress from the clinging hands, but they held too tightly.

"You—you are mad!" she got out at last, in a horrified voice, which she tried to keep steady. "I do not know you—I never saw you before! I know nothing of your husband! It's a mistake, all a mistake. Let me go, please, or I shall call some one——"

"No, no! Listen to me! Be patient with me!" pleaded the girl. "You do not know me, but I know you, though I only saw you and him together once. It was up the river. Oh, I should never, never forget you. Oh, be good to me! Let him come back to me! I am his wife—his wife! You will not, you cannot divide husband and wife!"

"Yes, you are mad!" said Margaret, with conviction. "You have never seen me with your husband!—never! never! Let go my dress!"

"Yes, you!" sobbed the girl. "Do you think I should mistake when all my life hung upon it? I have tried not to mention my husband's name, but you force me to do it. He may have tried to hide it from you—it is possible—but you may know it!"

"Yes, tell me," said Margaret, soothingly, feeling that it would be well to humor her, "tell me; but let go my dress—you frighten me—please."

"His name is Blair! He is Lord Leyton!" sobbed the girl.

Margaret uttered no cry. For a second she seemed as if she had not heard. The room spun round; the blue sky outside the window turned red; and the sofa opposite her seemed to heave as if shaken by an earthquake. Then she laughed.

"You are a wicked woman!" she said, in slow tones of cold anger and contempt—"a very wicked woman! Why have you come here with this story? Do you want money?"

The girl looked up at her with a strange look. Had she expected her victim to take the blow differently?

"You—you don't believe me!" she wailed at last.

Margaret laughed; a short laugh of scorn and contempt.

"Believe you!" she said, and that was all.

Her retort seemed to render the girl desperate.

"You know it is true!" she cried. "You knew that he was married—that I am his wife. He is Lord Blair Leyton; his uncle is the Earl of Ferrers. He is my husband, and you have stolen him from me— —"

"*You lie!*" burst from Margaret's white lips.

The passion that had been smoldering within her bosom leapt like an all-devouring flame to her lips, and she stood over the pale-faced, crouching girl like a goddess, her tall, graceful figure drawn to its full height, her eyes blazing, her hand outstretched as if it held the lightnings of Jove.

No wonder the girl shrank and cowered.

She did more than cower; she hesitated. For in that moment she quailed with fear, and half melted with pity, and shrank with loathing from her hellish task.

It was only for a moment. She had gone too far to go back now. To draw back would lead to exposure and ruin.

"Oh, hush, hush!" she whined. "You are too cruel! You know I speak the truth. We were married on the twelfth of March at St. Jude's—you do not believe me—see there, then; there is the certificate!" and she drew a paper from her breast and held it out, keeping firm grip of it, however.

Margaret stared at her without moving for a moment; then she bent down. For awhile she could see nothing, the paper and the characters on it danced before her eyes. Then her vision cleared, and she saw, still obscurely, the printed and written lines.

It was a certificate of the marriage of Blair, Lord Leyton—it set forth the long string of his Christian names—and Lucy Snowe, at the church of St. Jude, Paddington, on March the twelfth of the present year.

She tried to grasp the paper, but her fingers refused to close on it, and fell limp and useless at her side, and she stood glaring down at the crouching figure at her feet as at some monster.

"Are you convinced?" wailed the girl. "Do you believe me now? Oh, how *do* you think I should have the heart to tell you such a story? And now—what will you do? Oh, give him back to me! I don't utter a word of reproach against you! No! I know, I feel that he has deceived you—Ah!" she broke out as if she had been stung. "Don't tell me he has married you! If he has, if he has dared to, I'll punish him! I'll send him to penal servitude. I'll——"

Margaret's swooning senses caught the threat, and she held out her hand. It was her turn to plead.

"No, no!" she panted almost inaudibly, "he—he has not! He is nothing to me! You—you shall have him back! Oh, Heaven! Oh, Heaven!" and, with a cry that rang through the room, she fell forward on her face.

CHAPTER XVI

Lottie Belvoir looked down at the prostrate figure of Margaret with a pallor that made the carefully-applied paint on her face look yellow by contrast.

For a minute or two she felt frightened and had an idea of calling for help. Lottie was not altogether a bad girl; indeed, the persons who are either altogether bad or altogether good do not exist in real life, but only in the pages of some novels.

She had been brought up in a hard school, in which each has to struggle for itself, and where each knows that without doubt the devil will take the hindmost.

Mr. Austin Ambrose had worked upon her feelings and tempted her to do this thing, and she had done it. But in the doing of it she had felt distinctly uncomfortable, in the first place she had discovered that Margaret was a lady; if she had been one of Lottie's own class, Lottie could have had no compunction whatever. Then Margaret's beauty, which affected everybody more or less, had had its effect upon Lottie; then again Margaret had treated her so kindly and gently; and altogether Lottie Belvoir had not had a particularly good time of it.

She got the glass of water and sprinkled it over the white beautiful face, and chafed her hands and presently Margaret reopened her eyes, and smiling faintly, murmured—"Blair!"

Then, as memory returned to its seat, the white features were convulsed, and shrinking away from Lottie she said, in a ghastly whisper:

"It is all true, then? I—I thought that I had dreamt it."

"Yes, it is all true," said Lottie, rather sullenly. "And now I want to know what you are going to do, miss?"

Margaret winced at the "miss." More surely than any other word could have done, it brought home to her the fact of her ruin and degradation.

Slowly she dragged herself to a chair, and sank into it, refusing with a slight shudder Lottie's proffered arm.

"What I am going to do?" she repeated in a dull, benumbed fashion. "I do not know! Yes I—I must go away! I must go at once, before—before he returns."

"That is the best thing you can do, miss," said Lottie. "It goes against me to drive you away, but what can I do? He is my husband——"

"Yes, yes," gasped Margaret, as if she were choking, "he is your husband—he is nothing to me. I have no right to stay here now. I will go."

"Perhaps you'd like to see him again, like to see us face to face and have it out with him?" suggested Lottie, doubtfully, and watching Margaret's face covertly.

"No, no," she said, instantly, and with a shudder, "I—I never wish to see him again."

"He has behaved cruelly, shamefully to you, miss," said Lottie; "to both of us, in fact, and he isn't worth fretting about, though he is a lord."

Margaret sat staring at the gayly patterned carpet, almost as if she had not heard the last words, then she looked round the room in a kind of bewildered fashion.

Lottie rose and let down her veil.

"There is a train in an hour," she said, with a sympathetic sigh, "if you'd like to go to London, or perhaps you'd like to go abroad. If there should be money wanted——"

She had almost gone too far.

Margaret rose and looked at her with wild eyes.

"I will go," she panted, "do not be afraid. I will never see your—your husband again. But *leave me alone!* Do not offer me money"—then her face changed, and with a sob she cried—"forgive me. It is you who have been wronged as well as me. I—I did not mean to speak so—but, ah, if you would only go and leave me to fight against my misery."

Lottie turned pale again under her paint, and moved toward the door. There she paused, and a strange look came into her face. It was the shadow of coming remorse casting itself before its steps. Even then there was a chance for Margaret, for at that moment Lottie's womanly heart was beginning to assert itself, and the impulse to fling herself at Margaret's feet and tell her the truth—the real truth—was making itself felt; but at that instant she caught sight of a man's figure coming up the winding path, and with a quick step she came toward Margaret.

"I am going," she said, in her ear; "you will not see me again. Go to London—abroad—somewhere away from Blair, and—from *Mr. Austin Ambrose!*"

These last words were not in her part, but for the life of her, though she lost all, Lottie could not have helped whispering them. Then, without waiting for any response, she went out and turned down the path. A hundred yards from the gate, on the narrow path, she met Austin Ambrose.

"Well," he said, quickly, "is it over?"

"Yes, it's done," she said, looking at him with anything but a pleasant countenance; "and a nice job it has been! Why didn't you tell me she was a lady?"

He made an impatient gesture.

"What does it matter? Where is she?—how did she take it?"

"She is in there," said Lottie shortly; "and she took it—well, it would have been almost as easy to have murdered her! Indeed, I shouldn't be surprised if it *did* kill her. She fell at my feet as if she were dead."

"Tut!" he said, with a cold smile; "she is not of the sort that die easily. She will get over it. But there is no time to lose. You get over to Paris; catch the down-train to the junction, and travel by the night mail."

"And you—what are you going to do now?" she asked.

He smiled.

"You need not trouble about that," he said. "You have done your part, and I'll see that you get your reward."

She nodded.

"If it was to be done over again," she began; then she moved on a step, but stopped and, with a spot of red, said:

"I advise you to get away before Blair comes back. If he should happen to turn up"—she shrugged her shoulders—"I wouldn't give much for your life!"

He nodded and laughed, and his eyes flashed evilly.

"Blair will not turn up!" he said.

The tone of confidence startled her.

"Why? What have you done with him?" she asked.

"Now, my dear Lottie," he said in a low voice, and looking round cautiously, "don't interfere with my part of the play. It doesn't concern you. Get off as fast as you can, and make your mind easy. Stop! you'll want money," and he put his hand to his pocket; but, with a deep flush and a tightening of the lips, she refused it—as Margaret had refused hers!

"I've got enough money to go on with," she said. "You can send it to the Hotel de Louvre at Paris, if you like," and, with a nod, she sped quick down the path.

Austin Ambrose waited for a minute or two, looking at the sky. The blue that had been so unbroken a short time since was streaked with fleecy clouds, that might later grow black.

Then he opened the cottage door and walked into the room where Margaret sat, her head resting upon her outstretched arms.

While one could count twenty he stood and looked down at her, then he said, in a low voice:

"Miss Margaret!"

She did not start, but raised her head and looked at him, and a shudder seemed to convulse her whole frame.

"You here?" she said, scarcely audible.

He inclined his head with a sorrowful gesture.

"Yes, I am here. I have come to see if by any chance I can be of assistance to you."

"Then—then you have heard it?" she panted.

He dropped his eyes and sighed.

"Tell me," she cried, catching at his arm and holding it with a grasp of steel, "tell me the truth! Is what she said—this woman!—is it true?"

He waited a moment.

"It is true, alas!" he said.

Margaret's hand fell from his arm, and she shrank back.

"I only learned it just now," he said, as if in explanation. "Early this morning, Lady Leyton—I beg your pardon, but I fear it is her legal title—met me at the station, and recognizing me as a friend of Blair's, told me her story."

Margaret hid her face in her hands.

"She has been here, I suppose?" he said.

"Yes," breathed Margaret.

He sighed.

"I feared so! I wish that I could have reached you and broken it to you before she came, but I wanted to learn if her story was true, and I telegraphed to the clerk of the church at which she said she was married." He paused to see if Margaret was fully realizing his words, then went on slowly and impressively. "I received an answer promptly. They were married at St. Jude's on the twelfth of March."

Margaret remained motionless.

"But I need not have taken this precaution, for I met the one person who could set all doubt at rest."

She looked up and fixed her eyes upon him.

"I met Blair, and taxed him with his fiendish villainy, and——"

Margaret caught her breath.

—"He confessed it!" he said.

She uttered a low cry, and cowered against the back of the chair.

"I think I could have killed him on the spot," he went on. "He has played the part of a heartless scoundrel! Miss Margaret, do you remember how he started when I remarked how easy it would be for a man to commit bigamy at Sefton?"

The incident flashed back upon Margaret's memory, and she groaned.

"If I had only known what that start of his meant!" murmured Austin Ambrose. "Yes, he confessed the crime! He sent you a message by me——"

She looked up and put up her hand.

"Do not tell me! Do not mention his name again!" she cried hoarsely.

"I must tell you," he said gently; "I promised! He implored your forgiveness! Reparation, he knows is impossible; not even the remorse, which will haunt him as long as his life lasts, can invent any way of undoing the wrong he has wrought you! He consigned you to my care, Miss Margaret, and I have undertaken readily—yes, very readily—to see that your future is not further darkened by want."

Margaret rose and clutched the table.

—"You—you offer me money; you, too! And his money!" she panted.

Austin Ambrose hung his head and sighed.

"You will let me be your friend?" he pleaded in a soft voice.

Margaret pushed the hair from her white forehead.

"No!" she said; "I have no friend! I am alone in all the world! Tell him—yes, tell him—that I would not touch a penny of his if it were to save my life! Tell him that he has killed my heart and soul, but while there is life still left in my body, I will use it to crawl as far from him as I can! Tell him—" she broke down for a moment—"tell him that I forgive him, but that if he ever again sends me such a message as you have brought, the love through which he wronged and ruined me will turn to hate!"

"You are right!" he murmured. "But what will you do?" he asked, looking at her with anxious intentness.

Margaret moaned.

"Ah! What will I do?" she sobbed hoarsely. "Heaven knows! there is only one thing I can do, to creep away into some place where none may find me, and die!"

If Mr. Austin Ambrose had possessed that extremely awkward organ, a heart, he would—he must—have been touched by the sight of the misery and anguish of this innocent girl, whose happiness he had so carefully and skillfully plotted against; but if there was a heart in Mr. Austin's bosom, it existed there simply for physiological reasons, and not for those of sentiment.

"I think you must let me be your friend!" he said in a low voice, and keeping his eyes on the carpet. "I can quite understand what it is you are feeling and suffering, and I think your desire to get away from here, to get beyond the possibility of ever meeting with Blair, a natural one. If you will let me I will help you. You would wish to go at once?"

Margaret did not answer him, she was scarcely conscious of what he said. He waited a moment or two, then said slowly and distinctly:

"I think that the best thing I can do, Miss Margaret, is to leave you for a short time. The blow has been an overwhelming one, in very truth, it has confused and bewildered me; and standing here, a friend of the villain who has wronged you—alas! the friend who did all he could in all innocence to bring about the ceremony—I feel as if I were a sharer in his guilt."

Margaret tried to murmur "No," but the word would not come.

"I think it will be better if I leave you for an hour or two; I will come back in the evening, after having made all arrangements, and if you will be so gracious as to intrust yourself to my hands as far as the station, I honestly think you will find the journey made easier for you."

She tried to thank him, but she was not capable of doing more than incline her head, and with hushed steps—as if there were death in the house—Mr. Austin Ambrose went out of the room and down the path.

With a low, heartrending moan she threw herself upon the ground and, grasping her hair in both her white hands, hid her face—crushed with shame and the torture of a broken heart.

She lay thus prostrate in her anguish for some time, then she rose and staggered up-stairs. A sudden thought had smitten her.

Blair might come back—it might be that he still loved her! Was it not love that had tempted him to work her ruin? He might still love her passionately enough to come back and try to force her to remain with him. Or the woman—his wife!—she might hear what he had done, and in a fit of revenge drag her, Margaret, into a court to give evidence against him and convict him.

She must fly! She did not think of Austin Ambrose's offer of assistance; or if she had thought of it, she would not have remained for him to return.

To get away at once, to fly to some place where no one knew her, or could get to know about it; that was her instinctive desire.

She bathed her face until the fearful aching of the burning eyes was lessened, and tried to pack a small bag with the few articles that were absolutely necessary, taking care that nothing but that which had belonged to her went into the bag.

One by one she stripped off her rings—until she came to the wedding one—and placed them, together with the bracelets, chains and trinkets Blair had given her, on the dressing-table. The plain band of gold, inconsistent as it seemed, she allowed to remain on her finger. Then she changed her dress for the plain traveling costume in which she had been married.

In doing so, she saw the locket—Blair's first gift! With trembling hands she began to untie the ribbon, then she faltered. She had promised him that she would not part with this. Surely she could keep this to remind her of the time when she first tasted happiness, the time when she had thought him all that was true and noble.

The temptation to keep these two things that should seem as links between her and the past—so bitter, and yet so sweet!—proved too strong, and she let the locket fall into its place again over her heart.

The warm glow of evening was over the landscape by the time her simple preparations for flight were made, and drawing her veil on her pale and haggard face, she stole down the stairs.

In the narrow passage stood Mrs. Day.

"Are you going out, ma'am?" she said.

Margaret moistened her lips, and tried to answer carelessly:

"Yes, Mrs. Day."

"I don't think you ought to go far, ma'am," she said; "we are going to have a storm. Will you take an umbrella or your mackintosh?" and she looked toward the west, where a great bank of clouds seemed to rise from the horizon, as if about to swallow the sun in its inky mass.

"I will take my mackintosh," said Margaret.

Mrs. Day took it off the stand and folded it.

"I hope Mr. Stanley will be back before the storm breaks," she said. "You won't go far, ma'am?" she added, wistfully.

"No, not far," said poor Margaret.

She took the mackintosh on her arm and walked out and down the path. Then suddenly she heard the sound of a sob, and, looking back, saw Mrs. Day with her hand to her face.

Even in that hour of her supreme anguish, Margaret's gentle heart could beat in sympathy with another's sorrow, and she went back.

"What is the matter?" she asked hoarsely.

Mrs. Day forced a smile, but her eyes were full of tears.

"It's nothing—nothing much, ma'am," she said. "I beg your pardon for distressing you, but—but the boat hasn't come back yet!" and she looked beyond Margaret toward the sea.

"Oh, I hope it will be all right," Margaret faltered. "Do not be anxious, it will be back before the storm."

She could not trust herself to say any more, and turning, walked quickly away down the path.

She felt tired, but she reached the bottom by the aid of a handrail, and went toward the station. Then suddenly she remembered that she had forgotten her purse!

She had a few pounds in gold and a little silver in her pocket, but the purse, containing the bank-notes given her by the earl, she had left in a drawer at the cottage.

She stood, aghast and trembling. To go back she felt was impossible; and yet, what should she do? How could she accomplish her flight and hope to hide herself without money?

After a few minutes the dull roar of the rising tide seemed to exercise a fascination over her; and presently she felt no desire to reach the station, only a great longing to be alone by the side of the vast ocean, whose solemn, measured beat seemed like an awful voice calling to her.

She reached the foot of the rock, toward which the fisherman had pointed when he told her of the accident that had happened to the man and woman two years ago.

The tide had not touched it yet, and painfully she clutched its rugged surface up which a few hours ago she could have sprung easily.

At the top she sunk down exhausted, her face toward the sea, her eyes fixed on the bank of cloud, that like the giant in the Eastern fable, who escaped from the open bottle, had expanded and grown into a huge mass, which had ingulfed the sun, and threatened, as it seemed, to swallow the whole sky.

How long she lay there, hidden from the sight of the village, motionless and almost lifeless, she knew not; but suddenly she heard the lap, lap of water below her, and looking down, saw that the tide had crept round the rock, and was gradually but swiftly rising.

She regarded its sullen approach with heavy, listless eyes. All power of thought, much less appreciation of her peril, had deserted her. The sound of the waves, the dull booming of the wind fell upon her ear almost soothingly.

The day seemed to close and night to fall; the storm-clouds were right over her, and enveloped the earth as with a pall.

Suddenly the darkness was broken by a vivid flash of lightning, and the thunder roared and seemed to shake the rock on which she lay. At the same moment she felt her right foot grow cold, and looking down, saw that the tide had reached and covered it.

Then, for the first time, she awoke from her stupor, and realized that death and she were face to face.

With that instinct of self-preservation, that shrinking from the horror of death which comes to even the most miserable, she sprung to her feet and crawled to the highest point of the rock, and looked wildly round.

She had been cold the moment before, but now she seemed suffocating with an awful heat. With trembling hands she tore off her hat and waved it—Heaven knows with what desperate idea of attracting attention!—but the wind seized it and tore it from her hand. A moment afterward she felt the water lapping at her feet, and with an awful voice she called upon— Blair!

As if in answer to her appeal, the lightning shot out from the black sky and revealed her form as if carved in bronze on the top of the rock. The next moment she heard a man's voice, and a boat seemed to rise from the depths of the sea at her feet.

A lantern flashed in the darkness, and by its flickering gleam she saw a man rowing in the boat, and a woman crouching in the stern.

It was Day and his wife.

The woman screamed and pointed.

"There—there she is! For Heaven's sake be quick! Spring, Mrs. Stanley, spring! Oh——" and she moaned, "be quick!"

But, half mad with the insanity of mental and physical torture, Margaret drew back.

"No!" she cried. "I will not go! You shall not take me back to them!"

"Quick!" roared Day, with an oath, "or you will be too late! Here, hold the lantern, Jane! Hold it high!"

His wife seized the lantern and threw its rays upon Margaret's wild, white face. The boat, driven by the tide, struck against the rock, and Day, grappling it with his boat hook, sprung on to it.

For a moment or two there was a struggle between the weak and exhausted woman and the strong mariner. It lasted only a minute or two; then he lifted her bodily, and as gently as possible dropped her in the boat.

Springing in after her he seized the oars and began rowing to shore.

For a minute or two Margaret lay motionless, panting heavily, then she got to her knees and flung herself at Mrs. Day's feet, clinging to the woman's dress.

"Have pity on me," she moaned; "don't take me back! I will go anywhere else. I will do anything—but don't take me back to him! Oh, listen to me! You don't know how cruelly he has wronged me. I cannot go back. Stop!"— and she seized one of the oars. "You *shall* stop!"

Day stopped rowing, confused and bewildered.

"Is—is she mad?" he roared, hoarsely, at his wife.

Mrs. Day, white and trembling, threw her arms round Margaret and got her clear of the oars so that he might row.

"Oh, my dear, what is it? What has happened? Do you know that you have been nearly drowned? If I had not seen you and caught the boat just as it was coming to land—quick, James, quick!"

"No, no," sobbed Margaret. "Not back! I will not go back!" and she tried to free herself from the woman's grasp and throw herself into the sea.

"The poor lady's gone out of her mind!" said Day, pityingly. "Hold her, Jane, for Heaven's sake!"

"Yes, yes," panted Mrs. Day. "You row as hard as you can. I will hold her, poor dear. Oh, James, what can have happened? And she so happy a few hours agone!"

Day bent to the oars. Margaret had ceased to struggle, but Mrs. Day did not dare to relax her grasp. The boat forced its way nearer the shore.

Suddenly there rang out a sharp report, and a flash of fire darted from the beach.

Day uttered a cry and stopped rowing as if he had been shot, and Mrs. Day crouched still lower in the boat.

"It's the coastguard!" he said, bending forward and lowering his voice, though no one but the two women could have heard him. "It's the revenue men—*and I've got the things aboard!*"

There was silence for a moment, then Mrs. Day spoke.

"You must go to shore, James," she said, with the calmness of despair. "If we were alone— —"

She stopped and looked at the prostrate figure at the bottom of the boat.

"Go ashore!" he responded, with an oath. "What! and them waiting for me? I tell you I've got the stuff on board. It's ruin, blank ruin!"

Silence again. The wind howled, the boat tossed like a walnut shell upon the black billows.

"Oh, James, think of her—think of the poor demented creature!" sobbed Mrs. Day.

"Think of her! Yes, that be right enough; but I must think of thee, lass, and the bairns as well! I tell 'ee it means ruin! As well row straight into the jail's gates as go ashore to them wolves. No! I'm sorry, Jane; I'm main sorry; but I can't do it—for your sake."

There was that tone in the man's voice which quiets even the strongest and most determined of women, and his wife sank back and resigned herself.

The boat swung round, and Day, setting his teeth, pulled for the open sea.

"We'll never reach the schooner," panted Mrs. Day hoarsely.

"I'll risk it," he responded grimly. "Better trust ourselves to the open all night than run into the midst of the sharks there," and he nodded toward the shore.

"And this poor lady?"

He glanced at Margaret.

"Well, I'm but doing her bidding, beant I?" he retorted. "Didn't she pray and beseech me not to take her back? There, be easy! I've no breath for chattering, woman. Keep the lantern dark, and steer her straight out."

As he spoke there came another flash from the shore, and a rocket sped upward to the black sky.

Day uttered a grim exclamation of satisfaction.

"The fools!" he ground out; "they've showed me the way! The schooner lies due north of the customs, where that rocket started from! Keep her straight, lass, and we'll slip 'em yet. They won't risk their boat out—it's worse near the beach than it be here clear of the rocks. Sit still and fear nought!"

With the cool courage belonging to his class, he pulled steadily on, his wife grasping the tiller—for Margaret lay motionless and inert enough now—and peering into the darkness.

Suddenly she uttered a cry.

"The schooner, James! I saw her light for a moment!"

"Ay!" he responded coolly; "she's heard the gun and seen the rocket, and thinks we may be harking back. Show a glim of the lantern toward her, but keep it from the shore."

Cautiously Mrs. Day raised the lantern, with its light side toward the vessel, and an instant afterward a faint light appeared and then went out.

Day laughed cheerily.

"She sees us, lass. Keep up thee heart; it's all right. I've give them chaps the slip once more!"

"Yes, once more!" she responded, with a groan; "but some day or other——"

"Tut, tut! thee'st lost thee nerve, woman," he broke in, curtly.

She sank back with a heavy sigh and said no more.

Presently they saw the light again, this time close upon their bow, and in a few minutes the boat grated against the side of the schooner.

"Is that you, James?" inquired a voice.

Day answered in the affirmative.

"Yes; worse luck. Let the rope down the other side away from the shore; you can show a light then. I've got womenfolk aboard."

He pulled round to the larboard, and the lantern showed a rope ladder.

"Lend a hand here," he said, and he raised Margaret.

The man on board uttered an exclamation.

"Sakes a-mercy, James, what have you got there?" he demanded.

"It's my cousin," said Mrs. Day, before her husband could answer.

"Oh, and it's you, too, Mrs. Day, is it?" said the captain, in a tone of surprise. "Well, it's a rare night for ladies to be out in! And your cousin! Bless my soul, but she's swooned."

Between them they got Margaret on deck, and Mrs. Day had her carried down to the cabin, and then, asking for some brandy, locked the door on the men.

It was some time before Margaret recovered consciousness, and for some minutes she looked round with a listless indifference that was worse almost than the swoon from which she had roused.

At last she asked the inevitable question: "Where am I?"

"Here with me, dear lady," replied Mrs. Day, beginning to cry for the first time, "and Heaven be thanked that you are not lying dead in Appleford sands!"

Margaret drew a long sigh.

"I—I thought I had died," she moaned, and turning her face to the wall, said no more.

Mrs. Day sat down beside her, praying that she might sleep, for she knew that it was her only chance; and after a time Margaret fell into that stupor of exhaustion which is the nearest approach to nature's great restorer.

Presently there came a knock at the door, and opening it, Mrs. Day found her husband outside.

"How is she?" he asked.

"Better, poor soul!" she replied.

"Well," he said, "you'd better come on deck. The captain's upset and has been asking me questions about 'un."

"And what did you say?" she demanded anxiously.

"Well," he retorted, with a grim smile, "seeing as you've started the game, I thought as how you'd better continue it, so I left 'em to you."

She stood for a moment thinking deeply, then followed him on deck.

The schooner was scudding along at a pace which put all danger from pursuit out of the question; but the captain, who was leaning against the bulwarks smoking a pipe, did not look at all comfortable or amiable.

"Well, Mrs. Day," he began at once, "what's this yarn about your cousin? Sakes alive! I'm fond of your sex enough, but I like 'em best on shore. Who is she, and what is she doing out in the boat?"

"She's my cousin, Captain Daniel," said Mrs. Day promptly, "and she's in trouble. I don't know as I ought to tell you the story, but seeing that we brought her on board— —"

"Just so, and that's what I object to," he said gruffly. "It's work enough to take the trade quiet and snug, as it is, but with a woman aboard that nobody knows anything about— —" he puffed at his pipe significantly.

"You can trust her," said Mrs. Day; "there's no fear of her splitting, Captain Daniel."

"Oh, you think she'll die?" he said, looking mightily relieved.

"No, no! But there are reasons why she should keep her own counsel, though she is a woman. You wait until morning, captain, and you'll see whether she's to be trusted or not."

She spoke with such a confident air that he relaxed a little.

"Well, you and yours are in the same boat, remember, Mrs. Day, and if harm comes to us, your James will share it! Don't forget that."

"I do not forget it, captain," she responded.

"Very well," he said. "I'll leave it to you. Make the poor soul as comfortable as possible. The Rose of Devon wasn't chartered to carry lady passengers, but we'll do the best we can. You'll find some extra bedclothes, and that like, in my cabin; and I'll see to the supper by the time you're ready. As to liquor"—he grinned—"well, I dare say we can find a glass or two of that!"

"I dare say!" said Mrs. Day with an answering smile, and she hurried back to the cabin and to Margaret.

CHAPTER XVII

Blair rode on toward Ilfracombe, his cigar between his lips, his handsome face wearing its best and brightest look. He was, as he would have expressed it, as happy as a sandboy; and the only thing that could have increased his happiness would have been to have had Margaret with him.

It would be an exaggeration to say that he thought of nothing else but her as he rode along; but it is true that she was present in his thoughts nearly all the time, and that as he looked seaward, where the green water lay like an opal in the sun, or inland, where the yellow cornfields glittered like gold across the blue sky, he thought how much she would have admired it, and how her artist soul would revel in its beauty.

After riding some time he saw a couple of men lying by the roadside. They were fishermen from Appleford, who had, perhaps, been to Ilfracombe, and were resting.

"I'm right for Ilfracombe, I suppose?" said Blair.

The men touched their hats.

"Yes, sir, you're right," said one; "but you have come a long way round. You should have cut across the cliff by the narrow lane through Lee."

"Eh?" said Blair, standing in his stirrups and looking about him.

The man got up, and shading his eyes, pointed to the place indicated.

"That's the way; it's but a bit of a lane, but it saves a mile or more."

"Thanks!" said Blair. "I'll remember it, and come back that way."

As he spoke, a man, who had been climbing the hill behind Blair and the two fishermen, came suddenly, as it were, upon them. He stopped short, and in an adept fashion sunk easily to the ground, where he lay and listened, within almost touch of them, and yet unseen.

"Yes, I understand," said Blair; "nice day, isn't it. You fellows have a cigar?"

A fisherman may be a teetotaler, but he always smokes.

Blair took out his cigar case; there were just two cigars left, and he gave them to the men.

"Bean't we robbing you, sir?" said one of the men, rather shyly, offering the case back; but Blair pushed it toward them.

"Plenty more in 'Combe," he said, with a smile, "and this will last me some time."

Then he rode on, having made, by a few pleasant words and two cigars, two friends who would have risked their lives on his behalf.

He reached 'Combe at last, the colt having settled down to a steady pace, and putting him up at the hotel stables, he went into the town to buy Margaret's things, even before he had his lunch.

There was a very good artist's colorman, and he displayed a selection of portable easels, and canvases, and colors which bewildered Blair.

"Look here," he said, at last; "you know the sort of things a lady wants, don't you know. Just put up as much as I can carry on horseback, and send the rest to this address."

This being the kind of order a shopkeeper's soul delighteth in, the man beamed, and soon had a very bulky looking heap collected in the middle of the shop.

"All right," said Blair; "sure you have got everything?"

The man, after vainly endeavoring to think of some other useless articles, said rather grudgingly, "Yes."

"Very well then. What's the damage? I'll put the paint boxes in my pockets, and I can tie a small parcel of the other things to the saddle, and the rest you can send on; but mind, I want them sent at once! You people down here are rather slow sometimes. I can't have this lady kept waiting."

He gave the address, paid the bill, which did not in the least astonish him, though our friend had charged about fifty per cent. above his usual prices—and afterwards almost wept because he hadn't stuck on double!— and then went to the hotel and had his lunch.

He made a very hearty meal, for Blair, in love or trouble, being as strong as a lion and always on the move, was a capital trencherman, and then went over to look at the town.

He was in the humor to be pleased with anything, and the place, with its picturesque coast scenery and general air of brisk cheerfulness, just suited him.

"I'll bring Madge here, by George!" he said to himself. "She'll be delighted with it."

To give her some idea of the place he bought a dozen or two photographs and stuffed them in his pockets; then he saw a trinket cleverly made of the tiniest shells set in silver, and he bought that.

Some little time he spent sitting on a seat on the walk round the Capstan Hill, and would have stayed longer, but suddenly there came round the corner a figure he knew.

It was that of Colonel Floyd. Blair, forgetting that he was supposed to be on the Continent, was just jumping up to greet him with a hearty "Hallo, old man!" when he remembered himself, and catching up a newspaper, got behind it. The colonel lounged past in his languid, *nil admirari* fashion, and passed out of sight.

Blair let the paper fall, and for the first time that morning his face grew clouded.

"Confound all this mystery and concealment!" he muttered, impatiently. "By George! I'll have no more of it! I hate this skulking about like a bank-clerk who has bolted with the till and is dodging the detectives. I'll have no more of it! I'll take Madge to the earl next week, and make a clean breast of it. Even he can't be such a savage as not to melt at that smile of hers."

The resolution brightened him, as all good resolutions do, and considering that the colt had had rest enough, he went back to the hotel, and ordered him to be brought round.

The colt was in excellent spirits, and Blair rode along, humming a song and thinking of Margaret—and his dinner.

The color tubes rattled in his pockets, and his bulging pockets banged against his side, but he didn't mind in the least; he was doing something for his Madge.

By this time—he had not hurried going, and had been a good spell in the pretty town—the sun was setting, and the black mass of cloud was rising portentously.

"We shall get wet jackets, my friend," he said to the colt, and he put him to a quicker pace.

Mindful of the short cut which the men had pointed out in the morning, he rode up the rather steep hill, and without any difficulty found the lane.

It was, as they had said, a narrow lane, between two high banks. There was a tree here and there, and every now and then a gate opening into the fields on either side; it was steep, too, and not very easy, and Blair was obliged to go slowly.

"Seems to me," he said to the colt, "that we could move faster going across the downs, my friend. Never mind, it's a long lane that has no turning! Jove, here it comes!" he broke off, as a flash of lightning and a clap of thunder burst forth.

"Steady, old man, you are master, you know; I'm a stranger."

The rain dropped suddenly, in a sheet, as it seemed, and Blair stopped to turn up his coat collar, and see that Madge's tools were protected by the lappets of his pockets. He had very little objection to getting wet himself, but he meant to carry home the day's spoil to her uninjured, if he could manage it.

At the moment he was fumbling with the reins, held loosely in his hand, a shout, a yell was heard behind him.

It was man's voice, presumably; but it was so unearthly, so discordant, that even Blair started. As for the colt, he gave one side-way jump, then started off helter-skelter, mad with fright.

"Steady, old man!" said Blair, tightening the rein. "It was a rum noise, but don't lose your head. Steady!" and he laughed.

But the laugh died on his lips, for, while the horse was still on the bolt, he saw one of the field gates lying right across the narrow road.

Now, at any time, this is a sight which is calculated to make a horseman look and feel serious; because however slowly the horse may be going, if he is not pulled up in time before he reaches the prostrate gate, his legs will get entangled in the bars, and he must inevitably fall. But when a horse is bolting, the situation becomes dangerous and deadly.

To pull him up in time Blair saw would be impossible, even for him. He looked swiftly at the banks on either side, with the idea of turning him up them, but they were too high. There was only one thing to do, and that was to drop off as easily as possible as the horse fell.

A moment more and the catastrophe came. The runaway horse's fore-feet struck between the top bars, his off hind leg caught the lower one, and with a crash and a startled shake of the head, the colt came down all of a heap.

Blair had been ready a moment before, and as the horse fell he managed to get out of the stirrups and roll out of the saddle.

It was nicely and cleanly done, as only a steeplechaser could have done it, and he was on his legs and bending over the horse almost the next instant.

Plunging and kicking, the colt tried to extricate himself from the awful trap, and Blair had coaxed him on his legs, and was leading him out when he heard a strange noise behind him, and saw a tall form standing on the bank above his head.

At that instant, for the first time the thought of foul play occurred to him. Grasping the bridle with one hand and his whip with the other, he turned and looked up.

The sky was black as night, but a flash of lightning clove the heavens just then, and by its lurid light he saw the face of Jem Pyke. He thought that he was dreaming. It seemed too incredible. When last he had seen the man it had been at Leyton, where Pyke lived. How could he possibly be here?

He gazed up at him for a second or two, which seemed an age; then he opened his lips to speak, but the thunder roared and blotted out his voice.

With a wild laugh the man glowered down upon him motionless as Blair himself, then, with a spring, threw himself upon him.

Blair squared his shoulders to meet the shock, but Pyke, though lean, was tall, and his long form, aided by the impetus of his leap, bore Blair to the ground.

There was a terrible struggle, at which the frightened horse stood looking as if it were a horrified human being; then Pyke got his fingers round Blair's throat, and, pressing against it, shook him heavily.

"At last!" he shouted, between a hiss and a growl. "At last, mister! I've waited a long time, but it's my turn now, I think. You fine-tongued gentleman! I'll—I'll kill you. You thought I'd forgotten you, eh? You thought I was going to let you go scot free, did you? Ah! you'll know me better when I've done with you."

Blair struggled as hard as he could, but the man's long, bony fingers were like steel, and, with a shrug of his shoulders, he felt that his time had come. But even at that moment the old spirit came to the front, and, though he could not speak, he smiled up at the livid face of his assailant.

The smile seemed to madden the man.

"What! you grin, do ye?" he said, between his teeth. "I'll teach you! I'll humble you!" Then an idea seemed to strike him, and, kneeling on Blair's chest, he said, "But I'll give you a chance, my lord, even now, curse me if I don't. Say, 'I beg your pardon,' and I'll let you go."

With the intention of giving Blair an opportunity for the apology, his grasp slackened slightly.

It was a small opening, but Blair seized it.

With a tremendous effort he writhed himself free, and grasping Pyke by the forearm, raised himself to his feet, and forced Pyke to his knees.

"You miserable hound!" he said, with his short, curt laugh. "Beg your pardon, you mad fool! I'll teach you to set traps for a good horse, that's worth ten of you! You put the gate there, did you? Look here, I'll make you carry it back to its place before I've done with you! Ah, and beg my pardon, too, into the bargain!" and with a tremendous force he flung the man backward.

Pyke was on his feet instantly, and the two men confronted each other, not as they had done on Leyton Green, for then Blair's face wore a smile, and there was joy and contentment in his heart, at the prospect of a fair fight, but now he knew that it would be as foul as his opponent could make it.

The sky grew blacker; the rain pelted down upon them, but neither of them noticed the weather.

With a bound they sprung at each other, dealing heavy blows, and taking them as if they were feather-down. The result was a foregone one. Blair had been riding, the man had been walking, and was weakened by passion. His blows grew lighter and slower, his breath came in short, deep gasps; Blair knew that another minute would make him the victor, and, already relenting, he was about to call to Pyke and offer him quarter, when the man, stepping back, pointed beyond Blair, and shouted:

"Look! the lady!"

Blair turned. There was only one lady that could rush to his mind, and that was Margaret, and he thought, in the flash of the moment, that she had come to meet him. He turned, and Pyke caught up a heavy stick that lay where he had dropped it at his first spring, and struck Blair an awful blow on the back of the head.

Without a cry he went down face foremost, his arms outstretched, and lay like a figure carved in stone.

Pyke stood over him, looking down at him with livid face and panting breath.

There was a pause in the storm at that moment, as if the wind and the rain had stopped to look on; then the elements resumed their warfare, and a flash of lightning played over the prostrate man's head.

Pyke went down on his knees, and with trembling hands turned the motionless form on its face, and peered at it.

Then he started back with an oath.

"I've done for him!" he muttered, hoarsely, and the wind seemed to echo mockingly: "Done for him." "He's as dead as a herring! Curse him, it serves him right!" he ground out, and he raised his foot, but withheld the kick as a thought—the thought of self-preservation—came to him. "Looks ugly!" he muttered, "cursed ugly. There's more trouble in this than I thought on!"

He looked up and down the lane and across the hedge with the keen, fearful face of a man who already hears the pursuers; then buttoning his wet coat round him, and giving a parting glance at the still form, began to run—like Cain.

He went in the direction of Lee, and was so absorbed in the one idea of flight, that a dark object which stood beside the hedge just before him made him spring aside, and almost shout with fear.

But it was only the colt, which, too frightened by the storm, and disheartened by the rain, was cowering under the lee of the hedge.

Pyke was hurrying by it, when he pulled up suddenly, and struck his leg as if welcoming an inspiration.

"Dang it!" he cried, exultingly, "that's the game. Woa, horse, woa, horse," and he crept slowly up to the colt.

The animal was far too cowed to attempt flight, and Pyke got hold of the bridle easily. But he did not mount. Instead, he unfastened one stirrup and struck the colt with it. The horse, maddened by fear, started and shook, then tore down the lane at breakneck pace.

Pyke waited a moment listening to the clatter of its hoofs mingling with the rain and the thunder, then quickly retracing his steps returned to Blair.

He still lay where his assailant had left him. Pyke knelt down and thrust one unresisting foot into the stirrup, then he dragged the body for a few yards along the wet road and left it lying on its back, leaped over the hedge and fled. But once more he came back, and lifting the gate replaced it on its hinges and fastened it.

CHAPTER XVIII

Mr. Austin Ambrose was spending an extremely unpleasant evening. It sounds as if it would be a very nice thing to play with one's fellow creatures as if they were puppets—to pull the wires which govern their actions, and to make them dance to one's piping; but the wire-puller has sometimes a very uncomfortable time of it.

Mr. Austin Ambrose had up to the present found his puppets quite docile and obedient to the pulling of the wires. He had got Lord Blair and Margaret secretly married, he had hidden them away at Appleford; his puppet Lottie had played her part really quite admirably, and Margaret was fully convinced that she had been betrayed and ruined by the man she loved.

So far, so well; but still Mr. Austin Ambrose was uncomfortable. He had left Margaret to herself, knowing that if so left she would be more likely to carry out his desire and fly, than if he remained with her.

But he did not mean to lose sight of her; it was his intention to travel by the same train if possible, and to track her, unseen himself, to her place of refuge.

So he went and placed himself on the road leading to the station, and lighting a cigarette, waited as patiently as he could.

Hour passed after hour, and still she did not come. Then the clouds rose, and the sky grew murky, and presently the storm broke.

"Confound women!" he muttered, vainly trying to light the last of his cigarettes; "you can never count upon them. I would have sworn that she would have made for the station; and yet she hasn't. She's waiting to see Blair, after all. Well, I'll go and see. There'll be a scene presently, if she remains, and I hate a scene!"

With his coat-collar turned up he climbed to the cottage and knocked.

There was no answer; and after waiting and knocking again, he opened the door.

To his amazement, the cottage seemed deserted. He was calling Mrs. Day impatiently, when a woman came running with her apron over her head from the neighboring cottage.

"Mrs. Day's out, sir. She's gone down to the beach," she said in answer to his inquiries, "and I've got the children with me. It's lonely for 'em here, and such a storm raging."

"But—but Mrs. Stanley?" he said quickly; "she's in, is she not?"

The woman stared at him.

"Mrs. Stanley, sir—the lady, sir? Oh, no; she went out hours ago."

"Nonsense!" he said roughly. "I beg your pardon; I mean that it is impossible that she should be out in this storm."

"Yes, but she is, sir. I saw her go down the path in the afternoon with her mackintosh on her arm. I think she went to meet her good gentleman."

Austin Ambrose started, and his face flushed.

If she had, and they had met before—well, before something that he hoped had happened—all his plans, all his deeply and skillfully laid plots would be smashed and pulverized.

He turned his back to the woman, that she might not see his face.

"I—I think she must be in the house still," he said, with a sudden hope; "she may have come back, you know."

"She may, but I don't think she could without my seeing her. Howsomever, it's easy to find out." And she lit a candle and went up the stairs, calling respectfully, "Mrs. Stanley, are you in, ma'am?" while Austin Ambrose listened intently.

In a minute or two she came down.

"No, sir, she's not in the house. I'm afraid the poor lady's in the storm; leastways, unless she's taken shelter."

Austin Ambrose caught up his hat.

"If she should come in before I return," he said, hurriedly, "ask her to wait till I see her and speak with her. Do you hear? Do not let her go. You understand?"

The woman, frightened by his pallor and sternness, dropped a courtesy, and he rushed out and down the path.

If she had gone down the road to Ilfracombe, and had met Blair! His heart almost ceased beating at the thought. She would meet Blair, and, he knew too well, frustrate the elaborate plot, and ruin the plotter.

He gained the entrance of the road to 'Combe; two or three men were standing under the shelter of a shed, with their tools beside them.

"Have you been working here—in the fields?" he inquired.

"Yes, master, and we be drenched through, we be!" said one.

"Have you seen a lady—a lady with a veil—come this way—to Ilfracombe, I mean?" he said, trying to steady his voice. "I am afraid she has got caught in the storm."

The men shook their heads.

"No," said he who had spoken first; "no one has been along this road 'cepting the gentleman who rode Farmer James' colt this morning."

"I know—I mean I don't know," said Austin Ambrose, catching himself up. "Are you sure?"

"Sure and sartain!" said another man. "We've been working in sight o' the road all day, and the lady couldn't a passed without our seeing her. Have you got a bit of 'bacca, your honor?"

He tossed them a shilling, and hurried back. It was just possible that she may have gone to the station by another road than that which he had watched. Fighting his way against the wind and rain, he reached the station.

From one and another of the porters he inquired if she had been seen, and the answer was the same. No lady answering to Madge's description had reached the station. Half wild with impatience and fear—not for her, by any means, certainly not; but for himself!—he returned to the beach.

As he did so he saw a gang of fishermen and sailors standing under the lee of a rock, and peering out to sea.

They did not hear him approach, and, in his noiseless fashion, he got close up to them and within hearing unnoticed.

"No boat could put out from the beach, man," said the old man with whom Margaret had spoken that morning. "We've tried it with the best of them, the Lass and the Speedwell, and it ain't no manner o' use. 'Sides, where's the good? the tide have swept over the rock an hour agone!"

"And you're sure you seed her?" asked a man.

"Do 'ee think I've gone silly all in a moment?" retorted the old fellow, pettishly. "I tell 'ee, I seed her on the top, half a-sitting and half a-lying. I did think as I'd get up and go to her, but I'd warned her in the morning, this very blessed morning; and the missus come and called me in to tea, and— and bla'-me if I didn't forget her."

"Oh, she's lost! She's drownded, as sure as a gun! Well, sakes a mercy, but it's a pity."

"We've all got to die," remarked a man philosophically; "and most on us dies by drownding; but then we're used to it, which makes all the difference."

Austin Ambrose pushed his way into their midst, startling them not a little.

"Of whom are you talking?" he demanded, and his voice sounded harsh and stern.

The old man touched his forehead and puffed at his pipe.

"It's the poor young lady up at Mrs. Day's, your honor," he said; "she've been and got washed off the Long Rock——"

Austin Ambrose put his hand up with a strange gesture, as if to stop him, and his face grew livid.

"What?" he cried hoarsely. "You say—oh, impossible!"

The old man shook his head.

"It's the possiblest thing as can be," he said grimly. "Seed her there myself, and I thought she'd gone to look at the tide. I never thought as she'd stop there after the warning I give her. I told her about the lady and gentleman as was lost there two year agone," he added to the others.

Austin Ambrose rushed out to the rocks and stared before him like a man dazed. Then he sprung to his feet.

"I'll give any man twenty pounds who will launch a boat and search for her," he cried hoarsely.

There was a profound silence. Then the old fisherman said grimly:

"Twenty pun ain't much for a man's life, your honor."

"I will give fifty—a hundred!" he cried desperately.

"Bless your honor's heart," said the old man slowly, "no boat could live in this—that is, near the beach—it might in the open! It's to be hoped it will, for Day's out," he said significantly. "No, your honor, a thousand pounds wouldn't tempt us; besides, it's too late! too late! The poor lady is drifting out to the sands, and the last's been seen of her or ever will be seen on this earth!"

Austin Ambrose uttered a cry, an awful cry. They who heard it thought that it was that of sorrowing friend or relative; but the cry was one of pity for himself and all his shattered hopes. After all his cleverness, his deep-laid schemes and restless toil, he had been foiled—and by the woman he had fooled and deceived!

It was maddening. And indeed as he reeled away from the group he looked like a man demented.

Suddenly he heard a shout and staggered back.

A man came running toward them with something in his hand. He held the wet and dripping articles on high and surveyed his companions gravely.

"The old 'un's right!" he said slowly. "Here be the poor lady's cape and hat!"

Austin Ambrose tore them from the man's hand.

"Are you sure?" he gasped.

"Yes," came a grave chorus. "We've see'd her wear 'em, time and again. They're hers, and she's lost, poor soul!"

Austin Ambrose walked away with the hat and cape in his hands.

At the back of the beach, on the quay, was a small inn, through whose red curtains the light shone cheerily. He pushed open the door and entered with unsteady gait. The little place was full of sailors and fishermen, all talking about the sad event, and recalling the similar fatality of two years ago. As he entered they became suddenly silent.

"Give me some brandy!" he said, hoarsely.

The landlady mixed him a glass of hot brandy-and-water, and he took it in both hands and drank it; then he sank on to a seat, and with tightly compressed lips stared at the door.

For the time he was unconscious of the presence of the others, deaf to their voices, which arose again in a hushed tone.

"It's the awfulest night," said one, "the awfulest! The poor gentleman's out in it, too! Farmer James have gone down the road to look for him. He's afeard the colt will be skeared by the lightning."

"Ah," said another; "not come back yet, poor gentleman? What a terrible story it will be to tell him. They beant long been mated, have they?"

"Hush!" said a warning whisper, and the speaker nodded toward the crouching figure. "Her brother, most like," he added, in a whisper. "He's took all aback, poor fellow."

There was silence again, then they commenced to talk once more, and still Austin Ambrose sat still and motionless.

Suddenly the door was flung open, and a short, active-looking man dashed in.

"Why, Farmer James!" cried one of two, "what's amiss, man?"

"Give me time!" panted the farmer. "It's a night o' bad news, boys! The colt's come home—without him!"

The men sprung to their feet, and looked at the speaker aghast.

"Without the gentleman, farmer?"

"Ay," he said solemnly, wiping the perspiration from his face. "I met the colt tearing down the road to the stable with the saddle empty. A lantern, missis, quick. Who'll lend a hand, boys?"

One and all turned out and proceeded at something between a trot and a run into the road.

At a little distance the colt stood, wet and trembling, held by a boy. They paused a moment to stare at it and then passed on.

Austin Ambrose, uninvited by them, joined the group and ran with them.

They stopped a moment where the two roads joined, the one Blair had taken in the morning, the other he was returning by in the evening.

"Let's divide," said a man; but the farmer stooped down and examined the road.

"No occasion," he said; "here's the colt's hoof-marks. This is the road she come!"

Hurrying along, they climbed the narrow lane, and the foremost, a young lad carrying the lantern, stopped with a cry at the motionless form lying in the road.

There was a hush as the men crowded round. The farmer knelt down and examined it for a moment, then he looked up.

"I'm afeared he's dead," he said gravely.

"Is—is it foul play, do 'ee think, Farmer James?" inquired one of the men.

"Foul play!" the words ran round. "Why do 'ee say that?"

The man, a small, sharp-eyed old fellow, pointed to the road.

"Looks as if there'd been a struggle," he said. "But no matter now. Take that gate off its hinges, lads, and lay him on it. We'll carry him down to the Holme."

The gate was torn off its hinges—how little they guessed that it was not for the first time that night!—and some coats laid upon it; then they stooped to raise poor Blair.

As they did so, Austin Ambrose slid forward.

At the sound of the words "foul play," he had aroused. All was lost; Margaret dead, Blair dead; all his toil and ingenuity thrown away. But if these rustics were suspicious it was time to think of his own safety.

"Let me see!" he said, in a low voice. "He—he is a friend of mine. Who said 'foul play?' If I thought so—but, no! Look!" and he pointed to the stirrup through which the foot was thrust. "My poor friend was thrown from the saddle; the mare bolted and must have dragged him. His foot is still in the stirrup."

"That's true," said one. "Ah! if that stirrup leather had slipped out sooner——"

Almost in silence they carried him down to the small farm called the Holme; and the good-hearted people roused from their beds did their best for him.

In a short time he was undressed and put to bed.

Austin Ambrose, calm and self-possessed, but very sorrowful, showed the affliction of a brother.

"I am afraid it is all over!" he said, as they gathered round the bed and looked at the handsome face and stalwart form, which many of them had seen depart in the morning so full of life and happiness.

After a time the doctor came. He was an old man, who had worn himself out in the hard practice of a wild country-side. Accidents were his daily experience, and he fell to work in the cool, business-like way acquired by custom.

White and breathless, Austin Ambrose, who had been permitted to remain during the examination, waited for the verdict. It came at last.

"He's not dead," said the old doctor, gravely, "and that's about all that can be said. It was a terrible blow!"

Austin Ambrose's lips contracted, and his eyes sought the old man's weather-beaten face keenly.

"A blow, doctor?" he said, gravely.

"Yes," was the reply; "he was struck on the back of the head, sir."

Austin Ambrose uttered an exclamation.

"Oh, impossible, doctor!" he said. "Who should do such a thing? My poor friend had not an enemy in the world."

"Plunder?" said the old man, questioningly.

Austin Ambrose shook his head.

"His purse, watch, jewelry, even the things he purchased at Ilfracombe, are untouched. Besides, we found him lying, his foot still entangled in the stirrup, as you have heard."

"Humph!" said the doctor, still at work with restoratives. "Well, he must have fallen on the back of his head; but"—he looked puzzled and frowned thoughtfully—"but it's very strange. If I hadn't known what you have just told me, I should say that he had been struck, and that if he should die, the coroner's verdict would have to be 'Willful murder!'"

Austin Ambrose's lips twitched, but he shook his head and sighed.

"Thank Heaven that I have no such suspicion—it would be too dreadful! No, my poor friend was thrown and dragged by the frightened horse. It is, alas! too common an accident."

"Yes, yes, just so," said the doctor. "It's a pity, a thousand pities, for he is a splendid fellow," and he looked with sad admiration on the stalwart form. "What is his name?"

Austin Ambrose hesitated a moment.

"His name is Stanley. He is a very dear friend of mine," he added, "and only recently married."

The old doctor started.

"You don't mean to say that he's the husband of the unfortunate young lady who was drowned off Long Rock this morning?"

Austin Ambrose nodded, the doctor sighed.

"Well, sir, I'll do my best to bring him back to life; but it will be cruel kindness, I fear, under the circumstances. Poor young fellow! But if he should die he will be spared the misery awaiting him!"

"You—you think there is no hope of her escape?" faltered Austin.

The doctor shook his head.

"There may be a faint hope for him," he said, pointing to the bed. "But for her there is none, none whatever. She was seen on the rocks; they tell me that her cape and hat have been found washed ashore. No; if he should die they will not be long apart. But you look worn out, sir, you had better get some rest."

Austin Ambrose shook his head.

"I will not go until——" and he stopped significantly.

For the remainder of the night they watched beside the still form. Life was in yet, beating faintly, like a flickering lamp; but the dawn came, and Blair still remained hovering between the shores of the River of Death.

The morning passed. The whole village was in a state of excitement over the two accidents; that they should have happened on the same day, and to man and wife, seemed phenomenal, and every one of the inns drove a roaring trade with the crowds of excited men.

There was the chance, too, of another fatality, for the Days' boat had disappeared, and it was rumored that she had gone down in the storm.

Toward evening, however, the crowd collected on the beach, for the boat had been sighted.

Austin Ambrose had left Blair for a short rest, but he could neither sleep nor remain quiet, and his restless feet had dragged him to Appleford.

He stood just on the edge of the crowd watching the boat with lackluster eyes that shone dully in his pallid face.

There was a rush and a cheer as the boat came in, and two or three men ran out into the water—it was smiling calmly enough now—to haul her in, but as her keel touched the beach, Day held up his hand.

"Don't cheer, lads," he said, gravely; "I've bad news."

"Ay, ay, we can guess, James," said a voice, "you've seen the poor lady!"

Day started and glanced at his wife, who sat in the stern, her shawl to her eyes.

"Tell 'em, you," he said, in a whisper.

She raised her head.

"Yes," she said, with a sob, "I've seen the poor lady. We saw her on the rocks, almost at the last moment."

"And you couldn't get near?" said a man.

She looked round.

"Do you think we'd be here without her if there'd been half a chance?" she said, reproachfully.

"Ay, ay!" said the old boatswain. "Well, well, that settles it, and that's some'at of a comfort! The poor soul's gone! Don't 'ee cry, missis!" he added as he helped Mrs. Day out of the boat.

It so happened that as she stepped on the beach she was near Austin Ambrose.

He had been listening in a kind of stupor, his eyes wandering from Mrs. Day's face to her husband's.

At the moment of her landing he was so near that her arm touched his.

As it did so his eyes fell upon the shawl which she had been pressing to her eyes.

The sun was shining full on it, and in the dull vague fashion peculiar to his frame of mind his eye was following the pattern.

Suddenly he started, and a light shone in his eyes.

"Let me help you," he said, and gently but firmly he laid his hand upon her arm covered by the shawl.

And, as he did so, the light gleamed still more brightly in his face, for he discovered that the shawl with which she had been wiping away her tears—*was dry!*

CHAPTER XIX

Mr. Austin Ambrose walked back to Lee with a step that had regained its usual elasticity, and with hope again beaming in his eyes.

Few men would have been sharp enough to notice, in the midst of such excitement, so trivial a fact that Mrs. Day's shawl was dry; but Mr. Austin Ambrose was not an ordinary man, and in an instant his acute brain was hard at work.

If Mrs. Day had been out in the boat all night, as she would have them believe, then her shawl would have been still wet; but as it was dry, then Mrs. Day must have been somewhere to dry it, and Austin Ambrose felt, with that kind of conviction which is more a matter of faith than reason, that Margaret had been with her.

He felt as certain as that he was walking along the road that the Days had rescued Margaret from the rock, and had taken her to some place of safety, and that for some reason, best known to themselves, the Days had agreed to conceal the fact, and lead the public to believe that Margaret had perished.

"That woman wasn't crying," he muttered to himself as he walked along; "her eyes were as dry as the shawl! No; Margaret is in hiding somewhere, and those Days know where. Now, if Blair will only kindly pull round, I am all right."

When in the Holme, he learned that "Mr. Stanley" was still unconscious, and that there had been no change in his condition.

"Get some one from London," he said to the old doctor, with an energy which surprised him. "Get the best man—the very best: we *must* save him!"

"You can send for Sir Astley," said the doctor, quietly; "but if we send for the whole college of physicians, they can do no more than we are doing. It is concussion of the brain, and the poor fellow's magnificent constitution will fight for him far more effectually than we can. He shall have every attention, trust me."

Austin Ambrose acquiesced. Sir Astley might have seen Blair, and recognize him, and, in any case, might talk about the affair when he got back to London, and cause inquiries to be made.

So the days wore on. No man could have received more attention than Blair got at the hands of the old doctor, whose interest in the case increased as it became more critical.

Austin Ambrose, too, watched over him, as the people of the house declared, "like a brother!"

The case still puzzled the doctor, and he went one day and looked at the spot where Blair had been found; but the feet of the people who had searched for him had blotted out the impression of the struggle between Pyke and Blair, and there was no trace left of the murderous assault.

Chance had worked hard in Austin Ambrose's behalf, and if Blair should only recover, all might yet go well with his plans.

On the eighth day, toward evening, the doctor, who had been bending over the bed with his fingers on Blair's pulse, looked up suddenly, and motioned to the nurse and Austin Ambrose.

"Shut out the light," he said, in a low voice.

They drew the window curtains, and Austin Ambrose stepped up on tiptoe.

"Is—is he coming to?" he asked breathlessly.

The doctor nodded.

"I think so. Let no one speak to him but me."

They waited, and presently Blair opened his eyes and looked round with a dazed inquiry.

"Margaret!" he said.

The doctor held up his hand warningly to the others.

"Madge! Where are you?" he said again, almost inaudibly.

"Your wife cannot come to you at present," replied the doctor quietly. "Do not speak just yet."

"Where am I? Have I been ill?" inquired Blair, knitting his brows, as if trying to remember. "Ah, yes; the horse! Is the horse all right?"

"The horse is all right," said the doctor. "I will tell you all about it after you have had a good sleep. You have been very ill, and will be worse if you do not sleep."

"All right," he said, with a sigh. "Madge, my wife, is asleep, I suppose? Have I been ill long? Don't wake her or distress her; I shall be all right! Stop!" he exclaimed; "the paints and things, they are in my pockets, and the easel will be sent on to-day. Give them to her! I hope they haven't come to harm!"

"They are all safe," said the doctor soothingly.

"I'm glad," said Blair, with another sigh; "and the horse is all right? Well, it's not so bad! I thought he had settled me, confound him!"

The doctor thought he referred to the colt, but Austin Ambrose's cheeks paled.

He stepped forward noiselessly.

"I am here, Blair," he murmured softly. "Take the doctor's advice, and don't talk yet."

"You, Austin, old fellow!" exclaimed Blair, trying to hold out his hand. "Why, how did you hear of it? To come the same night. That's kind. But how did you get here? and Madge—have you seen Madge? Don't let her be frightened, Austin, I shall be up in an hour or two. Tell her—no, don't tell her anything; leave it to me."

"Very well," said Austin; "and now get some sleep, old fellow. I shan't say another word."

Blair closed his eyes, and presently the doctor looked up and nodded.

"He is asleep, and is saved, please Heaven!" he said in a grave voice.

All that Austin Ambrose had accomplished was as nothing to the task that loomed before him.

The time must come when Blair would ask for Margaret, and insist upon seeing her.

Many men would have shrunk from such an ordeal, but Austin Ambrose was not the man to allow sentiment, as he would have called it, to interpose between him and a long cherished design; so that, when, on awakening from the deep sleep which saved his life, Blair asked: "Where is Margaret?" Austin Ambrose was prepared.

"Blair," he said, laying his hand upon the sick man's, "are you strong enough to hear what I have to tell you? I trust so, for I cannot keep it from you."

"Keep it from me! What is it?" demanded Blair, trying to raise himself. "Is it anything to do with Madge? No, it can't be, of course. But why doesn't she come? Ah, I see—give me a minute, Austin," and he turned his head away. "My accident has frightened her, and she is ill."

"Yes, she is ill!" said Austin Ambrose, watching him closely. "Blair, for Heaven's sake, be brave, be calm."

"What is it? You haven't told me all," he exclaimed. "Don't turn your face away; tell me. Anything is better than suspense. Let me go to her— bring her to me. She can't be so ill— —" he paused, breathlessly.

Austin Ambrose laid his hand upon his shoulder.

"Blair, dear, dear Blair," he murmured; "she cannot come to you; you cannot go to her. She has been very ill—Blair, your wife is dead!"

The sick man looked at him and laughed.

"That's a pretty kind of joke to play upon a man lying on his back," he said. "Go and fetch her, and we'll laugh at it together—perhaps she'll see the fun in it; I don't!"

Then, as Austin Ambrose remained silent, Blair looked from him to the doctor, who had entered—an awful look of anguished, fearful scrutiny.

"I'm—I'm dreaming; that's what it is," he muttered. "Madge—don't leave me. Take hold of my hand I—I dreamt somebody had told me you were dead. Don't cry, dear. It's I who was nearly dead, not you; and I'm all right now. Did you find the painting things? They're all right, are they? I told Austin—I told— —" he stopped short suddenly, and uttered a cry, a heartrending cry, and raised himself so that he could see Austin Ambrose's face. "I'm not asleep," he moaned; "I am awake. And you are there—and you have just told me. Dead! Dead! Austin—don't—keep—it from me! Tell me all. Look, I'll be quiet. I won't utter a sound. Doctor, for Heaven's sake make him tell me."

The doctor turned his face away. It was wet with tears; there was not a tear in Austin Ambrose's eyes.

"Shall I tell him—or wait?" he whispered to the doctor. The doctor nodded.

"Better now than later; the shock will be less now he is weak. Poor fellow, poor fellow!"

Austin Ambrose bent down, and in a few words scarcely audible, told the story. He said nothing of the visitor who had come, nothing of Margaret's anguish. According as he told it, Margaret had strolled down to the rock and remained there too long, until the tidal wave had caught her and washed her out to sea.

Blair listened, his face pallid as that of death, his wide eyes fixed gleamingly on the speaker's face, his hands clutching the quilt. Every now and then his lips moved as if he were repeating the words as they dropped cautiously from Austin Ambrose's lips, and when he had finished he still leant upon his arm and looked at Austin with horror and despair.

Then, without a cry, he sank back upon the pillow and closed his eyes.

"He has swooned," said Austin. "It was too soon."

The doctor shook his head.

"No; better now than later."

After a moment or two Blair opened his eyes.

"Have you told me all?" he demanded, and there was something in the tone and the wild glare of his eye that smote Austin Ambrose and made him quail.

"Yes," he said, after a moment's pause, "everything has been done, Blair. Everything. I think you will know that without my saying it. There is no hope—there was none from the first. She was not seen after the tide reached her—she will not be seen again. Blair, you will play the man for— for all our sakes," and he pressed the hot hand clutching the quilt.

Blair looked at him and withdrew his hand; they saw his lips move once or twice, and guessed whose name they formed; then he spoke.

"Austin, did you ever pray?" It was a strange, a solemn question. "If so, pray now, pray that I may die!"

Over the weeks that followed it will be well to draw a veil; enough that during them the strong man hovered between life and death, at times raving madly and calling upon the woman he had loved and lost, at others lying in a stupor which was Death's twin sister.

As soon as he was able to walk with the aid of a stick, Blair got out of the house unnoticed and made his way to Appleford.

Pale and trembling he stood on the beach and looked at the rocks where Margaret had been seen—looked until his eyes grew dim, then he crawled back to the cottage.

"You have been to Appleford?" said Austin, who had watched him.

Blair lifted his heavy eyes.

"Yes, I have been to Appleford," he said in a hollow voice. "I have seen the last——" he stopped, and his breath came and went in quick gasps. "Austin, while I live, my poor darling will be with me in my thoughts but— but never speak her name to me. Never! I—I could not bear it."

"Yes!" murmured Austin Ambrose, sympathetically. "I understand. You will fight your sorrow like a man Blair. Time—Time, the great healer—will close over even so great a wound as yours, and you will be able to speak of her, poor girl."

Blair looked before him with lack-luster eyes.

"Do you think that a man who had been thrust out of Heaven could ever learn to forget the happiness he had lost?" he said, in a low voice. "While life lasts I shall remember her, shall long to go to her! That is enough," he added sternly; "we will never speak of her again!"

CHAPTER XX

What passed in the cabin of the Rose of Devon between the two women, Mrs. Day never told, not even to her husband.

In the morning, while the Rose was sailing along the coast, she went to the captain and requested that she and her husband might be taken as near Appleford as possible, that they might get back in their boat.

"My cousin will remain on board, Captain Daniel," she said. "She will go with you across the Channel, and land at the first French port."

Captain Daniel whistled.

"You settle things easily, Mrs. Day," he said, with a half smile; "how do you know I'll take her?"

"You'll take her for my sake and your own," said Mrs. Day quietly. "For mine because we are old friends, for yours because if she landed in England there'd be questions asked about the Rose of Devon that might be awkward to answer."

"And how am I to know that I can trust her?" he said.

"Because she has to trust you," said Mrs. Day. "Captain Daniel, my cousin has just come through a great trouble, and she's as anxious as you are that no one should know that she was ever aboard the Rose. If you don't mention it when you get back to England, she won't, wherever she is. You needn't require any oath; she's one whose word is as good as her bond; she's a lady and different to me. Just land her at the first place on the other side you touch, and say nothing. She'll pay for her passage— —"

"Thank you, Mrs. Day," said the captain. "I don't want the poor woman's money, and she's welcome to the run. As to keeping quiet, well, I think we can do that as well as she can; and if she will say nothing about the Rose, the Rose will say nothing about her. We know how to keep a secret, I think! If she's got in trouble and wants to show a clean pair of heels, well, I reckon we've been in the same plight, and may be, shall be again. Anyway, whether or no, Captain Daniel isn't the man to turn his back upon a woman in distress!"

Mrs. Day gave him her hand with a simple dignity which would not have shamed the first lady of the land.

The Rose beat about, and in another hour or two Mrs. Day and her husband got into their boat, and Margaret was left on the Rose of Devon, which, spreading all sail, was cleaving its way to the French coast.

For two days she kept to her cabin. There was a young lad on board, the captain's boy—a little mite of a fellow—and he waited upon her, carrying all sorts of delicacies from the cook's galley to her cabin; but Margaret, though she thanked him in a voice which made the lad's heart leap and brought the color to his face, could touch nothing but a little dry bread and tea, though she tried hard for the boy's sake.

The rough-looking skipper, with the truest delicacy, left her to herself, merely sending his compliments about twice a day, and a request to be informed if there was anything he could do for her.

On the third day she found courage to go on deck. The sailors looked at her curiously at first, but something in her beautiful, wan face appealed to their rough natures, and touching their caps, they went on with their work.

Margaret leaned against the bulwarks and looked out at the sea. She was a good sailor, and the vast expanse of cloudless blue above and the rolling water beneath her brought something of peace to her tortured heart.

Presently Captain Daniel came up with a deck chair in his hand and a thick rug over his arm. With a little bow, he put the chair right for her and spread the rug over it.

"Glad to see you on deck, miss," he said shyly. "The air's rather chilly; I'll fetch you another rug: there's plenty of them aboard."

Margaret thanked him, her voice sounding weak and hollow.

"I'm afraid I ought not to be here at all," she said, coloring; "you are very kind to let me stay. It will not be for long—you will land me soon, will you not?"

Captain Daniel took off his hat.

"You shall stay as long as you please, miss, and the longer you stay the better the Rose of Devon will like it."

"I am very grateful," she said in a low voice; "but I will not stay after we reach a French port. Mrs. Day has told you——" She stopped, and the captain took it up.

"Mrs. Day has told me nothing more than that you are in trouble, miss, and I reckon that's enough. There's no need for you to say anything! Me and my ship and my men are at your service, and if there's one place more than another you'd like to land at, say the word, and there the Rose goes, fair wind or foul!"

Then, without waiting for any response, he touched his hat and went aft.

As he had spoken so Captain Daniel acted.

The boy was ordered to make the cabin as comfortable as possible. An awning was rigged up on deck to provide shelter for her, and the cook taxed his inventive faculties to the utmost in the concoction of dishes which he deemed suitable to an invalid lady. The rough sailors lowered their voices as they went about their work, and even put out their pipes when she came on deck.

Their kindness, and the beauty of sea and sky, did more toward Margaret's recovery than fifty doctors could have effected, and by the time the Rose had sighted the French coast her face had lost something of its wanness, and a faint color had found its way to her cheeks.

She spent most of her time sitting on deck looking out to sea, trying to piece together the broken fragments of her shattered life.

For the future she had no plans, and could form none. Of what use or value could her life be to her when the man she had loved and trusted had broken her heart and left her desolate and utterly hopeless?

But as they neared Brest on the Brittany coast, she felt she must come to some decision.

She was alive, alas! and the future lay before her; something had to be done with it. Margaret, broken-hearted and weighed down by sorrow as she was, was still the same Margaret, strong of purpose and self-reliant. Love she had done with forever, happiness had passed beyond her reach, but her art still remained to her—the mistress whom those who serve find faithful to the end.

As the Rose sailed into the harbor, Captain Daniel came up to Margaret.

"We're nearing port, miss," he said, "but it don't follow that you and the Rose need part company. Brest's a poor place for a lady to be turned out in. If so be as you care to go on with us, why I'll pick up a few things in the port here to make the cabin more fit for you. I'm thinking, if you'll forgive me, miss, that the sea is doing you good, and that if you'd come on with the Rose as far as Leghorn in Italy— —"

Margaret's face flushed faintly, and a light, the first that had shone there for many a day, glowed in her eyes. The captain saw it and pressed his point.

"Italy's the place, miss!" he said, persuasively. "At Leghorn you'd be near Florence and Rome, and all the grand sights! But here, Brest, it's only a 'one hoss' place."

Margaret hesitated. The prospect of going to Italy contained as much pleasantness as any prospect could for her.

"Are you sure that I should not be in the way?" she asked, gently. "You are all so kind, and make such sacrifices for me——"

"Don't say another word, Miss Leslie," said Captain Daniel; for "Leslie" was the name Mrs. Day had given to her. "Me and my crew will be proud to have you with us!"

Margaret went ashore at Brest for a few hours, and got some articles of dress, and the Rose, staying no longer than was necessary to obtain provisions, set sail for Leghorn.

The weather was fine and the wind favorable, and in due course the Rose reached the Italian port.

Margaret's parting with Captain Daniel was characteristic of them both. When she offered to pay for her passage, the captain refused, at first politely, and then almost roughly and sternly.

"Why, Miss Leslie, sakes alive!" he exclaimed, "I'd rather see the Rose at the bottom of the sea than me or my men should take a shilling piece from you; and all I say is, if you want to pleasure us, why, when you're tired of Italy and I—talians, drop a line to Captain Daniel of Falmouth, and the Rose shall come and fetch you away, and be proud to do it."

Margaret could scarcely speak, but she managed to get out a few words of thanks, and the captain, almost crushing her hand—now very thin and white—turned to go, but he stopped at the last moment to add a word.

"And, Miss Leslie, don't be afeared of me and my men a-cackling. There's not a man as can't keep his own counsel, and there's not a man as wouldn't rather be strung up at the yard-arm than admit that he'd ever set eyes on you! No, miss, so far as the Rose is concerned, your whereabouts is as safe as if we didn't know."

Then he went, and Margaret was, indeed, left alone in the world without a friend!

Captain Daniel had engaged a room for her at the hotel, but to Margaret, whose wounded heart ached for quiet and solitude, the busy seaport seemed noisy and intrusive, and the next day she started for Florence.

Fortunately, she had some money with her; not a large sum, but the captain's hospitality had left it intact, and Mrs. Day had promised to send on the notes which Margaret had left behind directly Margaret sent her an address.

For the present, for a few months at any rate, she was secure from the dread attacks of that most malignant of foes—poverty. And she had her art; and she was in Florence, the Florence of painters and poets, the Flower City of the old world. The captain, who seemed as well acquainted with inland places as he was with the sea-board, had recommended her to a quiet little hotel overlooking the best view in Florence; and there, in a little room near the sky, Margaret found the solitude and quiet which she so much needed.

One morning, the third after her arrival, she roused herself sufficiently to go into the town and purchase some painting materials, and carrying them to a quiet spot commanding a view of the Arno and the wooded slopes above it, began to paint.

At first her hand trembled and her eyes were dim, for at every stroke of her brush the past came crowding back upon her, and she could almost fancy that Blair was lying by her side, and that she could hear his loving voice and bright laugh; but after a time she gained strength, and was gradually losing herself in her work—the work which alone could bring her "surcease from sorrow," when she heard voices near her, and looking up saw a young girl coming quickly along the path. She was a beautiful girl of about seventeen, with the frank open face of sorrowless childhood, and the springy step of youth and health. The day was hot, and she had taken off her hat which was swinging in her hand. Margaret had seen her before the girl had noticed Margaret sitting almost hidden behind a bush, and she came on, singing merrily and swinging her straw hat to the tune.

Suddenly she caught sight of Margaret, and she and the song stopped abruptly.

It was almost impossible for her to pass so close without saying something in the way of greeting, and so she made a little bow, and said rather shyly:

"I'm afraid I startled you. I didn't know anybody was near, or I shouldn't have made such a noise."

"I only heard you singing," said Margaret.

The words and the gentle tone, together with the beautiful face with its sad expression, seemed to fascinate the girl, and she drew nearer, saying timidly:

"But I was making a tremendous noise! You are painting?"

"Yes," answered Margaret, with a sigh, "I am trying to do so."

"What a lovely spot you have chosen!" said the girl looking round. "May I see what you have done? I am so fond of art myself, but"—and she made a little grimace—"I am a shocking stick!"

Then she colored furiously and laughed with pretty embarrassment.

"That's slang, I know. I beg your pardon! But I learn it from Ferdy! There—how stupid of me! Of course, you don't know who Ferdy is: he is my brother."

By this time she had looked at the canvas.

"Why!" she exclaimed, "that is beautiful! You are an artist!"

"A poor one," said Margaret, smiling in spite of herself at the girl's enthusiasm.

"Oh, no; you are a real artist!" she said. "I know the real from the sham; because we have so many of the latter staying in Florence. Poor Florence! They make daubs of her all the year round, and send them about the world as true pictures, while they are only libels. But yours will be a beautiful picture! How splendidly you have got those trees there, and that bit of cloud. Oh!" and she sighed, "I would give ten years of my life if I could ever paint like that!"

"That would be rather a heavy price if your life should be as happy all through as it is now," said Margaret, in her sweet, gentle fashion.

The girl looked at her and pondered for a moment, then she flung herself on the grass beside Margaret, and said:

"Do you know, you reminded me of mamma just then. That is just how she speaks when she wants to scold me for one of my extravagancies. Of course I wouldn't give ten years—or one year—of my life for anything; who would?"

Margaret sighed. How gladly would she have given all the remainder of her life to be able to wipe out the past! never to have seen Blair, or to have known those few short weeks of happiness.

"It all depends," said Margaret, gravely. "Some people's lives are not so happy that they could not spare a few years from them."

The girl glanced at Margaret's pale face and then at her black dress, and remained silent for a moment or two; then she looked up and said, timidly:

"Do I interrupt you sitting here? I will go at once if I am a nuisance."

"No, no," said Margaret, quickly, and with a wistful smile. "You do not interrupt me; pray stay!"

"I like to see you paint," said the girl, after a pause. "Somehow you remind me so much of mamma, though, of course, you are so much younger! I wish you knew mamma. Are you staying in Florence?"

"Yes," said Margaret, "I am staying at the hotel there," and she pointed with her brush.

"Really! Then you must be——" exclaimed the girl, quickly, but checking herself abruptly, and coloring with annoyance.

"I must be—what?" said Margaret, smiling at her embarrassment. "What were you going to say?"

"I was going to make one of my foolish speeches; and I'd better say it now I have gone so far, and get you to forgive me. I was going to say that you must be the young lady who lives so quietly at the hotel that they call her the 'Mysterious Lady.'"

Margaret smiled gently.

"Do they call me so?" she said; then she sighed, and went on with her work.

The girl sat and watched her for a moment, then she said:

"I'd better go now, I have offended you," and she half rose.

Margaret put out her white hand, and laid it on her arm with a gentle pressure.

"Do not," she said. "You have not offended me. And now, will you tell me something about yourself?"

She asked the question, not that she was at all curious, though the girl interested her, but to put her more at her ease.

"With all the heart in the world," was the instant reply. "Do you see that villa there—that one with the turrets? That is ours; mamma and Ferdinand, my brother, live there. It is called the Villa Capri; and, do you know, there are some beautiful views from it. If I were sure you wouldn't be offended, I would ask you to come and pay us a visit, and see if you could not make a picture of the river running below the woods. Oh, I would like that!"

Something in the girl's voice attracted Margaret's attention.

"Are you Italian?" she said.

"Half and half," was the reply, with a laugh. "My father was Italian, my mother is English. I call myself all English—please do not forget that!" she added, with all an English girl's frankness. "My brother, we say, represents the Italian side of the family. I should like you to know him. He is out riding this morning——"

Almost as she spoke a voice sang out clear and musical above the trees:

"Florence! Florence!"

The girl laughed and sprung to her feet, then she sunk down again as quickly.

"It is Ferdy!" she said. "Let him find me if he can!" and in a falsetto which rang quaintly through the hills, she called, "Ferdy! Ferdy!"

Margaret heard the dull beat of a horse's hoofs as the rider rode this way and that, misled by the echo, then, as, tired of the sport, the girl sprung to her feet and shouted with a full round tone, Margaret saw a handsome young fellow ride pell-mell at them.

"Oh, take care, take care, Ferdy!" shouted the girl; but the warning came too late; the horse struck the leg of the easel with its fore hoof, and over went the whole apparatus, paintbox, brushes, and the rest, leaving Margaret sitting smiling amidst the ruins.

The girl uttered a cry of dismay, and the young fellow, almost before he had pulled the horse in, flung himself from the saddle and stood bareheaded and penitent before Margaret.

"Oh, Ferdy, Ferdy, how could you be so reckless?" exclaimed the girl.

He put up his hand as if to silence her; then, as he went on his knees to recover the scattered implements, he said:

"Signorina, I am overwhelmed with shame! Believe me, I did not suspect that any one was here beside this madcap sister of mine! Pardon me, I pray you! Have I broken anything?—have I frightened you? I shall never forgive myself! Is that right?" and he put the easel in its place with the greatest and most anxious care.

"Thank you, yes," said Margaret. "No harm has been done. You did not see me, that bush hid me. Please do not mind; it does not in the least signify!"

"Oh, but——" he said, arranging the palette and paints with the nicest carefulness—"it signifies so much that I shall not sleep in peace unless you will forgive me!"

It was an Italian speech, but it was spoken with an air of sincerity that was singularly English, and the speaker's eyes were fixed so earnestly and pleadingly upon Margaret's face, that her color rose, and she bent down and got her brushes to hide it. The girl glided to her side.

"Poor Ferdy! But it was very stupid of him, and he might have hurt you as well as the easel, and then I should never have forgiven him, whatever you had done. But you will forgive him, will you not?"

She seemed to set so much value on the expression of forgiveness, that Margaret, with a soft laugh, said at once:

"Certainly, I forgive him!"

The young man's face cleared instantly, and with the slight foreign accent which was more marked in him than his sister, he said:

"I am deeply grateful! I do not deserve it. Florence, have you told the lady your name? Will you tell her mine?"

The girl at this direct invitation stepped forward, and with a little graceful movement of the hand, said:

"Madame, let me present to you my brother, Prince Ferdinand Rivani."

"And I, the Princess Florence, my sister," said the prince; and the prince bowed, and the young girl dropped a courtesy in courtly fashion.

"And now we have been formally introduced," said the girl, with a merry laugh. "We are friends, are we not, and you will come to see us? Ferdy, the lady——" she hesitated and looked at Margaret, and Margaret, with downcast eyes, said:

"Miss Leslie."

"Miss Leslie! What a pretty name! Why, it is more Italian than English, I think. Miss Leslie is staying at the hotel."

The prince drew himself up, and with the same fixed regard of respectful, almost reverential, admiration, said:

"I shall have the honor of waiting upon Miss Leslie to-morrow—if she permits."

A servant who had been holding the horse came up, and as the prince mounted, the princess drew near and bent over Margaret.

"Mind! We are to be friends, you and I! I shall come with Ferdinand to-morrow!" then, laying her hand upon the horse's neck, she tripped off beside her brother.

Margaret sat and looked at the view with eyes that saw nothing. She had come to Florence for solitude and seclusion, and already that solitude was threatened. What should she do? The girl was so lovable that Margaret's tender heart already felt drawn toward her. All the more should she guard against the possibility of an intimacy between her—nameless and under a cloud of shame—and these high-born Italians.

With a sigh she began to put her easel together, thinking that she must leave Florence in the morning, when she saw a newspaper lying on the ground.

It was folded up and had evidently fallen from the pocket of the prince.

Half mechanically she opened it and found that it was an English newspaper of some weeks back. Still mechanically she let her eyes wander over the columns, when suddenly she saw amongst the provincial news an account of her own death off the rocks at Appleford.

Trembling and shuddering, for the lines brought back all the torture of that day, she read the succinct narrative, and found that in very truth the world had accepted her death as a fact beyond question. But a strange coincidence awaited her, for turning to the births, marriages, and deaths columns, she saw this announcement—"At Leyton Court, on the 25th instant, Martha Hale, aged 68, the faithful servant of the Earl of Ferrers."

In one and the same paper was the account of her own death, and that of the only person whom she would have to acquaint with the fact that she was living! The last link between Margaret Hale and Mary Leslie was broken, and the past had slipped away as completely as if, indeed, the tidal wave had washed her out to sea!

CHAPTER XXI

It was autumn, but such an autumn as often puts summer to shame. The skies were as blue, the air as soft, as those of July; but that the leaves had changed their emerald hues for those of russet-brown and gold, one might well be tempted to believe that the summer was still with us, and the winter afar off.

The sun poured its generous warmth over the Villa Capri, laving the white stone front of the graceful house with its bright rays, and tinting the statues on the terraces, which, in Italian fashion, rose in three tiers from the smooth lawn to the *salon* and dining-room windows. On the highest of the three terraces, lying back in a hammock chair of velvet tapestry, was an old lady with a face of aristocratic beauty set in snow-white hair. At a little distance, pacing up and down, were two young ladies, the younger of the two with her arm round the waist of her companion, and her beautiful young face turned up with that air of pure devotion and affection which only exists in the heart of one woman for another.

The old lady was the Princess Rivani, the mother of Florence and Ferdinand; and the two girls were Margaret and Florence. It had come to pass that Margaret was an honored inmate of the Villa Capri.

The Princess Florence had fallen in love with Margaret's lovely face, and its sad, gentle smile, and still more with her sweet voice, and had taken a fancy that Margaret's presence in the villa was necessary to her existence; and as princesses' whims are born but to be gratified, Margaret was here.

The mother, who made a rule never to deny her darling child any innocent and harmless desire, welcomed Margaret with the gentle sweetness of a patrician, combined with the frank candor of an old lady.

"I am very glad to see you, Miss Leslie," she had said. "You have won my daughter's heart, and your presence seems necessary to her happiness. I trust you will not let her be a burden to you. Please consider the villa your home while it seems good to you to remain with us, and I hope that will be for a long period."

That was all; but as the signora—as the elder princess was called—always said what she meant, and never more than she meant, it was a good deal. She had scanned Margaret's face when she had been presented to her, and had listened to her voice, and was convinced that Margaret was a lady, and a fit companion for the princess, and she had said so in a sentence to her daughter.

"I like your friend, Florence, and I can understand the charm she exerts over you. It is a very lovely face, a— —"

"Is it not, mamma?" exclaimed Florence enthusiastically.

"—But it is a very sad one. I am afraid Miss Leslie has had some great trouble, one of those sorrows which set their mark upon the heart, as a fell disease brands the face."

"But you will not like her the less for that, mamma?" Florence had said, and the signora had replied with a sigh:

"No, rather the more, my dear," for the signora had suffered also in her life.

So the princess had her wish gratified, and Margaret came to the villa, and the princess, instead of growing tired of her, as one would be tempted to prophesy, seemed to grow more attached and devoted as the days rolled into weeks, and the weeks threatened to glide into months.

If it had not been for the experience of the grandeur of Leyton Court, Margaret might have been rather overwhelmed by the splendor of Capri Villa, for the Rivanis were great people, of the best blood in Italy, and lived in a state befitting their rank.

The villa was not so large as the Court—that Court which Blair had often told her she would one day be mistress of—but it was exquisitely situated, and the interior was replete with the refined splendor of a palace.

The suit of rooms allotted to Margaret were large and grand enough for a duchess, but when she murmured something in deprecation of such sumptuous apartments, the princess had opened her blue eyes wide and smiled with surprise.

"Oh, but I want you to be comfortable, dear," she said. "I want you to feel at home—that is the English phrase, isn't it?"

"Yes, but 'at home' all my rooms would have gone into the smallest you have given me," Margaret had said, smiling.

"Really! Well, at any rate you need large rooms, for are you not an artist, and do you not want a studio? Ferdinand has given orders that the large room with the big window is to be fitted up as a painting-room for you; and he promised to choose some pictures and some curios, and all those kind of things you artists love, to furnish it. He has gone to Rome, you know."

Margaret looked rather grave. A prince is a prince to us English people, and it rather alarmed her that she should be the cause of so much trouble to his highness.

The princess laughed at her serious countenance.

"Do not look so grave," she said. "It was Ferdy's own idea. He chose the rooms, and said how nice the big one would do for a studio. You can't think how thoughtful he is—when he chooses to think at all."

"His highness is very good," said Margaret, "but I am ashamed to give him so much trouble."

The princess laughed again.

"Ferdy loves trouble. His great grief is that he has nothing to do, for you see there is nothing to employ him here. The steward looks after the land, and the major domo does all the business in the villa, and there is nothing for poor Ferdy to do when he is away from the court. I want you to like my brother, Miss Leslie," she added.

"I should be very ungrateful if I did not," said Margaret.

All this had occurred on the first day of her arrival; since then the studio had been furnished and she had been made to feel as if she were part and parcel of the Rivani family. Just before Margaret's arrival, the prince had been called away by his duties to the Italian Court, and the three ladies were left alone, so that Margaret had as yet had no opportunity of thanking him for his kindness, of which she was reminded every time she entered the luxurious studio he had furnished for her.

Margaret's lines had indeed fallen in pleasant places, and if the possession of good and true friends and the comforts of a luxury brought to the highest state of perfection, could have brought happiness, she should have been happy. But the sadness which wrapped her as in a veil through which she smiled, and sometimes laughed, never left her, and she spent hours in her studio, with the brush lying untouched, and her dark eyes fixed dreamily upon the hills which rose before her windows. She could not prevent her thoughts from traveling back towards the past, that past with which she had done forever, and often in the gloaming of the late summer evenings she would see Blair's face rise before her, and hear his voice as she had heard it during those few happy weeks when she had believed him to be her lover and husband.

There was only one way of escape from these thoughts, this flitting back of her heart which brought her so keen an anguish, and that was in work.

She had come to the villa on the understanding that she should give lessons in painting to the princess, but Florence soon showed the futility of such an arrangement.

"Dear, you will never make me an artist," she said; "never, do what you will! I can learn to paint a barn, or a village pump, so that I needn't write 'this is a barn,' or 'this is a pump,' underneath them, but that is all. Don't waste your valuable time upon an impracticable—isn't that a splendid English word?—subject, but do your own work. I'll bring you my dreadful daubs, and you shall tell me where I am wrong, but you sha'n't work and drudge like an ordinary drawing-mistress. I daren't let you, for the last words Ferdy said were, 'Don't abuse Miss Leslie's good nature, and bore her! Remember that she is an artist, and she's something to the world that you must not rob it of!' and Ferdy said wisely."

"I think he spoke too generously, and thought only of the stranger within his gates," said Margaret.

"But mamma thinks the same," said the princess. "She has set her heart upon your painting a great picture while you are at the villa. You know that mamma and Ferdy are devoted to art; I think that either of them would rather be an artist—a true artist—than Ruler of Italy, and if you want to do them an honor, why paint a grand picture, exhibit it at the Salon, and date it from the Villa Capri."

Life at the villa, Margaret found, was one of routine—pleasant, easy routine—but still carefully measured out and planned.

At eight the great bell in the campanile rang for rising; at nine the household gathered in the hall for prayers; at half-past breakfast was served. At one o'clock the luncheon bell rang, and at seven the major domo, in his solemn suit of black, stood at the drawing-room door to announce dinner.

There was an army of servants, male and female, and the three ladies were attended with as much state as if the king were present.

Between breakfast and dinner Margaret worked.

Art is a jealous mistress; she will not share her shrine with any other god, though it be Cupid himself. If Margaret had remained the happy wife of Lord Blair, it is a question whether any more pictures of worth would have left her easel, but now, with her great sorrow ever present with her, she felt that her work alone would bring her partial forgetfulness.

And she did work. At first she thought she would paint a view of Florence from the hills, and she made a very fair sketch; but, about a week after her arrival at the villa she was sitting before a fresh canvas, and, her thoughts flying back to the past, she, all unwittingly, took up the charcoal and began to draw the outline of the Long Rock at Appleford. It was not until she had sketched in the whole of the scene that she became conscious of what she was doing; and when she had so become conscious, she took up her brush to wipe the marks out. Then she hesitated. A desire to paint the scene took possession of her, and she went on with it.

She painted the rock, with the sea raging round it, and the sky threatening it from above; and, as she painted, the whole scene came back to her, just as a scene which a novelist has witnessed with his own eyes comes back to him.

And as the picture grew, it exerted a fascination for her which she could not repel.

On this she worked day after day, carefully locking up the unfinished picture in the mahogany case which the prince had supplied with the rest of the furniture of the studio.

She felt that she could do nothing until it was finished. One day the princess knocked at the door, and Margaret, before she opened it, hurriedly inclosed the canvas in its mahogany case.

"Why, you have shut your picture up," said the princess in a tone of disappointment.

"I will show it to you, if you wish," said Margaret, laying her hand upon the key; but the princess stopped her.

"No, no," she said. "Do not. I think I understand. It is your great picture, is it not? And you do not want any one to see it until it is finished."

Margaret was silent for a moment, then, as the princess put her arm round her, and laid her cheek against Margaret's, she said:

"If I ever am so fortunate as to do anything approaching 'great,' this will be it, and I do not want you to see it until it is finished, princess."

"I would not see it for worlds until you say that I may, dear," said the girl, lovingly.

Day by day Margaret worked at the picture; it took possession of her body and soul. All the anguish of that awful night, when she battled against life and prayed for death, was portrayed in that savage sea and darkling sky.

She finished the scene, and was looking at it one day, with the dissatisfaction that the true artist always feels, when she thought of the words of Turner: "No landscape, beautiful as it may be, is complete without the human figure, God's masterpiece in nature."

She pondered over this for awhile, then, taking up her brush, she painted on the top of the rock the figure of a woman. It was that of a young girl, half kneeling, half lying, the water lapping savagely at her feet, her face upturned to the angry sky.

Half unconsciously she painted that face as her own—a girl's face, white and wan, marked with an agony beyond that of the fear of death. Despair and utter hopelessness spoke eloquently in the dark eyes and the attitude of the figure; and when she had finished it, she stood and gazed at it, half frightened by its realism.

She knew that if it was not a great picture, it was a picture at which no one could look at and pass by unmoved.

She locked the door of the cabinet which inclosed the canvas, and went on the terrace and found the princess waiting for her. The girl put her arm round Margaret's waist, and led her up and down, the signora looking on at the pair from her chair smilingly.

"And have you nearly finished your picture, dear?" asked Florence.

"Yes," said Margaret, dreamily, "it is quite finished."

"Oh, how splendid!" exclaimed Florence. "Ferdinand will be so pleased. He is coming this evening, you know, dear."

"I did not know," said Margaret, still absently.

"Ah, no, I forgot. I did not tell you, because mamma cautioned me not to say anything that might disturb you at your work. He is coming, and rather a large party with him."

Margaret, as the girl spoke, remembered noticing that some preparations seemed to have been going on in the villa for some days past, as if for many guests; she had thought little of it at the time, her mind being absorbed in her work.

"My brother often brings some of his friends back with him," said Florence; "they like the quietude of Florence after the fuss and bustle of the court. How glad I shall be to get him back, not that I have missed him so much this time, for, you see, I have had you, dear."

"I am afraid I have been a very poor companion," said Margaret.

"You have been the dearest, the best, and the sweetest a girl was ever lucky enough to find!" responded the princess, earnestly.

They walked up and down the terrace for some time, talking about the prince and his many virtues, as a sister who adores her brother will talk to her closest bosom friend; then Margaret went to her own room.

The thought of the coming influx of visitors disturbed her; like most persons who have endured a great sorrow, she shrank from meeting new faces, and she resolved to keep to her own rooms, as it was understood she should do when she pleased, while these gay people remained.

Toward evening the guests arrived, and Margaret, from behind the curtains of her long window, saw several handsome carriages drive up to the great entrance, and a group of ladies and gentlemen—most of the latter in military or court uniforms; in their midst stood the tall figure of the prince, towering above the rest, his handsome face wearing the grave smile of welcome, as he ushered his friends into the house, in which were the usual stir and excitement attending the arrival of a large party.

Margaret drew the lace curtains over her window, and took up a book. Presently the dressing-bell rang, then the dinner-bell, and soon after there came a knock at the door. In response to her "Come in," the Princess Florence entered in her rich evening dress, and ran across the room.

"Why, dear, aren't you dressed?" she exclaimed.

"I am not coming down to dinner to-night, Florence, if you will excuse me," said Margaret, gently.

Florence stopped short, and looked at her with keen disappointment in her blue eyes.

"Not coming down to dinner? Oh, Miss Leslie, I am so sorry! And Ferdy, he will be so disappointed!"

"The prince," said Margaret, smiling at the girl's earnestness. "I do not suppose your brother will notice my absence, Florence."

"Not notice!" exclaimed Florence. "Why, he asked after you almost directly after he had got into the house; and he has inquired where you were at least half a dozen times."

"The prince is very kind," said Margaret, "but I will not come down to-night, dear."

"You do not like all these people coming?" said the princess; "and yet you would like them, they are all so nice and—and friendly: it is a sort of holiday for them, you know."

"I am sure they are very nice, dear," said Margaret, "but I would rather be alone."

There was nothing more to be urged against such quiet decision, and the princess kissed her and reluctantly went down to the *salon*.

A maid who had been set apart to wait upon Margaret brought her her dinner, and Margaret took up her book afterward, and tried to lose herself in it. Now and again she took a candle and looked at her picture, and every time she looked at it the present faded and the past stood out before her.

What was Blair doing now? Had the woman, his wife, returned to him? Where was he, and was he happy? No, Margaret thought, there could be no happiness for him unless he were utterly destitute of heart and could forget the girl whose love for him had led her to ruin and dishonor!

From these sad thoughts she was aroused by a knock at the door and the voice of the princess calling softly:

"May we come in, dear?"

Margaret opened the door, and there stood the prince beside his sister.

He was in evening dress, and upon his bosom glittered a cluster of orders; he looked the patrician he was, but there was a deep humility and reverence in the manner of his bow and the way in which he extended his hand to her.

"Will you forgive this intrusion, Miss Leslie?" he said in his excellent English, which was made more musical rather than less by the slight accent. "I have come to beg you to give us the honor and pleasure of your company. Florence tells me that you are not ill, or I should not have bothered you."

Margaret made room for them to enter, standing with downcast eyes under his gaze, which was full of admiration and respectful regard.

"Pray come," he said with an eagerness only half concealed. "For all our sakes, if not for your own, and I should add for your own, too; for there are some people here whom I think you would like to meet." He mentioned some names of which Margaret had heard as those of great people in Rome. "And there are some artists, too, Miss Leslie; surely you will not refuse them the pleasure and honor of making your acquaintance. My mother, too, begs that, if you feel well enough, you will come down. There is Count Vasali, the great musician; he will play for us, I hope."

"Oh, do come, if only for an hour, dear," said the princess, adding her prayer.

Margaret hesitated, and while she hesitated the prince went slowly up to the easel upon which the picture stood, with the cabinet unlocked.

He started, and drew a little nearer, then looked from Margaret to the picture, and from the picture to Margaret again.

"Is this— —?" he said, in a low voice, then stopped.

"Oh, it is the picture! May I look now he has seen it?" exclaimed the princess; then she, too, drew near, and stood speechless.

"I—I hope you like it," said Margaret, with the nervousness of an artist whose work is being surveyed and criticised.

"Like it!" exclaimed the prince, gravely. "It is——" He stopped again, then turned to Margaret with almost solemn earnestness. "Miss Leslie, I am not an artist; I do not presume to be a critic, but I am convinced that this is a marvelous picture! It is, I think, a great work. I cannot tell you how it moves me! But there are others in the house who are more capable of judging and appreciating it. You will let me show it to them?"

Margaret flushed and then turned pale. She would have kept the picture to herself, for the present, at any rate; but then she considered the matter in the few seconds while he stood waiting. After all, she was an artist; it was by her art that she must exist, and it was well that her picture should be seen.

"I will do as you wish, prince," she said.

"No, not I, but you!" he said, gently, with a little thrill in his voice that touched Margaret, and made the princess turn and look at him.

"Take it, then," said Margaret.

He took it from the easel, and locked it in the cabinet carefully.

"And you will come down? You must!" urged Florence eagerly. "You must hear what they say. I know what it will be: they will say what Ferdinand said!"

"Very well," said Margaret, with a little sigh.

The princess clapped her hands.

"Oh, I am so glad. I will come for you in half an hour. Will that do?"

"Miss Leslie will understand that she will meet friends," said the prince, laying a delicate stress on the word, "though she has not seen them yet."

And with this courtly, kindly word of encouragement, he carried off the picture.

Margaret changed her plain black dress for one of black lace, which, simple as it was, and without ornament, lent to her graceful figure a distinguished air which even Worth himself sometimes cannot bestow, and before the half hour was up the princess came for her.

"Dressed already, dear! Oh, and how well you look! May I kiss you? Ah! after all, it is only the English who really know how to dress. Why, yours is the prettiest costume in the house——"

"It is the simplest, dear, I am sure," said Margaret.

The princess led her to her mother, and the old lady made room for her on the settee.

"I am glad you have come, my dear Miss Leslie," she said in her slow, gentle voice; "we should all have been so sorry if you had not."

Margaret said nothing, but presently gained courage to look round.

Some lady was at the piano playing, and there were a few persons round her; but the rest of the party was gathered together round some object at the end of the room, about which candles and lamps had been arranged, and she knew it was her picture.

Presently she saw the prince approaching, with an old gentleman at his side, an old man with long silvery hair and pale face, from which the dark eyes shone with a strange brilliance that was yet soft and dreamy.

"Miss Leslie," said the prince, "let me introduce Signor Alfero to you."

It was the great artist whose works Margaret had stood before with admiration and awe.

She inclined her head without a word. The great artist's eyes rested on her keenly for a moment, then he said:

"To have seen your picture, Miss Leslie, is to desire a knowledge of you. You are very young!"

It was a strange speech, and it brought the color to Margaret's face.

"I had expected to see an older person—one whose experience would account for her success; but it is always so, it is to youth all things are possible. My dear, you have painted a wonderful picture! It is a work of genius. I cannot tell you how it has moved me. How came you to paint it?"

Margaret looked up questioningly and fearfully.

"I mean," said the great man with a kindly smile, "where did you get your subject? Waves and rocks are old as the hills, but your waves and rocks are new because they are so terribly real. And the figure too! Why, yes—it is your own! Miss Leslie, your picture is a great one. I tell you this without flattery, and as one of our trade. It is great, and it will bring you fame."

Fame! Alas, it might bring her fame, but of what value would fame be to her now?

Perhaps the absence of all joy in her face as she received the tidings, touched the great man, for he said:

"But we do not care for that, do we? not so greatly, that is. It is the satisfaction in our work, is it not? Will you come with me and let me ask you a few questions about one or two things in your picture?"

He held out his arm, and Margaret, still speechless, let him lead her to the easel upon which the picture stood.

The group, clustering round it, made way for the pair, looking at Margaret, and whispering together in the well-bred way which conceals the act.

The great artist asked his questions—they related to various lights and shades, and wave formations—and Margaret answered modestly, in her low, sweet voice; then the prince, who stood on the other side of her, found himself besieged by applications for introductions, and quietly he brought one after another of the group to Margaret, and made them known to her.

It was evident that she was the celebrity of the evening. The fame which the great artist had prophesied had come already, for there was not one there who was not willing to blow a blast upon the trumpet which announces the appearance of a great one to the waiting and welcoming world.

It was not only the fact that she had painted a picture which Alfero had pronounced "great," but her beauty, with its touching air of subdued sadness, took possession of them.

They gathered around her, these noblemen and famous ladies, and made much of her, until the prince, fearing that she would be tired and overdone, offered her his arm, and led her, on the excuse of showing her the flowers, toward the conservatory.

Margaret was tired and excited, though there was no trace of it in the sweet, pale face, and she was glad of a few minutes' rest.

The prince led her to a seat placed amidst a cluster of ferns and exotics, and, taking up a fan, gently fanned her.

"I spoke truly, you see, Miss Leslie," he said. "I cannot tell you with what joy and pride—yes, pride!—Signor Alfero's words filled me. But we will not speak of them again to-night; though I trust they have made you as happy as they have made me."

There was something in his voice which half frightened Margaret, and, as she looked up to reply, she found his eyes fixed upon her with a light in them which caused hers to droop, though why she knew not.

"The signor—every one—has been too good to me," she said.

"No," he said, with a suppressed earnestness. "That no one who knows you could be."

He was silent a moment, then he looked round.

"Ah, how glad I am to be at home!" but as he spoke his eyes returned to her face.

"And they are all glad to have you, prince," said Margaret.

"All?" he said. "May I include you, Miss Leslie?"

A faint flush rose to Margaret's face, then it grew pale again.

"I?" she said. "Oh, yes, I am glad!"

"You make me very glad to hear you say that," he said in a low voice, bending down so that he almost whispered the words in her ears. "I have thought of you very often while I have been away, Miss Leslie, wondering, and hoping that you might be happy here at the villa, and longing to get back that I might see you again."

Margaret's heart beat fast.

She told herself that it was only the language of courtly kindness; warmer than an Englishman would use, but meaning no more than usual.

"What beautiful flowers!" she said, looking at a bunch of camellias before her.

He glanced at her dress, unadorned by a single article of jewelry, then crossing the conservatory, picked a snow-white blossom and brought it to her.

"Will you accept this?" he said.

"Oh, thank you!" said Margaret. "How lovely it is," and she held it in her hand.

"Will you wear it?" he asked, and his voice grew low and almost tremulous.

Margaret started and her face went white.

They were almost the very words Blair had spoken in the little garden at Leyton Court that never-to-be-forgotten night, and they brought back the past and her own position with a lurid distinctness.

"No, no!" she breathed, scarcely knowing what she said, and she let the flower drop into her lap.

The prince's face grew grave and pained.

"Have—have I offended you?—have I been too presumptuous?" he asked, humbly.

"No, no!" she said, again. Then she looked up. "Presumptuous, your highness? You! to me! The presumption would be mine if I—if I were to accept——" she paused.

"Do I understand you?" he said, drawing nearer, his handsome, patrician face flushing, his eyes seeking hers with an eager intentness. "Miss Leslie, my poor flower would be honored by the touch of your hand; will you honor me also by wearing it? Miss Leslie— —" he paused a moment, then went on—"I do not think you understand. Shall I tell you now, or are you too tired and wearied? I think you must know what I would say. Such love as mine will break through all guards, try as we will to hide it, and proclaim itself to the beloved one— —"

Margaret started to her feet with a wild horror in her eyes.

"Do not—speak another word!" she breathed. "I—I cannot listen! I— take me back, please, your highness!"

The prince's face paled, and his lips shut tightly; but with the courtly grace which could not forsake him, even at such a moment, he took her hand and drew it through his arm.

"Your lightest word is law to me," he murmured. "I will say no more— to-night; but I must speak sooner or later. But no more to-night! Not one word, be assured. You may trust me, if you will not do more!"

Margaret was speechless, her heart throbbing with a dreadful amazement and horror. That he—the great prince—should have spoken to her—to her upon whose life rested so dark a shame, almost maddened her.

In silence he led her into the *salon*. As he did so, a certain noble lady, an old schoolfellow of his mother, who was sitting beside her, looked up at them, then turned to the signora.

"This is a very beautiful girl, signora!"

The old lady glanced at Margaret and smiled placidly.

"Miss Leslie?—yes."

"Very," said the countess. "There is something sad and *spirituelle* about her which renders her loveliness something higher than the ordinary beauty of which one sees so much nowadays."

"Yes," said the signora. "I fear she has passed through some great sorrow. There is a look in her eyes when she is silent and thinking, which makes one tempted to get up and kiss her."

"A dangerous charm, that," remarked the countess dryly.

"A charm; yes, that is the word," assented the signora, smiling. "She has charmed the heart out of Florence, and has crept into mine, poor girl."

"Poor girl!" echoed the countess, dryly; then, as it seemed abruptly and inconsequentially, she said, "How handsome Ferdinand has grown!"

The signora let her eyes linger upon him with all a mother's pride and tenderness.

"Yes; has he not? He is like his father."

"And his mother," said the countess. "He is a great favorite at court, my dear. There is a career before him if there should happen to be a war, as I suppose there will be."

"I could do without a career for him if the price is to be a war," said the signora, sighing.

"He seems very attentive to Miss Leslie," remarked the countess, looking at the two young people as they crossed the room.

The prince had found a seat for Margaret, but still remained by her side, bending over her with that rapt attention which distinguished him.

"Oh yes," assented the signora, placidly. "He thinks a great deal of her. I imagine that he is very pleased at the success of her picture. Ferdinand is devoted to art; and says that the villa is renowned as the birthplace of so great a picture as Miss Leslie has painted."

"Hem!" said the countess; then, with a frown, she said, "Don't you think that the charm you speak of may exert itself over Ferdinand?"

"Over Ferdinand?" the signora glanced across at them with a serene smile.

"Yes, over Ferdinand," repeated the old countess, almost impatiently, "or do you think that the male heart is less susceptible than the female. Do you suppose that Ferdinand is blind to Miss Leslie's loveliness, and that it is only revealed to you and Florence?"

"What do you mean?" asked the signora.

"What do I mean? Why, my dear Lucille, aren't you afraid that, to speak plainly, Ferdinand may—fall in love with Miss Leslie?"

The old princess looked at her for a moment with a mild surprise, then she drew her slight figure up to its full height and smiled with placid hauteur.

"Ferdinand will not fall in love with Miss Leslie," she said, with an air of calm conviction.

"Oh," said the countess, dryly. "Does he wear an amulet warranted to protect him from such eyes as hers, such beauty as hers?"

"Yes," said the mother. "Ferdinand wears such an amulet. It is the consciousness of his rank and all its duties and responsibilities. Miss

Leslie is a most charming girl, and Florence and I are attached to her; but Ferdinand— —" she paused and smiled. "I know Ferdinand very well, I think, my dear, so well, that if you were to hint that he was likely to fall in love with one of the maid-servants I should be as little alarmed."

The countess looked at her with a strange smile, then glanced at the prince and Margaret.

"My dear Lucille," she said, "I beg your pardon. Of course, you are quite right, and there is no danger. There has never been an instance of one of our rank marrying beneath him, has there?" and she laughed ironically.

The signora smiled and shook her head.

"My dear," she said, "there isn't a prouder man in Italy than Ferdinand. I am not at all uneasy."

CHAPTER XXII

I do not think I have at any time held up Lord Blair Leyton as an example to youth, and I am less likely than ever to do so now, now that he has reached an epoch in his life when, like a vessel without a rudder, he drifts to and fro on life's troubled sea, heedless of his course, and perilously near the rocks of utter ruin and destruction. But at any rate, I can claim one quality for our hero—he was thorough.

A wilder man than Blair, before he fell in love with Margaret, it would be difficult to imagine; it would be harder to find a better one, or one with better intentions, than he was during his short married life; and, alas, no wilder and more reckless being existed than poor Blair, after Margaret's supposed death.

He was quiet enough while he was ill, for he was too weak to do anything but sit still all day and brood.

He would sit for hours staring moodily at the dim line where sea and sky meet, without uttering a word—all his thoughts fixed upon his great loss, the sweet, lovable, lovely girl whom he had called wife for a few short weeks.

He never mentioned Margaret's name, and Austin Ambrose was too wise to disobey his injunction as regards silence. He made no further inquiries, and even if he had been desirous of doing so, there was no one of whom to make inquiries, for the Days had left Appleford, and no one knew anything more of Margaret than the common record, that she had been seen on the rock, and then—not seen!

Emaciated and haggard, Lord Blair sat day after day waiting for the renewal of strength, his sole employment that bitterest of all bitter amusements—recalling the past!

Austin Ambrose was his only companion, Austin leaving him only for short intervals, which he spent in town.

Vigilant as a lynx, untiring as a sleuthhound, Austin Ambrose kept continual watch and guard. By a series of accidents, Fate had assisted his schemes, and he felt himself the winner almost already. A few turns more of the wheel, and he would have Violet Graham at his feet.

Revenge is a powerful motor, so is the love of money; but when they act together, then the man who harbors them is propelled like a steam engine— swiftly yet carefully, and, therefore, barring accidents, surely.

Gradually the long, absent strength came back to Blair. As the doctor had said, he had a wonderful constitution, and it did more for him than the great Sir Astley or the great "Sir" anybody else could have done, and at last one morning he remarked, in the curt manner which had now become habitual to him:

"I shall go up to town, Austin."

"To town?"' said Austin Ambrose, raising his eyebrows. "Do you think you are fit, my dear Blair?"

"Yes," replied Blair slowly. "I am sick of sitting here day after day, and lying here night after night. I think I could"—he paused, and smothered a sigh—"sleep in London. This place is so infernally quiet——"

"Very well. Only don't run any risks," said Austin Ambrose.

Blair looked at him with a hard smile.

"If I thought I should run any risk, as you call it, I should go all the sooner. Will you wire and tell them at the Albany that I am coming?"

"I'll do better than that," said Austin Ambrose, who did not by any means desire that their whereabouts should be known. "I'll run up and see that things are straight and comfortable for you, old man."

Blair looked at him moodily.

"I don't know why you take so much trouble for me, Austin," he said. "I've no claim upon you; you are not my brother——"

"Wish I were, especially your elder brother!" said Austin Ambrose, smiling, "then I should have all the Leyton property, and be the Earl of Ferrers, shouldn't I? Well, I don't know quite why I fuss over you; I've done it so long that I can't get out of it, I suppose. It is wonderful, the force of bad habit. So you have made up your mind to go to London? Well, heaps of fellows will be very glad. Violet Graham amongst them."

Blair frowned.

"Why should Violet Graham be glad?" he said, coldly. "Why should anybody?"

"Oh, I don't know." Austin replied, carelessly; "but I suppose they will. You always were popular, you know, my dear fellow."

So Mr. Austin Ambrose, impelled by his extreme good-nature and friendship for Lord Blair, ran up to town first, and saw that the chambers were put straight, and the valet, who had been put on board wages, and kept in complete ignorance of his master's movements, warned of Lord Blair's return.

And in the evening, after he had done all this, he went to Park Lane.

Violet Graham was still in London, although like the last Rose of Summer, "all her companions" had gone. She had pressing invitations to county houses in England, Scotland, and Ireland—shooting and fishing parties clamored for the presence of the popular heiress; but in vain. She declared that she hated eating luncheon in wet turnip fields, and that fishing parties were a bore, and intended remaining in London, at any rate, for the present. The truth was that she could not tear herself away while there remained a chance of Blair's return.

Austin Ambrose found her sitting before the fire in the drawing-room, crouching almost, her hands clasped in her lap, her eyes fixed on the glowing coals as if she were seeking the future in the red light; and she started and sprung up as he entered with an exclamation of surprise:

"Austin!" then she looked beyond him, as if she hoped and expected to see some one else with him, and not seeing him, her face fell.

"Well, Violet," he said, with his slow, calm smile.

"Where have you been?" she demanded, moving her hand toward a chair, "I thought you were dead!"

"I am alive," he answered, "and I have been wandering up and down like the gentleman mentioned in history. You are early with your fire, aren't you? It is quite warm out."

"It is quite cold within," she replied; "at least, I am cold, I always feel cold now. Well?" she added, with abrupt interrogation.

He smiled up at her.

"You want my news?" he said, shortly.

"Yes! Where is he? Where is Blair?" she demanded, and as she spoke his name a red spot burnt in either cheek, and her eyes grew hungry and impatient. "Why does he not come home or write? One would think you were both dead!"

"Blair is alive," he said, holding his hands to the fire, though he had said it was warm, and watching her with a sidelong look under the lowered lids. "He isn't dead, but he has been very nearly."

She uttered a faint cry, and put her hand to her heart.

"I knew it!" she murmured huskily, "I *felt* that something was wrong with him. Don't laugh at me," she went on fiercely, for the smile had crept into his face again, "I tell you I *felt* it. It was as if some one had passed over my grave. Blair nearly dead! And you never told me! What brutes men can be!" and the angry tears crowded into her eyes.

"Don't blame me," he said. "It was Blair's fault. I should have written and asked you to help me nurse him, but he wouldn't permit me to tell any one, even the earl."

"But why not?" she demanded.

He shrugged his shoulders.

"As well ask the wind why it blows north instead of south, or east, or west. Blair is whimsical; besides, he hates any fuss, and—forgive me, Violet—but he may have known that you would have made a fuss."

"I would have gone to him to the other end of the world, and have given my life to save his, if you call that making a fuss!" she retorted angrily.

"Exactly," he said; "and that is just what Blair didn't want."

"Where was he, and what was it?" she asked, dashing the tears from her eyes with a gesture that was almost savage.

"He got a fever at Paris," said Mr. Austin Ambrose promptly. "It was a narrow squeak for him; but we pulled him through."

Violet Graham's face went white, and her lips shut tightly.

"'*We?*' Then—then *she* was with him? She is with him now?" and her hands clenched so that the nails ran into the soft, pinky palms.

"She *was*," he answered gravely; "but she is not now."

"Not now!" she echoed, with a quick glance at the calm, set face. "Where is she, then? Has he sent her away? Tell me, quick!"

"He has not sent her away, but she has gone. Violet, prepare yourself for a shock. The poor girl is dead!"

She sprung to her feet, and stood staring at him for a moment, then sank into her chair, a light of relief and joy, almost demoniacal in its intensity, spreading over her face.

"Dead! Dead, Austin?" hoarsely; "you are not—not playing with me?"

"Rather too serious a subject for joking, isn't it?" he responded, coolly. "No, I am telling you the plain truth; the girl is dead!"

"When? How?" she demanded.

He was silent a second or two, then he said:

"Abroad. I don't think we need go into particulars, Violet."

She said nothing while one could count twenty, then she looked round at him with a glance half fearful.

"Did you—had you any hand——" She could not finish the sentence.

He looked her full in the face, then let his eyes drop.

"Better not ask for any of the details, my dear Violet! Take the thing in its bare simplicity. If I had, as you delicately suggested, any hand in bringing about this consummation you so devoutly desired, what would you say? Are you going to overwhelm me with reproaches and cover me with remorse?"

The two spots burnt redly on her cheeks, then, as she turned and faced him, her face went very white.

"No. Do you think I have forgotten what you said? You asked me if I was prepared to separate them at any cost, and I answered 'at any cost.' I have not forgotten. I do not retract my words. I said what I meant—-"

"Even if it meant—murder?" he remarked, coolly.

She shuddered, and glanced toward the door fearfully, then she met his gaze defiantly.

"Yes, even if it meant murder!"

He smiled at her thoughtfully.

"You are a wonderful woman, Violet," he said, reflectively. "One would not expect to find a Lady Macbeth in a delicately made little lady like yourself! You don't look the character. But don't be uneasy; there are other ways of disposing of a person who is inconveniently in the way, than the dagger and poison-cup. The way is——"

She put out her hand.

"Don't tell me."

He laughed sardonically.

"I told you that you would not want the details," he said, "and you are wise to let the fact suffice. Margaret Hale is dead, and Blair is free once more."

"Free!" she murmured. "Free!" and she drew a long sigh. "And where is he?"

"On his way to London," he replied. "He will be here to-morrow."

"To-morrow?" and her face flushed.

"Yes," he said, promptly. "But I do not know that he will find his way to Park Lane quite so quickly."

"No?" scornfully.

"No, not just at first. You see, Blair has been through a rather heavy mill, and he is—well, to put it shortly—rather crushed."

"I understand."

"Yes," slowly, "I imagine that he will fight shy of all his acquaintances for a time, women especially. Why, he can scarcely bring himself to say half-a-dozen civil words to me, his best friend."

"'His best friend!'" she murmured.

"His best friend," he repeated, with emphasis. "So that one must not expect too much from him just yet. In a week or two he will come round, and you will find him only too glad to drop in for afternoon tea."

She looked at him quickly, for there seemed a hidden meaning in his words, commonplace as they were.

He nodded.

"Yes, just that. He will drop in some afternoon and you will, of course, greet him as if you had parted from him only the night before. Make a fuss over him, and he will be off like a frightened hare, and you will lose him. But just receive him with the politeness due to an ordinary acquaintance, and he will not be alarmed. He will get accustomed to dropping in and—and—" he smiled significantly—"any further hint would be superfluous."

She sat silently regarding the fire, with this new hope, the news of Margaret's death, shining softly in her eyes, and he sat watching her.

"What fools women are!" she murmured, at last.

"I would rather you said that than I," and he laughed softly.

"We are like children," she went on. "The one thing denied to us, that is the thing we must have and cry our eyes out for! I wish—I wish that I were dead or had no heart!"

"The two things are synonymous," he said. "Without a heart one, indeed, might as well be dead."

She looked at him with momentary interest and curiosity.

"They say that you have no heart, Austin."

"But *you* know that I have," he responded at once. "But we won't talk about my heart, it is a matter of such little consequence, isn't it? And now I think I will go. I have come like the messenger with good tidings, and my presence is now superfluous. You will see Blair shortly. I need scarcely hint that not a word of the past should escape your lips."

He spoke as carelessly and coolly as usual, but his eyes watched hers closely as he waited for her answer.

"No, no," she said; "I will say nothing about—her," and she shuddered.

"Certainly not. Take care you do not. It is grewsome work raising specters, and I warn you that to speak of Margaret Hale to Blair would be to raise a specter which will send him from your side at once."

She sighed and bit her lips.

"He—he cared for her so much?" she murmured huskily.

Austin Ambrose shrugged his shoulders.

"Who can tell? I suppose so. Certainly, he raved about her enough. But all that is past, you know; the girl is dead, and Time—which, so they say, will wipe out anything save an I O U—will erase her from his memory!"

He got his hat, and stood looking down at her slight figure as she sat leaning forward over the fire.

Then she glanced up and caught his eyes.

With a little start, she rose and held out her hand.

"I—I do not know what to say to you, Austin," she said, falteringly. "To speak of gratitude seems a mere formal way of expressing what I feel. You have done me a great service——" She stopped and hesitated, embarrassed by his steadfast gaze. "If there is anything I can do——"

He shook his head.

"No," he said, with a smile, "there is nothing you can do for me, thanks, except win the day and be happy."

"And—and yet you spoke of—hinted at—some possible reward?" she said, wondering whether she should offer him money.

"Are you dying to make me a present of, say, a thousand pounds?" he said, laughing softly. "I am sorry to balk your generous intentions, but I do not want money—at present. I am not rich, excepting in the sense that the man whose requirements are small is never poor. No, I do not want your money, Violet. Some day I may—I only say I may—come to you and remind you of my share in this little business. Perhaps I may never do so; but at any rate, your bare 'I thank you' will reward me sufficiently now."

"Then, I thank you!" she said.

He pressed her hand, looked into her eyes with the same half-comical smile, and then left her.

CHAPTER XXIII

Blair came back to town, thin, and pale, and haggard, with only one desire in his heart: to forget the past and kill the present! He had been wild and reckless as a youth, and it had only been his love for Margaret that had checked him in his road to ruin.

If she had still been by his side, he would have swung round and become one of the steadiest of men—she would have been his saving and guardian angel. But he had lost her, and with her all that had made his life worth living.

So he came back to the old life in London, hating it with a weariness bitter as death, and yet not knowing of any other way in which to kill time and escape from the past.

As Austin Ambrose had said, his friends were glad to see him, but they were aghast at the change which a few weeks had wrought in the old light-hearted Blair; and the pace he was going alarmed even the most reckless of them.

They dared not ask him any questions, for there was something about him, a touch of savageness and smothered bitterness in his manner which warned them that any display of curiosity would be resented.

"I can't make Blair out," said Lord Aldmere to Colonel Floyd. It was at a well-known club which does not open its doors until well-regulated people have gone to bed. "What he has been doing, Heaven only knows; but I never saw a man so changed. Why it was only this summer that he was in the best of form bright as a—a star, don't you know, and now—look at him!" he concluded, glancing across the room at Blair, as he sat moodily over the fire, a big cigar in his mouth, his haggard face drooping on his breast, his sad eyes fixed gloomily on the ground. "Never saw such a change in a man in all my life."

"He has been ill, you know," said the colonel, eying the drooping, listless figure with a troubled regard; "had a fever and all that kind of thing."

"Yes—I know," said the marquis, stammeringly; "but other fellows have had fevers, and they don't cut up like that. I had the fever—no, I think it was measles, or mumps, or something, but I pulled round all right, and was as jolly as a sandboy after all. It isn't the fever that's done it, Floyd; there's something else, depend upon it. Where has he been all this time? nobody knows exactly."

"You'd better ask him," said the colonel, with grim irony.

"Ask him!" stuttered the marquis; "I dare say! I expect I should get my head snapped off! Some fellow said something about Paris yesterday, and turning to Blair, said: 'But you were there then, weren't you, Blair?' and Blair just turned and glared at him as if he was going to eat him! No, by George, you bet I don't ask him anything!"

"Perhaps you'd better not," assented the colonel. "Discretion is the better part of valor. But he isn't always like this, is he?" he asked, in an undertone.

"No, not always," replied Aldmere. "He'll wake up presently and pull himself together, and then he'll go into the dining-room and order some dinner, and as like as not when it comes he'll march out and leave it! I've seen him do it two or three times, by Jove! and then later on he'll take a big drink, and when he's livened up a bit, he'll go down to the Green Table."

The colonel whistled. The Green Table was the fashionable gaming club, and the proprietor might appropriately have inscribed over its handsome stone doorway, "Abandon hope, all ye who enter here!" for many a man had found cause to rue the hour in which he passed its portals.

There was no more dangerous place in all London than the Green Table, and Colonel Floyd's whistle was not by any means superfluous.

"And does he win?" he asked.

"Sometimes, but not often," replied the marquis. "Loses four nights out of five. Seems to have lost his game, too. You know how good he was at most things? First rate all round man, you know. But now he seems to have lost his head, and plays like a man in a dream. I saw him miss two points at baccarat last night. Poor old Blair!"

"Poor old Blair!" echoed the colonel. "Can't something be done?"

The young marquis shook his head sadly.

"Who could do anything? In the old times, Blair was as good-natured a fellow as you'd meet in a day's walk; but, by George! as I said, you dare not speak to him now. If one of us were to drop a word signifying that he was going to the devil—well, by jingo! he'd send us there ourselves, and pretty sharp."

"I suppose it was some love affair?" said the colonel, thoughtfully.

"Don't know. Perhaps so. There is one fellow who could tell us, and that's that fellow Austin Ambrose."

The colonel made a grimace.

"I hate that fellow more than ever," he said. "He's back, too, by the way. Shouldn't wonder if he has been with Blair all the time, and isn't, in some way or other, mixed up with the business. I never thought that fellow up to much."

"Don't see what harm he could be up to," said the young marquis. "And so the fair Violet won't go down to Scotland this autumn, eh, Floyd?"

"No," said the colonel, ruefully; "and so I can't, either, confound it! Not that there seems much use in hanging about, for one can't get a civil word from her lately."

"They say," whispered the marquis, "that she's still sweet on Blair."

The colonel glanced over at him and shrugged his shoulders.

"Then she's wasting that same sweetness on desert air, Aldy, for to my certain knowledge he hasn't been near Park Lane since he came back. Hallo, talk of the devil—here is that fellow!"

For Austin Ambrose entered the room in his peculiar noiseless fashion, and, bestowing a nod upon the colonel and the marquis, crossed the room to Blair's chair.

Blair looked up as Austin Ambrose greeted him, looked up with that listless, spiritless glance which speaks so eloquently of the wrecked hopes and consequent despair.

"Well Blair," said Austin Ambrose, with his slow smile. "Thought I should find you here! You've dined, of course?"

Blair thought a moment as if he were trying to recollect.

"No, I haven't," he said.

"No?" cheerfully. "Come and have some grilled bones with me."

"I hate grilled bones," was the listless response.

Austin Ambrose laughed and dropped into a chair.

"So do I, if it comes to that, but man must eat to live; but never mind the bones. Blair," and he leaned forward, "you have seen the evening paper?"

"No," said Blair, lighting his cigar, which he had allowed to die out.

"No! Then you don't know that Springtime has lost?"

"Has he?" was the indifferent response. "Did I back him?" and he passed his thin wasted hand over his forehead.

Austin Ambrose raised his eyebrows.

"Did you back him? My dear Blair, what a question! Didn't you tell me this morning to get what odds I could?"

"Yes, I remember," said Blair, leaning back and gazing into the fire. "That's the horse you thought so well of, isn't it?"

Austin Ambrose colored faintly.

"Well, I don't know. I would not put it exactly that way. But I did think he had a chance, and I backed him myself for as much as I could afford," he said in a much lower tone than Blair had used, for he did not want the marquis and the colonel to hear them.

"And he lost?" said Blair, indifferently. "Well, somebody must lose," and he shrank back in his chair as if he were both weary and cold.

"I suppose the money is all right?—I mean that you have a balance at the bank?" said Austin Ambrose.

Blair nodded languidly.

"I suppose so. Oh, yes, I think so," he said, carelessly. "If not, Tyler & Driver will see to it."

Then he relapsed into his old attitude, and into the silence which had lately become habitual to him. Presently he rose and absently took two or three turns up and down the room. He was the shadow of his former self in bulk, but the stalwart frame was there still, and the marquis and Floyd watched him sadly.

"Going home, Blair?" said the colonel, in that tone of forced cheerfulness which we use toward a friend that has been stricken down by illness or a great sorrow.

"Home?" he said, with a little start and suppressed shudder. "Good heavens, no! What should I do with the rest of the night?"

"It's morning now," said the marquis with a yawn. "Why not go to bed, old man?"

"No, thank you," said Blair with a grim smile. "Why should I go to bed?"

"Why, to sleep," replied the young lord.

"Yes, but I don't sleep," came the instant retort. "No, I think I'll go down to the Green Table."

"Oh, hang the Green Table!" exclaimed the colonel. "What's the use of going to that beastly place?"

"As for that, what's the use of going to any beastly place?" said Blair, and he rang the bell and asked for his overcoat.

"We'd better go with him, I suppose?" whispered the marquis; and when the footman had helped Blair on with his coat, they got theirs and followed him; Austin Ambrose walking by his side, his face calm and serene with its cool, set smile.

The tables at the gaming club seemed pretty well crowded, but Blair found a chair presently and began to play. The marquis and Colonel Floyd stood behind him with Austin Ambrose.

Neither of the men had spoken a word to him, beyond returning his greeting as he entered the club, but now impelled by his anxiety on Blair's account, the marquis addressed him.

"I say, Ambrose, you know," he interposed; "poor old Blair is going to the—de—devil, don't you know!"

Austin Ambrose shook his head.

"He was always very wild," he said in an undertone, without removing his eyes from Blair's cards.

"Wild! Yes; but not like this. What's come to him?—what's happened to him? He's like a man half off his head, poor old chap. Look how he's playing now! Why, a child could beat him. And he plays so confounded high. I've heard there's a lot of money in the family; but, hang it all, a gold mine couldn't stand it!"

Austin Ambrose heaved a deep sigh.

"I quite understand your feelings, my dear marquis; but what am I to do? If you think my poor friend is a man to be coaxed or managed, well, try it."

The marquis swore under his breath.

"I will!" he said, and laying his hand on Blair's shoulder, he said, in an undertone: "Old fellow, the luck is dead against you to-night; throw the cards up and come away."

Blair turned as a man might turn from a dream, and looked up at him.

"Oh, is it you, Aldy? I beg your pardon. Want to go? All right, just wait till I have had another hand. The luck is against me, as you say, but what does it matter?" and he smiled. "The next best thing to winning is losing, you know."

"You see!" said Austin Ambrose in a low voice. "What is to be done? I have tried everything, but it is of no use," then he bent over Blair, and said:

"Are you coming my way, Blair? I am going now."

"No, I think not," was the listless reply. "Going? Good-night."

The marquis and Colonel Floyd walked out of the club.

"I wonder what that fellow's game is," said the latter, "for, mark my words, Aldy, he has a game, all these sort of men have. Did you see his face when poor Blair lost?"

"No, I was watching the cards," said the marquis.

"Well, I wasn't. I was watching our palefaced friend, and if it was sorrow on his face, then I don't know joy when I see it. I don't know what his game is, and I can't even guess at it, but if he isn't winning it, then I'm a Dutchman."

Blair played on until the daylight came in faint streaks through the Venetian blinds of the card room, and the hour of closing arrived. Then he rose as listless and weary, as unmoved and calm as when he sat down.

"You have lost," said Austin Ambrose, who still stood beside him.

"Yes, I think so. Oh, yes, heavily."

"Heavily!" echoed Austin Ambrose. "My dear Blair! And you have had a run of bad luck all the week?"

"Yes, luck has been against me," assented Blair, and he beckoned to a footman who brought him some champagne.

"You don't know how much you have lost?" continued Austin Ambrose, watching him as he drank the wine.

"No, not exactly. I told them to send the I O U's to Tyler & Driver's. Are you going now? I am afraid I have kept you."

"To Tyler & Driver's!" said Austin Ambrose, as he strove to keep pace with Blair's long strides. "My dear fellow, Tyler told me only yesterday that you had overdrawn your account, and that he did not know how to arrange! And that was before this loss on Springtime! And there are those I O U's to-night! Good heavens, my dear Blair, you will be utterly ruined."

Blair stopped and took out his cigar-case.

"Got a light?" he said. "Never mind, I've found one. Ruined? Do they say that? Well, they ought to know," and he laughed grimly. "So they say I am ruined; well, what does it matter? If I am broke, I am the only person to whom it will signify. If I were a married man, now, and had got a wife— —"

He stopped, and the hand that held his cigar quivered in the lamplight; "but I haven't, you see. Ruined! Well, perhaps it's as well. What do fellows do when they go under, Austin? Why, go abroad, don't they? I'll go abroad. I'll go to Boulogne, and be a billiard marker, or I'll work my way out to Australia and turn cattle runner." He stopped abruptly and looked up at the sky, now streaked with the red rays of the coming sun. "Oh, Austin, if I could only go to some place where I could forget her! She haunts me— haunts me day and night! Go where I will, do what I will, I see her before me, just as she looked as she stood on the hill waving her hand the last morning"—his voice broke—"the last time I saw her. Oh, my darling, my darling!"

He stopped with a great sob, and then hurried on, drawing his hat over his eyes.

Austin Ambrose watched him with keen scrutiny, much as a surgeon might watch the subject upon which he was experimenting with saw and knife.

"Blair," he said, panting a little, for his victim walked fast. "You should fight against this weakness. It is ruining you, body and soul. It is not fair to yourself, or to your best friends. To me, for instance, or to the earl."

"The earl!" said poor Blair, with a bitter laugh. "What does he care?"

"Or to Violet. Don't be angry, now," for Blair had turned upon him almost savagely. "She is your friend, and you know it. Why don't you go and see her?"

"Why? Because I can go and see no one!" groaned the unhappy man. "I tell you my lost darling haunts me continually. I see her so plainly sometimes that I can scarcely believe she is really dead!"

Austin Ambrose started, then smiled reassuringly to himself.

"How can I mix with my fellow men in the state I am in? You must give me time, man!" he cried almost savagely. "Give me time!"

They had reached Blair's chambers by this, and with a nod he turned and slowly mounted the stairs.

Austin Ambrose, left alone, leant against the lamp-post and, panting a little, lit a cigar, his cold, gray eyes fixed upon the light that shone in Blair's window.

"You fool!" he muttered. "You simple fool! I've got you in my net—and her, too! Give you time! Yes, you shall have time, but whether you take long or come quickly I have got you!"

For a week after this Austin Ambrose saw nothing of him; he was missed at his club, and—very much—missed at the Green Tables. No one could tell where he had gone, but in truth he was wandering with a knapsack on his back through an out-of-the-way part of the country, solitary and companionless save by his own sad thoughts.

At the end of the week Violet Graham was sitting moodily by the fire, thinking of him and of the dark mystery of Margaret Hale's death, wondering whether all her passionate desires would be fulfilled, when a servant opening the door quietly, said:

"Lord Leyton."

She started to her feet, the blood coursing through her veins; then, suddenly remembering Austin Ambrose's advice, sank down again, and, looking over her shoulder, said, in a low and rather languid voice:

"Oh, is that you, Blair?"

Blair was very much relieved by the manner of his reception. He had expected, and dreaded, a fuss, and he was grateful to her for sparing him.

"Yes, it's I," he said, taking her hand, which trembled a little, for all her efforts to keep it steady. "You didn't expect to see me. I ought to have called before, but——" he hesitated and looked down, as men do who are bad at excuses.

"But you are given to leaving undone what you should do, and doing that which you should leave undone!" she said, with a soft laugh. "Of course, I am glad to see you. Come nearer the fire. It is an awful evening, isn't it?"

"Beastly!" he said, and he drew his chair up to the fire.

"You are just in time for tea. Shall we have lights?"

"No," he replied, "unless you want them. I like this firelight."

"It is rather cozy," she said. "I am fond of it myself. Will you ring the bell?"

He rang the bell, and the servant brought in the tea-tray, with its little silver kettle, and placed it upon the small table near by.

The fire burned brightly, the kettle sang, the richly yet tastefully-furnished room was redolent of luxurious comfort, and poor Blair nestled into his chair, and thought of the "beastly" weather outside.

Violet stole a glance at him as she busied herself with her tea-making, and a sharp pang shot through her as she saw in the firelight the pale, haggard face, which she had last seen so bright and careless.

She was just about to say: "You have been very ill, haven't you?" but once again she remembered Austin Ambrose's caution, and, instead, she said:

"Where have you been, Blair?"

He started, and roused himself.

"Lately, do you mean?" he said, looking at the fire still. "I have been wandering about Somersetshire."

"Not shooting with a party?"

"No," he answered. "I have been alone. Just tramping round to—to kill time. I have been rather seedy, you know, but I am all right now," he added, quickly, as if he feared she might question him.

All right! Her heart ached, but she forced a smile.

"You don't take any care of yourself, Blair," she said, lightly, though her soul was filled with bitterness at the thought that it was the loss of that "other woman" which had wrought such havoc with him. "Here is your tea; I think I remember how you like it."

"It is first rate," he said. "You always used to make good tea, Vi."

The color mounted to her face at the sound of the familiar name. How long it was since she had heard him use it.

"Did I? It is about the only thing I can do properly."

Then she went on talking in a light and cheerful tone, the sort of talk that exacts almost nothing from the listener—gossip about places and people he knew, the last scandal of the five o'clock teas, pleasant chat, to which he could listen or not, just as he chose. And Blair did not listen all the time, but sat looking at the fire, with his teacup in his hand, and marveling in a dreamy fashion at the faithfulness of women.

This girl—the most hunted heiress in London, pretty, accomplished, every way desirable, whom he had neglected, almost deserted—received him as if he had been most devoted and steadfast. It was wonderful!

His heart smote him, and he felt drawn toward her in a curious kind of way.

After all, it is to the women men go when trouble smites them. There is no heart so tender, no sympathy so sure as that of a woman.

"Oh, woman, in our hours of ease.
Uncertain, coy, and hard to please—

When pain and anguish wring the brow,
A ministering angel thou!"

What a brute he had been not to come near her all this time! he thought, and under the impulse of his self-reproach he felt inclined to tell her all.

"Vi," he said, abruptly, breaking into the middle of some story she was telling him.

"Well?" she said, turning her face to him, with a sudden light in her eyes, a light of hope and expectancy.

"I want to tell you," he said, passing his hand across his brow, "you know I have been in trouble lately. You may have heard something of it from Austin——"

"From Austin Ambrose?" she said. "No. Why should he tell me?"

"I didn't know. I thought perhaps he would. Vi, I have had a rough time of it—a very rough time of it. I don't think any man has suffered more than I have, during these last few months."

He leant forward in his chair, and put up his hand, so that it hid his face from her.

"Tell me, Blair," she said. "Poor Blair!" and stretching out her hand she laid it, softly as a feather, upon his.

Something in her voice, or perhaps it was the touch of her hand, reminded him of Margaret so keenly that he shuddered and his face went white.

She felt the shudder, and her acute sense saw the danger.

"Stop, Blair," she murmured. "Perhaps it is better that you should not tell me. Whatever it is—and it must have been something terrible—it will be well that you should forget it; and you won't forget it any the sooner by talking of it. No, don't tell me! But I am very sorry, Blair, very—very." Her face paled, and her lips, which were very close to his face as she bent forward, quivered. "I think I would go through a great deal to save you from pain, Blair. We are such old friends, are we not?"

"Yes—yes," he said, brokenly, and he put out his hand, and took hers and pressed it. "Yes, you were always good to me—too good, Vi. I don't deserve that you should be so kind now, after leaving you all this time!"

"Never mind that," she murmured, and her voice was as soft and tender as only a woman's can be to the man she loves. "Don't let us think of that. I will be as kind as you like, Blair!"

The poor fellow's wounded heart was aching; his strength, mental and physical, broken down by illness and the long, dreary tramp; something suspiciously like tears shone in his eyes, and he raised her hand to his lips in speechless gratitude for her kindness and gentleness.

"Oh, not my hand, dear!" she murmured, and slipping down at his knees, she put up her lips.

Blair bent down and kissed her, as he was bound to do. He could not have done otherwise, and by that kiss he sealed his fate. And yet, even as he gave it, the sweet face of Margaret rose as plainly before him as if it were she and not Violet Graham who knelt at his feet.

CHAPTER XXIV

Margaret went to her beautiful suit of rooms that night with a beating heart and a mind sorely troubled.

Prince Rivani had proposed to her!

It had come so unexpectedly that it overwhelmed her. There are a great many princes in Italy—they are commoner there than with us, but still a prince is a prince, and this one was amongst the best and highest of his order. Margaret had not dreamed that he would have condescended to bestow more than a passing and friendly thought upon the unknown English woman who dwelt in his house as the governess and companion to his sister.

And now, quite suddenly, without preparation, he had asked her to be his wife!

It seemed incredible, but it was only too true; and what was she to do?

It would have been bad enough if she had been an ordinary English woman, and her insignificance and poverty the only drawbacks; but her position was not so good as that even. There was a blot upon her escutcheon which made it impossible for her to be the wife of any honest man, however humble he might be, least of all the wife of so great a man as Prince Rivani!

She had so completely buried all thought of love in the tomb of the past, that it had never occurred to her that a man might fall in love with her, and now, as she stood before the glass and looked dreamily and sadly at her face, she was bound to admit, and that without vanity, that she was beautiful; but how beautiful, how supremely lovely, she herself did not guess.

But now what was she to do? Improbable and unlikely as it seemed, Prince Rivani *had* fallen in love with her and asked her to be his wife, and, as it was simply impossible that she should marry him, there was only one course open for her; she must leave the villa and Florence, and at once.

She sighed deeply as the conviction was forced upon her. She had been, after a fashion, almost happy; she had been at peace at any rate with these great people, who had lavished their kindness upon her and won her gratitude and love.

And now she must go! Must leave the kind old lady, who, with all her stateliness, had ever been tender to the unknown English girl; leave Florence who loved her with all the warmth of her young unscathed heart!

She sighed again, and, opening the window, looked out at the night, or rather morning, for midnight had passed some hours since, and as she did so the faint perfume of a cigar floated up to her, and she saw the tall figure of the prince walking to and fro on the terrace beneath. He, too, was sleepless, and thinking of her! She closed the window quietly and was beginning to undress, when there came a knock at the door and the Princess Florence entered.

For the first time Margaret was not glad to see her, but Florence unsuspectingly ran in and put her arm round the white shapely neck.

"Oh, forgive me, dear!" she murmured, with the impulsive enthusiasm of her age. "But I could not go to sleep until I came to you and told you how glad I am!"

"Glad?" said Margaret, flushing quickly, and tossing the long tresses of silky hair so that they hid her face.

"Yes, glad!" repeated Florence, joyously. "Why, you dear, sly girl, you are not going to be so wicked as to pretend that you don't know what has happened?"

"What has happened?" said Margaret, her face all aflame for a moment, then growing pale.

"I mean your great success to-night," said the girl, sinking at Margaret's feet and leaning her head against her knee. "I can't sleep for thinking of it. The countess says she remembers nothing like it, it is not only the picture, which was quite enough to make you famous, but yourself, dear—yourself! Isn't it almost too unfair for one person to be so lovely and bewitching and also so clever?"

Margaret forced a smile and smoothed the girl's rather rough locks.

"Are you making fun of me, princess?" she said pleasantly, and yet a little sadly.

The princess looked up at her amazedly, then uttered an exclamation.

"Then it really is true that you don't know that you have caused such a sensation?" she exclaimed. "Why, dear, it was a *furore*, it was a *'Veni, vidi, vici,'* as our ancient emperor said. Do you know that directly you left the *salon* everybody fell to talking about you, though they had done that while you were there under pretense of talking about your picture. They all talked about you as if you were something that had dropped out of the skies, and we Rivanis were lucky to own the particular spot of earth upon which your divinityship descended."

Margaret laughed softly. The girl's enthusiasm amused her, and yet it was honest enough.

"You may laugh, but let me tell you, you quiet little woman, that your name will be ringing all through Italy before the week is out!"

"I sincerely trust not," said Margaret.

"Oh, but it will!" retorted the princess. "Signor Alfero is going to send your picture to be exhibited, and he will express the admiration he feels for it all through Rome; and Rome—which is the art-center of the world—will spread it through Europe, and you will be famous! And then people will ask what the artist is like, and the countess and all those whose hearts you won to-night will tell what a lovely and charming girl you are, and you will have the world at your feet!"

"You talk nonsense very eloquently, princess," said Margaret gently.

"Is it nonsense? That is good! I will tell Ferdinand!"

"Ferdinand—the prince!" said Margaret.

"Yes," laughed Florence. "For if it is nonsense, it is his nonsense, for I heard him say it after you left the room; and he said it almost gravely, as if he were sad rather than otherwise. Now, why should he be sad?" she went on, looking up at Margaret's face thoughtfully.

"Isn't it rather too late for guessing riddles, dear?" suggested Margaret.

"Late! Who could sleep after such a night?" exclaimed the princess, with the sublime contempt for repose belonging to her age. "Why should he be sad, dear? I know he admires you, for when the countess asked him if he thought you pretty—pretty! What impertinence!—he smiled and said, 'No!' and he meant that he thought you more than pretty—lovely!"

"Do you think it is quite fair to construe his thoughts?" said Margaret.

"Oh, everything is fair in love and war——" She stopped suddenly and looked up at Margaret, and her face flushed eagerly. "Oh! Do you know a thought has struck me. Only think, if Ferdinand should——" She stopped, and clasped Margaret round the waist. "Why, I believe he does already. Oh, dear! It seems almost too good to be true. But fancy if you should, some day, become my real sister!"

Margaret's face crimsoned, then gradually grew pale and strained.

"Princess," she said slowly, "never jest on such a subject again—for my sake and your own."

Gently as the words were spoken, they frightened the young girl.

"Oh, what have I said?" she murmured. "Was it very wicked?" and her lips began to tremble.

Margaret forced a smile, and caressed the rumpled hair tenderly.

"A philosopher who was also a wit once declared that a thing was worse than wicked, it was absurd," she said; "and that is also my answer, and now go to bed, dear, or you will appear at the breakfast table and frighten all your friends, for they will think they see the ghost of the Princess Florence."

The girl thought that her incautious speech had struck some discord in her dear friend's heart, and, kissing her penitently, stole from the room.

"Yes," said Margaret to herself, "I must leave them—I must go into hiding again. Oh, Blair, Blair, you have not only ruined my past, but blighted all my future! It is not only that no love can ever visit my heart again, but you have made even peace impossible!"

Meanwhile the prince strode up and down the terrace, smoking his cigar and glancing now and again up at the windows of the room which contained the woman he loved.

Prince Rivani, the descendant of a noble race, was young, handsome, a favorite at court, a gallant officer, a popular young man all round, and yet he was neither vain nor a fool—which is singular.

To say that he had fallen in love with Margaret the first time he saw her, when he nearly rode her down, would be to say too much; but when she came to live at the villa, and he saw her day by day, her beauty, and grace, and that sweetness which is given to so few women, but which she possessed so abundantly, grew upon him, until he awoke one day to find that his heart had left him, and that he loved the young English girl of whose past he knew—nothing!

King Cophetua and the beggar girl is a very pretty story, and no doubt the king was very happy with his bride for a time, but the story does not go on to tell us that they were happy ever afterward, and as a matter of fact we may conclude that the monarch who marries a beggar maid commits a remarkably rash act. Such matches are not always happy ones.

Prince Rivani knew that he was expected to marry a lady of his own rank, or at any rate, of his own class. He knew that there were at least half a dozen beautiful women at the court, from whom he might choose a wife, and from whom he would be expected to choose one. "To marry beneath him," would, if it did not quite break her heart, make his mother, the signora, very unhappy, and would probably ruin his promising career.

He was a gentleman, and he was not a fool, so he went off to court determined to cure himself of the passion which had assailed him, and to forget the lovely English girl with the sad look in her dark eyes, and the sweet smile which made him long to keep it on her face forever.

It was a task beyond his strength, this forgetting her, but he had hoped that he was out of danger, when he returned and lo!—discovered that her love had taken too firm a hold upon his heart to be rooted out. The girl he had left unknown and of little account in the world, had suddenly, in a night, become famous. The glamour of her beauty, which had so affected even strangers, exercised a fascination for him, and he had spoken and avowed his love.

And she had refused him—or something like it. It was this refusal he was pondering over as he paced up and down, smoking cigar after cigar, long after the rest of the villa was hushed in quietude, if not repose.

Should he accept her refusal? No, he would not, he could not! She had become part and parcel of his very life; all his thoughts centered in her. At night he lay awake and called up her face; at day he thought of and longed for her. And to lose her at a word! She had said "No," because he had startled her. He had been too sudden and too abrupt!—the very first night of his return to the villa. He should have waited and prepared her by his attentions for the avowal he had sprung upon her last night.

No, he would not relinquish the hope which made life sweet to him so easily; he would win her even against herself if need were.

So, with one more glance at the window, the prince went to his rooms, to lie awake and watch the dawn creeping over the fair city which his race had helped to make illustrious.

Margaret did not appear at the breakfast table; but her absence was not commented on, for it was understood by all that the Villa Capri was Liberty Hall, and that each guest was fit to come and go as he or she pleased. So they made up for her absence by talking of her as they had talked the preceding night.

They were all curious, highly curious, to know something about her; but the signora, when appealed to, smiled her serene smile and shook her head.

"I can't tell you anything about her," she said; "I have never asked her for her confidence. She is a lady, and that is sufficient for me."

And they remained silent, for they could scarcely be so rude as to suggest that what sufficed for the signora did not satisfy them!

The guests dispersed after breakfast, the ladies to their boudoirs and the music-room, the gentlemen to the armory for their guns, for a shooting expedition had been planned.

The prince, as in duty bound, went with it, though he would far rather have remained at home in his study to think of Margaret.

They returned in time to dress for dinner, and the prince, who seemed tired, went straight to his sister's room.

"Oh, is it you, Ferdy?" she said; "you have just come in time to coil up this plait for me. My maid has run off to Miss Leslie's room; she is always so anxious to desert me for her. They are all alike—the servants, I mean; I think they worship her!" and she laughed with a poor imitation of a pout.

The prince gathered up a plait of the shining hair, and kissed it with brotherly affection as he attempted to arrange it.

"They all love her, do they?" he said; "and you, too, Florrie, eh?"

"And you, too, Ferdy, eh?" she retorted, glancing round at him wickedly.

He did not flush, but met her gaze steadily.

"And I, too, Florence," he said, gravely.

"Oh, Ferdy," she exclaimed, clasping her hands, "I am so glad!—I am so happy! I thought it was so, but I only thought. And—oh, I don't know what to say—and when are you going to tell her?" she demanded impetuously.

"I have told her," he said, quietly.

"And—oh!" for she read the result in his eyes.

"Never mind," he said, gently; "all is not lost yet. But do not speak of it—least of all to her. Have you seen her to-day—has she been down?"

"I have seen her, but she has not been down. She has kept her own apartments, and has been working; and yet only a very little, I think. Oh, Ferdy, it can't be because she doesn't love you; that's impossible."

"Thank you," he said, forcing a smile. "You will thrive at court, Florrie."

"But it can't be! There must be something else—somebody else!"

His face grew pale and his lips contracted, and he opened his lips as if to speak, but he remained silent for a moment, then said:

"I must dress, or I shall be late," and left the room.

On his way he passed the door of Margaret's painting-room, and as he did so the princess' maid came out. She started and stepped back with a courtesy, leaving the door open. Margaret came to the door to say something to the maid, and seeing the prince, stopped short.

For a moment they looked at each other without saying anything; then he bowed and drew a little nearer, and as the servant sped noiselessly away, said in a low voice, full of respect and reverence:

"Miss Leslie, will you forget what I said last night? No, not forget, but remember that I will not speak again without your permission?"

Margaret inclined her head.

"You are my mother's guest, as well as the woman I love, and I will keep the silence you commanded! You will honor us with your company at table?"

Margaret could find no words, but she inclined her head in assent, and the prince, with a low bow, which seemed as eloquent of gratitude and worship as the most ardent words could have been, left her.

That night, while the rest gathered round her, vying with each other for a word or a smile, the prince kept away from her side. Only twice did he address her; once to bring her a fan when the room grew hot; and the second time, to lay a shawl by her side when, the windows having been opened, the temperature changed rapidly.

The days glided on. Fresh additions were made to the party, but Margaret's popularity did not decrease. Fame, that had been prophesied for her, came, for her picture had been exhibited.

The great Alfero had expressed his admiration, and her name was ringing through Rome as that of the coming artist.

And through it all Margaret's heart was haunted by trouble. Day after day she met the prince, and his conduct toward her was the same. But though he refrained from paying her marked attention, it was evident to her and Florence—who watched him—that he was continually thinking of her.

Others might flock round her with the ready flattery of their ready tongues, courting the young girl whose picture had become famous in the world of art, and her beauty the theme in the world of fashion, but it was he who now and again stood with extended hand to help her into the carriage, or placed some choice blossom near her plate. No woman, daughter of Eve, could be insensible to devotion such as this; it would have touched a heart of stone, and Margaret's heart was anything but stony.

She scarcely exchanged three words a day with him, but she found herself looking toward him when he spoke to others, and meeting his gaze, which seemed to be always wandering toward her, her own eyes would fall, and her lips tremble.

Get away she must: and yet how? Night after night she lay awake trying to frame some excuse which would withstand the entreaties of the signora and Florence; and she decided to remain until the party broke up and the prince returned to the court, and then she would vanish—forever.

The last night arrived. The party had been out on the hills, and returned with the gayety of spirits which we English—alas!—know nothing of. The great banqueting hall was brilliant with light, and the guests in their magnificent costumes and gorgeous uniforms gave additional splendor to the decorations.

Margaret stole down to the drawing-room a few minutes before the gong sounded, and her advent was the signal for a crowd of courtiers to throng round her.

"I should think you would be glad when we are all gone!" said one, a white-haired veteran, who seemed to find it impossible to leave the side of the quiet English girl, with her sweet smile and rare eyes. "I know you artists so love quiet, and we make such a noise, do we not? Alas! we shall all be quiet enough to-morrow, for we shall be far away from the dear villa, and thinking of you——"

"Please include me, count," said the signora.

He made her a bow.

"I spoke collectively, of course," he said, amidst the general laugh, and not a whit discomposed. "If you knew how dreary you make the court after your villa, and how we pine after you all!" he said, with a sigh. "Why, I declare, to-day, if it had not been for the effort which becomes a duty, we should most of us have been in tears. I missed everything I shot at, did I not, prince? But, bah! I must not appeal to you, for you were as bad. Indeed, I do not know what has come to you lately; you have lost your own altogether."

"That is true," said a young *attache*; "and Rivani used to be the best shot amongst us; the best I know, except Blair Leyton."

The prince was standing beside Margaret, showing her some photographs of Rome which he had sent for, and was paying no attention to the general conversation.

"That is St. Peter's," he was saying, when suddenly Blair's name smote upon her ear.

She looked up, pale as death, and the photograph fell from her hand to the floor. Half a dozen hands were outstretched to recover it, but the prince stooped and picked it up, and stood in front of her as a screen.

"Are you ill?" he asked in a low voice; but Margaret did not hear him. She sat, leaning forward a little, her face deadly white, her eyes fixed upon the young *attache*.

The prince took up a fan and unobtrusively fanned her, his fine eyes fixed on her face with the tenderest regard.

She did not seem as if she were about to faint, but rather as if she had fallen into a trance.

"Blair Leyton?" said the count. "Blair Leyton?" and at every repetition of the name a tremulous quiver passed rapidly over Margaret's white face.

"Yes, Viscount Leyton, the Earl of Ferrers' nephew. Surely you remember him, general?"

"Oh, yes," said the count. "I had forgotten for the moment. Yes, yes! He was a good shot. One in a thousand. I was with him in the Black Forest—and in England, too. A wonderful shot! A wonderful young man, too," he added; then, as some reminiscence occurred to him, he warmed into enthusiasm. "A fine specimen of an English sportsman. I do not think I ever saw a young man ride as he rode. It was in one of the English hunting counties; and he was riding a perfect demon of a horse. There was no other man on the field who would have got into the saddle, and yet this young lord rode him as if he were a lady's palfrey. I saw him jump——" He stopped and smiled. "I am afraid, my dear signora, you would not believe me if I were to tell you. It was a tremendous jump, and to miss it meant a broken limb—or a broken neck."

He paused, and Margaret, who had been fighting against the terrible effect the mere mention of Blair's name had worked upon her, recovered, and with a sigh, withdrew her eyes from the speaker, and looked up at the prince.

"Are you better?" he murmured, still screening her from the rest, and affecting to examine the costly fan he held.

"I—I am quite well," she said, looking down. "It must have been the heat."

"Doubtless," he said. "I will see the dining-room is cooler."

The gong sounded at the moment, and he had to leave her and give his arm to the countess, but Margaret heard him give directions to the servants respecting the dining-room windows.

The dinner proceeded. Her chair was placed within about six of his at the bottom of the table, and sometimes he would lean forward and say a few words; but to-night, although he watched her with that tender scrutiny of which Love teaches us the secret, he said nothing. And she sat silent, not listening to the talk around her, but thinking of that past which Blair's name had recalled all too vividly. The splendid room, the brilliant company, faded from her sight, and in their place rose the inclosed garden at the Court, and in the moon rays stood close by her side the man who even then, as she thought, was plotting her ruin!

Suddenly she heard his name again. It was the old general, who, apparently, could not forget the young Englishman who had taken the big jump.

"Has any one seen Viscount Leyton lately?" he inquired.

Margaret had a piece of bread in her hand, and was breaking it, but the prince saw her hand fall, and her fingers close over the bread with a convulsive clutch.

"I saw him when I was in London a month ago, count," said the young *attache*.

"Indeed. And is he as strong and cheerful as ever? Dear me, I remember him singing a song—a stupid sort of song; but he sang it with that light-hearted *chic* which the French so pride themselves on, but which, after all, one sees oftenest in the English."

"Blair Leyton wasn't very light-hearted when I saw him last," said the young man. "He was awfully changed. He'd been ill, so they said, and very unlucky, too. Something had gone wrong with him, I fancy; an 'affection of the heart,' I suppose. Your Englishman, when he loses his mistress, invariably takes to drink or gambling. I don't fancy Blair would sink to the former, so I imagine he had been going in for the latter. You know the Green Table Club, general?"

The count made a significant grimace, and executed something very like a wink, and the *attache* nodded significantly.

"Poor fellow, he was always reckless and careless, but lately they say he was positively desperate. He must have been living pretty hard, for he is so fearfully altered; the mere shadow of his old self; and you know what a splendid fellow he was, general?"

"Ah, yes," assented the old soldier. "I thought when I saw him that I would give a good deal to have him in my brigade. And he was so altered and broken, you say?"

"Oh, terribly. I heard, too, that he had lost nearly all his property. He had a great deal in his own right, in addition to his heirdom of the Ferrers property."

"It is a dreadful thing to see a man so richly endowed go to the dogs in that fashion," said the general, who had borne anything but a character for steadiness in his youth.

A smile went round the table, and the *attache*, to close the subject, remarked:

"Oh, I hope the dogs will be disappointed yet. There was a rumor of a match between Blair and the great heiress, Miss Violet Graham; but I can't vouch for the truth of it, seeing I got it from a man whose word I wouldn't hang a dog on—Austin Ambrose."

"Austin Ambrose, a man with a face like a mask, and a trick of looking over your head while he is talking to you?" said the general. "Oh, yes, I remember him. He was always with Lord Leyton."

"And is still," said the *attache*.

The subject had run itself out, and the conversation took another turn, but all the time it had been dealing with Blair Leyton, Margaret had set, her eyes fixed on the cloth, her hand closed on the piece of bread, and when it had concluded she looked up and round about her, like one awaking from a dream.

The signora signaled to the ladies and rose, when the prince held up his hand.

"Pardon, my mother, but you have forgotten the toast."

"Ah, the toast, yes," she said, and with a placid smile sank down again.

The prince filled the glass of the lady near him with wine, and leaning forward poured some into Margaret's glass.

"It is our custom on the night before our departure, Miss Leslie, to drink this toast—'To our next meeting!'" and as he spoke he rose and raised his glass.

All rose, ladies included, and lifted their glasses above their heads, and Margaret did the same. But her hand felt weak and tremulous. Blair's name was still ringing in her ears, and almost unconsciously she let the glass slip from her fingers. The red wine ran down her dress, where it made no sign, but reaching the table-cloth marked it with a blood-like stain.

The party looked rather grave, for it was considered a bad omen, but the prince, with his ever ready tact, laughed.

"Bravo, Miss Leslie!" he exclaimed. "That is the Greek fashion; you have secured the fulfillment of the toast by pouring a libation to the gods."

She looked at him gratefully, as his "bravo" was echoed by the rest of the gentlemen, and then she passed out with the ladies.

As if to dispel the slightly grave impression which poor Margaret's accident had produced, the men were merrier over their wine than usual, and the prince seemed, as in duty bound, the brightest of them all; but at intervals his handsome face grew grave and thoughtful. At last they rose and sauntered into the *salon*; but the prince, instead of joining a group of ladies, walked through into the conservatory, and sinking into the seat on which Margaret had sat, folded his arms and gave himself up to reverie. He remained there for a quarter of an hour, then, with the firm yet light step peculiar to him, strode into the drawing-room, and going up to Margaret, who was seated, by herself for a wonder, in a shady corner, bent down and said:

"Will you give me a few minutes?"

Margaret looked up at him almost pleadingly, but he met her gaze steadily, and with a little sigh she rose and laid her fingers on his arm.

He led her through a doorway opening to a portion of the terrace, which was inclosed by glass and occupied by some palms and statuary. The moon shone through the brown leaves and fell in white gleams upon the marble figures. Through the thick curtains the sound of the voices and music in the *salon* came fitfully, but the prince and Margaret were as little likely to be intruded on as if they were in the midst of a forest.

For a moment or two he stood looking up at the moon, as if he were choosing his words, then he turned to her, and laying his hand upon her white fingers, he said in a low but firm voice:

"You know why I asked you to be gracious enough to come here with me?"

Margaret remained silent, her heart beating heavily.

"Miss Leslie, to-morrow I leave Florence. I may not return for months, or I may get leave of absence and come back within a few days. It rests with you. The words I spoke to you the other night, they are what I would speak again now. Miss Leslie, I love you; will you be my wife?"

Margaret raised her pale face, and regarded him sorrowfully.

"Prince, it cannot be," she murmured. "Oh, I wish—I wish you had not told me——"

"I could not do otherwise than tell you," he said gravely, and with a manly tenderness. "Why should I conceal that which my heart feels? And why cannot it be?" and his fingers closed over hers.

"You forget, prince, you are a nobleman, one of the noblest in Italy, and I——" She stopped.

If he but knew how far beneath and removed from him she was!

"It is true I am a nobleman," he said gently, his dark eyes seeking hers eagerly. "It may be true that you have no title, that to the world our rank may seem unequal; but I love you—you, Mary Leslie, and I should not love you better, it could make no difference to me if you were—well, Queen of England. Besides, have you forgotten that you have a rank that is all your own, won by your genius, a rank more exalted and worthy in my eyes than that of an empress. You are a famous artist, while I—I am but the wearer of a title and sundry decorations, which I share with a score of other men as insignificant in other ways. Ah, listen to me, dear Miss Leslie. I have never loved until I saw you. I cannot ever love any one else. I can never hope to be happy unless I win you——"

"Oh, no, no!" she murmured, with deep agitation. "Do not say that, prince, for it can never be, never! never! Even if my rank equaled your own; even if——" she paused.

"Even if you loved me! Is that what you were going to say?" he inquired, his voice tremulous with suppressed passion. "Ah, say it, dearest! Let me hear the sweet words from your lips! You *shall* love me! Yes, for I will win your love from you, even against yourself," and he made to draw her near to him, but Margaret drew back, her eyes regarding him pleadingly and sorrowfully.

"No, prince," she said, almost inaudibly. "Even if I loved you I could not be your wife."

He waited while she gained strength to go on, waited with that chivalrous delicacy and patience which distinguished him.

"It is impossible, prince. Think what it is you do. You are asking me to share your rank, your noble name, one who is a stranger to you, of whom you know nothing"—she paused—"who may be anything that is base and unworthy——"

"Oh, stop!" he said, pleadingly; "do I not know that you are all that is good, and true, and pure? Have I not lived in the same house with you, listened to your voice? A man blind to all else could not but see that you are worthy to be the wife of any one, be he whom he may."

"No," she murmured; "it cannot be. Let me go, prince. I will go away, far from Florence, from Italy——"

He stopped her with a sudden gesture, a glance of fear and dread.

"You—you are married?" he said.

Margaret started, then she shook her head.

"I am not married, prince; but there is a dark shadow in my life, a sorrow and a shame."

Her voice faltered and broke, and her hand closed on his with a convulsive grasp.

"Shame?" he breathed.

"Yes," she said, nerving herself; "shame! Now, prince, you know why it is that I cannot be your wife. Spare me, and let me go."

He stood, white as the marble faces looking down at him, his eyes fixed on her face, yet scarcely seeming to see her.

"Shame!" he repeated, like a man who speaks during some horrible dream.

Margaret tried to shrink from him, but his hand held hers in a clasp of steel.

"Shame and—you!" he said at last. "You! Oh, it is impossible." Then he looked in her face, bent low and humbly, like a drooping lily, and he uttered a faint cry. It was the cry of a man who has been mortally wounded.

There was silence for a moment, then he let her hand fall, and turned—not to forsake her, but to hide his face from her. Margaret waited a second, then crept closer to him.

"Will you—can you forgive me, prince?" she murmured brokenly. "I should not have come here, but—but I was sorely tempted. I was alone—alone, and craving for sympathy and love—and your mother and sister gave them to me. I had no right to enter their presence, much less to accept their love, but—ah, if you knew all!" and a sigh choked her voice.

"Tell me all," he said, turning to her almost sternly; "tell me all—all! The name of the man——" He stopped, and his hands clinched tightly at his side.

Margaret shrank back with a look of fear.

"No, no!" she gasped; "not a word. It is all past and—and buried. I am as one that is dead to the world, and he—he is forgiven."

"Forgiven!" he echoed. "Ay, by an angel; but we are not all angels. No; some of us are men."

His face was so awful in its wrath and craving for vengeance that Margaret sprung to him and seized his arm.

"Prince, what would you do?"

He took her hand and dropped it from his arm with a little shudder, as if her touch had stung him; then, half mad with love, half frenzied by the passionate desire for vengeance on her behalf and his own, he took her hand and pressed it to his lips.

"I understand!" he said hoarsely; "oh, yes; I understand! He has wronged you—but you love him still!"

Margaret shrunk back, and covered her face with her hands.

"Yes," he muttered: "you love him still. Heaven help me!"

Margaret's heart was wrung by the agony in that cry of a strong man mortally stricken, and in her anguish and pity she fell at his feet, sobbing bitterly.

He looked down at her for a moment, all his soul speaking in his white, working face, then he raised her and gently led her to a door leading to one of the staircases, and held back the curtain that she might pass through.

"Good-bye!" he said. "Do not be afraid that—that I shall torture you with my presence. You spoke of leaving the villa. Do not. I ask that much of you. Grant it to me."

With bowed head, Margaret passed through, and, letting the curtain fall, he stood for awhile like one of the statues surrounding him; then, with a gesture terrible in its intensity, he raised one hand toward heaven, and vowed that he would know no rest till he had avenged her.

And so sprung into existence a foe to Blair more deadly than he had ever known, a foe spurred, not by personal hate, but by the passionate desire to wreak vengeance on behalf of the woman of whose love he had been robbed, whose life this unknown man had stained with shame.

And on that day, miles away, at Leyton Court, lay the great Earl of Ferrers—dying.

"What is the use of being a king if one must die?" exclaimed the Emperor Nero, who had caused death to others too often not to know what it meant.

The great earl, with half a dozen titles to his name, and half a county owning his sway, lay upon a couch in his sitting-room, upon which flickered the rays of the setting sun, fitly typifying his own approaching withdrawal beneath the horizon of life.

At his side sat Violet Graham, who had been sent for in haste some few days back, and who had remained in close attention upon the old man.

Near as he was to that grim door through which all mortality passes never to return, the earl still bore himself as a patrician should. The face was drawn and lined, the white hands were gray and transparent, but the eyes still shone calmly and resolutely.

"Has he come, my dear?" he asked.

"Not yet, my lord," said Violet Graham, starting slightly and flushing faintly. "It is scarcely time, I think."

"I suppose he will come," said the earl, dryly, "or will he find himself unable to leave the gaming-table and his other pursuits for a few hours?"

"I—I do not think Blair plays much now, my lord," she said, in a low voice.

"You do not know," he said, grimly. "No one knows. His life is a mystery. Why has he not been near me—when did you see him last?"

Her face paled as she remembered the night Blair had come to Park Lane and kissed her.

"Not—not very lately, sir. Not for some weeks."

"Then he may be abroad—at Monte Carlo or some other congenial place?"

"No," she said, in a low voice; "he has not left London."

He looked at her with the shrewdness of old age.

"You keep yourself informed of his movements; you care for him still, Violet?"

She did not answer, but her keen eyes met his for a moment, and her small, restless fingers plucked at the edge of the silk shawl which she had thrown over him.

The earl sighed.

"The love of women!" he muttered. "It passes all comprehension. My poor girl!"

"Do not pity me, sir," she said. "Perhaps——" she stopped.

"You think all may yet be well?" he said, with suppressed eagerness, and with a sudden flash of light in his eyes.

She did not reply, but he read her answer in her downcast face.

"It would save him!" he murmured. "But would it make you happy? My poor Violet——"

"If not, then nothing else will," she said, a deep red covering her face.

Before he could make any response, the door opened and a servant announced Viscount Leyton.

Violet Graham turned pale, and rising, passed out of the room by one door as Blair entered by the other.

The earl held out his hand; Blair, advancing quietly, took it, and the two men, the great earl and the one who would so soon take his place, looked at each other; then the earl let Blair's hand drop, and sighed.

"Great heavens!" he said, in the low and feeble voice, "judging by countenances we might well change places!" and he looked at Blair's haggard but still handsome face.

Blair smiled grimly.

"What have you been doing? But no need to ask. Have you been trying to kill yourself?"

Blair smiled again, and then sank into a chair.

"Never mind me, sir," he said, gently, and his voice, for it was as soft as a woman's when he was moved, made the old man wince; "I am of no account. I did not know you were so ill until I got your letter—or rather Violet Graham's. Are you better? I trust so."

"Oh, yes, I am better. I shall soon be quite well—if there is any truth in the pleasant things good people tell us of the other land. But I did not ask you to exchange sickroom commonplaces with a dying man——"

Blair laid his still strong hand upon the thin, shriveled one.

"Don't talk of dying, sir! Please Heaven there are many years before you yet! You have not squandered your strength, as—as some of us have."

"Lord Leyton, for instance," said the earl, with a smile. "No, I won't talk of dying. We will talk of something more profitable. Blair, you will be the Earl of Ferrers presently; a few days, weeks, perhaps, and you will be the master of the Court. I have done my best for you, although you have done the worst for yourself."

"The very worst, sir," assented Blair, with the smile which, grim as it was, was still pleasant to see.

"The very worst! But it is not too late yet."

Blair looked hard at the carpet.

"Not too late! Blair, all your own property is gone, they tell me?"

"They tell you truly, sir," said poor Blair, gravely.

"But there is still the Court, and there will be my own money! I have saved for years. You will be rich, even as rich men go nowadays. Are you going to fling it all in the gutter, like that which has gone before?"

Blair remained silent. The old man watched the weary, haggard face keenly.

"I see! Ah, well! It will not matter to me, I suppose? But it is rather a pity, is it not? Ours is a good title, not a mushroom affair of yesterday. There are stones in the Court upon which time and history have set their seal, and they are to be flung in the gutter, eh? And with the heart of one of the best girls in England to be broken— —"

Blair started. For a second he had thought of Margaret, though he knew it was Violet Graham whom the earl meant.

"Poor girl! What fools men are!" Then his voice grew pathetic in its earnestness and entreaty. "Blair, is it too late? You owe me something, I think; I know you owe something to your name and all that belongs to it. Is it too late? Think! A woman's love, a good woman's heart is too priceless to be spurned with a light laugh. Blair, I, your kinsman, lying here dying, prefer one request. I do not ask you to spare this old roof or the wealth I leave you, but I do ask you to grasp the happiness within your reach. Will you make Violet your wife?"

Blair rose and paced the room. An agitation which seemed utterly beyond reason worked in his face. The old earl watched him in silence for a moment, then he said with a sigh:

"I understand. You refuse?"

"No," said Blair, "I consent. I will marry Violet, if she wishes it, and, please Heaven, I will try and be less unworthy of her."

The earl raised himself on his elbow, and touched a silver bell, and fell back panting on his cushions, and as Blair bent over him, the door opened, and Violet entered.

Her quick eyes glanced at Blair questioningly, but before either of them could speak, the earl took her hand and said:

"Violet, Blair has asked you of me for his wife. What have you to say?"

Her face went pale, then grew crimson, and she steadied herself by the head of the couch.

"Yes," she breathed, then just touching Blair's hand, she glided past him and fled to her own room.

The news spread with marvelous rapidity—for Violet told her maid within ten minutes of the proposal; but the interest that was excited was as nothing to that called forth by the further announcement that the marriage was to take place immediately.

The whims of dying men, especially when they are as great and as mighty as the Earl of Ferrers, must be regarded, and it was the desire of the earl that he should see his nephew, Blair, married to his ward, Violet Graham, before he died.

Under such circumstances it could not be anything but a quiet wedding; but even a quiet wedding between two young persons of their rank requires some preparations, and though these were hastened by the expenditure of large sums of money, a week had elapsed since their betrothal before they stood hand in hand before the altar in the little chapel of the Court.

Never perhaps had Violet looked handsomer. She had loved Blair Leyton for years with a passion of which, fortunately for the general peace, the fair sex alone is capable; and now she had got the desire of her heart, and he was her own. The fullness of her happiness almost frightened her, and as she found courage to glance up once at the pale, handsome face of the bridegroom, a sudden pang shot through her, the pang of a doubt and a dread which she strove to kill even as she felt them.

Would she be able to win his love, or, if after all her striving and its success, should she but own the shadow and semblance of the heart she craved for?

The little chapel was nearly empty, for only a few of the household had been permitted to view the ceremony, and no other guests had been asked.

At the request of Blair himself, an invitation had been sent to Austin Ambrose, but he had declined. It was, therefore, with some surprise, that Blair, as he returned from the altar with his wife—his wife—upon his arm, saw Austin Ambrose's tall, thin figure standing near the door. The sight of him gave Blair a sudden chill, for it recalled that other church in sleepy Sefton, and that other bride whom he had lost forever, but whose image was still enshrined in his heart; but he summoned up a smile, and held put his hand.

"You have come after all, then?" he said.

"Yes," said Austin Ambrose, with his calm smile. "I found that I could not keep away, and so ventured to look in, just to see the ceremony."

Then he turned to Violet Graham, who, rather pale now, had stood silently regarding him.

"One inducement, Lady Leyton," he said, his eyes looking over her head and carefully avoiding hers, "one irresistible inducement was my desire to be among the first to wish your ladyship the happiness and joy you so well deserve!" and he held out his hand.

Lady Leyton's face grew even paler as she gave him her hand, but as he grasped hers a shudder ran through her, and her eyes sought his face with a quick glance of alarm, for his hand was so cold that it struck like an icicle even through her glove.

And yet what could harm her? Was she not Blair's wife's, the Viscountess Leyton, the future Countess of Ferrers?

So, with a smile, she passed on.

CHAPTER XXV

Christmas had gone and there was a vague suggestion of spring in the air; but it was cold still, and a huge fire burned in the great drawing-room of Leyton Court. It was after dinner, and the room, though by no means full, contained a fair number of people representing a small house party which had been spending the Christmas with the new earl: for the old earl had died a week after Blair and Violet Graham's wedding, and Blair reigns in his stead. Not only is he in possession of the old title and the estates and the large sum of money bequeathed by the old earl, but he has married one of the wealthiest young women in England, and consequently the world speaks of Lord Blair with bated breath, murmuring, "Lucky beggar!" and sometimes adding, "Just in time, too! Another month and he would have gone under, by George!"

And so they point him out to country cousins as he walks down Pall Mall, and whisper: "The Earl of Ferrers—the famous Lord Leyton, you know," and his county neighbors regard him with awe not far short of adoration, and everybody, great and small, combines to envy him.

Some say that the long course of reckless dissipation has told upon his constitution and the general break up, which is always and inevitably the result of burning the candle at both ends, has arrived. And yet those who are intimate with him have never heard him complain, and it is notorious that there is no harder rider in the hunt, and that the earl can out-walk, out-box, and generally out-do any man of his age and weight, just as he has always done. There is not a stoop, not a sign of weakness in the stalwart, well-knit figure; the face is as handsome, is even more distinguished looking than ever; but there is a strange look upon it, an expression of utter weariness and lassitude, a far-off, preoccupied air which falls upon it whenever he is silent and alone.

And he is very silent of late, and very fond of being alone. Leyton Court is a charming place to visit, it is in very truth Liberty Hall, and so long as a guest does not bore his host or his fellow guests, he may do just what he pleases. And this freedom which is enjoyed by his guests, the earl claims for himself. Sometimes days will pass without his being seen, excepting at the dinner table, or for a few hours afterward in the drawing-room; but while there he is a model of what a host should be. Courteous, attentive, gentle mannered, everything but the smiling and light-hearted Blair who is still remembered in club land as the one man who never had the "blues!"

If he is attentive to his guests, to his wife he seems devoted. It is easy to gratify your wife's desires when you happen to be an earl, and wealthy to boot, but Blair, it would appear, aims at something higher than this—to anticipate the countess' wishes.

"Your rake makes the best husband!" exclaims a character in one of the old comedies, and it would really seem as if the saying were exemplified in Blair. The countess never leaves the room, but he is at the door to open it for her. In these days of sixteen-button gloves, that useful animal, man, has discovered a task suited to his energies, but no man save her husband ever buttons the countess' gloves; it is he who assists her with her pony carriage, rides beside her in her morning gallop, turns her music at the piano, and is ever at hand to perform those hundred and one little offices which render a woman's life so sweet to her.

For the rest, Austin Ambrose is as close a friend of the countess as of the earl, much to the surprise and annoyance of their friends, to whom it is still a mystery what those two young people can see in him.

It is he who assists Blair in the management of his vast estates, interviewing tenants, engaging servants, etc. And it is he who helps Lady Ferrers with her visiting lists, and executes all the little offices which a lady of rank and title is so glad to find some one to undertake.

This evening the countess is seated in her accustomed chair, exquisitely dressed—it is said that she takes Mr. Austin Ambrose's advice on this point also—and playing the part of hostess with admirable tact and judgment; but every now and then the keen observer might see that her eyes turned toward the earl, who leaned against the mantel, his hands folded behind him, his eyes bent on the ground, and that look on his face which had become habitual to it. Presently the tall, thin figure of Austin Ambrose came between her and the earl, and sauntering up, stood beside him.

"Blair," he said, "here are the letters."

There was a late mail, and the special messenger brought the letters from the office to the Court.

Blair awoke with a little start, and took them and glanced at the addresses indifferently.

"One from Tyler & Driver, isn't there?" said Austin Ambrose.

Blair nodded.

"Yes," he said, listlessly.

"I expect it is about the late earl's will," said Austin Ambrose.

Blair walked into an anteroom, and dropping into a chair, threw the letters on to a writing table.

"See what it is they want, will you, Austin?" he said.

Austin took the letter and opened it.

"It's about that five thousand pounds which the earl left to— —"

Blair turned and leaned his head on his hand, so that his face was concealed.

"Well?"

"They say that every effort has been made to discover Miss Hale's whereabouts, by advertising and inquiries, and that they can find no trace of her."

"Ah, no!" said Blair, with a deep sigh.

"And they give the usual advice, that the money should be funded. It is the best plan."

"Yes, unless we tell the truth," said Blair, in a low, sad voice. "Sometimes I think that I have been unwise, Austin, in keeping the story of—of my marriage and my darling's death from Lady Ferrers."

Austin Ambrose watched him closely.

"Take my advice, Blair, and while trouble sleeps let it sleep. The past— that past—is dead and done with. The poor girl is dead, and lost to human ken! Why provide the public prints with sensational paragraphs?

"No, I could not do it, and yet, I feel that it is due to my poor dead Margaret. I will think it over. If it should be done, if it is my duty to do it, I will do it," he added, with mournful firmness. "See what the other letters are about, will you, if it isn't too much trouble."

"Not a bit; it amuses me to flatter myself I am of some use to you," was the prompt reply, as the speaker sat down to the table.

Blair strolled back to the drawing-room. Some one was playing, and the vast room was filled with the music. For a moment Violet seemed left alone, and, with the courtesy which never deserted him, Blair walked across to her and took a chair by hers.

"You look tired, Blair," she said.

"Tired! Do I? I am not in the least," he replied.

"All this bores you, does it not?" she asked, glancing round at the company.

"Not at all," he replied, with a smile. "Why should it? They do not interfere with me— —"

"No, nothing is permitted to interfere with you," she broke in, with a sudden bitterness. "So that you are left alone, you are—satisfied. Is that not so, Blair?"

"What do you wish me to do?" he asked, with grave earnestness. "Believe me, Violet, you have only to express a wish— —"

"And you will gratify it. I know!" she retorted, with a laugh that seemed hard and cold. "You are the model husband they all declare you, Blair. No, I haven't a wish, excepting, perhaps—but it isn't worth mentioning."

"What is it?" He forced a laugh, and put his hand on her arm with a caress that was gentle enough, if it had no love in it. "Our old selves have a trick of disappearing, Violet," he said, "and once they are gone— —" he stopped significantly. "And I think most people would admit that it is a good thing my old self cannot come back!"

"Not I!" she said, in a low, quiet voice. "I would rather have you as you were. Yes; I know!—with all your wildness. I would rather you were unkind to me—struck me!—than as you are."

He half rose, then sank back again with a troubled sigh.

"You are wild enough for us both to-night, Violet," he said, trying to speak lightly. "Have you been reading some of the latest romances, or is it the professor's music that has affected you?"

She looked at him fixedly, and the color died out from her face, leaving it waxen pale.

"Yes, that is it," she said; "it is the music. It always did affect me," and she laughed.

He looked at her anxiously.

"Violet, this place does not suit you," he said. "You are looking pale and ill. It is my fault; I ought to have taken you abroad. You will go, will you not?"

She shrugged her shoulders.

"Oh, yes, if you like. I am perfectly indifferent. But I am quite well, all the same."

Some one coming up to them, he rose and surrendered the chair, as a matter of course, and a moment or two afterward he heard her laugh as if nothing had passed between them.

He walked about the room for some minutes, absently looking at the pictures, or exchanging a word with one person and another, then sauntered into the anteroom to consult Austin Ambrose as to the best place to take the countess, but that gentleman had left the room; and, ascertaining from a servant that he had gone into the library, Blair went there with the same listless step.

As he opened the library door he heard voices and saw that Austin Ambrose was not alone; a thin, gentlemanly man was seated opposite him, a stranger to Blair, and he stepped back.

"I beg your pardon; I thought you were alone, Austin," he said.

"Don't go," said Austin Ambrose. "This is the earl, Mr. Snowdon; this is Mr. Snowdon, the detective, Blair."

The gentlemanly man rose and bowed respectfully, and remained standing until Blair motioned him to resume his seat.

"Mr. Snowdon has come to report on his inquiries respecting Miss Margaret Hale," said Austin Ambrose, quickly but fluently, and giving the man no chance to speak. "He simply confirms Tyler & Driver's letter. No trace of Miss Hale can be found, unfortunately; that is so, I think, Mr. Snowdon?"

"Quite so," assented the detective, respectfully.

Blair stood with his hand pressed on the table, his face white and drawn.

"Thank you!" he said. "Yes, yes."

He stood silently for a moment, and then left the room without another word.

Austin Ambrose rose and slipped the bolt in the door.

"You were mad to come down here!" he exclaimed in a low and angry voice.

"I am very sorry," said the detective, humbly; "but you told me to let you know immediately if I got a clew, and I don't like writing; there's no knowing where a piece of paper will go to."

"Well—well!" said Austin Ambrose. "Now tell me as quickly as you can," and he sank into the chair with an affectation of indifference which the close compression of his hands and the glint of his dark eyes belied.

The detective took a note-book from his pocket.

"First of all, sir, I've to admit that you were right and I was wrong. The young lady was not drowned on that rock, and you were right in supposing that the Days had a hand in getting her away—not that I got any information from them; I'll do them that credit. Close as wax, both of 'em. I traced them down to Cardiff, and lodged in their house for a fortnight; but if I'd stayed twenty years, I don't believe I'd have got any light on the matter. If it hadn't been for an accident I'm afraid I should still be in the dark. If it hadn't been for spending the evening with the second mate of the Rose of Devon, I shouldn't have earned my money, Mr. Ambrose. I've had some tough business to do for you now and again, but this was the very toughest I ever had in hand."

Austin Ambrose sat perfectly still, and apparently patient, but his hands closed and unclosed with a spasmodic movement.

"From this sailor I discovered that the Rose had picked up the Days and a young lady one night, off the Devon coast, and an extra glass of brandy induced him to admit that she'd sailed in the Rose to Brest. At Brest I found that my man was correct. The Rose *did* have a lady on board. Two persons saw her land, and noticed her, as French people will! One of them, the harbor master, could even give me a description of her. There it is; you'll know best whether there can be any doubt!"

Austin Ambrose did not snatch the paper out of his hand, but let it lie on the table for a second or two, then he took it up and read it, and, self-possessed as he was, could not help an exclamation of triumph.

"It is she! She is alive! Well?" he demanded, quietly; "go on!"

"Well, sir," said the detective, "having made certain of the young lady's being still in the land of the living, I posted straight off for England. Your instructions were, Mr. Ambrose, that I was to come to you the moment I found out that she was alive. I could have traced her from Brest easily enough——"

"I know! I know!" interrupted Austin Ambrose. "You have carried out my instructions! A French *mouchard* will do the rest. She landed there—she did not go aboard again, you say?"

The detective hesitated for a second. As a matter of fact, he was not certain on the point; but your detective never likes to admit that he does not know everything, so, after the imperceptible hesitation, he said, glibly enough:

"No, Mr. Ambrose, she went straight on by land. She's in France, most likely Paris—for certain. Large cities are generally chosen by people who want to hide securely; every child knows that."

"Yes, yes," muttered Austin Ambrose, "she is in Paris."

He rose and took out his pocketbook.

"I am much obliged to you, Snowdon. The matter can rest here now. I wanted to be certain of the young lady's existence, and for the rest, well, I dare say I can find her if I should require her, which at present I do not. There is the sum I promised you, and there is a bonus. You will find it in your interest to deserve my confidence; and now make yourself scarce as quickly and quietly as possible."

"If you will kindly open that window, sir," said the detective, quietly, "I need not disturb any of the servants. I can find my way across the park," and with a respectful farewell he passed out.

Austin Ambrose stood and mused, his sharp brain turning the situation this way and that. Then he looked up and smiled at his own face reflected in the mirror over the mantel.

An hour afterward he re-entered the drawing-room, with his usual placid smile, and all his plans made.

Lying on the couch was the countess. Her fingers were picking restlessly at the edge of the Indian shawl, a habit she had, and as she looked up he saw her face was pale and troubled.

He bent over the head of the couch, murmuring softly: "Not in bed yet? You ladies are as dissipated as we men."

"Yes, this is dreadful dissipation, is it not?" she retorted, ironically.

"You look tired," he said. "Violet, I don't think this air suits you——"

She laughed sarcastically.

"Really you are too transparent. Blair has been telling you I want a change and you can't summon up courage to tell me so openly! What cowards men are!"

"Blair has not been speaking to me," he said. "But, all the same, I think you should go away, both of you. He looks bored, don't you think; rather off tone——"

"No, I don't think—I am sure," she retorted.

"Leyton never is very good in the winter, I believe," he said, hastily. "What do you say to—Naples for instance?"

"What do *you* say?" she responded, her keen eyes seeking his fixed steadily upon some point above her head. "That is the question, because whatever place you say, will doubtless be the one selected. I wonder why you take such an interest in us both?" and her eyes grew hard as steel. "You can say that I am pining for it, that it is the one desire of my heart, that I shall die if I'm not taken there at once——"

"Don't jest on such a grewsome topic," he said. "Joking apart, I will venture to prophesy that you will be happier at Naples than you have ever been in your life. It is so warm there."

"Even that will not be wonderful," she retorted; then suddenly her voice changed, and she looked up at him almost fiercely. "Do you think it will be warm enough to thaw Blair's heart? Austin, will he *never* forget that girl? Oh, Heaven! how I hate her."

"Hush!" he said, in a low voice: "you forget—the dead!"

"No," she retorted, the two bright spots burning fiercely on her cheeks, her eyes glittering like dagger-points; "I hate her more now she is dead, for if she had lived he would have tired of her, but now she comes between us like a ghost; and you cannot get rid of that for me, even you, clever as you are, Austin!"

CHAPTER XXVI

A month later, the sun, which in England was shining with a sickly affectation of geniality, was pouring a flood of warmth and light on every house and street in Naples. Color, warmth, brightness were all there, not in niggardly patches, but in lavish profusion, and in no spot of the enchanted city more profuse than in the palace in which resided the Earl and Countess of Ferrers; for to Naples they had come, and, needless to say, Mr. Austin with them.

But though he had prophesied that Violet should be happier there than she had ever been, his prophecy had not yet fulfilled itself, for even the Naples' sun could not thaw Blair's heart, and, as in England, there was still that weary, absent expression in his face which proclaims the man to whom life has become joyless and hopeless.

Of all the noble palaces which the Neapolitans so cheerfully let to the English visitors, the palace Austin Ambrose had chosen was the most sumptuous; and if rooms which emperors might have dwelt in, and surroundings which would have inspired a poet, could have made a woman happy, then Violet Countess of Ferrers should have been the most beatified of her sex. But on this glorious evening in spring, she was lying on her couch on the balcony overlooking the bay with the same restless fire in her eyes, the old red fever spots on her cheeks. Leaning over the balcony was Mr. Austin Ambrose attired in a spotless linen suit, with a cigar between his lips, and his eyes keenly noting the passers-by in the street beneath him.

"What are you staring at? Have you become suddenly dumb?" exclaimed Lady Violet, with irritability.

"I was looking at the beggars," he said, with a patience in a marked contrast to her impatience. "Naples is the paradise of the mendicant. Shall I wheel you nearer the balcony?—you would find them very amusing."

She looked over listlessly.

"They are not amusing," she complained, shrugging her shoulders.

"At any rate they are a study," he said. "There are beggars of every nationality under the sun, I should think. Strange how easy it is to distinguish them, even through their rags. There is the Neapolitan, for instance, that old man there with the boy; and there is a Spaniard, and there are two Frenchmen, and there is an English girl— —" He stopped suddenly, and let his cigar fall to the ground.

"What is the matter?" she asked.

"The matter?" he said, turning with a smile, though his face wore a strange expression. "What do you mean?"

"Why you start as if you had seen a ghost?"

"Oh, come; you *are* fanciful this evening," he retorted laughing.

"But you did start!" she persisted, listlessly.

"I never contradict a lady," he said lightly. "But believe me, the movement was unconscious," and he took out his cigar-case and languidly chose a fresh cigar; but as he did so, he leaned over the balcony, and keenly scrutinized the crowd beneath; for that which had caused him to start, and drop his cigar, was the form of some one who bore a strange likeness to Lottie Belvoir.

Mr. Austin Ambrose looked in the direction the girl had taken, but she had disappeared, probably up one of the narrow streets, and smiling at the fancied resemblance, he smoked on comfortably and devoted his attention to the crowd. Presently a servant came from the room behind them, and handed a card on a salver.

The countess took it languidly.

"What a nuisance people are! Did you say that we were not at home?"

"Yes, my lady," said the footman; "but his highness wrote on the card, my lady."

"His highness!" exclaimed Violet contemptuously. "Every second man one meets in Italy is a count or a prince! What is it he has written, Austin? Your Italian is better, than mine."

Austin Ambrose took the card.

"This is not Italian, it is English," he said. "'Prince Rivani begs the honor of the Earl of Ferrers' presence at a conversazione. Palace Augustus, this evening at ten o'clock.'"

"I thought it was understood that we did not visit?" said Violet languidly. "Why do people bother us? Prince Rivani! This is the second time he has left his card."

"His highness is very attentive, at any rate," said Austin Ambrose. "Shall you go?"

"Seeing that I am not asked," said Violet, "it is not very probable."

"Oh, I expect it is one of those gatherings which these Italians delight in: a little music, a little weak lemonade, and mild tobacco. Blair might like to go."

"Here is Blair to answer for himself," said Violet, as Blair strode on to the balcony.

"What is it?" he said, looking from one to the other.

"Only an invitation," replied Austin Ambrose. "I don't suppose you would care for it. You will be bored to death."

"'Prince Rivani.' He called the other day," said Blair thoughtfully, as he leant over the balcony. "Would you care to go, Violet?"

"I am not invited," she said impatiently. "Don't you see it mentions you only?"

"Ah, yes, a bachelor's party," said Blair. "I may go; it is a lovely day. I have been on the hills, and—Ah!" he exclaimed, and he leant over the balcony with a sudden appearance of interest.

Austin Ambrose glided to his side.

"What is the matter? Is it anything wonderful?" said the countess, and she rose from the couch and looked over.

Blair bit his lip.

"It is nothing," he said, "I thought I saw someone I knew."

"You are like Austin," she said, coiling herself on the couch again; "he started and dropped his cigar just now."

Blair walked out of her hearing, and beckoned Austin Ambrose.

"Do you know whom it was I saw just now?" he said.

"Couldn't guess," replied Austin.

"It was Lottie Belvoir," said Blair.

"Oh, nonsense; it's impossible!" said Austin Ambrose, lightly. "I tell you she is on an English tour at this present moment. How on earth could she be here?"

"I do not know, but I am certain it was she," said Blair, gravely.

"I'll soon convince you," said Austin Ambrose, and he disappeared. He mingled with the crowd for five minutes; then he was back again. "As I thought," he said, with a smile. "She is a Neapolitan girl with a face rather like Lottie's."

"Rather like!" said Blair, with a sigh of relief. "It was an astonishing resemblance, but if you saw the girl closely it is all right."

But the resemblance to Lottie of the girl in rags in the streets of Naples haunted him several times that evening, and on his way to Prince Rivani's rooms, he found himself unconsciously scanning the faces of the women who passed, as if he feared to see the girl.

Of Prince Rivani he had of course heard, but he had not seen him yet, and it was with a languid kind of curiosity that he followed the footman into the *salon*.

There were about fifteen or twenty gentlemen present, most of them smoking cigarettes, and from their midst a tall, patrician-looking figure came to meet him.

Blair, though he had heard of the prince's popularity and his good looks, was not prepared for so handsome a face; and he was looking at him with interest when he was struck by the expression of the prince's eye. It seemed as if he were regarding Blair with a scrutiny far and away beyond that usual on the part of a host greeting a guest for the first time. The prince's face, too, was pale, and his lips compressed as if by some suppressed emotion. But his courtesy was perfection.

"I am honored, Lord Ferrers," he said bowing, as he just touched Blair's hand. "Let me introduce you to some friends of mine," and he led Blair round the room, making him known to one and another. There were some Englishmen there—one meets them everywhere, from Kamtchatka to the plains of Loo!-and he got into conversation with one and another.

Presently, just as he was thinking of taking his leave, the prince came up to him.

"Are you fond of art, Lord Ferrers?" he inquired, in a grave voice.

Blair shook his head.

"I like a good picture, but I don't know anything about it," he said. "You have a very fine collection, have you not?"

The prince shrugged his shoulders.

"Not so fine as that at Leyton Court, Lord Ferrers," he said, with a bow. "But I possess one picture which I value above all the others. I am so attached to it that it travels about with me; it is here, in my writing room. Would you care to see it? I think it will repay you for your trouble."

Blair rose at once.

"I should like to very much," he said.

The prince led the way to a small room on the same floor, and stood before a picture, closely curtained.

"You will want plenty of light," he said, turning up the gas as he spoke, "and if you will sit just there, Lord Ferrers, you will be in the most favorable position."

At the same time he himself took up his stand by the curtain, with his eyes fixed piercingly upon Blair's face.

"Now," he said, "I want you to tell me exactly how this picture strikes you at first sight. You shall examine it closely and criticise it afterward. I ought to tell you that it has made the artist famous."

As he spoke, still keeping his eyes fixed upon Blair's face, he drew the curtain. Blair had not felt much interest in the proceedings, and expected to see some piece of artistic trickery, and so leant back to take it at his ease; when suddenly, as if the veil of the past had been rent asunder, there sprung upon his sight the picture of his Margaret lying on the rocks at Appleford; the exact representation of her death as he had pictured it, alas! how often!

Trembling and almost beside himself, he had forgotten the presence of the prince, who, mute as himself, stood with folded arras regarding him with a stern look.

"Does the picture please you, Lord Ferrers?" he said, and there was something ominous in his voice.

Blair started and turned to him.

"I—I beg your pardon. Yes, it is a marvelous picture. But there is something connected with it; I——" he sank into the chair and covered his face with his hands.

The prince stood regarding him in silence for a moment; then he drew the curtain over the picture and turned to Blair.

"My lord, you will understand why I showed you that picture. There need be not one word spoken between us in reference to it. Your face has told me all I want to know; my actions will explain my motives. Lord Ferrers will understand that if I treat him with discourtesy when we return to the company, that I do it to provide an excuse for our meeting to-morrow morning."

"Our meeting?" said Blair, who had scarcely listened to, and certainly had not understood, the prince's words.

Prince Rivani's face grew black.

"Lord Ferrers prefers to ruin women rather than fight with men! Ah, yes!"

Blair rose at once.

"I don't understand you," he said, quietly; "but if you wish to challenge me you need not be afraid that I shall decline. Why you should want to shoot me I scarcely know——"

"It is a lie!" hissed the prince, driven almost mad by what he considered Blair's prevarication.

"Thanks," said Blair, with a short nod. "At any rate, Prince Rivani, you have made it clear why *I* should shoot *you!*"

CHAPTER XXVII

Prince Rivani opened the door with a low bow, and the two men went back to the *salon*. The prince was pale but perfectly self possessed, and Blair very grave and quiet. The picture still floated before his eyes: the great black rock and the white, wan figure still stretched upon it, almost in the grasp of the cruel waves. His Margaret! Who could have painted it? And the prince had said that the picture had made the artist famous! He must find out that artist and get at the bottom of the mystery.

The *salon* was fuller than when he had left it, and he went and sat down in a quiet part of the room to wait until the prince had made some excuse for openly giving a reason for the duel of the morrow.

So he sat in his corner, outwardly calm and self-possessed, but thinking a great deal more of Margaret than the duel.

Presently Blair saw a tall, patrician man, with long hair and a beard, and the unmistakable air of an artist, enter the room, and absently noticed that he was instantly surrounded. He caught the name—it was Signor Alfero, the great artist; and scraps of the conversation floated to Blair's corner.

Suddenly he started. They were talking of the picture; he leaned forward and listened intently.

"What have you done with the masterpiece, prince?" Blair heard him ask.

"It is in my writing-room," said Prince Rivani.

"Oh, that is a pity! You should not deprive the world of a sight of its great treasures, *mon* prince."

"You still think as highly of Miss Leslie's picture, then, signor?" asked a gentleman.

"As highly?—more!" said the old man, turning promptly. "The more I see of it, the greater my astonishment grows that a woman so young could have painted a picture so old."

"So old?"

"Yes. We measure the age of a picture by the age of the thought it contains. There is a lifetime of suffering, and love, and despair in the face of the girl on that rock. Miss Leslie must have felt all that—ay, every heart-pang of it—before she could have painted it. It is—I repeat my verdict—a marvelous picture! She will, I trust, live to paint many other great ones; but never one that will go straighter to the heart than this."

"Where is Miss Leslie now?" asked another gentleman. "One sees and hears nothing of her."

"Because you do not go where she goes, signor. Miss Leslie is never seen in the promenade; you may drink your afternoon tea in all the palaces of Naples and not meet with her. But I venture to prophesy that if you will penetrate the slums of the city, the fever haunts, in which our poorest of the poor are awaiting the peace bringer, Death, you will find the great artist in their midst."

There was silence for a moment.

"Miss Leslie is a—philanthropist, then?" said the gentleman.

"She is a ministering angel," responded Signor Alfero, simply.

The prince stood by, white to the lips.

"What time she can spare from her work—and she works as hard as any seamstress in the city!—she spends amongst the poor. There is not a beggar in our streets who does not know her; not a blind man whose ears do not eagerly greet her footfall; not a sick child whose face does not 'lighten' at the sight of her smile. She is an artist—and an angel!" and the old man's lips quivered.

As if he could bear it no longer, the prince stood upright and approached Blair, his face white and set with the effort to suppress his thirst for vengeance.

"Referring to our discussion, Lord Ferrers," he said significantly, "are you still of opinion that we Italians have taken but a low place in the scale of nations?"

Blair started and looked up at him in surprise, then, understanding that the prince was going to make pretense of a quarrel, he replied:

"I cannot alter my opinion, even for so distinguished an Italian as Prince Rivani."

"That means that, as an Englishman, you regard us with contempt, my lord?"

Blair shrugged his shoulders.

"Your highness is at liberty to place any construction upon my words you please," he said.

"Thanks, my lord. Even if I assume that you charge us with cowardice?"

"Choose your own signification, prince," said Blair, beginning to grow warm, though it was only pretense.

"A nation of cowards!" said Prince Rivani, his eyes glittering at the success of the play. "That is a brave assertion; has the Earl of Ferrers courage to maintain it by the only consistent and appropriate argument?"

"I can maintain it at the sword's point, if necessary," said Blair, rising to his full height, and meeting the prince's deadly gaze with a steady, calm regard.

The prince bowed low, then turning slightly to the rest, said in a low, clear voice:

"Gentlemen, I call you to witness that the cause of quarrel is mine! Lord Ferrers has accused my country-men of a base and vile cowardice. I shall have the honor of defending them. As the Earl of Ferrers says, the argument is not one for words, but weapons! Is that so, my lord?"

"Your highness interprets me correctly," said Blair.

"Good! My friend, General Tralini, will have the honor of waiting upon your lordship at a later hour."

The prince drew him apart.

Blair got his crush hat and cloak, and approaching the prince, bowed low, then, with a general salutation, he left the room.

It was a lovely night, and the air blew upon his brow refreshingly, after the heat of the *salon.*

He paused outside the great doorway, and stood looking up at the sky— it was probable that it was the last time he would have the opportunity of seeing the stars.

Then he drew his cloak round him, and was going onward, when a woman, who had been coming down the street with her head bent and her face almost hidden in the thin shawl she hugged round her, stopped, and seeing him, held out her hand, murmuring something in broken Italian.

Blair stopped and looked at her absently; then he started, and taking her arm, drew her near a lamp.

"Lottie!" he said.

She flung her hands before her face and bent her head, almost as if she expected him to strike her.

The gesture amazed Blair.

"Lottie, Lottie!" he said, encouragingly; "it is you, then? I saw you this evening in the streets, my poor girl. But why do you shrink from me? What is the matter? Don't you know me—Blair?"

"Yes, yes!" she gasped. "I know you. I—I——Oh, Blair, don't kill me!"

"Kill you!" he exclaimed, with astonishment. "Why, Lottie, what is the matter with you?"

He took her arm as he spoke and drew it through his.

"You look ill. Lean on me. Don't be afraid."

She tore her arm from his and, shrinking back, leaned against the lamp-post, the light flashing on her face and revealing it in all its haggardness.

"Don't!—don't!" she said, with a catch in her breath. "Don't speak a kind word to me; I don't deserve it! Oh, Blair, if you knew all I've done——"

He sighed.

"Never mind, Lottie," he said, gently; "I'm afraid we have all done rather badly. But I'm sorry to see you looking so ill. Where are you staying? What made you come here? Come, tell me all about it."

"I can't! I can't!" she said, with a shudder and a fearful glance at his grave face. "I came here with a theatrical company—I got ill, and left behind. I wrote to *him* and asked for help, and he only threatened me——"

"Him! Who?" demanded Blair soothingly, for he began to think that illness and privation had turned poor Lottie's reason.

She shuddered and caught her breath.

"Austin Am——" she said, then stopped and looked up at him in sudden terror.

"Austin!" he exclaimed. "You wrote to Austin, and he——Oh, come, Lottie; that can't be true! But why didn't you write to me?"

"To you?" she breathed; "to you? Oh, Blair, Blair; if you only knew, you'd kill me where I stand!"

"Nonsense!" he said with gentle reproof. "Don't be silly, Lottie. Look here, you are weak and upset, and not in a fit state to tell me your story. Come to the palace, where I live, to-morrow, and let me hear all about it. Here is the address," and he tore a page from his pocketbook and wrote on it. "There it is. Now, mind you come; I shall be in all the morning—-" Then he stopped, for it suddenly flashed upon him that probably he should be where Lottie could not follow him. "Stay!" he said; "tell me where to find you, and I will come to-morrow—if possible."

"No!" she said with a shudder; "I will not! Go on and leave me, now."

"No, I won't," he said, and his voice sounded like the old Blair's in its hearty good-nature; "I shall stay here till you do tell me; and I warn you that we are keeping my wife up——"

She started and sprung back.

"Your wife!" she gasped. "Has she—has she come back?"

Blair turned pale, then forced a smile.

"My wife has not left me that I know of," he said. "I married Miss Violet Graham; you knew her, Lottie?"

"Violet Graham!" she panted. "Violet Graham! Oh!" and she put her hand before her eyes.

"Yes, and she is with me here at Naples, she and Austin Ambrose," he said. "He will be glad to see you and tell you that there is some mistake in your idea that he had refused to help you."

"She and he here!" she exclaimed hoarsely. "What does it mean? I can't think! I can't see what he wanted! It is all dark—all dark! Blair!" she exclaimed, seizing his arm. "That man—I tell you—I warn you! Oh, Blair, Blair! Take care! He means——" She broke off and almost groaned. "I don't know what he is working for, what he is plotting, but it is no good—no—— " She stopped again and drew her shawl round her.

"Whom are you talking about Lottie?" he asked. "Not Austin! Why, he was a friend of yours, and is one of the best fellows alive! My poor girl, what 'bee have you got in your bonnet?' What do you mean?"

"Nothing, nothing!" she said, breathlessly. "I am half mad with cold and hunger——"

"Yes, yes," he said, gently. "See here, Lottie; here is some money—get food and a lodging for to-night. Go to the Hotel Nationale. I will come to you to-morrow and you shall tell me all about it," and he held out some English sovereigns.

She looked up at him with a kind of wild horror, then with a cry of remorse, a cry that rang in his ears for hours afterward, she sped away. He threw off his cloak, and started after her, but she had gained one of the entrances to a network of dark and narrow courts, and Blair lost her as completely as if the pavement had opened and swallowed her up.

Lottie was not far off. Hidden in one of the deep doorways, she had watched him relinquish the pursuit; then, as if compelled to follow him, she crept out, and gained the large street again.

As she passed the Palace Augustus, the guests of the conversazione were coming out, and she drew back into the shadow of the doorway to let them pass.

They were all talking in an excited fashion, and two Englishmen, pausing quite close to the trembling girl, were speaking loudly enough for her to hear.

"Rum kind of thing this affair to-night," said one.

"Isn't it? But it's just what one expects in Italy. Gives quite a foreign flavor to the evening," and he laughed cynically. "Fancy two men fighting a duel on such a paltry excuse as that! Why, I didn't hear anything particularly offensive, did you?"

"Not half so offensive as one hears fifty times over at a political meeting in England."

"But then these Italians are all fire, aren't they? And glad of the excuse for a shindy, eh?"

"Poor Blair!" rejoined the other, with a sigh. "Seems rather hard when you are an earl, with goodness knows how many thousands a year, and a charming wife, to be spitted by a fire-eating Italian. But, there, we all prophesied that Blair Leyton would come to a violent end; either a cropper in the field, or the racecourse."

"That's all right and consistent enough, and would appear to be the logical conclusion of such a man; but to be pierced through the heart with one of those confounded needles! Bah! And he is such a fine fellow, too! Never saw a better made man! Don't wonder all the women of his set were mad about him!"

"Yes, Blair is a good type of our best men," said the other. "But he may not fall: he used to fence awfully well in the old days, at Angelo's fencing-school, don't you know."

"I dare say, but fencing at Angelo's is a very different thing to crossing swords with a man like Rivani, especially when he means mischief, and if Rivani didn't mean mischief to-night, then I'm no judge of a man's looks."

They passed on, and left Lottie amazed in her ambush.

Blair and Prince Rivani to fight a duel! She had been in Naples long enough to have heard of Prince Rivani's reputation as a swordsman. Blair was as good as a dead man when he stood opposite the prince's gleaming steel.

What should she do? What could she do?

Half wild, she stood wringing her hands, her black eyes gleaming with terror and despair, then, suddenly, worn out and exhausted by privation and the excitement of her meeting with Blair, and this subsequent discovery, she fell to the pavement in a deep faint.

CHAPTER XXVIII

Mr. Austin Ambrose was pacing up and down, in tiger fashion, the extremely luxurious sitting-room, waiting for Blair to return from the Rivanis'; and Austin Ambrose was anything but tranquil and at ease.

Hitherto fate had played into his hands so completely that he had run his career of villainy as smoothly as a well-oiled piston-rod works in its cylinder, but the sight of Lottie in Naples, close to his elbow, rather upset him.

The countess had gone to her boudoir some half an hour since; but she had languidly dropped a few words indicating that she intended remaining up for Blair, and Austin Ambrose listened intently now and again to hear if Blair went straight to his or her room.

Presently he heard a step upon the stairs; it was Blair's, but heavier and slower than usual, and it stopped at Austin's door, and Blair knocked.

Austin was almost guilty of an exclamation of surprise as Blair entered, for he handsome face looked so haggard and wearied that it might have been the face of a haunted man.

"You're late," he said, speaking lightly. "Had a pleasant evening, I hope?"

Blair sank into a chair, and his head drooped upon his breast; then he looked up and motioned to the table, on which stood a liqueur stand.

"Mix me something—anything, there's a good fellow," and his voice was dry and hoarse. "A pleasant evening," he laughed grimly, "you shall judge for yourself. Austin, I have seen Lottie Belvoir!"

Austin Ambrose started, and he set the glass down with a little thud. Then he smiled.

"Not really!"

"Yes. I was right, and you were wrong; it was she whom I saw. Poor girl! Lottie—who used to be the brightest and gayest of them—in Naples, starving and in rags."

"It is very strange! The last I heard of her," said Austin, his face pale with suppressed excitement and fear, "she was traveling with a dramatic company. Did she tell you— —"

"She would tell me very little or nothing," said Blair with a sigh.

Austin Ambrose drew a long breath. Lottie had stood firm, then!

"Little or nothing. Austin," suddenly, "did she ever apply to you for help?"

"To me?" he exclaimed, raising his brows. "Certainly not! Why do you ask?"

"Because she said that she had, and you had refused to assist her. But she was dreadfully incoherent, and I'm afraid that privation and trouble have upset her reason. She, poor girl, seemed possessed by some wild idea that she had injured me. She even feared that I should—strike her! When I offered her some money, and begged her to tell me where I could find her, she turned and bolted, and I lost her."

Austin Ambrose drew a breath of relief and mixed himself some brandy and water.

"Poor Lottie, she must be half mad! Thought she had injured you! Why, how could she do that?"

Blair shook his head.

"By no way that I know of. She behaved very strangely all through. She must be found to-morrow."

"Of course; and there's nothing easier. Don't make yourself uncomfortable about it, my dear Blair. I will set the police on her track at once, and we'll soon find her. But the meeting with poor Lottie hasn't spoiled your evening, I hope?"

Blair was silent for a moment, then he said, in a low voice:

"No, no; it was not that, painful as it was. I wish to Heaven it was no more! But—but—Austin, I have seen poor Margaret!"

Austin Ambrose sprung to his feet, and his hand slid like a snake into the bosom of his coat.

"Seen—seen— —!" he exclaimed, hoarsely.

"Yes," said Blair, whose back was turned toward him, and who did not see his white face and the movement of his hand; "yes, I have seen her in a picture."

Austin Ambrose dropped into the chair again, and lifting the glass to his lips took a good draught.

"In a picture, my dear Blair! You—you startled me! In a picture! A face that resembled hers. My dear old fellow, you are too sensitive. You must, really you must, fight against these feelings. They are ruining your life. In a picture——"

"Yes; not a face like hers, but her very own. I saw a picture"—and he stood and held out his hand as if he were pointing to it—"of Margaret, of my poor darling herself—lying on the Long Rock at Appleford!" his voice broke, and he turned away.

Austin Ambrose looked at him.

"He is going mad!" he thought.

"My dear Blair, impossible! This is the freak of a mind overwrought by sorrow and too much dwelling on the past. It is impossible. Where did you see this wonderful picture? I should like to see it."

"I saw it at Prince Rivani's. You can see it, no doubt. Do you think I am dreaming? That I have conjured the picture from my own imagination? Do you think I am going mad?"

Austin Ambrose certainly did think so, but he said:

"No, no; certainly not. But—but——"

"You do think so. Let me give you direct evidence that I know what I am about," said Blair. "The picture is Prince Rivani's; he took me to his private room to see it; it is the talk of all Italy, Europe, for what I know. It is a magnificent picture, terrible, moving, to any one; but judge what effect it must have had on me when I say that it was the place itself, the face and figure themselves of my poor lost darling."

Austin Ambrose stared at him.

"And Prince Rivani showed you this! What did he tell you about it, its history and so on?"

"Nothing," said Blair, gloomily. "I was so startled that I was almost beside myself, and I was about to ask him the history of the picture, and by whom it was painted, when he—you will think I am mad now, Austin!— refused to tell me anything excepting that the picture was a famous one. And he brought the interview to an abrupt conclusion by challenging me to fight him——"

Austin Ambrose's face worked.

"Which you refused?" he said.

"For which I asked his reasons. He declined to give me any one, calling me a liar, and so — —" he laughed, grimly—"provided me with an excuse for shooting him!"

"Well, and—and the artist, who is he?"

"It was not a man, but a woman—a girl," said Blair quietly and wearily.

Austin Ambrose started, and his eyes flashed. He saw it all in a moment. The picture had been painted by Margaret herself! The prince had fallen in love with her, she had told him her story, and the prince meant to avenge her.

"And—and this girl—this wonderful artist—where is she?"

He asked the question lightly enough, but his soul quaked as as Blair replied:

"Here, in Naples!"

"Here, in Naples?"

There was a moment's silence. Margaret here in Naples! Blair challenged by the prince! Any moment and his astute plans might be shattered at his feet.

He was not altogether a coward, but at the thought of the two narrow chances Blair had had of learning his—Austin's—villainy, he quivered from head to foot.

"And now you have it all," said Blair quietly. "Why Prince Rivani should want to fight me I cannot conceive, can you?"

"Yes," was the prompt reply.

Blair turned to him with weary surprise.

"The prince was an old lover of Margaret's."

The blood rushed to Blair's face, and his eyes flashed.

"An old lover? It is you who are mad! Margaret had no lover but me."

Austin Ambrose met his fierce gaze steadily.

"My dear Blair, I meant no kind of reproach against her! But think, is it not possible that the prince may have seen her before she met you? that, though nothing tangible may have passed between them, he may have fallen in love with her?"

"And she not tell me! Ah, how little you knew her!"

"She may not have thought it worth the telling! May have feared that you might think she was boasting of her conquest over a prince. But if you won't entertain this idea, what other reason can you find for his wanting to fight you? You know what these Italians are: they will fight for an idea—half a one! He may have got some inkling that you were her favored lover, he cannot possibly know that you married her, but he may see in you a rival, and these Italians consider it their duty to dispose of a rival in the most complete and expeditious way."

Blair leaned his head upon his hands.

"It is all a mystery," he said, wearily. "But the fact remains. I have undertaken to meet him to-morrow morning. You will be my second, of course, Austin? A General Somebody or other will call and make the arrangements presently."

Austin Ambrose got up and went to the window and rapidly mastered the situation. After all, Fate was working for him to the end! If the Prince Rivani would kindly kill Blair how easily the *denouement* would work out!

"I don't like this!" he said gloomily. "I am not thinking of myself, nor so much of you—for you are good at sword or pistol—but I am thinking of Vio— —of the countess."

"Ah, yes!" said Blair with a sigh. "Poor Violet! And yet, after all— —" he stopped, but the pause was significant. "I think I must go to the library, Austin," he said after a moment or two. "I have a few letters to write and papers to arrange. I may fall, you know."

"Oh, nonsense!" said Austin Ambrose. "Fall! You may be wounded in the arm, that's just possible— —"

Blair laughed grimly.

"If the prince wounds me anywhere it will be through the heart," he said quietly. "He means business, and I shall not balk him. At any rate, I'll have a fight for my life," and with a laugh on his lips he went out of the room.

Austin Ambrose walked to the window and looked out at the night, letting the cold air blow upon his forehead. A fever seemed burning in all his veins. All this had fallen so suddenly that there seemed scarcely time to think: and he had to *act*, and at once.

He poured out some brandy and drank it slowly; then, after a glance at his face in the mirror, he forced it into its accustomed smooth serenity, and going along the corridor, knocked softly at the countess' boudoir.

She was seated in a low chair beside the fire, her head thrown back, her hands lying listlessly by her side; but she turned with an eager light in her eyes, that died out when she saw who it was.

"Oh, it is you; I thought it was Blair," she said. "Where is he?—not back yet?"

Austin Ambrose bit his lip, and a savage light shot into his eyes.

"Always Blair!" he said softly. "No; he is not in yet."

"And why do you come here at this unearthly hour?" she demanded, pettishly.

"Violet, I have come to answer a question you have often asked me, and I have often parried. I have come to demand of you the reward you have promised me for the services I have rendered you."

She looked up at him in silent astonishment

"Question—reward! What are you talking about? Why do you look so strange?"

"Do I look strange? Forgive me. It is the only time I have allowed my countenance to incommode you. Have you forgotten—is it necessary to remind you of your promise? Is it necessary to remind you for what that promise was given? Ah, yes, I suppose so. Men and women have short memories. Violet, have you forgotten the day I undertook that you should be Blair's wife?"

Her face paled, but she laughed.

"How melodramatic you are. Of course. I was a poor little woman who set her heart upon something, and you were the clever man who offered to help me. Pray do not look so serious."

"I cannot help my looks to-night," he said, quietly, "for to-night you and I stand face to face, soul to soul. Violet, you had set your heart upon gaining Blair, and I have got him for you. You promised me at the time that you would give me whatsoever I should ask, and I told you that some day I should come to claim my reward at your hands. I have come. I will not tell you all I have done for you. You may have conjectured how dark and vile the work has been—no matter. I have succeeded; you have been Blair's wife through my agency. I come to claim my reward!"

She bit her lip and tried to smile.

"Well, well, what is it? It is awfully late, why not wait until to-morrow? Blair may come in at any moment, and though there is no impropriety in our chatting in my own room, still—what is it? Is it money? Are you in difficulties? How much is it?"

"It is not money," he said gravely.

"What, then?" she said, impatiently.

"It is yourself!" he said, his eyes flashing into hers, his pale cheeks suddenly glowing with fire.

CHAPTER XXIX

"It is yourself I want," said Austin Ambrose.

Violet looked at him for a moment as if she had not understood the purport of his words, then she raised herself on her elbow, and laughed.

"*What* do you say? Is this a jest? If so, it is in rather bad taste, don't you think?"

He looked at her steadily.

"Have I the appearance of a man who jests?" he breathed.

Her face paled.

"If it isn't a jest, what is it?" she demanded, querulously. "Why do you come at this time of night and say absurd things like—like that?"

"Is it so absurd, do you think? Consider. Violet, have you been dreaming all these months? You should know me well enough to feel that I am not a mere straw to be idly blown hither and thither, not a man likely to waste his life doing service for no requital. Let me take you back to the past. Do you remember the days and months and years I waited on you like a slave? Do you think it was done for nothing, with no hope of reward?"

His eyes shone with fierce determination, his whole manner proclaimed eloquently the dominant idea which had actuated him through the past, which was now so near its fulfillment.

"I never deceived you. Think! remember! Is it so hard to go back? I suppose it must be so! You are now the Countess of Ferrers, Blair's wife; you have obtained all you craved for, and, like all those who rise upon the shoulders or the hearts of some faithful friend and slave, you forget the aid by which alone you rose!"

He drew a little nearer, and stood upright before her, his face made almost handsome by the intensity of its expression.

"Violet, do you remember the day I knelt at your feet and poured out the love with which my heart was burning? I was no schoolboy, nor mere fortune-hunter. I loved you with an all-absorbing passion; I should have loved you if you had been a poor girl selling flowers in the streets, and I would have knelt to you if you had been such an one as humbly as I knelt to Violet Graham, the wealthy heiress, with all the world at her beck and nod! And you!—how did you treat me? Look back! You scarcely deigned to listen, and when at last you consented to waste a few minutes in listening to my prayer—ah! and what a prayer it was; the cry of a man begging for his life!—you answered me with a few half-contemptuous words, a smile wholly scornful, and a haughty request that I would never again so far forget myself. Forget myself! Violet, as I left you that day, I swore that if I lived I would win you; that every gift nature had given me, every talent I could acquire, should be pressed into the service of my oath, and that sooner or later I would come to you—not kneeling, as the humble suppliant, the slave craving for a boon at the hand of a tyrant, but as one having the power to command and exact that which he wanted."

"You—you must be mad, Austin!" she murmured, struggling with the terror his words produced on her.

"Wait!" he said, with the same deadly intentness. "Wait, as I waited! I knew that you had set your heart upon marrying Blair. Blair was in my hands. He trusted me implicitly; through him I thought that I might, perchance, gain a hold upon you. For days, through sleepless nights, I set myself to find some way of trapping you, some net which should catch and hold you fast. I knew that I could bring Blair to your feet sooner or later, but that was not enough, for, by doing so, I should lose you altogether. Violet, they talk of fate. If there be such a thing, then Fate took pity on me and worked on my side. It was Fate more than I, myself, which weaved the plot whereby I stand to-night before you as a victor, not kneeling, as I once knelt, your slave!"

He paused and smiled down at her, with the air of a man confident of his victim.

"You are tired, and it is time you got some rest. We start from here by five o'clock this morning. I will have a carriage waiting by the cathedral— but I need not trouble you with the arrangements. All that you have to do is to be ready; and I have no fear that you will disobey me."

She rose and looked at him with a flushed face and scornful eyes.

"Austin, you have been drinking," she said.

He started, but instantly recovered himself and shook his head slowly.

"It is the most charitable conjecture I can form," she said. "You have either taken too much wine, or you have lost your reason. I admit that I am indebted to you, but I will find some means of discharging that debt. I am rich—don't be offended—and an ambitious man like yourself needs money.

You shall have what you require; more, Blair shall exert all his influence and send you to Parliament—you will shine there, and may rise to any height you like. But, mind, I will do nothing if you do not go at once, and promise me never to come near me again. If you will not promise—why, then I will place the matter in my husband's hands." She paused.

"Have you finished?" he asked calmly, almost gently.

"Yes," she said, "only I may add that I think you know my threat is no idle one. Blair will know how to avenge an insult paid to his wife!"

His face grew hard, and his eyes dark with a flash of hate and anger.

"An insult paid to his wife! Yes! But one paid to Miss Violet Graham is another matter!"

"What do you mean?" she demanded, scornfully. "I am not Violet Graham, I am his wife."

"You are Violet Graham, but you are not Blair's wife; you are not the Countess of Ferrers, my dear!"

She looked at him, the blood rushing to her face at the contemptuous familiarity of the last two words.

"Leave the room, sir!" she exclaimed, raising her hand and pointing to the door. "You have abused my patience; go, or you will indeed compel me to forget your 'services,' and make it necessary that my paid servants should use force!"

He laughed softly, and his eyes glowed with admiration.

"Violet, I swear that every instant you make me love you more passionately! I see you think I lied when I said you were not Blair's wife, is it not so?"

"I know that you lied!" she retorted, as calmly as she could.

"How little you know me," he said, gravely. "Do you think I am so great a fool as to make such an assertion for the mere sake of making it?"

"If I am not Blair's wife, who is?" she demanded, as if humoring him.

"Come," he said, with a smile; "that is better, because it is more practical and business-like. Continue this tone, my dear Violet, and we shall speedily arrive at an understanding. You want to know who is Blair's wife? Certainly. It is a young lady who was Margaret Hale, but who became the Viscountess of Leyton and Countess of Ferrers."

She started, but it was only at the sound of Margaret's name.

"Margaret Hale! The girl——"

"Exactly. The girl he fell in love with at Leyton Court. What an excellent memory you find when you need it."

"And you say he married her? Oh, spare your breath!" she broke off, with a contemptuous gesture.

"Thanks; I will," he said. "Permit me to give you ocular proof. Here is the certificate of the ceremony; not a copy, please to observe: not a mere copy, but the original itself. The ceremony, as you will see, was performed at a charming old church, in a rural and secluded spot called Sefton. The date is set forth in plain figures, together with all the particulars even the most exacting lawyer could require."

She took the certificate, very much as poor Margaret had taken the false one from Lottie Belvoir, and looked at it with dazed eyes, then she crushed it in her hand, and looked up at him as a dumb animal looks up at the man who has struck it.

"Married to her!—married to her!" she murmured; "and he did not tell me!" A spasm of jealousy shot through her. "Then she was his wife?"

"She was, most certainly," he assented, watching her.

"But what has that to do with you and your plot?" she demanded, raising herself after a moment and facing him contemptuously. "This—this marriage is a matter between me and Blair. This certificate is not a forgery—I believe that."

He looked at her steadily.

"Thanks. You do me that credit, and safely. Of one thing you may be convinced, Violet, and that is, that I will not speak one false word to you to-night. By truth, and truth alone, I will win you. Do not doubt any one thing I tell you, for I swear that it is true!"

"I—I believe you," she said, almost involuntarily. "I believe this marriage took place, but what of it? The girl is dead. I am Blair's wife, and the offer"—she shuddered again—"the vile offer you made he will protect me from."

"Blair is not your husband, for Margaret Hale, the Countess of Ferrers, is alive!" he said.

He did not thunder it at her, nor hiss it as the serpent he resembled might have done; but he spoke the words almost gently and with a serene and complacent calmness.

She sprung to her feet and confronted him.

"What? Stop— —" and her hands went out toward him as if to shut from her senses any further words of his.

"I must go on," he said. "It is true. Margaret Hale is alive. Do you doubt me? Look in my face," and he drew a step nearer.

She looked at him with all her anguished soul in her eyes, then she shrank back.

"She is here, here in Naples. An hour hence, any moment, they may meet, Blair and she, and he will recognize her. Do you think that, after that, you have much chance of remaining as the wife of the Earl of Ferrers? You know best whether his heart has forgotten his allegiance to his first wife, his real wife, his present wife; for you are nothing whatever to him, remember. You are not the Countess of Ferrers, but simply—Miss Violet Graham!"

She sat staring at him, her hand clinched on the certificate.

"Why—why did she leave him? Does he know that she is alive?" she said hoarsely.

He laughed, and drawing a chair nearer, sat astride it and facing her.

"No, he thinks her dead," he said. "I see, you will not be satisfied until I tell you the whole of my little plot! Listen, then," and with his eyes fixed upon her watchingly, he told the story of the elaborate scheme which, helped by Fate, he had built up; of Lottie Belvoir's deception, and of Margaret's supposed death.

"And you did all this? You—you must be more devil than man!"

He smiled.

"I can claim to be a man who has devoted all his talents, and all his energies, to the attainment of one object. You call me names! Bah! my dear Violet, have you forgotten that evening in Park Lane, when I told you she was dead, and you thought I had murdered her? You did not call me rude names then, I think!"

She shuddered, and hid her face in her hands. When she lifted it, it was as drawn as if she had risen from a long and wasting illness.

"It is true! It is true!" she moaned, hoarsely; "and now you want me to— —" She could not go on, but her lips moved.

"I want you to keep your promise, that is all, my dear Violet," he said, coolly.

"And if I refuse?"

"You will not refuse," he said, quietly. "You dare not! If you are not ready to accompany me at five o'clock I shall go to Blair, and tell him all that I have told you.

"Come, Violet; you must know that it is of little avail to oppose me, much less to argue. Face the inevitable. You used to be a brave woman once, summon up some courage now. Consider, after all, what can you do better than fly with me? In an hour or two, at any moment, as I say, Blair and the countess will meet, the truth will be known, and you—what will you be? Nothing—worse than nothing! The law cannot give you redress, for Blair believed her dead; but none the less you will be—an outcast!"

She writhed and tore at the pillows in a frenzy of despair.

"Oh, please!" he murmured, reproachfully. "Is this the same woman who bade me separate Blair and Margaret Hale at any cost?—*at any cost*? Come, pluck up a little spirit. What must be, must be; and it is certain that you will have to yield to me."

"He can but kill me!" she moaned, desperately.

Austin Ambrose laughed.

"Nonsense! Blair will do nothing of the kind. He will simply repudiate you, and with many apologies, show you the door. But really it would be more merciful to kill you outright, than to leave you the butt of the whole of London! The great heiress, Violet Graham, wrongfully married to Blair Leyton, and discarded for his first and lawful wife!" and he laughed.

She put up her hand to silence him; and, his mood changing, he caught the hand and fell on his knees at her side.

"Forgive me, Violet! Do you not see that I am only seeming hard and cruel? Do you think that my heart does not bleed for you? But what can I do? You force me to tell you the truth in all its nakedness; for I know that if I do not convince you that you have no other alternative, you will not yield! Do not force me to say any more; accept the inevitable. Say the word; give me your promise to be ready at the time I have named, and I will take you with me— —"

"Never! never!" she said, hoarsely, and endeavoring to draw her hand from his grasp.

"What do you fear? Why do you shrink from me? Do you think that I do not love you? What stronger proof do you want than that I have given you? Have I not done more to win you than one man in a million does for the woman he wants? If it had been murder itself I would not have hesitated, I would not hesitate now! Ah, Violet! think of me a little. I, too, have suffered, suffered the tortures of the damned, for it was my hand that gave you—for a time—to him! I have stood by and seen you the wife of another, the man I hate— —"

"Hate!—you hate him?" she re-echoed.

"Yes," he said, a lurid light shining in his eyes. "I always hated him because you loved him! Many and many a time I have longed to see him dead at my feet—but no more of that! What does it matter? It is only of my love for you that I wish to think or speak. Trust yourself to my love, the deepest and truest man ever felt. I will marry you when and where you please; I will spend the remainder of my life in devotion to you; I will— —" he stopped breathless, and carried away by his passion, he threw his arms about her.

She struggled from his embrace, and even struck at him.

"Go with *you!*" she gasped. "Leave him for *you?*" and she laughed wildly. "I would rather die!"

"Very good. I may take that as your decision? In half an hour I take Blair to his wife; in half an hour I will tell him how he came to lose her, and that it was you—Violet Graham—who tempted and prompted me to carry out the plot which has nearly wrecked his life. And then I leave you to face him."

He took one step from her, but she sprung up and throwing herself at his feet clutched at his arm.

"No, no! Give me time! Wait, Austin! Only wait! I—I did not mean to be hard. I—I—oh, have pity on me!" and she turned her white face up to him. "Have pity on me! I was only a woman, and I—I did love him so! Yes, I know it was I who tempted you, but I did not know that you cared for me as—as you say you do, and—oh, Austin, look at me kneeling to you for more than life—ah, for life itself! Do not betray me! I will do anything— —"

"Anything but the one thing I want," he said, coldly. "You would offer me money, anything. Money! If you had all the wealth of the Rothschilds and offered it to me to forego the reward I have worked for, I would say 'no!' No, if I cannot have you, for whom I have plotted and planned, I will at least have revenge. You cannot rob me of that. Let go my hand and leave me free to join the early parted husband and wife."

"No!" she wailed, clinging to him. "Stay, Austin, I will—I will consent!"

He stooped down and looked at her face.

"Say that again," he said, eagerly. "You will consent? You will go with me?"

She rose, and with both hands pushed her disordered hair from her white face. Then, looking at him steadily:

"Yes, I will go with you."

"You—you will? Oh, my darling!" and he made to take her in his arms, but she put out her hands and kept him off.

"Yes," she said in a low, dull voice, "I will go with you. I see it is useless to fight against you."

"It is, it is!" he assented, intently. "And you will come to the cathedral——"

"No," she said, like one repeating a lesson; "come to me here at five o'clock. I—I am not strong enough to go out. Come at five o'clock, and—I will be ready."

He knelt on one knee, and taking her hand, pressed it to his lips.

"Violet, you know that I can keep an oath. I have proved it, have I not? Then hear me swear that you shall never regret your resolution. I will wipe out the past, I will surround you with a love that shall cause you to forget all that has happened, and that, that—must make you happy! At five! Go now and lie down, dearest! You will need all your strength, for the journey must be a long and a swift one. A few hours and we shall be beyond the reach of pursuit! And then—ah, then, your new life will commence! A life which my love shall make one dream of happiness! Go, dearest! At five! Remember!"

He led her to the door; she drew her hand from his hot, burning fingers, and pressed it on her forehead, then as she opened the door she turned and looked at him—a steady, resolute look.

"I will remember," she said. "I will be ready when you come!"

CHAPTER XXX

Ten minutes after Lottie fell senseless beside the stone steps of the Palace Augustus, a slight, girlish figure came quickly down the street. It was dressed in black, the only spot of relief being the fur lining of the hood which almost concealed her face. Though she was quite alone, she walked with a fearless and confident bearing, like one whose safety was insured. As she came near the gateway of the palace, a man, bearing the unmistakable signs of a footpad, approached her stealthily, but after a glance at the half-shrouded face, he made a bow, and spreading out his hands toward her, with respectful and almost awed deprecation, stood aside to let her pass.

Margaret, for she it was, returned the salutation with a gentle inclination of her head, and went on her way.

As she walked along in the starlight, a strange feeling of peacefulness, that for all its serenity had something of elation in it, pervaded her. She had just come from visiting a child down with the fever, which is as characteristic of Naples as its bay, or its volcano, and the blessings which the mother of the little one had called down upon Margaret's head, seemed to have borne fruit.

To-night, as she looked up at the stars, she could bring herself to think of Blair with a feeling of forgiveness and tenderness which she had not, as yet, been capable of.

In this life he could never be her own again, never; but perhaps in that mysterious after-life toward which they were all drifting, he would, in some way, come back to her. That he had loved her, even while sinning against her, she felt convinced; and to-night, as she walked through the silent streets, his face came before her, and his voice rose in her memory with a strange distinctness. In fancy she was back again at Leyton Court and at Appleford, and a reflection of these times, in all their glorious coloring of happiness, fell upon her spirit in the dark street, and illuminated it with a curious sadness that had a tinge of joy in it.

"Oh, Blair, my love, my love!" she murmured, looking up at the stars, very much as he had done about an hour before, "we shall never meet again here on earth, but who knows what may await us up there?"

As she lowered her eyes with a gentle sigh, she saw the figure of Lottie huddled up in a scarcely distinguishable mass beside the doorway of the Augustus Palace; she stopped immediately, and kneeling beside the unconscious girl, spoke to her gently. At first she thought that the girl was dead, but she detected a faint movement of the heart, and raising her head upon her knee, she moistened her lips with some eau-de-Cologne.

The light was so dim that she did not recognize her, and she was loosening the worn shawl and chafing the thin hands that hung limply at her side, when a man and woman came down the street.

Margaret beckoned to them. After a glance, they were keeping on their way; but she called to them, and hearing her voice their manner changed, and they hurried forward.

"A poor girl who has fallen in a swoon," explained Margaret.

"Looks like dead, signorina," said the man, shrugging his shoulders Italian fashion. "Best fetch the police: dead people give trouble to the most innocent."

"Oh, no, no; she is not dead, indeed!" said Margaret, earnestly.

"That's not what you said when the signorina nursed you through the ague, ungrateful pig!" exclaimed the man's wife, with charming candor. "What shall we do, lady?"

"If I could get her somewhere out of the street," said Margaret, anxiously. "I think she has fainted from hunger."

"Like enough," said the man. "It's a most popular complaint, lady!"

"I'll take her to our rooms, signorina," said the woman promptly. "Lift her, Tonelli!"

The husband obeyed with half sullen resignation, and the pair carried Lottie to a house in one of the small streets. They laid her on the bed; and Margaret, after dispatching the man to her house for wine and food, and setting the woman to light a fire, threw her fur cloak over the girl, and then, and not till then, carried a light close to her.

As she did so the lamp nearly fell to the ground, for she recognized in the girl she had rescued, the woman who had dealt her the blow that had wrecked her life. There, lying motionless and senseless, was Blair's real wife!

She set the lamp down and staggered back to a chair.

"The signorina is tired and ill!" exclaimed the woman of the house, gazing at her sympathetically. "Will not the signorina leave the girl to my care, and go home to rest? You wear yourself out for the poor, lady!"

"No, no!" said Margaret, fighting against the weakness which threatened to master her. "It—it is only a little faintness. Is the fire all right? Yes? Then will you go down and warm some of the wine Tonelli will bring, and bring it up to me?"

The woman left the room, and Margaret once more bent over the unconscious Lottie.

Yes, it was the same woman! But how came she to be lying in the streets of Naples, in rags, and evidently half-famished? Had Blair deserted her again?

All the while she was pondering she was using means to bring warmth and life back, and presently the woman of the house came up with the hot wine.

Margaret succeeded in getting some through the white lips, and after awhile Lottie opened her eyes. They rested upon the lovely face for some seconds vacantly, but presently a gleam of intelligence shot across them, and she tried to raise herself upon her elbow, staring wildly at what she took to be a vision.

"Do not move," said Margaret, softly. "You are weak and ill. Drink some of this wine."

Lottie took the cup and drained it feverishly.

"Give me some more," she gasped. "Give me anything to wake me from this dream. Do you hear? Wake me, or I shall go mad! I tell you I can see her standing there in front of me!" and she pointed to Margaret wildly. "I've often fancied I've seen her, but never so plainly as now. Wake me! for Heaven's sake, wake me!"

"Try and keep quiet," said Margaret, soothingly; but at the sound of her voice Lottie only grew more excited.

"There! I can hear her speaking! What is it she says? I know I did it! I plead guilty, my lord! But it was not me only. Where is *he*? Where is Austin

Ambrose? He is worse than I am, my lord. Send me to prison, if you like, but don't let him go scot-free. He is worse than I am! It was he who put me up to it—and now he leaves me to starve! Yes, he did! He threatened me, told me that he'd have me charged, and that he'd swear he knew nothing about it. Where is Austin Ambrose? He is worse than I am, my lord!"

Then she sank down, as if exhausted; but presently she started up with a cry of terror and clutched at Margaret's arm.

"Blair! Blair!" she shrieked, and at the name poor Margaret winced and could scarcely suppress a cry. "Blair will be killed! I heard them say so! Quick! Find him—stop the fight! The prince will kill him! Blair is no match for him—I heard them say so. Oh, for the love of Heaven, don't stand there doing nothing, but find them and stop them!"

The woman of the house crept to the bed, and looking down curiously shrugged her shoulders.

"She is English, lady, is she not? She is in the fever and raves; is it not so? What is it she says?"

"I—I am afraid she is delirious," said Margaret, scarcely knowing what she answered. "Will you go for the English doctor and beg him to come to me at once?"

Lottie caught the word doctor, and raising herself on her elbow, held out her hand imploringly.

"Oh, never mind me!" she panted. "What does it matter about me? It's Blair—Blair you must save! Don't you believe me? I tell you I heard them talking about it before I fell—where was it?" and she put her hand to her head and sank back with a groan.

Margaret sat beside the bed, with one of the girl's wasted, burning hands held tightly in her own.

She could not think—the meeting was too strange and mysterious to permit of her doing that—but she sat in a kind of dull stupor, even after the doctor had come and gone again.

The night passed away, and morning dawned, and with the first streak in the east Lottie awoke.

That she was no longer delirious was evident by her eyes, but she turned pale and started, as they fell upon Margaret.

"It was no dream, then!" she said, in a low voice, covering her face with her hands. "It was really you who sat beside me?"

"Yes, it was I," said Margaret, sadly and shyly, for it Came flashing upon her that this woman, after all, was Blair's wife. "I am glad you are better. I will go now," and she rose, a little stiffly.

Lottie put out her hand.

"No—stay," she said, with a frightened, nervous glance. "I—I have something to tell you! Oh, if I only knew how! Don't be angry with me more than you can help. Punish me if you like, but don't say much to me. I've done the cruellest thing that ever one woman did to another, and I deserve to be shot——" At the word she started up, and flung out her arms. "What is the time? is it morning? Not morning! Do not tell me that! Oh, great Heaven, how long have I been lying here? Oh, too late, too late!" and she rocked herself to and fro.

"Why are you too late, and for what?"

"To save him! To save Blair! Didn't I tell you? It seems to me that I have been raving about it for hours! He and the Prince Rivani are to fight this morning. This morning! It is light now!"

"Blair—Lord Leyton; your—your husband!" said Margaret, holding on to the bed to support herself.

"My husband!" Lottie almost shrieked; then she laughed wildly and hysterically. "No! not my husband, *but yours!*"

"Mine!" said Margaret, her eyes fixed on the flushed face and desperate black eyes.

"Yes; yours, yours, yours!" cried Lottie. "Oh, can't you understand? No! You are so good and true, that you cannot believe there are such fiends in the world as me and Austin Ambrose!"

"Austin Ambrose!" was all Margaret could falter.

"Austin Ambrose! The cruellest, cleverest scoundrel on earth!" cried Lottie, tearing at her clothes and flinging them on as she spoke. "It was he who tempted me to go down to that place in Devonshire, and pass myself off as Blair's wife——"

"Pass yourself off as——Then—then you are not his wife?"

"No, and never was!" cried Lottie.

"Then——Oh, stop!—give me a minute! No!—don't touch me! I'm not going to faint!" for Lottie had sprung forward to catch her. "I will not faint; only give me a minute. I am Blair's wife!—Blair's wife! Say it again!" and the poor soul, white and red by turns, held up her hands to the wickedly weak and erring Lottie.

"I'll say it a thousand times; I'll beg your forgiveness on my knees; I'll do anything to atone for what I've done—but not now!" she exclaimed fiercely. "For while we are talking here, murder's being done; for it is murder to pit a man against Prince Rivani, and that's what they have done with Blair—Lord Ferrers, I mean!"

"Ah!" Margaret caught her breath, and pressed her hand to her heart for a moment; then she snatched up her cloak and flung it round her, and sprung to the door.

Lottie had just succeeded in getting on her ragged clothing, and put out a hand, humbly and imploringly, to stop her.

"Where are you going?" she asked.

Margaret put her hand away with simple dignity, and, looking at her, replied:

"To save *my husband!*"

Mr. Austin Ambrose left the boudoir a happier man than he had ever been before during the whole course of his life.

There is a keener joy in the anticipation of success and victory which the actual success and victory themselves cannot produce. In his mind's eye he saw himself—as he had pictured to Violet—lying at her feet in some sunny, vine-clad villa in Spain. Those two by themselves, with no one to share or dispute his claim to her! With Blair either dead of Prince Rivani's rapier thrust, or away in England with Margaret! Yes, success had come to him at last. Not only would he have won the woman he loved with a passion which he had nourished and fostered and secretly fed during all those long and bitter months, but he would have secured wealth as well, for he had not managed Blair's estate for Blair's benefit alone, but had contrived to feather his own nest pretty considerably; besides, Violet still held her own money, and it would now become his!

He was so filled with the ecstasy of anticipation that he could have stopped on the great staircase, and raised the house with his exultant laughter, had there not been still something to do before he could admit that all was ready.

Always looking forward to this supreme moment, he had arranged with one of the drivers of the pair-horse carriages to expect a summons from him, and, slipping on a cloak, he went out to the corner of the street and gave the man his instructions. He was to wait at the corner of the cathedral until he, Austin Ambrose, arrived with a lady. The man was then to drive to the station as if for his life, and regardless of anything. Then he returned to the palace, and hastily packed a small portmanteau. He had scarcely finished it when Blair's valet knocked at the door, with General Trelani's card.

Austin Ambrose slipped on a dressing gown over the traveling suit, for which he had exchanged his other clothes, and received the general with calm serenity and dignity.

"You expected me, doubtless, and I will not detain you with apologies for the lateness of the hour," said the general, a stiff and soldier-like old man, to whom duels were very ordinary matters indeed. "I may add that my principal, Prince Rivani, will not accept an apology."

Austin Ambrose bowed.

"The Earl of Ferrers has no intention of offering one," he said, quietly.

The general inclined his head.

"As the person challenged, the earl has the choice of weapons," he said.

"Though, like most Englishmen, I am unfamiliar with the etiquette of the duello, I am aware of that. Lord Ferrers chooses swords."

The general looked rather surprised.

"Indeed! In honor, I am compelled to remind you, sir, that his highness is skilled with the rapier; if pistols would be considered more fair— —"

"Thanks, general, but the earl has made his choice."

"Then nothing remains to settle but the hour and place," said the general, suavely.

"Will half-past five be too early?" asked Austin Ambrose.

"No hour will be too early for us, sir," said the general, blandly, "and I would recommend the field behind the hospital. It is quiet and secluded at that hour — —"

Austin Ambrose assented, and the general looked at his watch.

"My mission is finished, sir," he said. "Pray convey my devoted respects to the earl."

Austin Ambrose bowed him out, and then returned to his room and completed his preparations. He sat down and wrote a short note.

"The meeting is for half-past five in the field behind the hospital. Do not wait for me. I have gone into the town and will join you to the minute."

He rang the bell and gave the note to Blair's valet, then locking the door, flung himself on the bed and closed his eyes, trying to force himself to sleep, but the effort failed for a time.

His acute brain was still at work picturing the incidents as he imagined them. At half-past five he and Violet would be speeding over the frontier. Blair would go to meet Prince Rivani; they would wait a quarter of an hour, half, perhaps; and then, the prince growing impatient, the general would offer to act as second for Blair; the two men would fight, and there would be no doubt as to which would fall. With pistols, Blair, who was a good shot, would stand something of a chance; but with swords, Rivani, whose skill was proverbial, must win. With his eyes closed he could see Blair lying stretched out upon the ground, with a thin streak of crimson creeping snake-like across the breast of his shirt, and at the vision a fiendish smile of satisfaction curved his lips.

Then he must have slept, for presently the sound of a church bell smote upon his ear, and with a start he sprung from the bed, and stealthily drew the curtains a little apart.

Yes, the dawn was breaking, the hour of his triumph was approaching.

Wrapping himself in his cloak, and with a fur over his arm for Violet, he caught up his valise, and with cat-like step made his way to the boudoir.

The door was ajar, as he had left it a few hours ago, but he paused and softly whispered her name.

There was no answer, and he crept in.

He had expected to find her there ready dressed, and waiting for him, but the room was empty. He went to the door of the bedroom and, knocking gently, cautiously called to her.

Still there was no answer, and after a moment's hesitation, he tried the door. It was unlocked, and he opened it and entered. The room was dimly lighted by a small shaded lamp, and for the moment he could distinguish nothing clearly, but the next he saw a figure lying on the bed. It was she. She was lying as if she had fallen backward in a fit of exhaustion, her pale face turned upward, one arm hanging by her side, the other thrown across the bed.

"Asleep? My poor darling!" he murmured. "But I must wake her! There is no time to be lost!"

Still she did not move, and he took her hand.

Something—its icy coldness, perhaps, or its irresponsive lifelessness—sent an awful pang of fear through him that was like the stab of a knife.

Still holding her hand, he caught up the lamp and held it above her head, his eyes scanning her face.

The next instant the lamp dropped from his grasp, and with a stifled cry, he reeled like a drunken man, and fell at her feet!

CHAPTER XXXI

Blair wrote his letters—there were not many, for Austin Ambrose had so entirely undertaken the management of the vast estates that Blair knew very little about any business pertaining to them.

He commenced a letter to Violet herself, but after several attempts tore it up. He would see her before he started for the meeting, and say good-bye as cautiously as he could.

Then he went out, and, leaving the city behind, wandered into the country beyond.

Still thinking of Margaret and the picture which in so mysterious and strange a manner photographed her and her death, he returned to the palace, and was surprised to find that it was past four.

He went straight to his rooms, and there, on the dressing-table, found Austin Ambrose's note.

Blair destroyed the note, then had a bath, and dressed himself with more than his usual care, doing it with his own hands, and without summoning the valet.

Then he sighed. He could not go on this errand of life or death without saying "good-bye" to his wife. And yet he shrank from it as he now shrank from nothing else connected with the affair. But it had to be done, and he went into her apartments and knocked at the bedroom door which Austin Ambrose had closed after him. There came no answer, and Blair, after waiting for a minute or two, turned away.

He went to the writing table, and taking out a sheet of the scented paper stamped with its gold coronet, wrote a line.

"Good-bye, Violet! Heaven send you every happiness.
Blair."

This he put in an envelope and laid it on the slope where she would see it when she entered the room; which she would do about ten o'clock. If he came out of this affair alive he should return long before that hour and could destroy the note.

Then he put on his cloak, and as quietly as possible left the house. The morning air struck coldly, and with a little shudder he turned up the collar of his coat and lit a cigar.

As the clocks chimed half-past five he reached the ground behind the hospital. A carriage and pair stood under the shelter of some trees, and near it was a group of three men. Blair distinguished the prince by his height; the second man was the general, and the third Blair judged to be the doctor; but Austin Ambrose was not there.

"My friend Mr. Ambrose has not arrived, I see," said Blair cheerfully. "I'm very sorry; but I have no doubt he will be here directly. He left word that he would be here before me."

"He will arrive in a minute or two, no doubt," said the general.

Blair went and leaned against a tree and smoked his cigar placidly. The prince stood at a little distance with folded arms, looking like a statue—a statue of implacability—the other two paced up and down.

A quarter of an hour passed, and the prince beckoned to the general.

"What is the meaning of this delay?" he demanded haughtily.

"His lordship's second has not arrived, your highness."

The prince's face darkened.

"It is a trick—a subterfuge!" he said, with suppressed rage. "When he comes, he will be accompanied by the police, no doubt."

The words were spoken with such an icy distinctness that they reached Blair.

His face flushed, and he flung his cigar away and approached the others.

"Some accident has detained my friend, general," he said. "It is getting late, and if we wait any longer we may be disturbed. Will one of you gentlemen do me the favor of acting for me?"

The two men looked blank; such an arrangement was utterly opposite to all etiquette.

Blair smiled cheerfully.

"Pray don't mind saying no. I am quite willing to dispense with a second."

This suggestion certainly could not be entertained, and after a hurried conference the doctor offered his services; the general and he selected a level piece of ground, and the doctor brought a couple of swords.

"You have brought no weapons, my lord," he said. "The prince begs you will make choice."

Blair chose one at haphazard, then took off his cloak, and coat and waistcoat, and turned up his wristbands.

The doctor eyed him approvingly.

"If the result depended upon strength, my lord," he said, "I should have little fear for you, but— —"

"Strength is little to do with it, I know," said Blair smiling; "never mind, sir, I will try not to discredit you."

"You are sure there can be no apology?" said the doctor earnestly.

Blair shook his head.

"I fear not. I think if I were to apologize, the prince would not accept it. He has set his heart upon a fight, and"—he smiled again—"I am not at all inclined to balk him."

The doctor shrugged his shoulders; there was a short and hurried conference between the two seconds, and then they placed their men.

The prince stepped up to his position slowly, and took his stand with that calm, resolute expression on his face which indicated a settled purpose. The gray of coming morning fell upon the open space, the white shirts of the duelists shining out conspicuously in the half light. The general stood at a little distance between them, his handkerchief in his hand, and both men fixed their eyes upon it. Then it dropped and they approached each other slowly and steadily, and looked into each other's eyes.

And in the prince's fixed gaze Blair read his intended death-warrant. He returned the look calmly, almost cheerfully, and the next instant the shining blades crossed with a sharp, hissing sound.

For a few moments each kept his guard, each man trying his adversary's strength.

It had occurred to Blair that he might succeed in wresting the sword from the prince's hand, and in doing it sprain his wrist, and so render him incapable of resuming the duel; but he was speedily convinced of the futility of such an attempt. Though so much slighter than Blair, the prince's wrist was like steel, and let Blair bear ever so heavily, his giant's force was met by its equivalent in steel. Of a certainty there was no chance of disarming the prince.

"His lordship is a better swordsman than I expected," murmured the general. "I always thought that Englishmen did not know how to fence!"

"This man is one of a thousand," said the doctor. "If the prince should only lose his temper he may stand a chance."

The general shook his head.

"He never loses either his temper or his head when he means business, and he means it this morning; look at his face," he added, significantly.

The doctor nodded.

"What can the earl have done to offend him so deeply?" he muttered. "Some woman, I suppose?"

The general nodded succinctly.

"*Per Bacco*! they are splendidly matched!" he exclaimed, in a low tone of admiration.

At present, indeed, it seemed as if the chances were equal, for, though the prince had made several passes that ought to have carried his sword through Blair's body, Blair had parried them skillfully and gracefully, and still stood untouched.

The prince's face darkened and he paused, for he thought he read Blair's intention. He would wait until the prince had scratched him or inflicted a slight flesh wound, and then declare himself satisfied, the seconds would interfere, and he, the prince, would be balked.

With compressed lips, he commenced the attack again, and, seizing a favorable opportunity, permitted his opponent's sword to cut his arm.

Blair lowered his weapon instantly, and the seconds sprung forward.

"A touch, your highness," said the doctor, in a tone of relief. "My lord, you are satisfied, I presume?"

Blair inclined his head, and wiped the tip of his sword, but the prince smiled grimly.

"Pardon me," he said, slowly, without removing his eyes from Blair's face. "It is a mere scratch, and will not serve as an excuse, *even for Lord Ferrers!*"

There was so deadly an insult in the tone as well as the words, that Blair's face flamed, and his fingers closed over his hilt.

"When his highness is rested, I am ready to resume," he said, quietly.

The seconds drew back reluctantly.

"Now he will kill him," muttered the general. "Mark my words! At the next thrust Rivani will run him through."

Cautiously, and yet with deadly intentions, the prince resumed the attack. The shining blades gleamed in the pale morning light, and hissed like snakes as they seemed to cling together; Blair put all the science he knew into it, but he felt that the moment would come when the sharp steel, that seemed like something human—or rather diabolical—in its persistence, would slip past his guard and finish the chapter for him; and presently he felt as if a hot iron had pierced his left shoulder; it was followed by the sensation of something warm trickling down his side, and he knew that he was wounded.

The two seconds sprung forward, but it was Blair who waved them back.

"Nothing, nothing!" he said. "Do not interfere, please!"

It would have been dangerous to have persisted in any attempt to stop the men, for the swords were flashing and writhing furiously; the prince was losing his calm; if it went altogether, it would leave him at Blair's mercy.

"By Heaven, it is my man who will be killed!" said the general, with an oath. "What possesses him? Look! he will be in the earl's power directly. Ah!—--"

The exclamation was wrung from him by a pass of Blair's that the prince parried so narrowly that Blair's blade cut his sleeve from elbow to wrist.

The faces of the two men were white as death, their teeth set, their eyes gleaming with that fire which springs from hearts burning for a fellow creature's life.

Another moment would settle it, one way or the other, and Blair, whose strength was beginning to tell, was wearing down the prince's guard; the seconds were, all unconsciously, drawing nearer and nearer in readiness for the fatal moment, when a woman's shriek clave the air, and two figures seemed to spring from the ground, and fling themselves upon the prince.

CHAPTER XXXII

Blair sprung forward and picked up the prince's sword, and was offering it to him when one of the women released her grasp of the prince, and turning to Blair with outstretched arms, uttered his name.

He started and shuddered as if he had been shot, then, with his eyes fixed on the pale, lovely face before him, began to tremble. The fact was, the poor fellow thought that he was dead, and that this was his Margaret coming to meet him in the other land!

"Blair!" she breathed, trembling like himself, and drawing a little nearer; "Blair, do you not know me?"

Then he uttered a cry—a cry of such agony, of doubt, and fear, and longing, that it went to the hearts of all who heard it. It touched two of them with pity, but the third—the prince's—it turned to fire.

"Stand aside!" he cried, passionately, and he thrust Lottie from his arm. "Stand aside! Your victim shall not save you, you heartless scoundrel! Here, in her presence, you shall pay the penalty!" and he sprung forward with his blade pointed.

The men rushed toward him, but Margaret was before them. With a cry she flung herself upon his breast, and seizing his arms, held them up with a strength almost superhuman.

The prince looked down at her face with wild anguish.

"You, you!" he uttered, reproachfully. "You step between me and this villain!"

"I see no villain, prince!" she said, panting, her eyes fixed on his face. "He who stands there is—my husband!" Then she slid from him and sank with an indescribable cry of love and joy upon Blair's breast.

The prince leant on his sword, and he stood looking at them with a wild amazement that seemed to hold the general and the doctor as if in a trance.

The general was the first to recover himself. With his eyes still fixed on Blair and Margaret, who stood gazing into each other's eyes speechlessly, he went up to the prince, and gently took the sword from his grasp.

"Come away, your highness," he said, in a whisper, "this is no place for us."

"Her husband! Her husband!" breathed the prince, like one in a dream. "Impossible!"

"It looks only too possible," said the general gravely. "Doubtless Lord Ferrers will offer a full explanation later on, but this is no time for it."

"That it isn't, but you can take my word for it that it's true!" said a voice, broken with a sob.

It was Lottie's. The general turned and stared at her.

"You are Miss Leslie's—that is, the countess'—friend, madam?" he said, still staring at her in amazement, that overwhelmed his politeness.

"No, her worst enemy, but one," said Lottie, in her old curt manner. "Oh, I can't tell you half of the story, but if you want to know, it was I who separated them," she said defiantly, through her tears. "But," she added pathetically, "it was I who brought them together again!"

"This is strange!" murmured the general. "Come away, Rivani!"

The prince started as if from a trance and strode toward Blair and Margaret.

"One word, my lord!" he said hoarsely. "You know, you have known from the first, the reason for our meeting. Will you tell me, as man to man, that it had no basis? Will you pledge me your word that you have not injured this lady, for alas, I cannot trust her! It is her heart that has spoken— —"

"As man to man I pledge my word that I have not knowingly injured this lady," said Blair brokenly. "She is my wife, Prince Rivani!" then his voice failed him, and he drew Margaret closer to him with a passionate pressure.

The prince bowed, his face white as death, his lips quivering.

"That is sufficient," he said. His eyes turned to Margaret. "Madam, will you forgive me? It was for your sake— —" he stopped.

With a sob. Margaret put out her hand to him. He took it, bent over it as if to kiss it, then, as if he could not trust his forced composure another moment, he let it fall and strode away.

Two minutes afterward Blair and Margaret and Lottie were left alone.

What pen could describe the joy which fell upon those two hearts, so long parted by worse than death, but now reunited! Mine shall not attempt it. For a time they stood, her head resting upon his breast, his arm holding her tightly, as if he feared that the next moment he might lose her again. For a time they could only speak in broken, passionate murmurs and it was not until Lottie timidly drew near them that Blair led Margaret to a fallen tree and implored her to tell him how it came to pass that she, whom he had mourned as dead, was now again in his arms.

For an hour they sat, while with many breaks and much faltering, she told the strange story, he listening the while in an amazement that almost overwhelmed his joy. He forgot Lottie, forgot that the city had awakened into its daily life, and above all, he forgot that another woman claimed to be his wife; that, at no great distance, Violet Graham was awaiting him.

It came upon him suddenly, so suddenly that he almost sprung to his feet with a cry of terror and agony.

"Oh, Blair, be calm!" said Margaret, clinging to him, for she thought that he had suddenly realized who it was that had wrecked their lives, though she had cautiously and carefully refrained from mentioning Austin Ambrose. "Be calm, dearest. All our trouble is over now. Let him go. What does it matter? Promise me, Blair—Blair, my love, my husband!"

He groaned, then he started.

"Let him go! Him? Who?"

His wildness frightened her, and she would have soothed him and put the question by, but Lottie was within hearing, and it was too much for her.

"Who? Why, Austin Ambrose!" she exclaimed.

"Hush, hush!" said Margaret, warningly, and she held up her hand haughtily, for, much as Lottie had done to restore her to happiness, she could not endure the sight of her or the sound of her voice.

"Hush!" exclaimed Lottie, half indignantly. "What! are you going to let him go on trusting that wolf in sheep's clothing any longer? Why, it's past reason! Give him a loophole, and he'll ruin everything yet. I know him and you don't, no, neither of you, and Blair—I mean Lord Ferrers—least of all. Why, my lord, you two would never have been parted but for Austin Ambrose."

"Austin! Austin!" echoed Blair.

Then Lottie poured out the story of her villainy and her weakness. Out it came, despite Margaret's commands and entreaties, and, like a lava torrent, it seared Blair's heart.

White and speechless he listened, until, almost breathless, Lottie cried in conclusion:

"And he is down at the palace still, and he'll ruin everything yet if you don't crush him. Oh! I know what he is. He is there with her— —"

"Her! Who?" asked Margaret, bewildered.

Lottie stopped short and looked aghast. She had forgotten Violet Graham, the woman who stood before the world as the Countess of Ferrers, as Blair's lawful wife.

Blair held up his hand.

"Not a word more!" he said. "Go, now, Lottie. I—I will send for you later."

Lottie hung her head and left them, and for a few minutes Blair sat silent, feeling as if some fiend had dashed the cup of joy from his lips again.

How was he to tell this lovely angel whose image had never left his heart's throne, this lovable woman who clung to him as if to sever from him would be death to her, how could he tell her that, thinking her dead, he had taken another woman as his wife!

He could not then, at that supreme moment, at any rate.

He rose, still with his arm round her.

"Dearest," he said in a whisper. "You must go home—to your own home for the present— —"

Margaret started and looked at him, then her face went white, but she said nothing, not one word.

"For the present," he repeated, almost beside himself. "In an hour or two I will come to you. Tell me where?"

She told him falteringly, yet calmly.

"You can trust me! Surely you can trust me! Ah, if you knew what it costs me to part with you for a single second! But it must be—it must be!" he groaned. "Believe in me, trust me, dearest Margaret, my wife, for a few short hours longer! You will?"

She looked up at him for a second with a deep earnestness, then she laid her head upon his heart and he kissed her.

With a consideration and a delicacy peculiarly Italian, the prince had left his carriage, and Blair led her to it. He stood and watched it as it drove away, with all that he cared for in life, with the treasure so marvelously restored to him, then he turned toward the city.

He seemed to be walking in a dream. What was this task that lay before him? He was to go to Violet Graham and say, "you are no longer my wife—

you never have been my wife! Begone!" It was true he owed her no pity, for she had gained her ends by an unscrupulous alliance with the traitor who had marred and ruined so large a portion of his life; but—still—it was from love of him that she had sinned! And now to go to her and tell her that Nemesis had fallen upon her, and that henceforth she must go before the world a thing for scorn to mock at.

With Austin Ambrose, Blair knew how to deal; there would be no hesitation there. Two or three short words, followed by one blow. But Violet——!

Slowly he made his way to the palace. Servants were running to and fro in the vast hall, the sounds of life were filling the air which a short time back was so still and quiet.

He entered the hall and mounted the stair with dragging step. In the corridor his valet stood aside to let him pass, and regarded his pale face with covert curiosity.

"Is—is her ladyship down yet?" asked Blair.

"No, my lord; it is not her ladyship's time for rising yet."

Blair glanced at the clock.

"No, no," he said. Then his face darkened. "Will you go to Mr. Ambrose's room and send him to me?" he said.

"Mr. Ambrose has gone into the city, and has not returned yet, my lord," said the man. "I thought your lordship knew——"

"Wait in the hall until he returns, and ask him to come to me," said Blair.

He passed on and entered Violet's boudoir. His note lay on the table where he had left it, and he tore it in pieces and dropped it on the fire. Then he paced to and fro, stopping to listen now and again.

All was still in Violet's room, and he began to ask himself the question if it was necessary for him to see her. Could he not write and tell her all that he had discovered; could he not break it to her in some way? Why should he not leave the place with Margaret alone, within an hour or two, and see Violet no more?

But his spirit rebelled against the suggestion. It seemed unmanly and unworthy. No, he would go through with his task to the bitter end. First Violet, then the other conspirator, Austin Ambrose. Still he waited. The hands of the clock toiled round the dial, and chimed the hour. With a start he nerved himself and knocked at the door. No response followed, and he knocked again and again, more loudly. Then he opened the door and entered.

The next instant he staggered back with a cry of horror.

Stretched upon the bed was the woman he had made his wife, and lying at her feet was the man who had been at once her dupe and her master. As Blair bent over to raise her, he fell back shuddering, for he saw that she was dead! At the same instant the white hand of the man lying at her feet dropped lifelessly and slid away. Blair, who had been about to strike him, saw a small vial lying at his feet.

Small as it was, it had contained sufficient poison for Austin Ambrose. It was the vial he had carried in his breast for months past, for which he had felt that night when he thought that Blair had discovered his villainy. It was for this that he had plotted and schemed with a heartless ruthlessness that an Iago might have envied! To find the woman he had loved and entrapped snatched by Death from his grasp in the very hour of his triumph, and to finish his career—a Suicide!

CHAPTER XXXIII

About twelve months after what the newspapers called "The Mystery in High Life at Naples," on a very bright day in June, the Earl of Ferrers and Margaret, his wife, were standing at the open window of the drawing-room at the court.

This window commands the best view of the drive, and it seemed by the intentness with which the two pairs of eyes watched it that they were expecting some one.

Leyton Court always looks at its best in June, and it has never looked better than it did this year, for the earl had spent a great deal of money on the place—"a small fortune," as it was said. A new wing had been built; the old part of the house redecorated; but above and beyond all, an addition had been made to the picture-gallery, which raised it to the first rank in England.

This had been done "to pleasure" Margaret, the countess, whom the world rightly regarded as one of its best and noblest artists. This same world, too, had gone slightly mad over the countess, and would have been delighted to make her the sensation of the season. For, consider! she was not only the wife of a wealthy earl, but the heroine of as romantic a history as the modern world wots of. Even now people did not know the full particulars, did not know more than that the countess was supposed to have died, and that the earl had, in all innocence, married Violet Graham; and that Violet Graham had died of heart disease at Naples, and Mr. Austin Ambrose had poisoned himself—for love of her. All this the world knew, but it was still ignorant of the details, of the diabolical plot which Austin Ambrose had woven, and so nearly successfully. But it knew enough to make Margaret a "sensation," and it was quite prepared to meet her in saloons and ballrooms, and point at her in the park, and fight for introductions to her, and intrigue to get her to its concerts and dinner-parties.

But Margaret had declined to be made a sensation of. Immediately after the tragedy at the palace at Naples, both she and Blair disappeared, not together, as the world hinted, but separately; and it was only through the appearance of her pictures at the various European galleries that people were made aware of her existence.

For months Margaret lived in a seclusion as impenetrable as that of a Trappist, and it was not until Blair had fallen ill and sent for her that she had gone to him. Then the rumor went round that Leyton Court was being done up, and that the earl and countess were going to live there just like an ordinary couple who had not been the hero and heroine of romance.

"I hope they won't be late," said Blair, looking at his watch and then staring down the drive.

"The trains are always late—unless you want to catch them, then they are fatally punctual!" said Margaret. "I feel as if I were growing *old* waiting for them!"

He turned and looked at her with that smile of combined devotion and admiration which the man wears who is both husband and lover.

"You don't look very old, Madge," he said. "In my eyes you seem younger than when I saw you first. What is it you use? Some magical cosmetique, eh?"

"I don't generally tell my toilet secrets, but I will just this once. It is a capital preparation, Blair, and, but that you look so ridiculously boyish yourself, I'd recommend you to use it. It is *Cosmetique de Felicite——*"

"Which translated means——? You know I don't know two words of French."

"Which translated means 'Cosmetic of Happiness,' you ignorant young man!" and she stole a little closer and looked up at him invitingly.

He put his arm round her and kissed her, and of course she pretended to be indignant.

"Right, before the window, and these people likely to come at any moment, sir!" she exclaimed.

"I wish they would come," he said. "I hate waiting for people. Let us go out and meet them."

"Very well!" she responded, and dashed off for her hat.

In two minutes they were walking side by side down the avenue, and they had not got very far before the Court carriage came bowling up the smooth road.

"There they are, Blair! Hold up your hand or they'll pass us! Florence! Florence!"

At the sound of her musical voice a girlish head appeared at the carriage window, and a girlish voice shouted an eager greeting. The coachman, looking rather scandalized at this want of ceremony, pulled up, and Prince Rivani and the Princess Florence sprung out.

The two men shook hands warmly, each looking into the other's face with that frank, steady glance which denotes a stanch friendship; and the two girls embrace, and laugh, and almost cry in a breath.

"Oh, you dear creature!" exclaimed the princess. "Isn't this just like you to come and meet us? And we thought it was only a young couple love-making as they strolled along, for you had got hold of each other's hand, just like two sweethearts; did you know that?"

Margaret blushed.

"We are two sweethearts," she whispered, almost piteously.

Then Margaret turned to the prince, who was waiting for his share of the greeting.

The prince looked older than when we saw him last, but as he took Margaret's hand in his and pressed it warmly, he was able to meet her clear, pure eyes without a trace of embarrassment or reserve. Good blood has many advantages over the ignoble sort, and not the least is the power to conquer self. In the twelve months that had passed since he stood opposite Blair, and sought to take his life, Prince Rivani had fought a sterner fight even than that memorable one at Naples; the fight with a passion which had threatened to absorb his life, and he had conquered so completely that he could return the gentle pressure of Margaret's hand with one of brotherly affection.

"If I cannot have her for lover and wife," he had sworn to himself, "at least, I will have her for friend!"

It was a noble and unselfish vow, and he fought for strength until he had accomplished it.

"And now, when you can tear yourselves apart, you two," said Blair, with a smile, addressing the two ladies, who displayed a great disposition to linger under the trees, and talk for the remainder of their lives, "perhaps we'd better go to the house."

"And what a lovely place it is!" exclaimed the princess. "I always thought the Villa Capri the beautifulest house in the world, but it is a *hovel* compared to this. Oh how happy you must be, dear!" she added in a whisper.

"Yes," said Margaret, with her quiet smile; "yes I am very fond of the Court, but I think I am happy because I am the wife of its master!"

Florence glanced at Blair as he strode along beside the prince in earnest conversation.

"What a splendid fellow he is, dear," she said in a low voice, not altogether free from awe. "Do you know, if I weren't so fond of him—you aren't jealous?—I think I should be a little afraid of him. The stories we are always hearing about him since we came to England! It is always how Lord Blair—they always call him Blair!—rode in such and such a race, and how he swam such and such a river, and fought such and such a man, and what a magnificent place Leyton Court is, and how lovely and famous the Countess of Ferrers had become! Why, when some people heard we were coming to stay with you they looked at us as if we were going down to Windsor Castle!"

Margaret laughed with all her old light-heartedness.

"You always were a terrible flatterer, Florence!" she said.

"Now, that's a shame, for it prevents me saying what I was going to remark; but I'll say it all the same. Margaret, do you know that I should scarcely have known either of you?"

"Really? We have both grown so gray!"

"You have both grown so ridiculously *young*!" retorted the princess emphatically. "I don't mean that you ever looked old, that's absurd of course; but you were so grave and quiet and sad. Don't you remember the first day I saw you I said you reminded me of mamma? That you were so—so—what is the word you English are so fond of?—so sober! That's it! And now you speak and laugh like a young girl again!"

And Margaret answered her almost as she had answered Blair.

"Do I, dear? It must be because I am so happy!"

And indeed it was a very happy little party in the small dining-room that night. Blair was like the old Blair, full of stories of his wild youth, ready with the old light laughter; just the same Blair who used to win the hearts of old and young in the time before Austin Ambrose had commenced to set his snares.

They were so merry in a wise fashion, so light-hearted, that they had forgotten the past entirely; and it was not until the two ladies had left the room—the princess beseeching the two gentlemen not to leave them alone in the drawing-room *too* long, in case they should quarrel—that Blair grew suddenly quiet.

"I can't tell you how I have looked forward to this visit, Rivani," he said. "I have been looking forward to it since that day in Florence when we shook hands at parting, and you promised to come and stay with us."

"I am very glad to come," said the prince, with sincere earnestness. "Gladder still to see you so well—and the countess."

"You thinks she looks well?" said Blair, his face lighting up at once.

"She looks the picture of youth and health and happiness," said the prince, quietly, "and more beautiful—you will pardon me—than ever in my eyes."

"And in mine, old fellow!" said Blair, holding out his hand.

There was silence after that significant meeting of the palms, then Blair said, "Any news?"

The prince was silent a moment.

"No, not much," he answered, after a pause. "All you wished done I have had carried out."

He referred to two graves in the cemetery at Naples which he had undertaken to keep in order—two graves covered with huge slabs of black marble, one bearing the initials "A. A." and the other "V. G."

Blair nodded, and his face grew cloudy for a moment.

"And Lottie?"

"Lottie doesn't need your generous assistance any longer," said the prince, with a smile. "She is now one of the most famous young ladies in Italy. I forgot to send you the paper containing an account of her great success in the new spectacular play"—he had not forgotten, but had remembered with some consideration that the paper would only recall the past and its old bitterness—"she took them by storm, I assure you, and for weeks our volatile people were raving about her; for that matter they are raving still," and he laughed.

Blair smiled, but his face was still clouded, and the prince laid a hand on his shoulder.

"Blair, forgive me, but I think the time has now come when the past may be allowed to bury its dead. That it may do so the more completely I want you and Lady Ferrers to assist me in a short ceremony."

Blair looked at him inquiringly.

"Will you ask her ladyship if she will kindly show me round her studio?" said the prince gravely. "She knows how devoted I am to the art of which she is so great a mistress!"

"Certainly," said Blair, rising, and still puzzled.

They went into the drawing-room, where Margaret and the princess were sitting very close together, and Blair whispered a few words to Margaret.

She got up directly, and drew the princess' arm through her own.

"Follow me," she said; and she led them to the magnificent studio which Blair had built for her.

Here, amongst costly pictures and rare statues gleaming in the reflected light of antique curtains of deep reds and blues of Oriental dyes, she showed them her latest work.

"Beautiful!" exclaimed the prince. "Beautiful! Ah! if Alfero could but be here! Do you know what he said when I told him that I was coming to see you?"

"No," said Margaret; "but everything that was kind and thoughtful I am sure," she added.

"He told me to convey his devotion to you, and say that he looked forward to the hour when he should be able to kiss your hand; then he sighed and added, 'and tell her not to forget that she is an artist as well as a great English lady. Anybody can be a countess, but Heaven only sends us such a painter as she is at long intervals. Tell her to put the paint-brush and the palette first and her coronet afterward!'"

"That was like him!" said Margaret softly. "How much I owe him! You shall take my answer back, prince. But, see; do you think I have been idle?" and she looked modestly at the pictures on the wall and on the easel.

"No," he said. "No," then he was silent a minute; "but there is one thing I wish you would do—it is for myself. I want you to alter a picture of yours I have got."

"Really!" she cried eagerly. "Of course I will!"

"Thanks!" he said gravely, "I knew you would not refuse me. I will go and fetch it, for I have brought it with me."

He left the room, and the other three waited expectantly. While he was gone, Margaret took up her palette and brush, and absently began mixing some colors.

He re-entered the room presently with a canvas-inclosed case, and, unlocking it, placed upon the easel the famous picture of the Long Rock.

Blair uttered an exclamation, but Margaret stood and regarded it in silence, though her face was very pale.

"I want you to alter this for me," said the prince, gravely and gently. "Can you not guess how?"

She looked up at him inquiringly, then, reading his meaning in his eyes, she took up a large brush, filled it with black paint, and in another minute the picture had disappeared.

Florence uttered an exclamation of dismay, but the prince inclined his head, and as Margaret turned and hid her face on Blair's breast, he said:

"That is what I wanted. Now, in deed and in truth, my friends, we may say that the past is blotted out; not even the shadow of it can mar the happiness of your future; a future made bright with a love that has been tried in the furnace and found not wanting."

And this is the reason why Lady Ferrers' great masterpiece, which set all Italy talking and made her famous, can never be found, and some art critics are beginning to doubt whether, after all, it could have been so good as Signor Alfero and others declared it to have been; and whether some of her later pictures, which dealt with the bright side of nature, may not be far better than the mysterious work which has disappeared so strangely.